ZANITA:

A Tale of the Yo-semite

THERESA YELVERTON

(Viscountess Avonmore)

INTRODUCTION BY
MARGARET SANBORN

PREFACE BY KATE REED

A DOUBLE ELEPHANT BOOK

■ TEN SPEED PRESS ■

The publisher gratefully acknowledges Kate Reed for bringing this novel to our attention for historical reprint.

Originally published in 1872 by Hurd & Houghton, New York.

↑☯
TEN SPEED PRESS
P.O. Box 7123
Berkeley, California 94707

Book Design by Hal Hershey
Cover Design by Nancy Austin
Cover illustration from *Hutching's 1867 Yo-semite Almanac*,
    courtesy of The Bancroft Library

Library of Congress Cataloging-in-Publication Data

Yelverton, Theresa, Viscountess Avonmore, 1832?–1891.
    Zanita: a tale of the Yo-semite / Theresa Yelverton (Viscountess
    Avonmore).
        p. cm.
    Includes new introd. by Margaret Sanborn.
    ISBN 0-89815-410-3
    I. Title.
PR5909.Y45Z26 1991
823'.8—dc20   90-42653
                                                    CIP

First Printing, 1991

Manufactured in the United States of America

1 2 3 4 5 — 95 94 93 92 91

ZANITA:

A Tale of the Yo-semite

PREFACE.

by Kate Reed

ZANITA: A TALE OF THE YO-SEMITE was originally published in 1872. A novel of and for its day, its plot is romantic and melodramatic, its prose florid—*Zanita* serves as a window into the past, through which we can catch glimpses of life in Yosemite and its environs as it was more than a century ago. It casts as its main characters many of Yosemite's important historical figures, including John Muir. And, moreover, its descriptions of Yosemite itself are timeless.

In 1870, when *Zanita* was written, Yosemite Valley was still relatively unknown as a travel destination, although word of its natural wonders was spreading. Congress had granted the valley and the Mariposa Grove of Big Trees to the state of California in 1864 "for public use, resort and recreation . . . for all time," but those who lived there still harbored proprietary feelings towards it. Travel into the valley from any "civilized" location took several days over rough roads, and those who visited felt themselves to be a select, fortunate few. These were the conditions under which *Zanita* was written; in fact, the narrator and her friends seem to have Yosemite Valley virtually all to themselves. Fortunate, indeed!

John Muir was, at that time, an unknown naturalist employed at Hutchings' sawmill, and that is how he is portrayed in *Zanita*, bearing the pseudonym Kenmuir. Most, if not all, of the characters in the novel were based on people that the author, Theresa Yelverton, met in and around Yosemite, and her depictions of them are, apparently, fairly true to life. Her descriptions of Muir imbue him with the vivid, even virile, vigor of his pre–Sierra Club youth. Some of Kenmuir's words and many of his sentiments are recognizably Muir's, and a great deal of the book's appeal comes from the fun of, in David Robertson's phrase, "watching [this] hero in action."

The novel's chief joy, ultimately, is its principal setting: Yosemite Valley. Yosemite's charms are changeless, and, despite more than a century of visitor use, those scenes of natural splendor described in

Zanita can still be experienced today. The reader should be able to recognize the paths rambled, the peaks scaled, and the majestic panoramas surveyed and admired.

Although the topic of minorities does not constitute a major element of the story, a few words should be said regarding their depiction in the novel. Yelverton's descriptions of the African-American child, Beppo, are presumably humorous, but, while representative of the era and relatively brief, they remain indefensible. Her discussions of Yosemite's Native American population, whom she calls "Payutes," are, however, more sympathetic than prevailing attitudes and government actions towards them. Several characters argue forcefully on behalf of Native American lifestyles and practices and when taken in their historical context and recalling, in retrospect, the wars of attrition that had been waged against the Native American populations and which were still being conducted against the Plains Indians, these arguments seem unusually enlightened for their time.

A final note: Throughout the book, the author used Ahwahneechee names, or her versions of them, for the natural landmarks that she encounters. Thus, "Pom-pom-pas-us" is the Three Brothers; "Pal-li-li-ma" is Glacier Point; "Tu-tock-ah-nu-lah", El Capitan; "Py-wy-ack" and "Yo-wee-ye", Vernal and Nevada Falls, respectively; "Tissa-ack", Half Dome; "To-coy-eeh", North Dome; "Hunto", Basket Dome; and "Tah-mah", Liberty Cap. "See-wahlum" is Washington Column, and "Hum-moo", Lost Arrow.

INTRODUCTION.

by Margaret Sanborn

LATE IN THE SPRING OF 1870, the Honorable Theresa* Yelverton, author of *Zanita*, arrived in Yosemite Valley by horseback, for an indefinite stay. Although her name and her story were known the world over, for she was one of the most noted women of her day and the press reported her every activity, she had managed to leave San Francisco secretly and reach Yosemite without being recognized, which was how she wanted it to be—for she lived in dread of being tracked by her estranged and vindictive husband. She was in search of a remote and peaceful retreat where she could find diversion in the out-of-doors after a successful but exhausting tour of the Eastern United States as a public reader and lecturer; try to forget the fiasco of her San Francisco debut, and start writing a book about her American experiences. Yosemite had been recommended as the ideal refuge by the young San Francisco poet and musician, Charles Warren Stoddard.

In 1864 Stoddard was in Hawaii, visiting his sister Sara, who was married to a plantation owner. Charlie, as he was always known, sat on their cool, vine-shaded veranda "facing the sunsets and within sound of the sea," reading Theresa Yelverton's first book, *Martyrs to Circumstance*, recently published in London. He found it hard to put down this exciting tale of adventure and conflicting passions, set in wartime Asian Turkey. He admired its "superb description" and its atmosphere "rich and mellow as the Orient itself." But the greatest wonder to him was that every word was true, for it was the author's own story. "I remember I longed very much to meet this lady—this martyr to circumstance; to take her by the hand, to know her and call her friend."

Five years later this opportunity came when she arrived in San Francisco to give a series of dramatic readings. "Nothing could have been easier. I wrote to her." It was the kind of letter "an enthusiastic young

* Professionally she generally spelled her given name Thérèse, but in private life, she was Theresa Yelverton.

fellow would write to a modern female martyr whose trials and triumphs were at that time almost a household word." He mentioned the fragrant bower by "the sobbing sea, where my heart was first touched by her sorrows," begged to know more of her "mysterious history," and offered his help in publicizing her readings. She must consider his "loyal pen as being ever at her disposal." Her reply came by return mail. She accepted his "kind offer, with pleasure," and would be happy "to favor you with any number of 'historical curiosities' relating to my life. I think my *début* in the House of Lords is perhaps as interesting and singular as any, and very much to the point. As I am about to give readings here . . . the public might like such a guarantee of my power of elocution." To save a great deal of writing she suggested that he call, "when I could narrate events more easily, and you might ask any particulars you wished.—-From the tone of your note, I shall be glad to know you."

Stoddard called at once. "Who could have hesitated?" His timing, however, was unfortunate, for that morning there had been a strong earthquake, something she had never experienced, and he found her in a state of near hysteria. In spite of her excitement, her conversation impressed him as being the product of "a thoughtful and highly cultivated mind," and he noted that she was often singularly brilliant in repartee. As to her person, he thought her "attractive in an uncommon way and to an uncommon degree." But he left that first meeting in low spirits for he knew that she had come to the last place on earth where her readings could be financially successful.

With the expansion of Virginia City's great Comstock Lode and the founding of new fortunes, there was a resurgence of wealth in San Francisco after several years of depression. In the midst of unbridled prosperity, theatrical productions flourished, and 1869 saw the opening of the new California Theatre, a richly appointed and spacious house financed by the local banker William C. Ralston. It immediately became the home for a strong and well-trained stock company and featured a procession of visiting celebrities: Frank Mayo, Mrs. Judah, Edwin Booth, Julia Dean, and the inimitable Lotta Crabtree. Night after night the theater was packed with a discriminating audience, dressed in the height of fashion, sparkling with jewels, expecting to be entertained by only the best. The repertoire included Shakespeare and the most popular New York plays. Competing at smaller theaters were such sell outs as minstrel shows featuring Billy Birch and David

Wambold; extravaganzas like "The British Blonde Beauties"; or the spectacular "Imperial Troupe" of Japanese jugglers and acrobats. Then in the fall of 1869, just when Theresa Yelverton planned to start her series, Lotta Crabtree opened at the California Theatre in *Little Nell and the Marchioness*, an immensely popular piece that she had been playing for months to overflow audiences in New York. There was no place in this galaxy for poetry readings, even though the work of San Francisco's own Bret Harte was included. Acting jointly as her manager, Stoddard and his friends did what they could to arouse interest in her program, but the public remained apathetic. Undeterred, she hired Platt Hall.

Charlie Stoddard remembered that during the "decisive day she fasted upon limes and oysters; for her voice, which was of exquisite quality, required the utmost care to keep it in perfect tune." By this time, he and Theresa had, as he said, become "close friends," and after she had dressed for the performance—she wore what he described as a "*souffle* of lace over trailing ivory satin"—he helped her select her jewels. They decided on an heirloom necklace of "superb opals." Her appearance was striking. He thought that "she might have stepped back into a 'Book of Beauty' and put some of her rivals to shame."

At the appointed hour "I escorted her to the stage door . . . and she was preparing for her grand *entrée* when it was discovered that there was not a corporal's guard in the house." (Only a year before Mark Twain had had to stop the sale of tickets for his lecture at Platt Hall because he did not want to be bothered with standees. San Franciscans had flocked to hear the humorist because he was the talk of the country.)

Stoddard and the group of admirers who were there accompanied Theresa in a body back to the hotel, where "in a private parlor, she gave us a taste of her quality; and, between the smiles and the tears, the chagrin and the champagne—the latter was served with the compliments of the sympathetic landlord—we had a rather pleasant night of it, after all." She made no further attempt to give public readings in California.

Charlie Stoddard had noticed that she had a good deal of the Bohemian in her makeup, which enabled her to fit well into the city's active literary life and encouraged her to write again. Full of promise, Stoddard was the youngest member of what was known as the Golden Gate Trinity (along with Bret Harte and the gifted poet Ina Coolbrith), who kept the newly founded *Overland Monthly* lively. Harte, then editing the magazine, was making it and himself famous with such local color stories as "The Luck of Roaring Camp" and "The Outcasts of Poker Flat." Theresa was asked to contribute to the *Overland*, which she did, and, through her contacts there, met nearly all the literati in the Bay Area. One of the most interesting and important friends she made was the dynamic Jeanne Carr, botanist, educator, and feminist, whose husband was on the faculty of the new University of California. Their Oakland home was a gathering place for the intelligentsia, local and visiting, and there Theresa became acquainted with still other notables in the arts and sciences. One who impressed her greatly was Dr. Joseph LeConte, a physician and a professor of geology, zoology, and botany, also a faculty member. He had the additional distinction of having studied with Agassiz at Harvard and to have been associated with him personally on scientific expeditions. Later Theresa used Dr. LeConte as a character in *Zanita*.

But it was Charlie Stoddard, described as a man of "great sweetness, kindliness, and gentleness," with a generous gift of whimsical humor, upon whom she depended most for companionship. He observed her closely as they "rambled about the ragged edges of town . . . clambering among rocks and sand" (for she was most content out-of-doors), satisfying their appetites with crackers and cheese. At such times she might say, "O if my friends were to see me now!" and then she would laugh and run off in mock horror. She was thinking of her friends abroad. It was satisfying to have their conversations take profound turns at times, and to explore such a concept as she offered: "I have often thought that Mozart and Beethoven must have had some of their most tender and pathetic melodies inspired by the various harmonies of mobile water." They also talked about books—right then she was reading Buckle's *History of Civilization in England*.

He realized that, having been uprooted and cast among strangers, she was a lonely woman longing for affection, and saw that she was lavish with hers for those who offered sincere friendship. She took a deep interest in her younger friends who were talented and ambitious, and tried to inspire and advise them. From Sausalito, where, to save money, she had rented rooms in a house built picturesquely over San Francisco Bay, she wrote Stoddard about the necessity of contributing regularly to periodicals. He would then have "a handsome income on which to travel, stopping at different points on the way to pick up touches of life." She suggested that he go to Hawaii and Australia, then on to England. "What charming papers you could write from there!" He took her advice the next year and sailed for Hawaii and Tahiti. Sketches born of those experiences were collected into a volume called *South-Sea Idyls*, a work that inspired favorable comparison with Pierre Loti's gift for describing exotic scenery.

During their frequent visits, Theresa supplied him with enough material about her life—some in the form of notes, some printed, some personal correspondence (including love letters), some oral (which he wrote down)—to fill a volume. After reading everything, he realized that although only thirty-three, she had crowded a lifetime of experience and adventure into that short span.

She was born Marie Theresa Longworth, in Cheetwood, Lincolnshire, the youngest child of a wealthy English silk manufacturer and merchant, Stoddard learned. When she was very young, her mother was forced to leave home with her three daughters and go into hiding to escape persecution from her husband, turned atheist, who refused to tolerate the Catholicism of his wife and children. When her mother died, Theresa was placed in an Ursuline convent in Boulogne, where both her sisters were being educated.

In the summer of 1852, Theresa finished her convent schooling and sailed for England to visit a relative, the Marchioness de la Belline, who had given her mother and sisters sanctuary during those days when they lived like hunted criminals. A sister, married to General Leferve of the French army and living in Boulogne, provided an escort and saw Theresa safely on her way. Aboard the steamer, her escort introduced a Captain William Charles Yelverton of the Royal Artillery, in his late twenties, who was heir to the impecunious Irish viscount, Barry John Yelverton. He was captivated by the beautiful, naive sixteen-year-old and never left her side. Theresa remembered that when they reached London he was "most polite and attentive in looking after my luggage, and getting me a cab." The next day he called and met Theresa's other sister, also a houseguest, now married to a Mr. Bellamy whose ancestral seat was Abergaveny Castle, in Wales. Yelverton admitted afterward that he was greatly impressed by the rank and style of living of Miss Longworth's kin and, being in search of a wealthy and genteel wife, wished for some excuse to become better acquainted. But there was no opportunity for he was almost immediately assigned to duty in Malta.

In the spring, Theresa went to Naples to study painting and vocal and instrumental music, for which she had real talent. Her sister, Mrs. Bellamy, went with her. Obviously Theresa had found Captain Yelverton attractive, for while in Naples she made the first overture by writing him, asking that he forward through military channels an enclosure for her brother, then a British consul in Greece. This opening led to a correspondence that turned rather quickly into a regular exchange of love letters.

After two years in Italy, Theresa sailed back to England, with the encouragement of her voice instructors, to make a career in opera. Meanwhile, the Crimean War had begun, and Yelverton, now brevet-major, was sent to the front in command of a battery of siege artillery. Theresa, deeply in love, decided she must find some way of getting to the seat of war, in the hope of being near him. Learning that several nuns from her Ursuline convent were going as nurses to the French hospital at Galata, she sent an urgent request to join them, but she was refused on account of her youth. Even an application made to the pope was turned down for the same reason. Friends suggested that she appeal to Empress Eugénie, but when that beautiful Spaniard with the Scottish grandfather met her, she was "so charmed with the fair English girl" that she invited her to become a maid of honor. Theresa accepted and spent a number of happy months at the brilliant court in Tuileries. Unsuccessful in her attempts to dissuade Theresa from risking her life in the war hospitals, Eugénie found her a place as a lay member of the French Sisters of Charity. Dressed in their habit, she was soon on her way to Constantinople.

It was in the hospital at Galata that Major Yelverton found her. Right away he proposed marriage, and she accepted him as her fiancé. He begged her to leave the hospital because of the danger of disease, but she told him she intended to stay until the war was over. He visited her regularly at the quarters of General and Lady Straubenzee who were acting as her protectors. Then one day he confessed that he was under "pecuniary difficulties" and would be unable to marry her because he had promised his father never to choose a wife who could not pay his debts—the old viscount spoke from experience. About three thousand pounds would cover his needs at present. In that case, Theresa told him, the engagement was broken, for her modest property was in trust, and the interest could never meet that sum. When he left she begged him not to return, but within a week he was back. He "could not keep away," he explained, and suggested that she live with him as his mistress. When she refused, he proposed a secret marriage at the Greek church in Balaklava. But she was a Roman Catholic (as he claimed to be also), not Greek, she objected. She asked him to go and not try to visit her again, a request he seems to have respected.

For two years she continued nursing and proved to be skilled and hardy. Nothing daunted her. Once after a battle, when a ship carrying a thousand Russian prisoners, most of them wounded, came into port, everyone was warned away because there was cholera aboard. Packing a bag with medical supplies, Theresa ordered a caïque to take her to the anchorage, climbed swiftly up the ship's side, and went right to work among the most seriously wounded.

In January 1857 she returned to England and, after visiting in Portsmouth, traveled on to the home of a friend, Miss MacFarlane, in Edinburgh. "I went into society in Edinburgh," she wrote, so it was only natural that she would meet Major Yelverton, for he was stationed at Leith, Edinburgh's port. Shortly he was calling daily at Miss Mac-Farlane's, and one afternoon suggested a Scottish marriage. "He said the marriage could be constituted by mutual consent, without priest or ceremony. He said this could be done in the room where we were sitting." He had only to read the ritual aloud in the presence of a witness and then acknowledge Theresa as his wife. She told him flatly that she did not want such a marriage. To her it was a sin not to be married by a clergyman, in her case a Roman Catholic priest. Marriage was a sacrament. Yelverton insisted that they conferred the sacrament upon themselves—the priest did not. She disagreed. But on April 12, 1857, over her protest, he read the Church of England marriage rite in Miss MacFarlane's sitting-room, with others present. "This makes you my wife, according to the laws of Scotland," he announced. She refused to live with him. Finding her adamant, he at length agreed to a Roman Catholic ceremony, and, traveling separately to Ireland, they were married by the parish priest in the village of Rostrevor. There were two witnesses. The only flaw was Yelverton's refusal to allow his surname to appear on the certificate. But that was shortly rectified.

As soon as they were alone he made Theresa promise not to disclose their marriage until he gave permission, yet throughout their wedding tour of Scotland, England, and France he acknowledged their marriage by signing "Mr. and Mrs. Yelverton" in hotel registers and guest books, while on her passport she appeared as Theresa Yelverton.

He left her at Bordeaux, sick and pregnant. He had to return to duty at Leith. Later he was to testify that by this time he had grown "tired of her," and was glad to have this reason to separate. Before going he reminded her to keep the marriage secret. She pointed out the impossibility: to register a child's birth in France it was necessary to present proof of marriage. He warned that if she defied him, she would repent it all her life. As soon as he left, she wrote to the Reverend Bernard Mooney, who had performed the ceremony, explaining her need for an amended certificate: "I must now confide to you my husband's surname, which I was allowed to do only under the seal of confession." The priest complied promptly.

After recovering from a stillbirth, she wrote Yelverton that she was determined to save her honor at any cost and would publish their marriage if he did not. He replied that such an act on his part would ruin him. He had no wish to see her again and advised that she marry a rich man and "go to New Zealand or to the ends of the earth," and hide herself to spare him, Yelverton. She returned to Miss MacFarlane's house, and from there wrote him:

"You are like a child who has pulled a watch to pieces and cannot put it together again; and, fearing to ask assistance, throws it away and tries to forget the mischief he has done. You meddle with the human heart without knowing the depth, strength, or the complicated machinery contained therein . . . You did not know the strength of hope or the length of patience of a woman's heart; and now you want to throw it away and forget you every played with it. Do so, *mio bene*, if you think you can forget. . . ."

And again: "Caro mio Carlo: . . . Have you not made me endure the torments of Tantalus over and over again? Have I not expressed to you that I had but one wish; that if you would gratify that one I would never trouble you to all time and eternity with another—'only to see you once'? . . .

"My kismet at present is to float around you in ambient air—to hover near you, unfelt, unseen. Through forests I'll follow, and where the sea flows; through dangers, through whole legions of foes,—with no hope, no home, no refuge on earth but that ill-requited love. You could comfort me with a word of kindness, and you refuse it. God, too, must have abandoned me, or I never could feel so utterly desolate— *semper a te*."

Then she learned that on June 26 of that year, her husband had formally married, at the Trinity Episcopal Chapel near Edinburgh, a Mrs. Emily Marianne Forbes, a young woman of "large fortune," and debt-free ancestral estates, who was the daughter of Sir Charles and Lady Ashworth. She was also the widow of the famed invertebrate paleozoologist and biogeographer, Professor Edward Forbes of the University of Edinburgh, who had recently died at age thirty-nine. Major Yelverton had been willing to commit bigamy in order to marry the woman of wealth and rank he had promised himself and his family. He expected, because of his station, to clear himself easily of charges by denying the legality of his two marriages to Theresa Longworth and to destroy her credibility through slanderous statements, which made her no better than a prostitute.

But his arrogance was due a fall. He had not counted on Theresa's beauty, charm, and candor making her a hugely popular public figure, and he was cast in the role of a scoundrel. As soon as Theresa learned of her husband's marriage, she sued him for alimony. He allowed judgment to go by default and paid the money. Then, hoping to discourage her from further action through attrition, he instituted a series of vexatious appeals denying the legality of both marriages, which dragged her from court to court—from England to Scotland to Ireland, and back to England, submitting her to seventeen protracted trials. But he failed to break her spirit. She once said that she liked nothing better than "the rush and strife of battle." Little did he know that he would spend the next ten years in litigation; that he would be suspended from military duty; that he would be burned in effigy and forced to go into hiding on the Continent. What must have been a severe blow was his discovery that all of Mrs. Forbes' wealth and real property was held in trust entirely for her own use.

Throughout the siege, public sentiment was solely on Theresa's side, and "sympathizing strangers and titled men" deposited large sums of money for her expenses. A beautiful young woman wronged and maligned by a blackguard was an ever-popular theme, and periodical readers the world over eagerly followed the developments in what was known as "The Great Yelverton Marriage Case," heralded as "the most extraordinary trial in modern times."

Once, during the progress of a court action, Theresa met Yelverton in a railroad car. They were alone, and he immediately demanded the marriage certificate, which figured so prominently in every trial. He tried to get it by persuasion, then bribery, and finally by threat. She told him that "no living power could ever, by any means, tear from her that proof of her wifehood." Furious, he pronounced a curse: May she know every sorrow and misery as long as she lives and die an agonizing death alone and far from help.

Then, in 1861, an action was brought in the Dublin Court of Common Pleas by Theresa's landlord, a John Thelwall, who, as her champion, was wanting to collect over two hundred and fifty-nine pounds for Mrs. Yelverton's board and room. The object was to try and force the major to acknowledge Theresa as his lawful wife.

The trial lasted ten days, and public interest grew rapidly, for "her story is one of the most romantic that has ever seen the light," the *Dublin Morning News* reported. "The Hon. Mrs. Yelverton . . . has been three days under examination, two of which have been occupied by one of the severest, closest, and most searching cross-examinations, conducted by one of the ablest lawyers, that has ever taken place in a public court. During that prolonged ordeal Mrs. Yelverton was never for a moment deserted by that dignified and ladylike demeanor which has characterized her throughout these three days. She has maintained an imperturbable coolness, without the least appearing too confident or too clever, while her self-possession has elicited the highest admiration from all who have been able to procure admission to the Court. . . . The seemingly unreserved, candid, and outspoken frankness of her replies call forth the warmest approbation, and prove that the Hon. Mrs. Yelverton is not only a lady most highly educated, but that she possesses an intelligence, a quickness of comprehension, and a power of language rarely met with in a lady, even in the present intellectual age, when the education of females receives so much attention." Her defense was marked by "self-command, wit, and coolness."

She was probably in her twenty-fifth year, the reporter continued; was under middle height, and "admirably proportioned." The smallness of her hand "is indeed one which your fair readers would admire." Her face was oval, with a delicately pointed chin. Her blue eyes were "large, beautifully set, and indicative at once of mental vigor and great tenderness. Her glance penetrates, while it charms with a spell. . . . It is the eye that lights and makes beautiful the whole countenance." Her abundance of golden hair was of that "rich and glowing hue which Titian . . . delighted in." It was worn brushed back "in the French style, displaying an unusually broad, calm and intellectual forehead." Her attire showed impeccable taste: on the first day she wore a "black moiré antique dress," a black velvet mantilla, a fashionable French bonnet in white, and mauve gloves.

"But how shall I describe what constitutes the greatest charm about her? The perfection of graceful motion in the simplest movement; and the voice—such a voice!—clear, soft, liquid, and musical."

An hour before court opened on the morning of the fourth day, the space in front of the doors was blocked by a throng, milling about impatiently. When at ten-thirty an order was given to open the doors, the "police whose duty it was to see that the court should not become overcrowded, were swept aside by in-rushing thousands. Several people were dashed down and trampled under foot . . . So terrible was the confusion that his lordship the chief-justice was compelled to adjourn the court for half an hour . . . .

"Upon such a stage now enters the Hon. Mrs. Yelverton. Her appearance in the witness-box excites the greatest curiosity; then a breathless silence falls upon the assemblage as she begins to speak:

"My maiden name was Theresa Longworth. I was born in Cheetwood, in Lincolnshire. My father is dead; my mother is dead also . . . "

Father Bernard Mooney was called next, and testified to having performed the marriage ceremony and signed the certificate. Then it was Major Yelverton's turn to be sworn. He was described as being about thirty-seven years old, "a little over medium height; tolerably good-looking but by no means handsome. His hair was of a dark brown color, his eyes deeply set, and his expression care-worn and anxious. He wore heavy whiskers and a moustache."

In his opening statement he said that he had met this pretty girl, taken a fancy to her, noticed her "passion" for him, and resolved to seduce her. "He had done so. He had never married her. When he grew tired of her, he had left her at Bordeaux in France. He had never wished to hear of her since." His cross-examination began ominously for him when he was asked if he had ever loved Theresa Longworth "purely and honorably," and he replied that he had not. "Then your love for her was always founded in dishonor?" "Yes." "Do you think it a laudable thing to seduce a woman?" "Upon my honor I do not." "Upon your oath—I do not want your notions of honor—is it laudable?" "I do not think it is." The examiner pressed him closely on the "laudability" of seduction, and Yelverton finally admitted that in his opinion laudability depended entirely upon "whether it was found out or not," words which produced a "sensation" in the courtroom.

Although the major knew that Theresa Longworth was an orphan and a gentlewoman of high accomplishment and education, had he considered it laudable to take base advantage of her youth and innocence, and "follow her persistently and perseveringly with the intent . . . to dishonor her?"

He avoided a direct answer with an attempt to prove that she was not a "gentlewoman." *Harper's Weekly* commented: "There are many other parts of Major Yelverton's evidence which are painfully interesting, as showing the brutal purpose of the systematic seducer, and the abominable selfishness of the man. But they are not for reproduction." He was "often hotly hissed by the throng present and reprimanded by the Lord Chief-Justice."

When the legality of the Catholic marriage was being investigated, he was asked if he had gone inside the church at Rostrevor, to which he replied that he had. "You went to the altar?" "Yes." "The priest went inside?" "Yes." "And stood before you? " "Yes." "And you and she knelt down?" "Yes." "Side by side?" "Yes." "Listen to me! Did you at the altar, before that priest, take her to be your wedded wife?" "I did." "Did she take you to be her wedded husband?" "She did."

Yelverton objected at once that the ceremony was meaningless because he was not a Roman Catholic. The examiner pounced: "But had he not disclosed earlier to the court that at the altar, when the priest asked if he was a Catholic, his reply had been, 'I am, but a poor one. I am no Protestant.' Was it the Major's regular practice to deceive members of the clergy?"

The eminent Right Honorable James Whiteside, Q.C., M.P., Theresa Yelverton's counsel, skillfully reviewed all the points of the case in a speech of great length. In his appeal to the jury he said: "How stands the question, now that the whole of this great trial is before you—now that you have all these facts? . . . I ask you to judge that woman as she came before you, and then say do you believe her? Trace her conduct from the first hour she sat within the walls of the convent until she came to this box to tell the story of her multitudinous sorrows, and ask yourselves what fact is proved against her with any living man save this defendant. Her crime is that she loved him too dearly and too well. . . . Therefore I now call on you to do justice to that injured woman. You cannot restore her to the husband she adored or to the happiness she enjoyed. . . . You may, by your verdict . . . restore her to that society in which she is qualified to shine and has ever adorned. To you I commit this great cause. . . . She finds an advocate in you; she finds it in the respected judge on the bench; she finds it in every heart that beats within this court, and in every honest man throughout the country." The old account concludes: "Mr. Whiteside resumed his seat amidst loud demonstrations of applause, which were continued unchecked for several minutes. Cheers were also given for the Hon. Mrs. Yelverton."

The jury had three questions to decide: Was there a Scottish marriage? Was there an Irish marriage? Was Major Yelverton a Roman Catholic at the time of the latter marriage?

When the jury returned, the foreman announced: "First, that they had found the Scottish marriage a valid one; and, secondly, that there was a good Irish marriage; and thirdly, they had found the defendant a Roman Catholic."

As the final words were spoken, "the joy and approval of all found expression in a most enthusiastic burst of cheering, again and again renewed. . . . Hats and handkerchiefs were waved; the members of the bar stood up and joined heartily in the public manifestations of delight; many of them . . . took off their wigs and waved them with energy. Ladies wept for joy. . . . " Outside, over fifty thousand people waited to hear the verdict, and when word was brought that Mrs. Yelverton "had triumphed and was declared a wife," there was further cheering. Hats were tossed in the air; men shook hands with people they did not know; women hugged one another. Vehicles of all sorts went dashing off in every direction to carry the good news to distant parts of Dublin; the telegraph offices were besieged in order that the whole empire might learn the outcome of this great trial.

Around seven o'clock the police cleared a path through the waiting throng for Theresa to reach her carriage. The horses had been removed so that the people could pull it themselves. She left the courtyard in a storm of cheers and applause. The multitude moved with the carriage, sometimes lifting it bodily from the pavement. The streets leading to the Gresham Hotel "were covered by a solid mass of humanity."

Once she was inside the hotel, there were repeated calls for her to appear. In response she came out on a balcony and spoke to the crowd:

"My noble-hearted friends, you have made me this day an Irishwoman by the verdict that I am the wife of an Irishman. [Vehement cheering.] I glory in belonging to such a noble-hearted nation. [Great cheering.] You will live in my heart forever, as I have lived in your hearts this day. [Tumultuous applause.] I am too weary to say all that my heart desires; but you will accept the gratitude of a heart that was made sad and is now made glad again. [Loud cheer.] Farewell for the present, but forever I belong in heart and soul to the people of Dublin."

She withdrew "amidst tremendous and prolonged applause."

That night Major Yelverton was burned in effigy.

Bitter and angry over Theresa's triumphant victory, Yelverton vanished. He knew that if he could not be traced, he would escape the bigamy trial that would automatically follow. His disappearance would also make it impossible for Theresa to collect income from her trust. For her, one hope remained: to outlaw him and recover the rights to her property. It was for this purpose that the eighteenth and final suit was instituted, and brought her into the House of Lords as a speaker, where only the peers of the realm were permitted to speak, and where but one woman's voice was ever heard, and that was the queen's. By choice she was her own counsel and prepared her plea in the House library, familiarizing herself with the thousand intricacies of the law.

She opened the case and spoke from ten o'clock in the morning until four in the afternoon, with only half an hour's intermission. The next day she spoke from ten o'clock until one. Her voice, it was observed, was "almost trumpet-toned at times, then cadenced to liquid melody that touched the depths of the heart."

When the distinguished attorney Sir John Ralt rose to reply, he made his plea in Latin, hoping to fluster her. Unruffled, she asked for a translation, then refuted all the errors in fact. Her whole speech took four days to deliver. Each night as she sat in her drawing room at work on her notes, she heard the shrill cries of newsboys running through the streets, shouting the headlines of the extras carrying the text of her day's talk.

Although the House was sympathetic, and Lord Brougham declared in her favor, the majority voted against outlawing William Yelverton, who was heir to their distinguished title.

In July 1862, an appeal instituted by the Yelverton family to the Scottish court of sessions was successful, and the Scottish marriage was annulled. But the Catholic marriage would always remain binding. Theresa's attempt to reopen the case at Edinburgh in March 1865 failed. Then, in October 1868, she tried once more, making an appeal to the court of sessions to set aside the judgment of the House of Lords, but it was rejected. However, public sympathy never wavered, and a subscription was raised for her in Manchester, near her childhood home.

Fiction writers found inspiration in the story of her double marriage, and as early as 1861 James Robert O'Flanagan published a novel he called *Gentle Blood, or The Secret Marriage*, while in 1867, Cyrus Redding's novel, *A Wife and Not a Wife*, appeared. Meanwhile, Theresa's close friend, the famed beauty and wit Caroline Elizabeth Sarah Norton, poet, novelist, pamphleteer, and editor, who was also the granddaughter of playwright Richard Brinsley Sheridan, got her information from the source and published *Lost and Saved*. In telling Theresa's story, Caroline Norton had another advantage in also having been persecuted by a brutal husband who took the income from her inheritance, forced her to support herself and their children, seized her copyright interests, and then sued her for debt.

In 1870, Wilkie Collins, the friend of Dickens, published his novel *Man and Wife*, about the Yelverton case, which became so popular it was dramatized. When Theresa was in San Francisco, an impresario, planning to produce the play, offered her "a goodly sum of money" to take the leading feminine role. She indignantly refused to enact herself, declining to make a fortune out of her misfortune, as she explained to Charles Warren Stoddard.

Although Major Yelverton continued to deny the legality of his Catholic marriage, he asserted his right as Theresa's husband to keep her property and collect the income. Robbed of her inheritance, she was forced to support herself and wrote the autobiographical *Martyrs to Circumstance*, followed by *The Yelverton Correspondence*, in 1863. Calling upon her talent for speaking, she decided to lecture and give dramatic readings, which were so successful that she was encouraged to tour the United States.

After a few months in Sausalito, California, Theresa was ready for a change. She wrote a letter to Charlie Stoddard on the back of her Platt Hall programs: "Dear Friend: We have taken, I fear, the last of our pleasant rural strolls. . . . I do not as yet know where I shall go; I feel in rather a desolate and forlorn condition—as though there was not a place for me in this great world. . . .

"I have just taken a walk over the hill, and looked my last on Tamalpais. And I have felt very melancholy; for I have become strongly attached to the place. . . . I establish strong local friendships with whatever is about me—with a crooked old tree, with the . . . animals, with the slope of the mountains, and especially with all the flowers. . . . "

Stoddard urged her to go to Yosemite, where he had spent six regenerating months. It was the very place "in which to restore one's soul," he assured her. She decided to go, and followed the route he had taken, which brought her to the log cabin inn of Galen Clark, at what is now Wawona. She stayed several days and, with Clark as her guide, explored the nearby Mariposa Grove of Big Trees of which he was co-discoverer. She wrote Stoddard: "Your spirit is hovering still around this place; I have been living in intimacy with it ever since I arrived, and so am in peace and happiness. . . . Galen Clark is a gem I can both understand and enjoy. . . . He remembers you kindly, and we talked about you."

As soon as Theresa Yelverton signed the register at the Upper Hotel in Yosemite Valley, the owner, James Mason Hutchings, an English journalist, recognized her name. Relishing celebrities, he invited her (as he had done with Stoddard), to become a member of his household, which meant taking meals and spending evenings with his family at their cabin. His family included his young wife, Elvira, who painted, wrote poetry, composed for the guitar, botanized, and collected material for a book on the local Indians; their two daughters, Florence (Floy) and the younger Gertrude, always called Cosie. There was also Elvira's mother, a talented woman, Florantha Thompson Sproat, whose father was Cephus Thompson, the noted portrait painter. For the sake of comfort and privacy, Hutchings suggested that Theresa rent a cottage rather than a room in the hotel.

"When shall I see another such cabin as that one—with its great fireplace, and its loft heaping full of pumpkins?" Stoddard wrote nostalgically of the Hutchings house. "O halcyon days! and bed-time at eight P.M., tucking in for ten good hours of delicious sleep, and up again at six; good eatings and drinkings day by day, mugs of milk, long strips of baked squash, and plenty of butter to our bread. . . . a fowl of our own raising, a pie. . . . Then the evenings, so cosy around the fire. H. reads Scott; we listen and comment." Saturday nights when their neighbor James Lamon left his "hermit-like solitude" to join them, were devoted to cards and song.

Charlie Stoddard believed he knew just how she spent her days—writing, sometimes in the shade of sweet-smelling alders beside the river, hearing the warbling of grosbeaks and robins; wandering in meadows carpeted with shooting stars and violets; walking through the pine woods to the waterfalls; riding horseback to the heights; most of her excursions solitary, as his had been. Actually, her presence created quite a sensation, for everyone who lived in the Valley knew her story, and Hutchings saw to it that all distinguished visitors met her. She proved extremely popular for those reasons Walter Leman, the noted actor and close friend of Mark Twain, remembered. Leman rode into Yosemite Valley that July with a party of literary men: "We lingered . . . a week and our visit was made doubly pleasant by the company of a lady we met there . . . the Hon. Theresa Yelverton. . . . Her conversational powers were wonderful, her affability was endearing, and her lovely face was a pleasure to the sight. . . . She was a companion in our rides and walks, an associate in our junketing and picnicking, and will ever be a sweet and gentle 'memory' of our visit."

Instead of leading the reclusive life she had anticipated, she became very active socially and made several intimate friends. One was Mary Viola Lawrence, a handsome young woman with sparkling eyes, a ready smile, and a crown of short curls. She was San Francisco correspondent for the Sacramento *Union*, signing "Ridinghood" to her weekly letters on social matters. She also contributed to San Francisco's *Alta California*, *Bulletin*, and *Examiner*. In 1871 the *Overland Monthly* published "Summer With A Countess," which told about her happy association with Theresa Yelverton in Yosemite.

Mary Lawrence was well known to James Mason Hutchings, for she came to Yosemite often and had written many articles about it. When she registered at his hotel, he purposely assigned her to the unoccupied half of the double cottage where Theresa was staying, but did not tell Mary who her neighbor was. Riding with her guide to "the picturesque cottage, nestled in among the purple rocks," Mary saw a woman sitting on the porch with two children (the Hutchings girls) nearby, stirring mud pies. Mary admired the woman's "delicate complexion of snow and roses," and "the wealth of golden hair negligently looped back from a classic brow." As Mary went into her room, she heard her neighbor ask the guide, "'Any letters?'—Oh, that voice!" I thought; "only two words . . . yet such a magical singing tone!"

A day or two later Mary heard her addressed as Mrs. Yelverton. "I hadn't come lion-hunting, but had made this pilgrimage with *dolce far niente* intentions, neither wanting to seek new friends nor to be bored myself." But the proximity of their quarters brought them into frequent contact, and soon "the bonds of friendship were sealed. We rode up the trails, climbed the heights, walked the meadows over, and boated on the river, again and again, the summer through. For her my admiration was unbounded, being, without exception, the most interesting woman I ever knew. Others think likewise; so this is not alone the impression of enthusiasm and partiality."

One moonlit night Theresa agreed to entertain a party at Mirror Lake, famous for its echoes as well as its reflections. The event was organized by Hutchings and included Mary Lawrence, each of whom left a record. "So, on a cool evening, a merry company went down the meadows, past new-cut hay, fragrant as a 'clover farm,' up the banks of white violets, enjoying the gurgling freshness of the wood-streams, and the tunes in the air from fall, and cataract, and tree-top . . . by an Indian camp with its glowing fire . . . and barking dogs, finally climbing among the rocks that let us out at the borders of the lake," wrote Mary. "Here we stood on a projecting rock and tried the echoes. 'Tallyho!' shouted one with stentorian lungs. 'Ho—ho—ho—o!' repeated the cliffs. Mrs. Yelverton warbled a Tyrolean melody, the echo accompaniment being delicious over the waters. A great pyramid of wood, already arranged, was set on fire at the water's edge, and the party embarked in the boat, to take a sail. We made the mountains re-echo with songs, for ours was a musical band."

After they returned to shore, Theresa walked out on the rock over the water, "and by the light of tapers gave us 'Excelsior,' in her original style. 'Excel-si—or!' was sung back from the great heights . . . we all held our breath, completely lost in the poem realized. Then Tennyson's 'Bugle Song' indeed 'set the echoes flying,' as her bugle-notes leaped over the lake." Hutchings noted that she paused a little longer than the music called for, so that nine distinct echoes could be heard. Afterward, by the light of a full moon, the party sat around the glowing embers toasting the performer with "Mr. Hutchings' sparkling champagne."

Theresa discovered a new and lasting interest after she met Harry Edwards, the San Francisco actor, described as "a remarkable man, a finished artist in his profession," whose avocation was entomology. He owned the finest private collection of butterflies and beetles in the world, and came often to Yosemite to add to it. He invited Theresa to accompany him to the high- and lowland meadows where these insects were found. He taught her how to collect, and she evidently became adept, for not long afterward, she sent him from Hong Kong a case containing "a most wonderful collection of Beetles and butter-flies," which she had gathered in Hawaii and China.

Before the poet and novelist Anna Cabot Lowell Quincy (Mrs. Robert C. Waterston, who wrote under the initials A.C.Q.W.) left Oakland for Yosemite in the summer of 1870, her hostess Jeanne Carr told her about John Muir and let her read his letters. This daughter of the second Josiah Quincy described them as "poems of great and exquisite beauty." Jeanne urged her to make his acquaintance, and so "one morning about sunrise an old lady came to the mill and asked me if I was the man who was so fond of flowers, and we had a very earnest unceremonious chat about the Valley and about 'the Beyond'," Muir reported to Mrs. Carr. After the "chat," Anna Waterston talked enthusiastically to her friend Theresa Yelverton about that young man who worked at Mr. Hutchings' sawmill and told her she must meet him.

With her background it was only natural that Theresa Yelverton would be conscious of rank, and on first meeting John Muir was prejudiced against him because of his "tattered trousers, the waist eked out with a grass band," his "hay-rope suspenders," and "a long flowering sedge rush stuck in the solitary button-hole of his shirt, the sleeves of which were ragged and forlorn." But she admitted that she forgot all this as soon as she looked into his "bright, intelligent face . . . and his open blue eyes of honest questioning," noted his "glorious auburn hair," and heard the poetic flow of words as he talked about Yosemite Valley's geological origin. She soon realized that his "refinement was innate, his education collegiate, not only from his scientific treatment of his subject, but his correct English." What was important to an Englishwoman of her time and station: he was a "gentleman."

Their friendship developed rapidly. "We are pretty well acquainted now," Muir wrote Jeanne Carr not long after they had met. "I was glad to find that she knew you." Shortly he was acting as her guide on excursions around the Valley and to the high country. He was, she admitted, unlike anyone she had ever known, and, being interested in character and personality, she began studying him. She made notes on his manner of expressing himself in both words and gestures; his opinions about the universe; even his "joyous ringing laugh." For him, she found, the spirits of the wild were angels—angels who lifted and carried him over perilous places and showed him where to put his feet. As he raced ahead in their climbs, she admired his "lithe figure . . . skipping over the rough boulders, poising with the balance of an athlete . . .

never losing for a moment the rhythmic motion of his flexile form . . . His figure was about five feet nine, well knit, and bespoke that active grace which only trained muscles can assume."

Most writers on Muir have made this relationship ridiculous by picturing Theresa Yelverton as a foolish older woman infatuated with the handsome young Muir, who, tiring quickly of her brazen and unremitting pursuit, runs away from Yosemite in desperation. This concept was formed carelessly, without any investigation of existing evidence, and ever since it was first published it has been accepted without question and repeated constantly. One Muir biographer thinking to make Theresa appear yet more absurd in seeming to deify Muir, quoted from her first impression of him in which she said that his face, "shining with a pure and holy enthusiasm," reminded her of a small painting of Christ she had seen in an old Italian village. She had never forgotten that face because of its "tender, loving, benignant expression."

Interestingly, when Jeanne Carr sent her painter friends William Keith and Benoni Irwin to meet Muir in Yosemite, she instructed Irwin to sketch him in his ragged attire with the "hay-rope suspenders." What impressed both artists strongly was not Muir's tattered clothing, but his striking resemblance to classic renditions of Jesus.

This accepted view of Theresa Yelverton and John Muir is highly unfair to both. First, Theresa was only two years Muir's senior (she was thirty-four). Second, as has been amply shown, she was a brilliant woman and far from foolish. John Muir's scholarly friend, Professor William Frederic Badè, who edited Muir's unpublished papers and wrote the first biography, stated that Mrs. Yelverton and John Muir became "warm friends," meaning the admiration was mutual. It is only reasonable to suppose that they did, for Muir would have appreciated her exceptional mind; her candor, her courage, independence, and those talents that set her apart as a remarkable person. He would have relished her repartee, for he was witty himself, and appreciated her Bohemian traits, for he was unconventional. Certainly he was not indifferent to the personal charm that everyone who met her remarked upon. He was openly attentive enough to arouse jealousy in one of Theresa's admirers who thought Muir's eyes "were too bright blue" when he talked to her; "that was because *his* were green, no doubt," she quipped.

She and Muir found a strong common bond in their interest in botany, natural history, and the wonders of Yosemite, and in her faculty for also finding spiritual solace in the out-of-doors. Muir would have been pleased to find what might be least expected—that she was a good listener. Mary Austin remembered Muir as "talking much" and having "the habit of soliloquising." In fact, he often monopolized the conversation in a room where such fluent intellects as Ina Coolbrith, Stoddard, William Keith, and Jeanne Carr were gathered.

In her turn, Theresa would have appreciated his gentle nature and forthrightness, qualities lacking in those men with whom she had been closely associated in the past. Muir offered her a warm, candid friendship she could trust.

In Theresa's surviving letters to Muir (the only evidence that exists), there is no suggestion of any feeling for him beyond deep affection. "You had an existence in my heart," she once told him—as she must have had in his. Typical of her letters (they corresponded long after she had left Yosemite), is one she wrote him in the early fall of 1870 after Muir had supposedly run away to escape her unwanted attentions. Actually, he had followed the Merced River out of the Valley on foot, through all its canyons to the plains, as part of his geological studies. She described for him the first touches of autumn—bracken turned golden, and oaks and maples every shade of yellow. She sent news of local doings and a little gossip. They had their private and sometimes unflattering names for certain permanent residents of Yosemite, about whom they made sharp or amusing remarks. These appear in this relaxed letter. She signed herself, "Very sincerely yours, Mrs. Brown." Mrs. Brown was to be the narrator of *Zanita*.

If John Muir were trying to extricate himself from a situation "daily becoming more melodramatic," as some biographers claim, it seems entirely out of character for him to encourage Theresa's attentions by continuing to write to her. And finally, if he had unpleasant feelings about their relationship, it is most unlikely that he would have carefully preserved her letters.

Convinced that his glacier theory concerning Yosemite's origin was sound, Theresa made notes on his explanations and went with him to examine the proof. They planned to ride one day across the Sierras to follow the evidence of ice erosion and see the wonders of Mono Lake and the eastern slope. With his help—he lent her his herbariums—she studied local plants. One day in late October Mary Lawrence saw her coming "across the rustic bridge, bearing bunches of autumn ferns, and trailing vines, and frail blossoms, looking like Flora gathering in her truant children from the coming winter storm." She was intending to identify and press these specimens.

In spite of her many activities she was still able to report to Charlie Stoddard: "I have set you an example by writing a novel to be called 'The Daughter of Ah-wa-nee: A Tale of Yo-semite.' It happened this way: I was finishing my book on America with a chapter on Yo-semite, when I was suddenly seized with the desire to write a story; it was like possession. I at once set to work, and have written two hundred and fifty pages in four weeks."

When the idea first came to her, she spoke of it to Muir who sent the news on to Jeanne Carr, in a letter dated July 29: "Mrs. Yelverton . . . told me the other day that she was going to write a Yosemite novel!! and that 'Squirrel' and I were going into it." "Squirrel" was Floy Hutchings, who earned this nickname at an early age because of her lightning-quick movements. She was the first white child born in Yosemite.

"Dear little Squirrel! she knew nothing of the world but what she saw of it within her mountain-walled horizon; such an odd little child as she was, left quite to herself and her fancies; no doubt thinking she was the only one of her kind in existence . . . making long, solitary explorations, and returning, when we were all well frightened, with a pocketful of lizards and a wasp caged in her hand—they never stung her," Charlie Stoddard remembered from his long stay at the Hutchings cabin. "She was forever talking of horned toads and heifers; was not afraid of snakes not even rattlers." When she was happy she imitated the birds in song; when displeased, she growled like a bear. When old enough to have her own way entirely, she put on trousers, freeing her to ride her horse bareback and astride at top speed over the meadows—a favorite pastime. John Muir spoke of her as "a rare creature," "a tameless one," "a smart & handsome & mischievous Topsy" whose appearance in the novel "can scarce be overdrawn." So it was Florence, Floy, or Squirrel, with yet another name, Zanita (short for Manzanita), who became the leading feminine character in Theresa's book and, at the publisher's suggestion, gave her name to the title.

Keeping these descriptions of Floy Hutchings in mind as one reads about the child Zanita, it is clear that her personality and character— even her talk, have not been overdrawn. A photograph taken about the time Theresa Yelverton met her indicates how accurately she described Zanita's physical appearance. The slender oval face, the Grecian brow, the determined chin, the brunette complexion, and the dark, silky hair are there. With remarkable prescience she had Zanita meet a tragic death in Yosemite as the result of an accident, a fate that overtook Floy Hutchings nine years after the novel was published.

Theresa's principal male character was John Muir, whom she called Kenmuir, a name which may have had special meaning for them because her letters to him always began, "My dear Kenmuir." To lend reality to his dialogue, particularly his reverence for nature and his explanations of Yosemite's origin, she worked from her records of his conversations and soliloquies and from his notebooks, which he lent her. Kenmuir's talk about the importance of glaciers in Yosemite's formation has given *Zanita* historical significance in the knowledge that John Muir was aware at least as early as 1870 that ice had overridden Glacier Point.

He read some of the manuscript and admitted, "she had a little help from me." He felt that she had pictured his appearance accurately, for "I have often worn shirts, soiled, ragged and buttonless . . . with a spray [of greenery] stuck somewhere, or a carex, or chance flower. It is about all the vanity I persistently indulge in, at least in bodily adornments." But he was not sure that she knew enough of "wild nature" to understand and draw the complete man.

But Theresa Yelverton knew him far better than he suspected, as is shown by other perceptive descriptions of him made at this time. The popular poet, essayist and newspaperwoman, Sara Jane Lippincott (known best as "Grace Greenwood"), who was staying at Hutchings' hotel, wrote:

"Among our visitors in the evening was Mr. Muir, the young Scottish mountaineer, student, and enthusiast, who has taken sanctuary in the Yosemite, who stays by the variable Valley with marvelous constancy, who adores her alike in her fast, gay summer life and solemn autumn glories, in her winter cold and stillness, and in the passion of her spring floods and tempests. . . . Mr. Muir talks with a quiet, quaint humor, and a simple eloquence. . . . He has a clear blue eye, a firm, free step, and marvelous nerve and endurance. He has the serious air and unconventional ways of a man who has been much with Nature in her grand, solitary places."

Professor Joseph LeConte, who supported Muir's glacier theory and invited him to join him and a party of his geology students through the high country to trace the evidence of ice striations and glacial polish, wrote in his journal on August 8, 1870: "After dinner, lay down on our blankets and gazed up through the magnificent tall spruces into the deep blue sky and gathering masses of white clouds. Mr. Muir gazes and gazes and cannot get his fill. He is a most passionate lover of nature. Plants and flowers and forests, and sky and clouds and mountains seem actually to haunt his imagination. He seems to revel in the freedom of this life. I think he would pine away in a city or in conventional life of any kind. . . . He is really . . . a man of strong, earnest nature, and thoughtful, closely observing, and original mind."

The narrator of *Zanita* is Mrs. Sylvia Brown, the wife of a professor of geology in "a College of California," who lives in Oakland and spends his summers in geological field work, sometimes accompanied by a group of his students. When the book opens, he is planning to go to Yosemite. "Professor Brown" is Professor Joseph LeConte of the University of California, who lived in Oakland and made his first trip to Yosemite in 1870 with a party of nine students. In the journal he kept of those "ramblings" he mentions Theresa Yelverton as being among friends he met at Hutchings' hotel, where he stopped for his mail.

In an attempt to disguise LeConte, Theresa makes him disagree vehemently with Muir's theory of Yosemite's origin and set forth the conclusion developed by Josiah Whitney, head of the California State Geological Survey.

Elvira and James Mason Hutchings are prominent in the novel as Zanita's parents, Placida and Oswald Naunton. Gertrude Hutchings, the younger daughter, as Rosalind Naunton is developed into a rather important character, who at the book's end marries Kenmuir. Two other well-known Yosemite residents appearing in *Zanita* are the Vermonters Albert and Emily Snow who built a chalet on the flat between Vernal and Nevada Fall and opened it in April 1870. Emily, known for her "piquant pleasantries," becomes Nell Radd, while the husband she orders about is simply Radd. They have a sagacious St. Bernard named Rollo, who is the counterpart of the equally wise St. Bernard Carlo, who was John Muir's companion in the High Sierra during the summer of 1869, when he was tending sheep. He must have told Theresa a great deal about Carlo's intelligence and capacity for learning.

James Lamon who spent every Saturday evening with the Hutchings family, appears in the book as the aged giant, Methley. John Muir described Lamon as "a fine, erect, whole-souled man, between six and seven feet high." After homesteading in Yosemite Valley in April 1859, he built a ten-by-twelve-foot log cabin, located a vegetable garden and orchard opposite Half Dome, set out apple, pear, and peach trees, and berries of many kinds, which bore so heavily he sold the fruit to tourists. Theresa, as Mrs. Brown, tells in the book about visiting Methley's plantation and tasting the raspberries. The talus cave below the Royal Arches that she identifies as Methley's dwelling was actually Lamon's storeroom. She also took poetic license with his age, for he was fifty-two when she met him.

The Galen of Galen's Rancho is Galen Clark with whom Theresa visited on her ride into Yosemite. "Horse-shoe Bill" was modeled after "Pike," a competent guide who was popular because of his familiarity with the name and history of every landmark in the area; because of his amusing observations, his fund of tall tales, and his skill with the fiddle.

"I can not tear myself away from the purple rocks, the golden ferns, the rosy sunsets on the great South [Half] Dome," Theresa wrote Charlie Stoddard that autumn. She planned to winter in the Valley, where she felt at ease and safe from her nemesis, finish *Zanita*, and possibly write another novel. No reason not to stay on forever, Stoddard reflected. These months had been the happiest in her entire life, she told Hutchings.

Then one day in early November, letters bearing a coat-of-arms arrived for her through the British consul. Mary Lawrence was with her and noticed how her hand trembled as she tore the covers off, and that she became "so agitated" after reading the contents (they announced the death of the old Viscount Avonmore and her husband's succession to the title), she hurried off to her room and remained shut in for hours. Staying at the hotel was an earl whose advice to Theresa was, when he heard the news, hasten "home" and claim her rightful title and inheritance.

Although she decided against following his suggestion, she changed her mind about wintering in the Valley. Yosemite's spell was suddenly shattered. Her inner peace vanished, and she grew restless. Very soon she was packed and ready to ride out with the earl and a party of his peers who had invited her to join them up the mountain trail to Clark's and accept a seat in their private carriage to Mariposa.

It was an overcast morning when Theresa, dressed in a blue bloomer suit, took her place with the horsemen. She very soon discovered that the saddle was uncomfortable, and Hutchings, who was seeing them off, insisted upon changing it.

"Ride along, gentlemen," she said to the others. "I will overtake you at Inspiration Point in time for luncheon." A superb horsewoman, well-acquainted with the trail, she knew she could easily catch up. But by the time the saddle was replaced the sky had darkened and a light snow was falling. Elvira and Hutchings did their best to persuade her not to leave, but fearful that this might be the start of winter in earnest and the blocking of the passes until spring, she set off at a canter across the meadows. Once she began to climb, the snowfall increased, the wind-driven flakes became almost blinding, and progress was slow. When she reached Inspiration Point, no one was there. Her escort, having expected to be overtaken long before, decided that she must have wisely stayed at the hotel. Afraid of being stormbound, they had waited only a few minutes before riding on.

Although it was by then snowing harder, and dusk was nearing, Theresa was reluctant to turn back toward the Valley and risk the hazards of the steep downhill trail in the dark. Holding some hope that she might still overtake the party, she pressed on to Peregoy Meadows, but when they reached the boggy grassland the storm suddenly worsened and her horse refused to cross. Theresa was wet to the skin and shivering. Knowing she must remain active to keep from freezing, she dismounted and, leading her animal, began retracing her steps, searching all the while for some shelter in which to pass the fast-approaching night. At length she sighted an upright hollow tree. Removing the saddle blanket, she wrapped it around her shoulders, and keeping a firm grip on the bridle, crawled into the hole. She then drew the horse's head inside and rested her cheek against his for comfort and warmth.

The sleepless night seemed without end. Cold, hungry, and desolate, she thought many times of Yelverton's curse during those lagging hours. In the morning a bright, cloudless sky brought hope of finding her way back to the Valley, but when she started off she saw that snow covered all identifying marks. Still leading her horse, she tried every direction, uphill and down. Once she heard rustling behind some high boulders and, thinking it might be Hutchings who was supposed to go to Mariposa that morning, she called his name and hurried toward the sound. Rounding the rocks hopefully, she came face to face with a large black bear. Her horse snorted and, breaking away, made for the heights. The bear, equally frightened, turned and fled. Theresa, also startled, began to run, broke through the snow, and tumbled twenty feet down a cliff. Bruised, cut, and bleeding, she got to her feet and began climbing slowly to the top, but suddenly becoming weak, she collapsed. Certain her end had come, she thought once again of the curse, and then lost consciousness.

The Yosemite innkeeper George Leidig, on his way out that morning, noticed the fresh trail of footprints going this way and that. Aware that Theresa Yelverton was the last person to leave the Valley the day before, he knew she must have missed her escort. Following the prints to the cliff's edge, he saw her lying motionless below. Climbing down, he was able to partially restore her and, with the help of Hutchings, who had by then come along, got her up the slope and back to the hotel.

A few days of rest restored her, and as soon as the weather settled, she set out again for San Francisco. But while still in the Valley she wrote an account of this experience for John Muir, who had not yet returned from his pedestrian exploration of the Merced River.

"It seems strange to me that I should not have known and felt her anguish in that terrible night, even at this distance," he wrote Jeanne Carr, for he was clairvoyant and could cite many instances when his premonitions regarding people with whom he had an affinity were correct. He sent off a letter to Theresa as soon as he received hers.

The press made much of this latest adventure of the Viscountess Avonmore, as they called her, and sensational stories illustrated with "frantically melodramatic" woodcuts appeared throughout the country. Charlie Stoddard remembered that after she returned to San Francisco they laughed until they were in tears over those accounts.

She was in no hurry to leave the city. She finished *Zanita* and placed it with the same New York publisher who later issued John Muir's books. She worked on the travel book she called *Teresina in America*; wrote an article for the *Overland Monthly*, and arranged to contribute to it regularly, as she did with the San Francisco *Daily Evening Bulletin*.

Then, in the fall of 1871, she set sail in a clipper ship at midnight in the midst of "a dreadful storm and fog," for Canton rather than England. She left a letter for Stoddard, who was out of town: "You can not think how distressed I am to leave without seeing you again . . . ," words he read with "a heavy heart." But she said that through her articles for the *Overland*, "I shall be with you in spirit, though I am elsewhere in the flesh." From Hong Kong she wrote him:

"What an age ago it seems to me since I left the California world! . . . I have . . . lived an entirely new life, full of excitement, full of interest, and also full of struggle. . . . You like the *dolce far niente*; I, the rush and strife of battle. And yet, somehow, we sympathize; we are links of a chain that fit well together." She had spent a month in Canton, "reveling in Orientalism. How much you would enjoy it! . . . but all this I shall put in a book for you, and we will talk it over by and by. . . . " Although they continued to correspond, they never met again.

On January 22, 1872, she wrote John Muir from Hong Kong:

"My dear Kenmuir:

How I have wished for you, and sometimes longed for you avails not to say. It is sufficient to make you comprehend that I never see a beautiful flower or a fine combination in nature without thinking of you and wishing you were there to appreciate it with me." She would like to send him specimens of the many varieties of ferns, flowers, and moss she has gathered, but can compress only a few into the envelope. She pictures him in Yosemite, reading her letter "in some quiet spot with all nature as calm and still as your heart. I used to envy you that, for mine will not be still but is restless and unquiet; yet I have enjoyed a great deal lately." If, in his rambles, he discovers "a new Valley as beautiful as Yosemite, I will surely come and see it and pitch my tent for a time." She was leaving shortly for Saigon and Bangkok, where she expects to find "wonderful things" about which to write. Then she will return to England by way of the Cape of Good Hope, where he must send a letter, for she will be staying awhile.

"And now good bye for a time but remember that your letters and proceedings have always a deep interest for me." She signed herself, "Your sincere friend, Theresa Yelverton."

Her harrowing adventures were not over. The sailing vessel taking her to Saigon was dismasted in a typhoon and nearly wrecked. Theresa, "a prisoner in the cabin, was dashed violently about, and rescued with difficulty from what might have resulted in serious injury, if not disfigurement or death," reads an old account. The story of that narrow escape received wide news coverage and made its way to her friends in California.

After returning to England in 1873, she soon discovered that to try and claim her title and recover her property would require years of litigation, which she could not afford, especially because the prospects for success seemed hopeless. The second Mrs. Yelverton, who already had two sons by Theresa's husband, was the accepted Viscountess Avonmore. Theresa continued to use her rightful title and turned her thoughts to planning her future. She placed two book manuscripts with her London publisher: *Teresina Peregrina, or Fifty Thousand Miles of Travel Round the World*, which was issued in 1874, and the work on her stay in the United States, which came out in two volumes in 1875. The author's name appeared on the title-page of each volume as it had in *Zanita*: Thérèse Yelverton (Viscountess Avonmore). Over the years she varied her title, sometimes calling herself Lady Theresa Avonmore, Thérèse, Lady Avonmore, or Theresa, Countess Avon-more.

Once her books were in production she began to lecture and give dramatic readings. Her talks about the countless exciting adventures she had met during years of world travel to exotic and inaccessible places (she was the first white woman to push up the crocodile-infested rivers through the heart of the jungle to explore the newly discovered ruins of Angkor Wat), were immediately popular and she was engaged to tour England. She was billed as "Thérèse, Lady Avonmore."

In 1873 Charlie Stoddard was staying in London with Mark Twain when he learned of Theresa's arrival. The humorist, then lecturing there, had hired Stoddard as his secretary because he delighted in Stoddard's company and enjoyed listening to him play the piano. Of Theresa, Stoddard wrote: "Often we had planned to meet—somewhere, somehow, sometime; and I tried to reach her by letter addressed in care of her London publisher. In vain: even her publisher was unaware of her whereabouts," for she was on the road speaking. She tried to locate him, but was equally unsuccessful, for right after the new year Mark Twain sailed for home, and Stoddard began flitting about England, first to worship at Shakespeare's grave and, with permission, sleep in Anne Hathaway's bed for several weeks. Eventually he turned his steps toward Rome, arriving after a time without his coat, his pocket-book, his luggage, or his ticket, all of which he had lost along the way.

Of Theresa Yelverton he wrote: "Evidently it was our destiny never to meet again."

By writing, lecturing, giving dramatic readings, and elocution lessons, Theresa earned enough to live comfortably and afford to take those long ocean voyages which satisfied her restlessness and her love of adventure. It was her ambition, she once said, to "live always at sea." During the next few years she sailed over the Pacific, traveling as far south as New Zealand, where she visited her brother, Jack Longworth, who was living there. In all of her wanderings she seems never to have gone back to California.

In 1880 she toured India and Ceylon, then returned to South Africa. On May first of that year, the press in Natal announced the arrival of Lady Avonmore at Durban. Shortly she moved on and rented rooms in the best part of Pietermaritzburg, the capital city, where she had a circle of friends made during previous visits.

On January 15, 1881, the newspaper *Natal Witness* published the first in a series of columns titled, "Pen and Ink Sketches," that appeared nearly every Saturday. The author (Theresa Yelverton) signed herself "Kate the Critic," and her identity had to be carefully guarded, for each article lampooned one of Natal's prominent men. She began with "His Worship the Mayor of Maritzburg," a success that was followed by a piece about someone she called the "usurping" Bishop. Few were spared—not even the editor of the *Witness*, who could only laugh with the others because "Kate's" sketches increased his paper's circulation manyfold.

That February she wrote of being "racked with pains in every limb," and to be suffering from fever and edema. "My doctor tells me I must not excite my mind; it is the first time I knew I posessed such a piece of furniture." Within a month she had recovered, but in May all of the symptoms returned. Then, on August 27, "Kate" announced: "I have been ordered complete change which will prevent me from continuing for a time at least, 'The Pen and Ink Sketches.' But at some future period I hope again to hold up Natal's public men to the gaze of their fellow colonists."

She grew steadily worse with what was diagnosed as dropsy, and in early September a friend, Joseph Mason, had her moved from her rooms to his home, where a married daughter came to stay and nurse her.

On Tuesday evening, September 13, Theresa Yelverton, Viscountess Avonmore, died at age forty-five. She was not alone and untended as her husband's curse had stipulated, and she had dreaded for so long, but with a group of close friends. One of these admirers wrote at the time: "Her mind was clear and vigorous up to the last moment."

She was buried the next day in Pietermaritzburg's Church of England Cemetary. The Reverend Joseph Rice, curate of St. Paul's Cathedral, conducted her funeral service.

ZANITA:

A Tale of the Yo-semite

CHAPTER I.

KENMUIR.

SOME OF THE MOST potential episodes of our lives are ushered in by apparently trivial circumstances. A fancy, a whim, a caprice, even a movement without any separate act of volition, an accidental glance across the street, a false step over the stones, are often the foundations upon which some vitally important bridge of our lives has to be constructed.

Trifling incidents not infrequently give birth to the most stupendous events.

Thus the life-drama which I am about to narrate fell out in consequence of the gratification of what might have appeared at the time a very innocent whim.

Caprice had been attributed to me all my life through: as a school-girl, by my companions, and as a woman, by my husband; until I had come to believe it formed a part of my character.

Yet any individual exercise of the propensity never warned me at the time, and it was not until my husband classified my action as a piece of caprice, that I came to regard it in that light.

The very beginning and root of my story grew out of one of these trifling fancies. My husband was a Professor of Geology in a College of California, and much of the pleasantest part of my life was spent in bearing him company in his geological excursions.

We usually spent the vacations in delightful rambles, occasionally accompanied by a few of the more studious and inquiring of his pupils, sometimes by a fellow Professor, and sometimes alone.

I used to long for Commencement Day quite as eagerly as any over-worked student. The city, and everything connected with the city, had by that time become abhorrent to me. I hated the noise, the dirt, the talk, the dress, my household cares, and the dry parched look of everything, and longed for the fresh green sward, the music of streams, the song of birds, the sunset rambles and the still hush of moonlight nights; in fine for all the delights of the country.

For, although a most practical body in the matter of shirt buttons, darning, and improvised dishes of unctuous flavor, yet there was a latent stratum of romance in my composition which, *de temps en temps*, would bubble up amid my daily cares and wrestle for a recognition, and enfranchisement of its own.

What then was my disappointment when the Professor announced that he would be detained by business for a week or ten days after the term had closed.

"This is a terrible disappointment to you I know, my dear," said my husband, who never thwarted me in anything. "But do you not think you could make a start on your own account, and stop at some pretty place for a few days, when I could join you?"

Of the two evils this seemed to be the least objectionable. And so it was settled that I should start for Mariposa alone, where I duly arrived, and was enjoying myself with my usual zest for the country, when the idea, or caprice, seized upon me that it would be a very pleasant thing to go on a little exploring expedition on my own behalf, and prospect for the Professor ere he arrived. I thought if I could secure a horse and guide, I would wander forth in search of that marvelous Valley of Yosemite, so recently discovered by white men, and already exciting so much interest in the world at large, as well as in scientific circles.

I knew my husband had some intention of measuring the colossal trees, reported to be three or four hundred feet in height, and the granite giant, showing a vertical front of four thousand. I thought it would be pleasant to forestall him. Acting upon this freak of fancy, I set out with my guide, Horse-shoe Bill, who, as he informed me, derived his title, like many of the nobility, from having located in, and possessed himself of, a certain Horse-shoe Bay.

We rode from early morn until eve through the most glorious country it had ever been my fate to traverse. Mountain rose above mountain, and tower above tower of rocky peaks; and, away up, mingling with the snowy clouds, peered the no less snowy caps of the distant Sierra Nevadas. Here and there we could see green valleys nestling in among the mountains, and deep cañons filled with dark pines.

"O, them's nowhar to the Valley whar I'm agoin' to take you; and we can most see some of it now. Them three peaks as you see a topplin' over one another, a sort of playin' leap-frog, the Indians call Pom-pom-pas-us."

Looking in the direction to which he pointed, I beheld a chaos of mountain tops and deep chasms, all seemingly thrown inextricably together, and apparently inaccessible. My heart began to fail me as to my further progress, when a peculiar looking object foreign to the scenery caught my eye.

"What on earth is that?" I exclaimed, reining up my not unwilling mustang, and pointing to the singular creature extending itself as though about to take wing from the very verge of a pinnacle overhanging a terrific precipice. "Is it a man, or a tree, or a bird?"

"It's a man, you bet," replied my guide, chuckling. "No tree or shrub as big as my fist ever found footing there. It's that darned idiot Kenmuir, and the sooner he dashes out that rum mixture of his he calls brains the sooner his troubles'll be over, that's my idee."

"It's not mine though," I said decisively, "for if he is really crazy we are the more bound to take care of him. Suppose you give a shrill whistle to attract his attention."

"He'll not bother for that, he'll know it's me; but if you ride around this here point he'll see you belike; that'll be a novel sight for him," said the guide, who was by no means an ill-natured man: only thoroughly imbued with a recklessness of human life, which years spent in the wildwood seems to engender in the most humane.

Adopting his suggestion, we quickly rounded the point, when the singular figure was seen swaying to and fro with extended arms as if moved by the wind, the head thrown back as in swimming, and the long brown hair falling wildly about his face and neck.

The point on which he stood was a smooth jutting rock only a few inches in width, and a stone thrown over it would fall vertically into the valley five thousand feet below. My heart beat fast with horrible dread as my guide coolly explained this fact to me. I hardly dared to fix my eyes upon the figure lest I should see it disappear, or remove them, lest it should be gone when I looked again. In my desperation, I exerted that power of will which is said to convey itself through space without material aid. I strove to communicate with him by intangible force. The charm seemed to work well. He turned quickly towards me, and, with a spring like an antelope, was presently on *terra firma* and approaching us.

"There, you'll have plenty on him now," said Horse-shoe Bill. "He loafs about this here valley gatherin' stocks and stones, as I may say, to be Scriptural, and praisin' the Lord for makin' of him sech a born fool. Well some folks is easy satisfied!"

As the lithe figure approached, skipping over the rough boulders, poising with the balance of an athlete, or skirting a shelf of rock with the cautious activity of a goat, never losing for a moment the rhythmic motion of his flexile form, I began to think that his attitude on the over-hanging rock might not, after all, have been so chimerical; and my re-solve, as to how I should treat this phase of insanity, began to waver very sensibly, and I fell back on that mental rear-guard—good inten-tions; but when he stood before me with a pleasant "Good day, madam," my perplexity increased ten-fold, for his bright intelligent face revealed no trace of insanity, and his open blue eyes of honest questioning, and glorious auburn hair might have stood as a portrait of the angel Raphael. His figure was about five feet nine, well knit, and bespoke that active grace which only trained muscles can assume.

The guide increased my confusion by exclaiming, "Hallo, Kenmuir! the lady wants to speak to you."

I wished the guide at Jericho for giving me such false notions. Why had he induced me to believe this man a raving maniac, only to compel me, like old Dogberry, to write myself down an ass. I could have as soon reproached one of the clouds gyrating round the crest of the mountain with running into danger.

"Can I do anything for you?" asked Kenmuir gently.

"She wants to know what you were doing out on that bloody knob overhanging eternity?"

"Praising God," solemnly replied Kenmuir.

"Thought that would start him," interrupted the guide.

"Praising God, madam, for his mighty works, his glorious earth, and the sublimity of these fleecy clouds, the majesty of that great roaring torrent," pointing to the Nevada, "that leaps from rock to rock in exul-tant joy, and laves them, and kisses them with caresses of downiest foam. O, no mother ever pressed her child in tenderer embrace, or sung to it in more harmonious melody; and my soul joins in with all this shout of triumphant gladness, this burst of glorious life; this eternity of truth and beauty and joy; rejoices in the gorgeous canopy above us, in the exquisite carpet with which the valley is spread of living, palpitat-ing, breathing splendor. Hearken to the hymn of praise which re-sounds upwards from every tiny sedge, every petal and calyx of myriads and myriads of flowers, all perfect, all replete with the divine impress of Omnipotent power. Shall man alone be silent and callous? Come, madam, let me lead you to Pal-li-li-ma, the point I have just left, where you can have a more complete view of this miracle of nature, for I am sure you also can worship in this temple of our Lord."

Here was a pretty fix for a Professor's wife, and a sensible woman! I was about to put myself in the identical situation which but a few moments before had induced me to consider the man who occupied it a lunatic.

Horse-shoe Bill remarked my puzzled expression, and laughed, "Ho, he'll guide you right enough; he knows every inch of the road as well as I do. You needn't be afeard; he'll take you to the shanty I told you of, where you can locate for the night, and I'll make tracks back again, if so be you don't want me."

One thought of the maniac shot through my mind, not as a fear, but a souvenir. I looked on the face of Kenmuir, shining with a pure and holy enthusiasm, and it reminded me of the face of a Christ I had seen years ago in some little old Italian village; not a picture of any note, but possessing such a tender, loving, benignant expression, that I had never forgotten it; and had then thought that the artist must have intended it for the Salvator Mundi before he became the Man of Sorrows.

With this picture brought forcibly to my mind, I resigned myself cheerfully, and followed his lead to the great projecting rock called the Glacier Point, or Pal-li-li-ma, where I had first seen him, and where there are still traces of ancient glaciers, which he said "are no doubt the instruments the Almighty used in the formation of this valley."

As we proceeded slowly and carefully, my thoughts dwelt with deep interest on the individual in advance of me. Truly his garments had the tatterdemalion style of a Mad Tom. The waist of his trousers was eked out with a grass band; a long flowing sedge rush stuck in the solitary button-hole of his shirt, the sleeves of which were ragged and forlorn, and his shoes appeared to have known hard and troublous times. What if he had been, at some previous period, insane, and still retained the curious mania of believing that human beings might through righteousness float in ambient air? What if he should insist on our making the experiment this evening together? What would my husband say if he knew all, and saw me here committed to the sole care of this man with the beautiful countenance, and with no other guarantee, in a wilderness of mighty rocks, gigantic trees, and awful precipices, a hundred miles from anywhere! This was a very awkward thought to deal with, and there was no justification I could think of. What inconvenient but useful creatures husbands are sometimes! If we should go over the rocks together, of course there would be an "end of everything," as Sir Peter Teazle says; but in case I should survive, and recount the whole matter to him, as I could not help doing, then he would upbraid me with riding off at the risk of my neck, on my favorite hobby-horse, Physiognomy.

But, in the course of conversation with my *cicerone*, I soon divined that his refinement was innate, his education collegiate, not only from his scientific treatment of his subject, but his correct English. Kenmuir, I decided in my mind, was a gentleman; and behind this bold rampart I resolved to intrench myself against the sarcastic tiltings of the Professor.

As we approached the point, Kenmuir said, with a gleeful laugh, "I do not intend to take you out on the overhanging rock, where I was standing, but to a very nice little corner, where you can sit your horse comfortably, unless you really want to dismount."

I thanked him, and, smiling at the arch allusion, said I would remain seated. The scene from Pal-li-li-ma was a marvel of grandeur and sublimity, and fully warranted the lavish enthusiasm of my new friend. Around us vast mountains of granite arose one above another in stupendous proportions, and over them leaped the mighty cataracts with majestic sweep.

"These are the Lord's fountains," said Kenmuir, clasping his hands in the intensity of his delight, "and away up above, elevated amid clouds, are the crests of the God-like peaks covered with eternal snows. These are the reservoirs whence He pours his floods to cheer the earth, to refresh man and beast, to lave every sedge and tiny moss; from those exalted pinnacles flow the source of life, and joy, and supreme bliss to millions of breathing things below; to the dreamy-eyed cattle that you see four thousand feet in the valley beneath us, standing knee-deep in the limpid pool; to the tiny insects that are skimming in ecstatic merriment around every glistening ribbon of water as it falls. Look! and see these silvery threads of water all hurrying down so swiftly, yet so gracefully, to bathe the upturned face of nature, and varnish with new brilliancy her enameled breast. Beyond is the Lord's workshop. With these resistless glaciers he formed a royal road,—from the heights of the topmost Sierras which you now see covered with snow, roseate from the sun's last beams,—into the valley at our feet. Yet all is lovely in form, and harmonious in color. Look at that ledge of rock—the hardest of granite—how exquisitely it is tapestried with helianthemum. Would you like a bunch?"

And before I could reply, the rash man had leapt down, and alighted like a bird on a perch, and grasped a bunch of ferns, which he stroked affectionately, and carefully stowed away in the grass cincture, whilst there was but a half foot of rock between him and "etarnity," as the guide expressed it.

CHAPTER II.

A STRANGE GUIDE.

"Now," said Kenmuir, "lest you should think I have brought you to this wilderness to make you be food for ghouls and water kelpies, I will point out the spot where you are to spend the night, and as many more as you wish."

I looked round in dismay. "We seem a million miles from anywhere."

"Upwards, yes." he replied,—"but look down, and you will see a yellow spot, surrounded by what appears a few willow sticks, but which are in reality tall pines, with the river winding round like a golden cord,—that is the homestead. We will go down by the trail, which is almost level."

By which I found he meant a pathway, next thing to stairs, down which my horse clambered very adroitly.

And thus through forests of gigantic pines, which Kenmuir would climb like a cat to reach some particular cone, and point out its wonderful structure; through groves of azalias, making the air heavy with odorous sweetness, where Kenmuir would disappear altogether, returning with some precious specimen, all which he carried to me like a faithful dog, going twice the actual distance in his erratic gyrations. Then we came across a patch of great tiger-lilies which we were both anxious to cull; and at last we entered on a green sward smooth as any lawn, set round (as in a garden) by Mariposa lilies, so called from their resemblance to a butterfly.

The piece of level ground was in front of a massive rock resembling an old country house, with gables and quaint chimneys overgrown with honeysuckle, which completed the delusion. Kenmuir threw up his arms in ecstasy, and declared it was a fac-simile of his father's manse in the braw old country of Perthshire.

"Then you are a Scotchman?" I exclaimed.

"Yes; did you not know that by my name?"

"Names," I said, "are not so indicative in this country as in yours. There you may almost tell if a man comes of a good stock, by his name. Whereas, here the greatest aristocrat might rejoice in the name of

Squaddles with impunity. The old country is more fastidious about euphonious sounds, and I think they are right; for I cannot help attaching a peculiar quality to peculiar sounds."

"What would you judge your host of this way to be,—his name is Oswald Naunton?"

"That is a name which requires a great deal of consideration. It is original. I never heard it before, and I am sure he will not be a commonplace man. Then there is poetic rhythm, which would suggest something harmonious and symmetrical in the character. Both smartness and pride combined; a man from whom you might safely ask a favor, but from whom you could extort nothing."

"Ha! ha!" laughed Kenmuir, "you're a fine guesser."

"I am not guessing in the least. You give me a real name and I will give you the rhythmical interpretation."

"Then you don't believe a rose would smell as sweet if it were called a tulip?"

"I will not discuss botany with you; but I say the rose by another name would not have played the same role in the world, would not have had the same poetical *entourage*. Lovers would not have offered it to their belles as emblems of their passion had it been called catnip!"

The twilight now had deepened to moonlight. For although we could not see any moon, she had risen, and was taking a ramble behind the cliffs. Yet her light swam over the whole scenery in magic waves, transforming it to the most unearthly vision of weird enchantment. Every notch and projection caught the soft loving light which fell in perfect streams over the mighty Tu-tock-ah-nu-lah, which seemed to have pierced the pale clear blue of the heavens and let out floods of its glistening moonlight.

"Do you not perceive the balmy odors of the pines? They also mark the height and distance of these stupendous adamantine bulwarks. What are the towers of Notre Dame, which they so singularly resemble, compared to these cathedral spires rising in proud majesty three thousand feet with the flying buttresses and ancient caryatides supporting the projecting arches!"

"Yes," I put in. "I believe I see a procession of monks ascending to the great entrance of the church."

"Those are pine-trees two hundred feet high, growing up the ravine. Look at the rich carving and fretwork on the walls, and the tall minarets dazzling in the moon's rays."

11

"And I hear the *muezzin* calling to prayer."

"That is an owl," answered Kenmuir; "and he says, 'Do! do! oh, do do !' *Do* what, I wonder?"

"Go on," I suggested, "for we have stopped here a full quarter of an hour, and our host will have retired for the night."

"We will wake him up," said Kenmuir, "but he will not be asleep such a night as this, he has too much soul."

"Still we had better move on," I said, recollecting what my former guide had turned back to say in a stage whisper,—"Don't let him stop, or he'll talk till judgement day; and don't let him stoop to pick up any new specimen, or you'll never be through with him for a month."

So we moved on softly, listening to the crackle of the pine straw which covered the earth through the park-like forest.

Kenmuir had got one more temptation—the moonflower.

"Did you ever see them open to the moon? They gradually untwist the outer leaves, then suddenly burst right open like a flash of light. I have watched them many an hour; they belong to the family œnothera."

"Stay! I'll hold your horse," he said, as I made a quiet attempt to keep jogging on.

"Now, my dear sir," I exclaimed, "How long do you think it will take the flower to open? or do you think you can inspire it with the amiable idea to do so within sixty seconds, because longer than that I cannot wait, and I'm all on the *qui vive* to see if my *nomenclatology*, that is what I call my new science, for it has a right to an 'ology, is correct as regards Mr. Naunton."

The flower did not open, and we sped on again, our shadows clearly defined on the grassy meadows which were studded with flowers, whose broad discs were like stars of the first magnitude.

"Do you see that light? That proves they are not gone to bed, and your fears may rest."

Through the trees a bright light was glimmering; not unwelcome it appeared, for beside the excitement which so much novelty and magnificence are sure to arouse in certain temperaments, the bodily fatigue of so many hours of up-hill and down-hill climbing on horseback, made the prospect of rest very thoroughly congenial.

What romantic temperament has not fed the soul with the marvelous and supernatural on such a night as this; when arriving either late at night or by moonlight in some unknown part of the country, he has pictured himself benighted and lost in the forest or the fog; the night owl, or the will-o'-the-wisp, has been his only guide, and when a light as at length startled his aching sight, has imagined it the gleam of the lantern of some midnight assassins burying their dead; or fancied it proceeding from some monastery, where silence was the discipline, and where the brown cowled monk, who attended upon us dumbly, pointed to the pallet in a bare cell as the resting-place for the night.

Who has not frightened himself with a vague superstition, like children with a made-up bogle, the more to enjoy the pleasures of security.

But this evening there was no need to conjure up any phantom of the brain; no occasion to counterfeit any romance; the reality was too importunately present.

Here was I, a lone woman having transgressed her husband's directions to await him in a civilized place, alone in the wildest part of the wild world, with a stranger—the like of whom I had never met in all my travels—wandering on an untrodden path to a habitation of which I knew next to nothing. It was certainly as extraordinary and romantic a situation as any lover of fiction could have framed. But my ruminations were cut short by our actual arrival, and a wild hallo from Kenmuir to arouse the inmates.

CHAPTER III.

THE DAUGHTERS OF AH-WAH-NEE.

A MORE CHARMING ABODE never gladdened the eyes of the weary traveller, than that which rose before me as I saw it in the moonlight.

An Italian cottage, with wide and tasteful veranda, over which grape-vine and wisteria were contending for each morsel of trellis-work. It was constructed of the rich yellow cedar, each knot and contortion of grain showing out like lumps of burnished gold; the pointed gabled roof was shaded by an enormous oak, with trunk some twelve feet in diameter, whose broad leaves lay on the yellow shingles, like sea-weed on a sandy beach.

In a semi-circle grew tall pines, the Douglas fir, and cedars, the lower spaces filled in with maples, and occasionally a *quercus virens*.

A small plot of garden, with choice flowers clustered around the veranda; and beyond, the river wound in serpentine curves green and clear, silvered here and there by the moonlight, and reflecting the summits of the great mountains. Such a fairy-like site I had never even read of in my youthful story-books.

"And how did it get here?" I exclaimed, "that beautiful *bijou* cottage amid these fierce and ragged rocks? Was it borne through the air from Italy or Switzerland, on the wings of seraphs, like the *Casa Santa de Loretto*."

"You've got to see my saw-mill, and then you will know how it all came about."

"For goodness sake," quoth I, "don't destroy my poetic hallucination by suggestions of a saw-mill!"

Kenmuir laughed one of his joyous, ringing laughs, and mine host appeared at the door. Little introduction seemed necessary; he had me off my horse in the twinkling of an eye, seated in one of the easiest chairs I know of,—and I am a connoisseur in those articles,—with a pinkish-colored California wine sparkling in an antique glass before me. And here I was in two minutes as cosy and comfortable as though I had called a queen my cousin.

Mr. Naunton was a tall, spare man of fifty, but looking ten years older, from his long snowy beard and the few white locks which still adorned his fine phrenologically developed head; his brilliant dark eyes shone with charity and humor. There was a benignant sweetness about his whole demeanor that made you feel at once that he would become the best friend you ever had, and I longed to import to Mr. Kenmuir the correctness of my divination.

He wore no coat or vest; and his trousers, which were very loose, had the same tendency as Mr. Kenmuir's, requiring to be hitched up, which I subsequently found was an epidemic in the Valley among the nether garments.

Upon his shoulder he carried, as a part and parcel of his natural appendage, a lovely child about two or three years old, who poised herself on her elevated station with one little dimpled hand on the top of the bald head. She was a fair, blue-eyed, flaxen-haired little creature, the living picture of one of Raphael's angels; cheeks like two luscious ripe peaches, and rounded limbs dimpled all over.

Before my eyes could satiate themselves with this lovely vision, I was interrupted by a sharp little nip on my arm, and turning, beheld the most midnight prototype of face I have ever seen in a human being, much less a child of six years.

It had all the character of the portraits of Mrs. Siddons taken as Lady Macbeth, where she is washing out the "damned spot." Her face was thin but oval, the eyes piercing black, with delicately penciled lines, squaring a Grecian brow, broad and low, with that fixed limning which gives a stare or habitual frown to the face. Her complexion was the richest brunette hue with a pure vermilion tinge on the cheeks, which had little of the roundness of childhood; her mouth was small, with thin, compressed lips, but her chin was of extraordinary depth and power. The hair was dark, fine, and silky.

A more startling little vision, as she emerged from the shadow into the blaze of the great fire, never roused into activity a weary traveller whose sensational emotions were nearly all exhausted.

The little hand with which she had pinched me to call my attention, was long and slender, the fingers so tapered that it looked like the hand of some little hobgoblin.

"Say!" she ejaculated, with another pinch.—"listen! Where do you come from, where are you going, what made you come; do you want to camp out? I'll go with you. We had better start before the moon goes down; have you plenty of blankets? It's only twenty miles to the top of Tis-sa-ak. I'll show you the trail. I've just come down to-day; me and my sister have been camping up there some time; we killed twenty bears. You are not afraid of rattlesnakes, I suppose; there is one just below here that has bitten me three times, but I always cut the piece out with my jack-knife, and it did me no harm."

"What is your name?" I asked, by way of mingling in the talk.

"My name is Zanita, because I was born amongst these rocks, which are all covered with Manzanita. It bears a pretty white blossom; and mamma, who is crazy for flowers, called me Zanita after them. Do you like it?"

"Very much," I said; "both the name and the idea are beautiful."

"Say!" she went on, "do you like me?"

"I shall tell you to-morrow; if you are good I shall like you."

"I'm not good," she answered, rapidly. "Do you want a polecat skin? I'll just go out and catch and skin one alive, and bring it to you."

"No, no, thank you, certainly not!" I replied, in some horror, lest the offer might be put into execution by this wonderful little Flyaway.

A mischievous elfish light gleamed in her black eyes for a second; it was not a laugh, and could hardly be called a smile, for the mouth did not move, yet it was the nearest approach to either that I ever saw pass over that handsome little face.

"Suppose I shoot it, and keep it off, far, far away, so that you can't smell it."

"That will be much better," I replied.

All this she snapped out in a short, rapid way, with the utmost nonchalance, as if it were the common matter-of-fact proceeding of everyday. Her voice was wiry, and sounded more like that of an old woman's than a child.

All my phrenological faculties were brought to instant play, and I was so preoccupied in my new human specimen that I did not at first notice the entrance of another personage, who seemed to glide rather than walk, and about whose every look and motion there was such a calmness and repose, that she might have represented the Goddess of Placitude.

She was introduced to me as Mrs. Naunton, and she uttered a few gentle words of welcome in a tone which sounded like the vibration of an Æolian lyre, so soft and musical was her voice.

She was a young woman, looking little over twenty, a slight, semi-girlish semi-matronly figure, with a Madonna cast of countenance, deep, pensive hazel eyes, a blush-rose complexion, and brown hair.

She moved dreamily, as if under a spell; and as she stood speaking to me, plucked meditatively the remains of a flower which she seemed to be studying botanically. She conducted me to a quaint bedroom that I found would take me all night to investigate, the scrutiny of which, therefore, I postponed until the next day.

After I had taken off my things, and refreshed myself with a wash, I returned to the sitting-room, still accompanied by the small sprite, who kept up a continual rattle of propositions, all of the most fabulous nature, for scaling rocks and fording rivers, as though we had been born elves instead of flesh and blood creatures.

A Chinaman was laying the table for supper, with the gliding aid of the Madonna. While she was thus engaged, I had time to examine the room, which was a singular admixture of rustic simplicity and modern refinement. It was a large chamber opening on the veranda, and its walls running up to the full height of the house without the intervention of any ceiling; the massive rafters illumined by the flickering flame, displayed some curiosities of natural history,—such as hornets' nests, which, after remaining tenantless for several years, had again become inhabited by sundry enterprising yellow-jackets; a few lichens had vigorously contrived to struggle through some crevice, and garland the antique roof; and part of the vine which wreathed the porch had found some tiny nook or crevice through which to twine its delicate tendrils. The walls were of the same rich yellow cedar as the outside, and were paneled with the deep claret-colored Manzanita wood, and decorated with pictures, some fine engraving of the best masters, or an oil painting of a striking scene in the Valley. On one side was a bookcase stocked with choice volumes of standard works, literary, scientific, ideal, and artistic; at the opposite side was an enormous chimney-place formed of four slabs of granite; the hearthstone, a great slab of the same stone extended some five feet into the room. Great logs, five or six feet long, raised on antique irons, blazed and crackled, and sent forked flames high up the capacious chimney.

It was a treat to see that fire burn; it seemed so thoroughly in earnest to enjoy and lavish itself in such a luxurious splendor; it roared, and sparkled, and leaped for gladness; the light white ash fell so soft and tenderly around, like some cozy old grandmother hemming in her unruly, frolicsome children. The furniture was principally rustic: a broad divan covered with handsome skins; the easy-chair before mentioned, made of the gnarled branches of Manzanita, and lined with white woolly skins; an *étagère* filled with wonderful fossils and crystals, specimens of gold and silver quartz, feldspar, and stalactites. A magnificent eagle, the defunct veteran of Eagle Point, spread his giant wings in one corner of the room, and a comical old cinnamon bear, with very red glass eyes, sat up on his haunches in another; his paws and snout served for a coat and hat-rack.

In a deep frame, covered with glass, was a dried bouquet of the wild flowers of the Valley. It was easy to see the feminine hand which had been here. There were rustic tables, and an escritoire decorated with pine cones, acorns, and hickory nuts, and yellow pine bark, resembling the most elaborate oak carving. There were delicate baskets, suspended from the roof, of gray and yellow fungi, and containing great flourishing bunches of the wood warelias, forming a living Prince of Wales's feather.

Each window was a separate conservatory, where grew the singular blood-plant, so called from its stem, leaves, and flowers being all of a flesh and blood color. A bobolink and grossbeak rivaled each other in an opposition duet. A guitar, and a few scraps of manuscript, might have told more for the talent than the tidiness of the author. Such was the general *coup d'œil* which riveted my attention.

With the gliding aid of the Madonna an excellent supper of cold venison pie, smoking hot new potatoes, and green peas, was soon on the table. To which, after the entrance of Kenmuir and Oswald Naunton, with the Rosebud perched aloft on his shoulder, I addressed myself in real earnest, believing meanwhile that I had actually penetrated into fairy land, or, more vulgarly speaking, "fallen into clover." Kenmuir and the Madonna entered into a most intricate botanical discussion. The former all vigor, and arguing in little puffs and dashes, while the latter glided out her sentences like soft falling snow.

I explained to my host the reason of my sudden advent, and the joke I had played upon the Professor; which he applauded, and praised my courage in pioneering my own way. He expatiated, with great fluency and perfect knowledge of his subject, on the marvels, geological, botanical, and natural, of the Valley.

"You need not tell me of the flowers, if these two have bloomed here," I said, indicating the Rosebud and Sprite.

"Yes," he said, "these are the daughters of Ah-wah-nee. They were born in the Valley, and have never been outside its granite fastnesses."

"I thought," I remarked, "that my guide had called the Valley Yosemite."

"Yes," replied my host, "that is the name which custom has now sanctioned. It means 'great grizzly bear,' and the name arose from a celebrated Indian chief having killed one with a club, a wonderful feat in this valley. But the original Indian name previous to that was Ah-wah-nee. We have called the children after the most profuse flowers here—the manzanita and rose—Zanita, and Rosalind. But Rosalind is such a contented happy little creature that Cozy seems the most appropriate appellation."

As I looked upon this artistic group, lit up by the varying flame of the pitch-pine fire, I could not help believing that this family, shut in from the outer world, yet with all the refinement of civilization, was surely one of the natural wonders of the Valley.

In spite of the adventures of the day, we still sat up round the fire until late in the night. The conversation was sparkling, and certainly original; and it was difficult to believe that I was a stranger amongst them, and had not been with them all my life. The little chubby rosebud lay asleep in her mother's lap; and the elf, with unwinking eyes, kept her post at my side, every now and then, *sotto voce*, hazarding a plan for a new expedition.

Kenmuir's laugh rang clear up to the rafters as he promised to induct me into the mysteries of the saw-mill on the morrow.

But once under the snowy sheets, I slept the sleep of the just, dreamless, and without waking, until the sun shone bright through my vine-latticed window next morning.

CHAPTER IV.

A DAY'S PLEASURE.

WHERE WAS I? Was it all a midsummer night's dream? The question was answered by a little sharp voice snapping out,—

"Don't you want to come and bathe? The river is just deep enough to drown father in some places; but you can take your shoes and stockings off." And through my half-closed lids I saw my fairy of the previous evening, with the miniature frown still on her face, and a worried look, as though she had the cares of the world on her slender shoulders.

"Hurry up!" she said; "we have to catch the fish for breakfast. I can hook five or a dozen" (her conception of numbers was not very profound), "and if that is not enough we can get them from the Indians. You need not be afraid of that Indian squatting on the rock with his bow drawn; he'll not shoot you unless you cross their trail. He's waiting for a Payute to come; they've been at war. I'll take care of you. They always shoot with poisoned arrows; do you know it? I'm not a bit afraid of them," she said, and the same uncanny light, which symbolized a smile, shot from her eyes.

Upon the most positive promise that I would prepare immediately if she would leave me, I succeeded in sending her forth to collect fishing tackle; and shortly after breakfast was announced by the sweet voice of Madonna.

Looking through my trellis work of vine leaves, my eyes wandered up what appeared a mile of perpendicular rock, without ever meeting the sky. The morning sun was bringing out upon it the softest gray tints streaked with burnished silver. Here and there a tuft of spirea was clinging, by some occult process, to the smooth rock; and the feathery branches of the spruce and tamarack were defined against its glistening surface, as though they had been frescoed there. I could hear the booming of the great Yo-semite fall like a distant park of artillery.

The breakfast did as much honor to the housekeeping as the supper of the previous evening. Fresh trout, poached eggs, fried ham, strawberries with the morning dew upon them, and delicious cream and butter, made a meal for a sybarite.

Then arose the different proposals for the day's entertainment. Mr. Naunton offered to saddle my horse and convey me to a near view of the magnificent double waterfalls, the Py-wy-ack and the Yo-wee-ye, which I had seen in the distance the day before. Kenmuir was full of some aeronaut scheme to the clouds somewhere between Tissa-ack and the moon. Mrs. Naunton insinuated that as I must feel fatigued after my long journey, we had better meander round the pleasant meadows, and curves of the river, and watch the trout if we could not catch them.

Miss Zanita was eagerly bent upon a bear hunt, herself to be armed with a double-barreled rifle. Cozy prattled off that portion of each proposal that her coral lips could turn the easiest, and lisped out, "saddle horse, fissis, big bear, and sifle," at which her great blue eyes sparkled with rapture, and she clapped her little dimpled hands and laughed like the ripple of summer water.

Amongst all these inviting tenders of amusement it was difficult to choose. Kenmuir's celestial trip, as being the most impracticable, was the first to fall through.

Zanita paced to and fro in the heat of her argument in favor of the bear hunt, urging how easy it was to kill the bear before he could come upon us.

Mr. Naunton's journey having been reckoned at fourteen miles, there and back, besides a good deal of hard climbing, was voted too fatiguing for the second day's excursion; and the Madonna, like all quiet, soft spoken women, gained her point.

Zanita was pacified by the offer of the porter's place in bearing a long fishing-rod and basket.

And there tantalizingly, skimming from pool to pool in the limpid water, were scores of speckled trout, all singularly cognizant of the fact that our admiration for them was of that ardent nature that we longed to eat them.

As Mrs. Naunton, whom we shall call by her given name of Placida, glided gracefully on with one golden haired child in her arms, and the other with its deep midnight gaze clinging to her dress, she seemed to me the model for the poet's lines:

> "And dark against day's golden death
> She moved where Irudis wandereth.
>
> A sweeter woman ne'er drew breath
> Than my son's wife Elizabeth."

"Very probably," replied Mr. Naunton, amused by this suggestion, and a humorous twinkle came in his bright eyes, "with the slight difference that she is my wife, not my son's."

This matter of relationship having been settled, we set forth upon one of those delightful strolls which must live in the twilight remembrance of every one, unless a Cockney or a Parisian, who have never been outside of their capital, who are so satisfied to see their peas ready shelled and their chickens ready trussed, that they are contented to believe they actually grew that way.

A pious London cook once remarked to her mistress, as she was about placing a large turkey to the fire, "Ain't this a blessing of Providence, ma'am, for this here skiver to grow right in the middle of this fine fat turkey? Why without that I never could get him all roasted." She had never seen a live turkey in her life, though she had roasted five hundred.

But outside the Cockney and Parisian world, every man, woman, and child ought to remember a holiday in the country, when they gathered wild flowers for their sweethearts, and wild berries for their children. Who has not felt as if translated into a new state of being, to a higher existence, when suddenly transported from the noise and turmoil and worry of a city, the incessant clang of machinery or the monotonous roll of street cars, to some peaceful Arcadia. And then what ecstasy to breathe in the stillness of the country, to listen only to those ethereal tones which may be the whispering of beatified spirits around us, or the tread of angels. There is a music in the hushed calm which speaks to the soul with an intensity of vibration, unaroused by the most stirring scenes of city life; awakening emotions too deep and spiritualized to be interpreted to the outer world, and which, though never appearing in garish day, dwell ever in the *chiaroscuro* of that dreaming spirit within us, to whom we all bow down in reverence. And on such days as these we commune with this mystic indweller of our interior life as with our guardian angel, and sweet and holy is the converse.

We walked upon a carpet of greenest sward, besprinkled with blossoms of nature's brightest dye. Many of the valley flowers were as yet unknown to botanists; and it was amusing to hear Kenmuir disputing with himself as to what genus they appertained.

"Now, you would never believe, madam, that this tiny fellow belonged to the family of the composite! and yet you perceive"—

"O, I am credulous to any extent," I interrupted, "and am prepared to believe any proposition you may lay before me to-day. I feel in too placid a state of mind to dispute on any topic; but when we get the Professor here, he will fight you tooth and nail as to the origin of everything. There never was such a man for doubting; he is not satisfied yet whether he is dreaming a life, or living a dream! You will find him delightful company."

"I am sure I shall," replied Kenmuir.

"I hope," said Mr. Naunton, "that he will give us some satisfactory theory about the formation of the Valley."

"O, I can tell you his opinion about that. He believes it was the bed of a great river from which the bottom fell out in the wreck of creation; the water subsided to the present level, and gradually dried off to this little river, vegetation taking its place everywhere."

"Good gracious!" exclaimed Kenmuir, "there never was a 'wreck of creation.' As though the Lord did not know how to navigate. No bottom He made ever fell out by accident. These learned men pretend to talk of a catastrophe happening to the Lord's works, as though it were some poor trumpery machine of their own invention. As it is, it was meant to be.

"Why! I can show the Professor where the mighty cavity has been grooved and wrought out for millions of years. A day and eternity are as one in His mighty workshop. I can take you where you can see for yourself how the glaciers have labored, and cut and carved, and elaborated, until they have wrought out this royal road."

Here Placida come to the rescue with a delicate perception, that I might feel hurt by this wholesale destruction of my husband's theory.

"Do you notice the peculiar spring of the branches out of the cedar? Unlike other trees, they appear as though a hole had been made in the main trunk, and the bough fitted in like the socket of a Dutch doll's arm."

"Yes," I replied, "and also how singular is the horizontal growth of the limbs, while the main body is so perpendicular."

"Some of these trees are little short of three thousand years old," said Mr. Naunton. "And if we understood the low murmuring of their branches, they could doubtless explain many a mystery we now puzzle our brains over."

"They tell it to the birds," put in Zanita, "and the birds will tell it to me. I know what the birds say; Mu-wah, our Indian, teaches me."

"Well, what is that bird saying now? That bright little fellow," I said, pointing, "with the top-knot of blue plumes."

Her eyebrows contracted as she looked earnestly at him, and I thought for a moment the little sorceress was at fault. I was mistaken.

"He says," she interpreted, " 'Yonder is a strawberry patch with fine ripe strawberries.' Don't you hear him? It's real plain."

The same dark twinkle shot from her eyes; she knew well she had triumphed. We all laughed, and asked to be escorted to the patch of fresh fruit whose fragrant bed she needed no bird to help her to find; in fact there was scarcely a spot high or low that those venturesome little feet had not explored.

The Valley was some eight miles long, and about a mile and a half in width, inclosed by immense bulwarks of granite, always precipitous, and sometimes ascending vertically a mile in height; occasionally advancing into the greensward in a stupendous colonnade, or massive single tower; sometimes receding into a cavernous amphitheatre, like the interior quadrangle of some ancient chateau-fort, simulating the domes of cathedrals, and minarets of mosques, and Chinese pagodas. Both ends of the Valley were closed by a cañon, or deep ravine; on the one end the river entered from the top. It came with a leap from the Cloud's Rest, the highest point seen from the Valley, and dashed down in two falls and a series of cataracts into the plain below, where it meandered round white sandy banks, the most tranquil and peace-loving little river in the world, shimmering coyly as for the sole benefit and habitation of the speckled trout jumping in its limpid waters. At the other end it stole quietly out through a rugged fastness, and was lost sight of in the deep cañon.

Upon which ever side we gazed, these towering battlements met the skies. Their jagged summits cutting the horizon in clear, pointed slants and zigzags, carved it into the curious form of a dandelion leaf. The blue vault above was the exact size and shape of the green valley below; so much of earth and heaven was encompassed by the granite walls, and all the rest of the great world was excluded. No sound but of Nature's broke the stillness.

"And yet one might fancy there were a number of carpenters at work," I said, as we paused to listen to the rap-a-tap-tap of the woodpecker.

"There he goes," said my host; "you can see him at work with his long chisel beak and scarlet hammerhead, working away faster than you can count the evolutions; he has bored a hole in that tree as rapidly as a joiner with his auger, and he has made it the exact size to fit in his acorn. I can show you trees perforated with a thousand holes as close as a honeycomb; for these little birds have not only to provide their own winter food, but are fully conscious of the fact that the squirrels will rob them of the greater portion of their stores. And so it is in human nature," continued Mr. Naunton; "one half the world labors from dawn to dewy eve, and often by midnight oil, that the other half may prey upon them, and despoil them of the fruits of their labor. It is a common saying, that one half the world does not know how the other half lives; but it is a problem easily solved. They live *upon* the said other half, as do the squirrels on the woodpeckers. Take the father of a family. For years he has passed six days of every seven sitting on that hard stool in that dismal counting-house, and has induced five or six young men, upon the alternative of keeping their spirit within their body, to do likewise; for the sole end and object that his lady wife and elegant daughters may sweep the street with their silks and velvets. He takes a hurried meal at a chop-house on week-days, and a cold slice on Sundays, in order that the servants may get out the sooner. Upon that day of rest he leaves his hard stool and perambulates to church, and during the service has a quiet time to himself, to arrange for the coming week, and speculate how he can best utilize his time by making a review of the past, and prudential resolves for the future. Yet he is an independent merchant, with a heavy account at his bankers. There is no difficulty in discerning that he is the woodpecker, and his lady wife and daughters are the squirrels. There is 'the man of enterprise,' fashionably dressed, with the weightiest diamonds in his shirt-front; his buggy, or saddle-horse, awaiting his pleasure. He has started every sort of 'company' that a high-sounding name could be tacked to. He is a great talker, with an immense flow of language, and delights in the display of it. He has talked every one's money out of their pockets to supply his need. He never did one hour's labor, mentally or physically, but has lived all his life in affluence on his neighbors' acorns. Sometimes it falls pretty hard on the woodpeckers; some ravenous squirrels will not only help themselves to the superfluities laid by, but eat up the hard-earned share of the laborer. Look into that wretched garret, where dwells a mother, a son, and two daughters. The son, with his hands in his pockets, is loafing round the corner of the street, waiting for acorns to turn up without the seeking. The mother is trimming her pretty taper nails, and explaining to her daughters how she always kept them unsplit, and of perfect filbert shape. The elder daughter is arranging dead men's beards into pads in her hair, to give her head the proportions of an idiot's. But the second daughter, who is the woodpecker of the family, is stitching away at the bodice of a dress, others lying about half completed. Her nimble fingers, filbert nails all cut short, go as fast as the head of the little woodpecker boring his holes, to complete those seams, and bring home the acorns, upon which the rest of the family live idly; the share remaining for the woodpecker is infinitesimally small.

" 'Jane, how can you sit over those seams and flounces day after day, and night after night? I am sure it would kill me. I would let the people wait!' exclaims the sister.

"She may be quite sure in process of time it will kill Jane, and she will *wait* for her acorns. But they soon look out for another woodpecker, for people *never* change their natures, anymore than the Ethiopian his skin."

Whilst Mr. Naunton had been speaking, we had all gathered round the strawberry patch, and been fed by Zanita and Rosalind with the choicest morsels. But here the dulcet voice of Placida broke in with the suggestion that if we were going to continue such disquisitions, we had better adjourn to a seat near the Yosemite Fall, "where the roar," she added, naïvely, "would serve for applause at the end of Oswald's speech."

"There is Zanita, like a tricksy squirrel, far away up the rocks already," I exclaimed.

"I hope she is not in search of that polecat she promised you," said her father, laughing, "for it would be the most uncomfortable present I ever heard of."

CHAPTER V.

SQUIRRELISM.

WE MADE OUR WAY toward the foot of the Falls, over rugged rocks garlanded profusely with the most exquisite flowers. Kenmuir soon became rapturous in his intense enjoyment of the music of the falling water,—falling as it seemed from the very heaven above us, almost three thousand feet,* to where it broke at our feet in a whirlwind of spray.

"It is the most glorious orchestra in the world," he exclaimed. "Listen to the wondrous harmony! No instrument out of tune, none wiry or reedy; all is pure, rich, full, and resonant. Hark to the trombones! how they boom out their parts; and the delicate, rippling flute, too, is as clear and prominent as any! All the stringed instruments surge through, as if with one bow and set of strings, in a rush of liquid melody. There is no wavering in time or tune. And the fugue is led off by the clarionets (those streams of silver just divided from the main fall) with a precision that is followed up in the *allegro*, enough to drive an *impressario* frantic with excitement and delight. Mark you that lyre-like boulder upon which the principal bulk of the water falls; there is no silver kettle-drum to equal it in its full volume of harmonious roar, in perfect accordance with the rest of the instruments. Observe, Mrs. Brown,—you who are a musician,—that chromatic scale, executed by the first and tenor violins! Cremona never made such perfect instruments, nor has Paganini executed such perfect performance. It is effected by the wind raising the whole body of water, and switching it over the rocks. O, I love to climb up into that top chamber,—the great Concert Hall,—and hear the liquid roll of music all night long!" cried Kenmuir.

"Of course you cannot sleep," I said, "with the noise and the damp?"

"O yes; and believe myself in something brighter than what you call Paradise, with angels playing harps and cherubims singing eternal hallelujahs."

---

* Twenty-seven hundred feet in one continuous leap.

We all laughed at the idea of the Yo-semite Fall making better music than the cherubims and seraphims.

"Tell me," cried Kenmuir, a little irritated at our seeming skepticism, "do you believe that hallelujahs and harps could be finer harmony than this water music?"

"Upon my word," I replied, "from my knowledge of instruments, as you have enumerated them, I do not think any could be finer in the form of natural music than this."

"Then, why do you set up artificial before natural music? Man's trumpery inventions, before God's great works!"

"Heaven forbid that I should! But you premised the harps in heaven, and asked my opinion thereon, which was favorable to your water-music theory."

"Yes, yes!" replied Kenmuir, pacified; "but since you admit the superiority of this music, will you not also acquiesce in my doctrine, that the Paradise which our preachers are always locating here and there out of reach, and furnishing with harps, and fountains, and jewels, and gold, is often in our very midst, ringing in our ears, flashing under our eyes, if we were not so stupidly deaf and confoundedly blind as not to perceive it. The greatest truism ever written, is,—'Having eyes and seeing not, having ears and hearing not.' Man might as well be born without—

'Eyes which only serve, at most,
To guard their master from 'gainst a post.'

For my part, I would never pray the Lord for a greater display of grandeur than that with whose fulgency my soul is satisfied. Moses was an arrogant ass to ask the Lord to *show* him his glory! Could he not see it all around, if he opened his eyes?" wound up Kenmuir, in a state of excitement with that biblical autocrat.

"Well, well!" laughed Oswald Naunton, "your Bible reading does not seem conducive to your patience; but let me remind you of one thing in your Eden, which you seem to have forgotten. Where are your angels?"

I believed Kenmuir to be in a dilemma, and came jokingly to the rescue. "Angels are said to be 'few and far between,' but here is one," touching Placida, "and here is a cherubim, as round and fair as ever Guido portrayed on canvas."

The angel thus indicated suffused a rose-blush very angelic to behold, and warbled out, in her luscious voice, the little ditty,—

" 'If I'm an angel, where's my wings?
Tiral la, tiral li.'
Kenmuir, can you furnish me with flying epaulets?"

The cherub, from the effects of a titillating pinch, trilled out a stave of honeyed laughter, her blue eyes radiating mellow beams of sunny mirth. But our Eden, as of yore, was presently invaded by the unrestful spirit of Zanita, who came flying down over the rocks in hot haste after a squirrel she had unearthed; his bushy tail, like a bright silver spray, was to be seen bounding from rock to rock, in desperate effort to escape his equally erratic pursuer. One bound brought him in the midst of us, and then the plumy tail disappeared altogether.

"O, papa! Kenmuir! shoot him! catch him!" screamed Zanita, her black eyes flashing with eager thirst for her prey. "I want his tail for a broom, to sweep out my stable with!"

"O no, not shoot him!" sobbed the cherub, her soft eyes looking piteously through their humid glow.

But Zanita stamped and chafed with the discomfiture and vexation.

"What a subject for an allegorical picture of Pity and Sport," I said to Kenmuir, as the mother pressed the little tender heart to her own, "and what a contrast between the two sisters."

"Yes," he replied, gathering a small plant at his feet. "Do you see the exquisite form and redundance of grace in the petals and lobes of this flower, growing upon the same stem with this other mean, shabby, gnarled, and twisted one, adding lustre to the other by mere force of contrast?—yet, nevertheless, the poor little scraggy fellow contains a fine fruit, which he will develop at the proper time. The Lord is never unjust: it is we who lay down such narrow premises, and draw such puny inferences."

"By the way," I said, turning to Mr. Naunton, "that squirrel recalls our moral squirrel conversation, and I want to ask you if this squirrelism is not practiced to a great extent amongst the Indian tribes in and about the Valley?"

"No," replied he, stroking his white beard thoughtfully. "No, I cannot say it is to a greater extent than in civilized life. It is true that the women carry the heavy burdens, whilst the man walks at his ease, with his bow and arrow, or rifle. But if he were burdened, he could not pursue the game whenever it should appear, which is often the only flesh meat they know. If we consider that the Indians approach the nearest in their practice the pure idea of republicanism,—equality, fraternity, and indivisibility,—we shall see that the squaw is only a detail, and matter of necessity, to the carrying out of the system. They live in tribes with *biens en commune*, and labor in common, too. The man takes the most arduous portion, procuring the food in the most toilsome and hazardous manner; whether he scours the plains, and risks his life in contact with the horns or deadly hoofs of the buffalo, or scales the frowning cliffs in search of game, or sits with enduring patience by the side of a stream to catch the shy trout; his life has dangers and vicissitudes which many civilized citizens would shrink from.

"But when he has strained his sinews, and torn his flesh in hunting down the deer, his female helpmeet will carry it home, cut it up, and cook it for him. She thus takes her share in the labor of life, yet does not work nearly so hard as the citizen's wife, who scrubs his house floor, washes his clothes, and tends his offspring, whilst the husband is carrying the hod or using the plane. True, that this difference increases as we emerge into the upper ranks of society; the wife of the citizen who has made wealth, and is able to hold on to it, lounges in her *causeuse*, and wears lavender kid gloves. But here Republican *égalité* ceases; for her fellow-citizen scours down her frescoed walls with chapped, bleeding hands, and aching bones; and the lavender kids can write tirades on the Indian's barbarity to his squaw, because he allows her to carry a funnel-shaped basket filled with household necessaries on her back, or a little coffin-shaped ditto with the papoose. Yet, with the Indian we have no records of the husband beating out the wife's brains with the iron heel of his boot, or smoothing her hair with a hot flat-iron, such as the journals often notify us as occurring in civilized lands.

"If the Indians are at war, they thirst for their enemies' blood, and spill it the first opportunity; taking a savage delight in bespattering his brains to the wild winds or carnivorous animals. We call this atrocious, but we invent machinery for the same purpose; we hate to dabble our white kids in human gore, yet we plant ourselves behind a secure bastion and blow our enemies to fragments, or mangle them by the thousand in agonized torments. And our lamentation over the frightful slaughter caused by the *chassepot*, or revolving cannon, is mere mawkish sentimentality. We do not wish to kill—we only wish to show our strength and conquer.

"Then you argue, why not decide the question by personal combat and individual prowess; why not test the courage and power after the manner of the Horatii and Curatii,—increasing the number to as many hundreds or thousands as each standing army of a nation could muster: this would be consistent and comparatively humane. By this principle the millionth part of the suffering of war would be curtailed. But the fact is, that destruction is the incentive of the white man as it is of the primitive savage, and he carries it out with as much zest though in a different way.

"Furthermore, argues the philanthropist, woman, being the weaker vessel, should be surrounded with care and tenderness, and shielded from the roughs of life like the shorn lambs. But all men are not philanthropists, some partaking more of the nature of grizzly bears, with a taste for devouring lambs who cannot take care of themselves; and society becoming overrun with these helpless creatures, who have to be clothed and fed and lodged, the poor woodpeckers have hard times. Nor does physiology prove that woman, though more graceful and beautiful than man, is so much more fragile, as we are accustomed to think. The Indian women, from constantly exerting their muscles in building their bark or pine-brush wigwams, carrying their goods and chattels, and cutting up the animals for food, are quite as strong as the men in any of these occupations; they can walk as far, and ford rivers with the same ease. She, in truth, plays a more prominent part in life, and is more on an equality with her spouse than a white woman who is entirely dependent on her husband to lace her boots."

"That," I said, "is a very strong argument for woman's rights,—that in the primitive state a woman should be more equal than in the position in which civilization has placed her. Have they a vote, do you know?" I asked laughingly.

"I believe," he rejoined, "that some of the older and wiser squaws have 'a say' in the 'big talk,' and according to their capacities and superiorities exercise a great sway in their tribe. With these tribes it is a more even division of labor, and the man, in fact, takes the most dangerous and active part, although combined with intervals of ease and leisure. Yet I have heard white women complain that their work was never done. Now two Indians whom I have in my employment perform any and every work indifferently, and seem to recognize no distinction between a man's and a woman's work; and, in fact, the nineteenth century ought to blush to have to learn a woman's rightful sphere from a wild Indian.

"There are a few occupations that I can call to mind that a woman would not fulfill as well as a man if she were trained to it as early and assiduously as a man. In farm-houses, women born and bred there tend the cattle as well as man. Milkmaids are proverbial. Welsh farmers' wives and daughters harness their own horses, ride on them to market, and transact the business of the farm. In Europe, in the provinces, women take their turn with the men in the field, especially at time of harvesting and haymaking. In France women hold their position in the country house and office public and private, can keep any description of store,—even take charge of tailoring and clothing stores. As in the case of the Indians, there is no reason why labor should not be shared between the sexes without making one a slave and the other a drone."

"This world affords suitable occupation for all if they would only attend to it," said Kenmuir.

"But, although there is a great outcry about the Indian's distaste for work, I know a good many white folk who labor under the same indisposition."

"If they were cleaner I should feel more attraction to them," I remarked.

"All barbarous nations wallow in dirt," said Mr. Naunton, rising to his full height with a peculiar jerk, as if to emphasize his remark,—"unless, like the Mohammedans' frequent ablutions, it is part of their religion to be clean. Cleanliness is a very modern virtue, and one which we should no more expect these uncivilized foresters to possess than the art of printing or photographing."

"The Jews could not have been very clean camping out so long," laughed Kenmuir, "and yet they are said to have been God's chosen people. Clean linen becomes an unknown luxury after many days of mountaineering; men and ducks are the only creatures whom I know to be seriously given to washing operations."

"And I do not think it is nature to the former," cried Mr. Naunton; "for I can recollect when no such thing as a bath, public or private, was in vogue, and when a washhand-basin was about as large as a saucer."

"Which dimension it remains in many parts of France to the present day," I ejaculated. "Clothes' washing is an operation indulged in once in six months."

"Which naturally circumscribes the soiling of them; whereas," said Placida, "in this country ladies of leisure and fashion vie with each other in how much bathing they can perform in the day; and how many dozens of soiled clothes they can send to the laundress. Laundries are quite an institution of this country, and a large population is engaged in rumpling and soiling, whilst an equal proportion are laboring to straighten and whiten; if the statistics were taken as to the number of people employed in this way, the figures would astonish all."

We all smiled at this original view of the case. The very clear view of such a virtue carried to a mania made me regard its laxity with less distaste.

Zanita having become impatient of a conversation she could not understand, tugged away at my hand until she started us all *en route* for the cottage.

"For," she kept on chattering, "we have everything to pack up: flour, and tea, and sugar, and potatoes, and a frying-pan, and a tea-urn, and bacon; and we must start a good hour before sunrise, as we shall be scorched going up that cliff right exposed to the sun without a bit of shade. Now when I get to that bit of rock I can build a fire, and you can go wrap yourself up in your blanket and go to sleep, while I take care no rattlesnakes come to you."

Thus she continued to rattle on, her imagination working and contriving, and fretting, and torturing itself over the difficulties and untoward accidents of her perilous exploits and dangers; whilst the little one would toddle along rejoicing in some flower, nursing it tenderly, smiling upon it, and looking up with deep delight in her heaven-lit eyes, exclaiming, "So pretty, so pretty!"

Thus unconsciously, and without effort, had I drifted into this family, and become absorbed into their whole existence, like a chip washed into a narrow cleft of rock. Here I had floated without helm or sail; here landed high and dry, never to sail out again, never to be distinct from those lives and fortunes until mother earth had taken them to her bosom and wrapt them in her softest bed, and laid a mossy pillow over them.

And yet we persist in believing that we are guiding our own destinies, working out our own ends, and bearing our own responsibilities.

CHAPTER VI.

THE FALL OF
THE MERCEDE.

THE FOLLOWING MORNING, as had been agreed, I set out with Mr. Naunton to visit the double fall of the Mercede, where it makes its triumphal entry into the Valley by leaping a precipice of about four thousand feet.

The morning was bright and clear; the air exhilarating and bracing; and we cantered along briskly.

"I must take you," said Mr. Naunton, "as you are a lover of physiology and psychology, and natural curiosities of all sorts, to see the 'Man of the Mountain.' Methuselah we call him; for, according to his recollection, he must have lived a century or so. His real name, I believe, is Methley; and he has lived in this singular formation in the granite mountain for fifteen years, without going outside the Valley; and sometimes has gone a twelvemonth together without speaking."

"What an extraordinary character! Pray tell me more; he will make a charming study."

"There are many different stories about him, and his motive for his singular seclusion. The Indians regard him as a great 'Medicine man,' and hold him in some awe and veneration for his great prowess and contempt for all danger. When the floods were in the Valley some years ago, and the water swept down from a hundred cataracts, and roared through the plain like a storm-lashed ocean; when immense trees were torn up and floated down like straws; when huge boulders came toppling over with the crash of an iceberg,—this man piloted himself on a log with a long stout sapling for an oar; and picked out from a watery grave some Indian children, and even animals which had been hemmed in by the flood before they could escape up the mountain. Powerful, skilled, and reckless of life, he is a wonderful man in time of danger."

"And what is the secret of his life, that he hides it away here?—a kind of entombment before life is extinct."

"Very much like that," said my host, "for all he sees of humanity he might as well be buried. Disappointment, no doubt, is the poison he has sipped; perhaps in love, perhaps in ambition,—or both. Possibly, but not probably, in grief for some loved one, for a man rarely becomes a hermit in grief for another, but rather in pity and compassion for himself. A woman, like Niobe, may weep herself to stone; but a man shuts up his heart with a bitter resolve that grief shall never more enter there, even though he should exclude all joy with the same iron door.

"But here we are at his castle gate, and I must sound the horn to gain admittance or bring him forth. Do you see those two projecting rocks? between them is a cavern some ten or twenty feet in circumference, and that is his town residence. When he wishes for a change of air he mounts up by that staircase hewn in the rock, and there is another chamber which is fashioned by that huge boulder, which, having rolled so far, has settled upon those two projections, leaving even a loophole for a window, from which it is said that Methuselah shot a score of red men at a *battue* as they came in Indian file, dressed in their red paint and feathers, to scare him off their territory. They had no means of reaching him except by this path, for the river is deep and forms almost a moat round his castle, so that he could pick off his besiegers one by one, whilst he was inaccessible and his castle impregnable.

"Having established this salutary awe, peace was concluded between himself and the tribe of Payutes. That is many years ago,—before we came to settle in the Valley."

"Halloa there, Methley!" he cried. "Halloa!" And presently something peered from the aperture.

"Methley, how are you!" called Mr. Naunton.

"How's your health?" replied a voice; and an object very like a white mop ascended about a yard. Then it rose another piece, repeating, "How's your health?" and showed a human face lengthened out, and displayed the figure of a man with very white hair, and long beard. Giving himself a jerk, he rose another foot.

"Dear me," I whispered, "how much higher is he going to rise? Is he a telescope, that shoots out a foot at a time?"

"Something on that principle," replied my companion, with a merry twinkle in his eyes; "but he has not done yet."

And the Man of the Mountain continued to hoist himself up in short lengths, hitching up his nether garments along with him, until he had reached the great height of six feet eleven, as I was afterwards told.

"Good-day, madam," said the giant, coming forward with the air of a *grand seigneur*, without expressing the smallest surprise or embarrassment at the apparition of a strange lady, perhaps the first who had ever entered his domain.

"May I help you from your horse, and offer you some raspberries, and wine of my own vintage?"

I at once accepted the courteous invitation, and was led by my singular host into a very fine fruit garden, trim and in order, as any market gardener's. Here were peaches, and gooseberries, and apples, and pears, and raspberries, all on the same gigantic scale as the proprietor.

"These are all my family," he said, pointing to them. "These raspberries," gathering me a large vine-leaf full, "are red Antwerps,—the best stock grown in New England. These gooseberries came from Old England, brought over by my ancestor. These strawberries were first cultivated by Martha Washington. This was Lafayette's favorite pear, the Duchess d'Angoulême. They are not ripe yet, or I would ask you to pass your opinion upon them."

Thus he chatted on, piling up fresh fruit before me, his conversation underlying two thirds of a century, which seemed to him but as yesterday.

"I should like to see the Duke of Wellington, if he should ever come over to this country. I should like to make his acquaintance."

"He has been dead at least twenty years," I exclaimed, involuntarily.

"I'm sorry to hear that; he is a man I have the greatest respect for. Lord Chatham is also a great man; if you have been in Europe, madam, you have doubtless met him."

"I think," I said, laughing, "he died some twenty years before I was born."

"How very singular," he observed. "How do you account for these great men dying so young?"

"The Duke of Wellington must have been over seventy," I hazarded.

"Just so," he answered; "the prime of life—the prime of life."

"They had not found the *elixir* for keeping young like you, Methley," said Mr. Naunton.

"Now, Naunton, none of your jokes; you know I am growing old. I feel that my youth is past, madam, and age fast creeping on. I have to

THE FALL OF THE MERCEDE

take care of myself, in fact, and indulge in certain luxuries which the young had better avoid."

I looked at his raiment, and at his habitation, and could not help exchanging looks with Mr. Naunton, who seemed to relish the joke amazingly.

After we had satisfied ourselves with fruit, he conducted us to his castle. It consisted of a spacious apartment, if I may use the word for a place that could not be called a dungeon, not being underground, and scarcely a cavern; but yet I could believe that a grizzly bear, in good circumstances, might have a more comfortable lair. In one corner was heaped together on some logs a quantity of spruce branches, which formed his bed, the covering consisting of a wretched old cinnamon bear-skin. An old chair constructed from unhewn boughs of trees, and covered with sheep-skin for a seat; a tin plate and cup, a large jack-knife, a two-pronged fork, cut from Manzanita bush, a kettle, and a frying-pan, seemed to constitute the whole of the furniture of the room. The fireplace was outside, on account of there being no fissure in the rock to admit of a chimney; in a large iron pot he was baking a loaf, which he regretted was not sufficiently cooked for us to partake of with our wine,—which, I ought to have mentioned, was drawn from a large barrel which stood in the corner, and which was presented to me in a goblet without a foot, so that it had to be drained ere it could be set down. To think of a human being, much less an educated man like Methley, living for fifteen years alone in a crevice of the rock such as this, was to me the most melancholy thing conceivable; and my heart ached as I looked at the gaunt old Methuselah, with his still handsome features, and daring eye. I wondered what terrible misfortune, or cruel fatality, had driven him to this fifteen years of practical despair. I yearned to pour out sympathy over that poor white head, though it did look so like a mop!

Mr. Naunton noticing my pained expression, led the way to a conversation which he knew would bring the old man out in a humorous light. "When you have leisure, Methley, you must come up and see us whilst Mrs. Brown and the Professor are with us; you might step in on your way to the East."

"I shall certainly make time for that visit," he said, brightening up. "I am trying to make a holiday for myself to go to the East, madam; at a certain time of life, a man begins to want change."

"That's right," put in Naunton; "and you are going to bring home that young lady with you. Well, give us timely warning, and we will meet you with wreaths of syringa, a good substitute for orange blossom, to deck the bride."

"We shall see, we shall see," rubbing his hands, like two old gnarled branches, together, and chuckling with delight; which goes to prove that even in this rugged old rock of humanity the sweet well of love could still spring up, and refresh the dried up ruin with a bliss fit for angels.

"Well, come and see us any way," reiterated Mr. Naunton, and we rose to resume our journey.

"I wish some one would come and take care of him," I said to my companion as we rode on.

"I question," replied he meditatively, "whether any reality would now be as pleasant to him as the ideal he has cherished for the last sixty or seventy years. Once he did leave the Valley, giving us to understand that he should not return alone. However, when he resumed his old life he evinced no disappointment, and explained that he had seen so many ladies who more or less reached his *beau ideal* that he was obliged to take twelve months to decide amongst them. The ladies' ages varied from sixteen to twenty."

"But," I argued, "he might be taken ill and die all alone without a creature to help him."

"That, in all probability, he will do," resumed Mr. Naunton philosophically. "But is that a misfortune? or is it worth while to regret the inevitable? A wife could not prevent his death, and at his time of life he is not likely to have a long sickness. For my part I think those who die alone are better off than such as have their death-beds surrounded by weeping and wailing friends."

"How do you maintain that hypothesis," I exclaimed.

"Firstly, because there are few who at the hour of death realize from their own sensations that they are dying, unless well versed in the symptoms, and die as they would go to sleep; whereas in long and fatal maladies persons are given frequent warnings by their friends in order that they may *prepare* themselves, as it is called, though how they are to prepare for the great unknown future is difficult to say; but in default of knowing how, the mind plunges into the vaguest unrealities of horrors and fears and intangible miseries. Their lives, if evil, rise like avenging furies goading them to coward words of repentance, which they feel comes too late, for deeds of restitution are rarely executed if life should be prolonged; whilst on the other hand those whose lives do not rise in judgment before them have their last moments harassed by the misery of those relatives who mourn their loss, which like all emotion is infectious, and the acuteness of sorrow is increased tenfold by the communicated sympathy of both parties. Death is very much what we choose to consider it. A dead child looks as sweet and pleasant as when asleep. I have seen scores of men shot through the heart or brain who suffered nothing in death, and it is so with most diseases. They suffer from the disease which carries death upon its fatal wings, but the death itself is painless; and except in a very few cases, the disease abates some hours before dissolution, and the parting of body and soul is calm and even pleasant. I have often seen persons pass away with a smile on their lips."

"There is a great deal of truth in what you say," I observed, "for I have often seen persons hastened out of the world by the agonizing thoughts suggested to them by injudicious and timorous friends, and the appalling thought of the mystic future kept constantly before their minds. Yet we remain in the hands of the Creator whether in the flesh or out of it, and his mercy is not of to-day or yesterday but endureth forever."

"Therefore," interrupted Mr. Naunton, resuming a gayer tone, "if no wife turns up, let the old man die in peace when the Lord shall call him."

We had for some time been riding in the open meadows over a mosaic of nature's choicest labors; but we now arrived where the river was fordable, and our horses made a decided halt to enjoy a cool draught of the limpid stream.

What rider has not known the pleasure of sitting on horseback in the midst of a clear stream or river watching the eddies over the rounded pebbles, calculating the amount of treasure it may be hurrying down to the all absorbing ocean, and listened to the rich mellow sound of the horse drinking—slew-eesh, slew-eesh, slew-eesh? Whether it is sympathy with the dumb beast thus made happy for a moment and communicated back to me through his medium, or whether there is some intrinsic pleasure in the thing itself, I know not, but I never could urge my jennet across a stream without stopping to let her drink, if she wanted so to do.

After crossing we skirted the river as close as its serpentine course would admit,—the valley becoming every mile narrower until it merged into a ravine on whose rugged side a horse trail had been cut. The rock rose in gigantic tiers, bunch after bunch, crowned with the richest verdure, and tall pines, which nevertheless looked like mere twigs when seen from above or below, so exalted are the heights that sustain them. Masses of rock and huge boulders, some of them worn round by the action of the water, lay in chaotic confusion, as though the Titans had been at war across the ravine, or had playfully been trying to stone out the course of the river, which, just below so placid and tranquil, came roaring and foaming with a crash and a bound incredible in that erst meek and gentle stream. By degrees, as we ascended, the mountains interlaced, forming a deep dark cañon, through which only the silver thread of the Mercede caught the light; and now we could hear the thunder of the great Py-wy-ack echoed a thousand times from each separate niche and cavernous hollow, till the whole blent in a solemn roar like hoarse waves booming to the ocean's shore.

No longer grassy green or silvery sheen in the moonlight enwrapping the glistening trout or caressing the smooth, white sand. It now bids defiance to the sternest scaurs and cliffs, strikes them as with an anvil, cleaves them apart in its headlong course, moulds their jagged points into polished roundness, dashes through the smallest fissures, and upheaves great mountains with its mighty strength; boils over from bottomless pits, and flings itself wildly from crag to crag, with a whoop and a clang that startle the stillness in the unsearched dome of Tis-sa-ack. Here it wrestles in a chasm of dark granite, and seems well-nigh overpowered and inclosed, never to sing its wild song again but in rumbling depths of the earth. But anon it has sent up a column of fleecy white foam, curving over the boundary wall, and is off again in its mad career to the valley below, where virgin lilies are awaiting its murmuring ripple, and merry buttercups its laughing kiss.

All the granite walls in the world cannot hinder it any more than wise saws can stay the youth in love. Days and weeks, and months and years, and centuries, aye, millions of centuries it has leaped those iron barriers, battering them with diamond spray of liquid hail, sharp and strong, and torn down the adamantine wall.

All this is only the prelude to the sweep of the huge cataract of the Py-wy-ack, which, seven hundred feet above, takes its triumphal leap, spurning the rocks behind it, and, spreading like a vast fan, casts itself over in a million tons of dazzling spray.

As we escaladed the dizzy height to the hanging head of the cataract, tethering our horses some distance below, a thin mist, like illusion tulle, enveloped us, together with the surrounding scenery,—like the nuptial veil suspended over the high altar whilst the sacred hymeneal rite is performed,—and when we emerged from its folds at the top, the whole scene was changed. A brilliant sunlight illuminated the very depths of our emerald lake, without a ripple or movement upon its surface. Nevertheless, it silently fed that fierce Py-wy-ack, and was the mute cause of all this clamor and tumult. We approached the very brink of the fall and looked down upon the avalanche, leaning on a stone balustrade. We needed Kenmuir here to dilate upon the sumptuous glory of all around which steeped my every sense in silent beatitude: the music of the waters, the coloring of the sunset, the perfume of the syringa.

In rival towers on either side rose the lofty Tis-sa-ack and coneshaped Tah-mah; and leaning its spiral head against the blue heavens loomed the Clouds' Rest, well named by the Indians from the nebulæ which makes its home about it.

At our feet the cascade of diamonds gradually melted into a chain of twinkling gems, as it wound through the stern and rugged ravine we had just traversed; and the narrow opening was graced with the blood-red disk of the setting sun, looking in as through an oriel window of rock to take his evening farewell of the earth.

Then we turned, and through the gnarled boughs of the oak and cypress we could see the second cascade, the Nevada Fall, nine hundred feet above us, pouring out of a white fleecy cloud which hung right above and seemed to form a part of it, as though it fell from the very heavens an avalanche of eider-down clouds: so pure, so silky white was the gossamer foam which rolled in soft cadences with slow and graceful motion like the silver stars of rockets. So exquisitely symmetrical were the figures, descending in a single span from heaven to earth, that it might have been the realization of Jacob's dream,—

> "The ladder of light,
> Which, crowded by angels unnumbered,
> By Jacob was seen as he slumbered
> Alone in the desert at night."

There was so much of beauty above, below, and around that I said:—

"I shall feel quite bewildered unless I can have longer opportunity of gazing upon it and examining it at my leisure. A *coup d'œil* is very unsatisfactory to me. To see a beautiful object once and away is nearly as bad as not seeing it at all."

CHAPTER VII.

THE RADDS
AT HOME.

"IN THAT CASE," said my host, "our best plan will be to ascend to the Upper Valley, and if you can content yourself with hermit's fare, and a bed of pine boughs, I think you may pass the hours until morning and see the cascades by moonlight."

"Why here comes the sole inhabitant thereof," he cried, as an individual with a very uncertain step moved in sight.

"Ho, Radd!" shouted Mr. Naunton, hailing him in the distance, "How are you!"

The man named gyrated toward us taking off his tattered hat with a courtly air. He looked to me like the figure of King Lear. His face had a wild majesty; his long beard, and elf locks streamed on the wind. His costume was that of the Valley, shirt and trousers, with the extra feature of rents and gashes. He was followed by a fine dog of the St. Bernard breed, which kept close to his heels, executing the same evolutions as his master, and maintaining a careful watch upon him, as though he feared that every movement he might be called upon to help him, and that it was necessary to be at hand.

"Madam," said Mr. Radd with a deferential obeisance, "at your service. What though a stranger in these unexplored wilds, you are as welcome as flowers in spring."

I thanked him, and Mr. Naunton took up the *parole*.

"Well, then, I am sure you will do your best to accommodate this lady for the evening, for she wishes to enjoy this glorious scenery to the full. Can you make her a bed of pine boughs?"

" 'Aye, aye, master, that I can'—
'Strew then, O strew
The bed of rushes;
Here shall she rest
Till morning blushes.' "

Broke out Mr. Radd in a rich baritone voice that woke the echoes.

43

"Do you think she can manage to climb the rocky steep to your valley?"

> " 'As with his wings aslant
> Sails the fierce cormorant;
> So to my rocky haunt
> Bear I the maiden.' "

"Sixteen years a matron," I laughed.

"You had better not let your wife hear you say that," cried Mr. Naunton.

Mr. Radd shrugged his shoulders as though warding off an imaginary broomstick; made three zigzag steps forward and three ditto backward, followed by Rollo, and said, plaintively,—

> " 'Come where the aspens quiver.' "

"Here, Rollo!" he said, addressing the dog, "carry the lady's satchel: show your gallantry, man!"

Rollo approached deferentially with an expression that said, "I am only too happy to be useful to a lady, but do not wish to intrude myself unnecessarily." He took the bag gently and walked behind his master.

We followed him above the Wild-cat Cascade and on by the rapids, until we neared the foot of the Great Fall we had seen in the distance, and right at the foot of the Mah-tah, thence up the steep side of jagged rocks and huge boulders where a "fierce cormorant" to bear me up would have been no mean assistance.

Sometimes the poetic Radd would improvise a rustic seat from whence we had a fine view of the roaring cascade. Sometimes he would conduct us into a cave, introducing us with—

> " 'Here, in cool grot and mossy cell,
> With woodland nymphs and fairies dwell.' "

Thus by degrees we wound up the rocky path, for far away above the topmost cataract of the Nevada is a delicious little valley where the Mercede, once more a pure and peace-loving stream, flows through a green flowery dell.

Soon we were pressing the primeval turf of this Valley which few human feet had ever trod.

"This indeed is a surprise," I exclaimed, as I cast my eyes around on the magic scene of higher mountains, fresh cataracts, new groves, and again a lovelier phase of the river.

"Yes," said Radd, "Nature has donned her brightest garb to welcome the Queen of May."

"Bravo, Radd! Then how do you account for its being June?" said Mr. Naunton.

"June it may be with you down below in your march of civilization, but with us it is still May."

We now perceived a habitation something like an Indian wigwam, constructed partly of the bark of trees and partly of canvas.

"I will not ask you to share my humble cot, but with these hands will build you a palace of art," said Radd, and he oscillated from side to side and finally dived into the wigwam.

"He is afraid to take you in suddenly," whispered my companion, "on account of his wife Nell, who has not the most placable of tempers in the world."

Presently we heard a shrill voice coming from the hut, exclaiming,—

"I'm downright 'shamed of you, Radd. You know we hain't no 'commodations for folk as you goes picking up by the highways and by-ways a bidding to the marriage feast when there ain't none: not unlike as there might be if you was like any other man. We might 'commodate folks as comes as well as other folks down in the Valley. There's them turkeys I had this here spring as was as fine turkeys as ever was and laid as first-rate eggs. Why, them eggs in cakes was as rich as ever you tasted, and you let them hawks carry them all off just because you wouldn't shoot 'em, and you would go on with your humbug a calling of them falcons."

Here Radd made his appearance bearing a three-legged chair, formed from the gnarled bough of a tree, with a sacking bottom.

"I prithee be seated on this rustic bench, and I will twine for thee a bower of eglantine and roses."

Presently Mrs. Nell made her appearance, her face and arms shining brightly from a fresh scrubbing down. She was an ungainly woman, as I had expected from the tone of her voice, with angular limbs and harsh features; one large tooth protruding seemed anxious to make up for a gap in her mouth, through which she seemed to speak without the trouble of opening it.

"Good day, ma'am," she said, making an attempt at a bob curtsey; "good day, Mr. Naunton; yer welcome to the top Valley: we hain't to say much 'commodations as you have below. Some folks has a way of 'cumulatin' things around, and some has a way of slatterin' around."

Here she cast a reproachful look on Radd, the twist in her mouth strongly indicating the twist she seemed inclined to give his neck, round which a blue neckerchief was tied in the form of a halter.

"But you are welcome to all the 'commodations we have."

Meantime Radd was busy with his hatchet, felling pine boughs to construct the bower, a feat which he accomplished in a surprisingly short time.

"I'd like a drink of water," said Mr. Naunton to Mrs. Radd.

"Well now, Radd!" exclaimed Mrs. Radd, extending both arms toward him with the fists partially closed, "have ye been and brought up them lone folks and never taken 'em to the spring of as fine water as there is in the country round. Why, you'd bring folks past the gates of Paradise, that's what you would, and never let them know, if you was a mooning over some of your crack-brained nonsense: the idee of bringing folks past the spring when I left a tin cup there a'purpose, as mebbe there might be folks a coming up, but you never think of nothing."

"Rollo!" she shrieked, "take the pail and go and get some water, do! and make yourself useful, forever maundering about at your master's heels, lazing around. I shouldn't wonder if some day you began to spout pottery!" and with grim chuckle she flung him a pail which he took demurely and walked off.

"That there dorg has more sense nor most Christians," she remarked approvingly, "but I'm obleeged to keep him up to his work and not let him guess how smart he is."

Her green eyes twinkled, and the long tooth thrust itself forward an eighth of an inch. "Why," she continued, "if it warn't for Rollo I should never know where that crazy fellow had been. He might put hisself, p'raps, over a precipice or down a cascade: the Lord knows what sink he'd tumble into if it warn't for Rollo: why he's better nor a nurse-tender to him. For Mr. Naunton knows well that he never goes down to that there Valley below to trade off his skins but what if there's a drop of whiskey in fifty miles he'll have it, and if Rollo didn't bring him home he'd have been lying at the bottom of the Specific Ocean, or somewheres else, this many a year; and if he war, I'm not the woman to cry for him. I've not lived around in mountains for a matter of fifteen years not to know how to 'commodate myself to circumstances. I don't want no lazy men around me anyways, but if it warn't for Rollo I might mebbe stand waiting around thinking he'd turn up somewheres."

Here the subject of the eulogium appeared, steadily bearing the bucket of cold spring water.

"There," she exclaimed, as she wiped a cup on her apron and presented me the cool sparkling water, "there's a 'commodation you can't get in the Valley below. Mr. Naunton, you've no water to beat that, I guess."

"Certainly not," said Mr. Naunton, "it is delicious; the upper Valley excels in springs."

"Here! Rollo, where are you off to?" as the dog was furtively stealing away to his master.

"I guess this lady's to be accommodated now she's here, and mebbe you think I'm to do the whole business myself, but I'm not; so just you grind this coffee, and look likely about it!"

Rollo winked compliance, and mounted upon an old stump and commenced pushing with his two front paws a double handled coffee-mill ingeniously nailed against a tree, and constructed on the principle of a water-wheel. Rollo ground away, nodding his sagacious head all the while, and made me think of the French satirist, "Plus je connais les hommes, plus j'admire les chiens."

Upon this hint of the division of labor, Mr. Naunton commenced building the fire.

"O, you're a handy man," said Mrs. Nell, "but I guess I can 'commodate you all round; I'll just set you to tend this meat and see it doesn't burn; I guess I can fix it so it will be broiled in a jiffy," and she placed a fine venison steak upon a forked stick before the fire thrusting the other end into the earth.

"I guess you smelt my baking in the Valley below; you were right smart to hit on baking day."

She uncovered a pan of smoking hot biscuits which looking temptingly white to mountain travellers.

Rollo had ground his coffee, and the fragrant fumes were soon wafted to our nostrils. A table was constructed of a plank of pine between two great oak-trees, which formed over our heads a canopy a king might envy. Here Nell spread her stores amid a constant fire of invectives against her two companions and grumbling at the want of "'commodations."

"I ain't got no sarce to give ye with your meat; that tomato sarce as your wife sent me is all gone down the mountain. Rollo broke the bottle as he was bringing it up the Wild-cat Falls, so you might have got it back again in your water," said Mrs. Radd facetiously, again protruding the front tooth.

Rollo hung his head dejectedly, as though overcome by the guilty memory of the bottle of tomato sauce.

"Ho! Radd," shrieked his loving helpmeet, making a horn of her hand; "that man's never ready for his meat when his meat is ready for him," complained Mrs. Nell, as she invited us to draw around her hospitable board. "Rollo! off and fetch him this minnit; don't let him be dangling about there: I could a' gathered a bushel o' berries by this time."

With these words, Rollo in three bounds was on the opposite side of the smooth flowing river, and in a short time we saw him carefully superintending the passage of a raft, by means of a rope drawn across it, which conveyed Radd, who was carrying an armful of blackberry bushes and two or three young spruces over his shoulders.

"There is 'Birnam Wood moving on the castle,'" quoted Mr. Naunton; "Radd is going to make you as high a bed as they make for a princess in France."

"Well, I guess the lady don't want to sleep on fifteen mattresses," said Nell, as Radd threw down his load; "you'll pile her up as high as Mah-tah."

Radd, casting away his tatterdemalion hat, took a seat, and Rollo, giving himself a shake as a toilet preparation, took another, and looked as demure as though he was saying grace.

Our dinner party was now complete, and we enjoyed it as no royal repast was ever relished. The forked flames of the fire flickered over the foliage and brought out a thousand fantastic forms and colors from the surrounding scenery; but long before our banquet came to an end, the silver moon shone our brightest lamp, and again the soft, weird, mysterious aspect I had admired the evening before was transmuting the rugged rocks into smooth mountains, and the frowning heights to delicately penciled cliffs, against the deep blue sky; as she sailed slowly toward the peak of Clouds' Rest she seemed to dwell upon it, and two tall pines growing on the very summit were as clearly traced upon her burnished disk as though they had been transplanted there.

"Well, well," said Mr. Naunton humorously, as he called our attention to this singular phenomenon, "the man who was taken to the moon for gathering sticks on Sunday must surely have planted them, and these trees are the result."

"I can't say as I believe about that," said Nell sharply. "I guess if he were here he would have to gather sticks most every day, and I guess he'd be hard set to know rightly when it was a Sabbath if he'd nothing exacteter nor Radd to wind up the clock; for he lets it run down, and we have to start the week like on Monday or Tuesday, just as may be."

"Time is made for slaves," muttered Radd softly.

But Nell had keen ears as well as sharp eyes. "I'm ashamed of you, Radd, talking of slavery, after living a spell of fifteen years with a wife as comes from an abolition State. I make no account on these Maryland folks; they are neither one thing nor t'other, neither fat nor lean," she said, looking fiercely at Radd, who continued to sip his coffee stoically.

We walked down to the falls in the moonlight; they fell like an avalanche of silver spray glittering like globules of quicksilver, the whole arched by a delicate lunar rainbow.

"A real *pluie de perles*," I exclaimed.

"Or Naiad's tears," responded Radd, "weeping that Venus has usurped the loves of the golden backed dolphins."

"Then it is not true of the dolphins, 'qu'on retourne toujours à ses premières amours?' "

"No," rejoined Radd; "*amour* only returns when the *amourette* is a"—

"Mrs. Brown," I put in mischievously.

"Ah, that's too bad," laughed Mr. Naunton, "to spoil the phrase and the compliment; it should have run, 'When the *amourette* is a Sylvia,' for that is your name I believe."

We turned to retrace our steps, although I could have spent an hour or two in contemplation of this fairy-like spectacle; but I was laboring under some dread that Mrs. Radd, having accomplished the washing up of dishes, in which operation she had declined both Rollo's and Radd's assistance, might be getting impatient, and consider that we were "loafing about" the falls, instead of going to bed like decent folk.

We heard her voice long before she was discernible.

"Well, so you've come'd at last. I thought mebbe as Radd had persuaded you to sleep there, to hear the roar or see the *linear* rainbow, or some highfalutin' notions. I guess you'll conclude to lie down, ma'am."

I assented.

"I should say," she continued, "that a smart woman like you would conclude to take a stretch in our hut sooner than that ramshackle thing Radd's been piling up for you; but 'commodate yourself anyway."

" 'It's a bower of roses by Bendemeer's stream,
        Where the nightingale sings to you all the night long,' "
quoth Radd.

"Bendamore, indeed! it's the crookedest piece of water in these diggings, you bet."

Here we arrived at the bower: it was a sort of arbor constructed of the *arbor vitæ* and hemlock, covered with branches of the *pinus ponderosa*, which formed a roof like a Gothic cathedral, with pointed corbels, hanging in live tassels.

The bed was made of spruce, with a splendid cinnamon bear-skin for a covering. A miniature mirror—no doubt Radd's shaving glass, whenever he performed that operation—was suspended in a frame of oak leaves, and a bouquet of wild roses in a vase, made from a curiously shaped pine-knot, chased in delicate arabesque, was placed upon what I was pleased to call my toilet table,—a very handsome *buffet* made of a clean square-shaped pile of *arbor vitæ*. The whole apartment was trellised by the moonbeams, forming exquisite patterns over all.

This was really the poetry of camping out, and when once Mrs. Radd's shrill voice was silenced in slumber the romance was complete. I lay watching the stars as they shone across my horizon through the pine boughs; and inhaling the balmy odors from my fragrant bed.

The next morning I awoke with the roseate beams of day slanting gayly through my lattice-work. I saw Nell in the distance cooking another venison-steak for breakfast, and scolding all the time,—at least I concluded she was from the motion of her head and arms.

Poor Radd, as usual, was not ready for his breakfast when it was ready for him; but just at the close appeared with two chipmunk skins, which he had been preparing as a little offering "to the first angel," he whispered very low, "who has ever alighted in the Valley." He took the opportunity whilst Nell was throwing a heap of brushwood on the fire, which roared and crackled briskly.

The skins were sewed neatly together, making a bag; the two little heads formed the opening, and the bushy tails made a handsome tassel.

I said I would keep it as a souvenir of the Valley.

"What of the Valley?" echoed Mrs. Radd, who never could keep out of any conversation whether she understood it or not. "I guess you might have found something better to give the lady nor them bits of varmints; there's the big cinnamon bear-skin," she called after Radd, as he slunk away, and, as he did not stop, she made two long strides, and seizing him by the sleeve, she hissed into his ear, "Mebbe she'd pay for it; you never brought a cent back for the last you traded off for whiskey."

Radd gave himself as violent a shake as Rollo when he prepared his toilet for dinner, and walked on unmindful of her.

We soon began our descent of the mountains, again crawling to the very verge of the rocks forming the Nevada Falls, in order to look down over its rolling foam, which tumbled like avalanches of snow, and dispersed into mist as it touched the chaos of rocks below.

We gathered some scarlet humming-bird trumpets, growing on the ledge sweetly innocent of the tremendous torrent rushing within a few inches of their birthplace, that might any moment engulf them.

"Thus," I said to our friend Radd, who accompanied us so far, under strict injunction from his wife to make "right smart tracks back again,"—"thus do we often loiter over the brink of the greatest catastrophe of our lives, careless of the gulf in which we are about to be precipitated."

CHAPTER VIII.

THE EPISODE
OF A KISS.

WE HAD DESCENDED the steepest portion of the mountain, and had reached one of the level benches on which are situated those marvelous and fantastic grottoes that must be seen to be realized.

The entrance is draped with the royal plumes of the *fernus gigantia*; the walls elaborately tapestried with bright green mould moss, the product of damp and wet. The ceiling is decorated with lichens that droop in architectural wonders. The floor gleams in crystals and glittering spars, like a pavement tessellated in gems.

We had just emerged from examining one of these homes of the Naiads, when Mr. Naunton threw up his arms in surprise and amusement, and exclaimed,—

"Well, well! if there is not Zanita coming to camp out with us. How in the name of wonder has she got Billy up that tortuous track?"

I looked, and there was the sprite riding a calf, tricked out as a packmule, with a milk-pail on one side and her father's hunting-bag on the other. She was quieting and driving him by dint of kicks with her little feet, and thumps with a broken broom administered at the four points of the compass upon the wayward calf; and was actually at the moment piloting him under an immense boulder which overhung the trail, leaving scarce two feet of path above a fearful precipice, at the bottom of which the Mercede roared in one of its deliriums of fury.

"Good heavens!" I screamed, "she will be killed."

"No," resumed her father composedly; "a child that can guide a calf up such a trail as this will never meet her death among the mountains."

"Where are you going, Zanita?" he called out.

"Coming to camp out with the lady. O, don't go back yet. I have brought you bacon and potatoes," and she produced from the milk-pail a very dirty ham-bone, rescued from the dogs, no doubt, and a living root of potatoes, with soil and fruit clinging to it fresh pulled from the earth.

She was greatly disappointed to have her calf turned back again, though Billy seemed to relish the descent mightily, switched his tail, and trotted on briskly.

As we traversed the park-like meadows, studded with massive oaks, and Mr. Naunton was expatiating upon their girth and height as compared with trees in other portions of the Continent,—these present averaging ten feet in diameter,—a sudden light broke over his face (brighter, I thought, than the circumference of a tree could animate), and following the direction of his eyes, I perceived the gliding figure which had power to call it forth.

"My Placida," said Mr. Naunton, in the most mellifluous tone of his voice, indicating his wife to me; "she has walked out to meet us."

When we approached, Mrs. Naunton murmured something about having come to look for Zanita. But her husband sprang from his horse and kissed her; and the sweet upturned face told me precisely, and without any circumlocution, what she had come for. She had come for that kiss; walked three miles to have it thus much sooner.

She must have longed for it and wanted it, from the pink glow of happiness which radiated her whole countenance. If ever I should be tempted to envy a woman anything, it would be such a meeting as this. If ever I coveted anything, it would be such a destiny as this. They had only been separated twelve hours, and yet the time had been all too long; and that she had hastened to shorten it was an evidence of that perfect union of soul which makes corporal absence so unendurable; that wonderful unity of two in one called wedlock.

I thought that here was fully realized the beautiful German appellation of "*mine man*," that seems to complete the full measure of everything,—not merely the endowing with worldly goods and body-worship, which the marriage ceremony enjoins, but "*mine man*" comprehends all his soul, his manhood; his whole being is included in this possessive case.

How few marriages ever bring about this real possession. Of husbands more or less exacting, more or less indifferent, selfish, unfaithful, there is always an abundant harvest; but of "*mine man*'s" how few! And as Mr. Naunton placed his wife upon his vacated saddle, and walked beside her, Zanita scrimmaging around in abortive efforts to make the calf keep on the path, I fell into a reverie on connubial bliss in general, and that kiss I had just seen exchanged in particular,— upon all it meant and contained for her, or any one whose soul is in a condition to accept and realize so much felicity cemented with another soul twin-born. Under such auspices I am of opinion with Kenmuir, that we can realize upon earth something of the delights of heaven, which preachers so kindly inform us is so far away as to be nearly out of our reach.

I look upon kissing as rather a psychological demonstration than a physical performance; for creatures without souls do not kiss, and the lower grades of humanity, said to possess soul in a minor degree, but rarely, and it is a mere rubbing of noses together like horses. Kissing is the specialty of the human race, and has been held as sacred from time immemorial. The blackest crime on record was rendered more heinous by the treachery being ushered in with a kiss, and the tenderest devotion and most sublime self-sacrifice is tendered with a kiss. It is one of the grand dividing lines between the animal and man; and the higher a man's nature becomes, the more spiritualized and refined, the more perfect is the beatitude of the divine essence of his kiss. Then, if in "the land for which we wait" we are to enjoy what we like best, surely it would be more delightful to perpetually kiss than continually sing; and as to playing harps, though melodious and graceful, a serious drawback is in blistered or hardened fingers. The kiss between friends is pleasant; the kiss between sisters and brothers is sweet; the kiss of a mother and child is a delicious rapture; but the kiss between wedded lovers is bliss unspeakable,—"Heaven on earth," as Kenmuir would call it; the spiritual commingling of kindred souls and of all the divinity within us; the welling up of pure ecstasy, from the eternal living fount of love, that God, the beneficent Creator, has blessed us with. No wonder, then, that the faces of Oswald and Placida beamed with such infinite radiance and light of joy. It is a talisman that beautifies all it reaches. A woman may not have a symmetrical line in her face, yet will she blossom to the beauty of an angel when touched by the magic of a kiss. How often it is asked, What can that man see in the woman to love—no one else sees anything? True, no one else; he alone sees it all, for he produces it, and the glory of that reflection more than compensates him for the symmetry of a Venus. Phidias was wretched because he had created all that was lovely except the divinity of love. That comes alone from the Omnipotent.

In a few days my husband made his appearance, and there was great joking about the important discoveries and contributions I had made to the science of geology. My husband said he had no doubt that I should be made a fellow of no end of societies, and have to tack the whole alphabet to my name.

I retorted that I could well afford him any witticism, for all is well that ends well. But I adroitly set Kenmuir off upon a geological discussion about glaciers and moraines, etc., etc.; for I knew they would disagree upon every point, and thus I turned the flank of the Professor's attack upon me.

After his arrival excursions became quite the order of the day. Climbing days, walking days, riding days, and boating, occupied our heads and our feet. We visited all the points of interest,—in fact all was interesting for twenty miles around,—gaining health and strength and happiness to the full, and we laid in a bountiful stock of all for the winter.

Thus in content and gladness our Valley-life sped on from days to weeks. When first I saw the Yo-semite temple, summer seemed to be brimful of all the beauty and joy that any summer land could accomplish. Young birds were tasting life in every grove. The great ocean of insect existence flowed on with amazing life and motion; multitudes of flowers had ripened and planted their seeds; and each day developed a new glory. Brighter glowed the meadows with starry composite. The deep places of unmingled green became yet more unfathomable; groves of purple grasses, tall as bamboos, waved in thickets of mint and golden-rod; and every plant of Californian summer waxed to corresponding greatness.

I was charmed and almost bewitched by such a *luxe de beauté*, and my whole soul flowed out blending with the grandeur, like clouds among the tallest mountain pines. When my enthusiasm had reached its highest point, fanned to red heat by Kenmuir, and Mr. and Mrs. Naunton, for they were all Valley worshippers, the Professor proposed a visit to the alkaline plains of Mono as a counter irritant,—"for my dear," he said, "you are just at that period of insanity when people form new religions. You might call yours *Sylvia-Brownism*, or 'Landscape Religion.' You can make yourself high-priestess. You would start with more capital than Mohammed, for you have three followers, whilst he had only two, his wife and his cook. Yet he converted a third of the intelligent world."

"For that impetuous speech," I said, "you shall go alone to Mono. I came to worship in these high places, and my devotions are not half complete."

"Why not finish them some four thousand feet higher? Mount Dana, for instance, whose brown top is up in heaven always. You can build your altar there; and if you want fire for sacrifice, some of the extinct volcanoes might be induced to explode and lend you their assistance. You could get up a tidy little miracle, if you thought well of putting that in the programme."

"You have not the ghost of a chance of my accompanying you now," I exclaimed.

"I knew I never had from the beginning, or I should not have so recklessly hazarded the chance. But I know who will go," he said, looking toward Kenmuir.

The latter nodded assent.

"Yes," I rejoined, "and you will dispute over every stone you come to: how it came there! what it was doing there! its component parts, and if it would not have been better had it not come there! I think, as there are a million tons of stones, you will get on remarkably well together." For, although the best of friends, they were the bitterest opponents that ever came together. But after a lapse of ten days' wanderings they returned, their *entente cordiale* being in no way destroyed, and shortly after we quitted the happy Valley.

CHAPTER IX.

A RETURN
TO THE VALLEY.

IT WAS A BRIGHT autumnal morning in the early part of November,—the season we call our Indian summer, and so richly prized in the Eastern States, partly because it is of a certainty the last bit of pleasant weather we shall have for six months to come, and partly because it is such a charming season in itself, combining all the tonic of invigoration with the pleasant warmth of comfort. It is indeed the perfection of atmospheric combination, as though it were a compromise between the heat of summer and the cold of winter, to produce a short spell of at least respectable weather, in order that humanity might stop grumbling for a while.

I was sitting in my husband's study in Oakland engaged on some manuscript. The sun's rays streamed in through the window, transmitting diamond-like lines from every lucent medium. It was now more than two years since we had visited the happy Valley of Ah-wah-nee; for although a correspondence had been kept up amongst us, and the Professor had intended returning there the following, and the present, year, yet his researches elsewhere had monopolized his leisure, and I had not, since my valley escapade, undertaken another solitary journey. The gorgeous coloring of some maples near the study window made my thoughts take a retrospective course to the Valley, and picture how beautiful it would look in its autumnal gala dress. I was interrupted by Martha opening the door, and turning, who should meet my gaze but Kenmuir. There was no mistaking his face anywhere, or I should not have known him in his broadcloth suit and white shirt front; but there, still holding its own, amidst the fashionable city dress, was the little mountain flower in his buttonhole.

I held out my hand with a glad welcome, and his old smile brightened his face; but I noticed that it had faded before he had taken the seat I offered him.

"I have come upon a melancholy errand," he said; "Mrs. Naunton is seriously ill."

"I feared so. Do you believe it is really consumption?"

"There can no longer be any doubt," he answered. "She is wasted to a shadow, and for more than six weeks has not been able to walk about. Naunton keeps on repeating that she only wants strength; but she will never be strong again in this world, and I doubt if she has many weeks to remain with us. I fear she will go, as she often says herself, 'with the snow-flakes,' for in the Valley," continued Kenmuir, running off into his beloved subject, "the snow does not drop down as in other places, but seems to be floating in the air in large flakes, like a cloud of white doves just let loose from the Almighty hand."

"But when did the malady assume a serious form?" I interrupted.

"It is difficult to say. I presume it was one of those fatal cases from the beginning. She never seemed seriously ill, and never was to say perceptibly worse,—yet she is dying; and my message is, that she would like to see you once more before she goes; and if you can, you must get in before the storms commence, or the Valley will be snowed up, and the trail impassable. I have come to escort you in if you can decide to go without delay."

"Poor thing!" I said, "it would grieve me deeply to refuse her dying request; and even at the risk of being snowed up in the Valley all winter, I must make the attempt to see her."

Kenmuir held out his hand and shook mine. "God bless you!" he said. "I thought you had courage enough to do a noble act, and she is worthy of your sacrifice."

"Indeed she is, and of ten times as much. I will go and speak to the Professor at once."

My husband never exercised any authority over me in his life, and never opposed any project in which I even imagined I had a good object in view.

Thus the evening of the same day saw us *en route*, and the following morning we lost not a moment in taking horses at Mariposa. But as we ascended the mountain, the wind began to rise, and presently some heavy drops of rain denoted a storm. It was, however, too late to return, and we whipped on our mustangs in order to reach Galen's Rancho before nightfall. The path was steep and rough, and with our best endeavors and willing animals we made but little way; whereas the storm came on with a rush and a vehemence that left us little hope of escaping its full rigor. Still we struggled on, till a gust of wind and hail nearly bore me from my saddle; and a flash of vivid lightning at the same time caused Kenmuir's horse to shy, nearly throwing both steed and rider over a declivity some eight hundred feet in depth. We, therefore, decided to take shelter under a mighty hemlock, that would, at least, screen us from the heaviest of the rain and the keenest of the wind. We drew a thick California blanket over our heads and took patience. The roaring of the storm through the forest giants was terrific; the creaking and splitting of the boughs was like the screeching of demons in their agony. The bellowing of the thunder, peal on peal afar, and the mournful reverberation of the mountains, might have well represented the denunciation pronounced upon the fallen spirits.

Our horses quivered and started with every fresh explosion, and shook their heads under every new gust of rain and hail, which rattled on the broad leaves, that still clothed the forest, like rifle balls on a casemated fortress.

Close to us an immense oak was torn up by the roots, and fell with a tremendous crash that shook the mountain like an earthquake, carrying with it two or three handsome pines and spruces. So fearful was the uproar, and the whirl of hail and soil thrown up from the widespreading roots, that for a moment I thought the earth had given way beneath us and that we had been hurled into eternity.

I clung tightly to Kenmuir, for our horses swayed to and fro as though unable to keep their feet.

I was nearly terror stricken, but my companion threw up his arms in a paroxysm of enthusiastic reverence. "O, this is grand! this is magnificent! Listen to the voice of the Lord; how He speaks in the sublimity of his power and glory!"   .

"I declare I am frightened, Kenmuir," I whispered.

"O, nonsense!" he cried, "there is nothing to be afraid of when the Lord manifests himself in his omnipotence."

"Well, I don't know," I said, a little waggish humor taking possession of me. "Tam O'Shanter thought on such a night as this a child might understand—

"   'The deil had unco business on his hand.' "

"That was a drunken man's fancy," cried Kenmuir impatiently,— "the result of false teaching. If they would leave the devil out of their Sunday-school tracts they would make many a wiser and better man. By cultivating a fear of the devil they excite the lower faculties instead of the higher ones. They blind the young mind to the grandeur of the Lord by arousing his terrors of the prince of darkness. For my part I would not have missed seeing this marvelous physical phenomenon, this wondrous handling of these clashing elements in harmonial splendor: though I had to die next week, I should thank the Lord for permitting me to adore this new display of his universality."

Presently the rain abated, and although the lightning flashed from pole to pole, and the thunder rolled like a mighty bombardment, the wind was not so fierce.

"We had better try and move on," said Kenmuir, "lest you get a chill from standing in the cold."

The horses went willingly, foreseeing a speedy termination to their troubles.

We had proceeded about a quarter of a mile when both horses backed and sprang round.

My heart stood still with fright.

A most unearthly wail rent the air and mingled with the rumble of distant thunder.

"That," I cried, "is not the voice of the Lord. What under heaven is it? There it is again," I added, growing cold with terror.

It was not the crash of trees, nor the yell of savage animals, but sounded like the wail of human creatures in anguish.

"Do not be alarmed," cried Kenmuir, catching my bridle and turning my mustang round. "It is something human, for there is a fire ahead of us. Let us go on and see. It must be the Macbethian witches, or else 'Auld Nick, in shape o' beast, playing his pipes to the warlock dance.' "

We advanced two or three hundred yards on the road and turning a corner, we suddenly came upon a small plateau of greensward and pine straw, when a scene met our astonished gaze which might have dazed Tam O'Shanter. A number of semi-nude figures were dancing, and shrieking, and waving old rags, skins of animals, and eagles' wings around an enormous blazing pyre, on which was a human body tied up in a bundle with knees and arms bound tightly above the breast; and as the motley group danced around they uttered the fearful wail which had so appalled us. As my eyes took in the diabolical scene I wondered if I still had my senses, or if, like poor Tam, my brain was playing me some wild phantasmagorical trick, so fearful was the sound and awful the sight. But Kenmuir pressed my arm and whispered,—

"It is an Indian funeral. They burn their dead, and this is the funeral coronach. They believe that the heart is the immortal part, and that when the body is consumed the heart wings its way to the everlasting hunting-grounds. There is, however, a peril of the evil spirit intercepting its journey, and the friends are therefore doing all in their power to distract his attention in order that the heart may effect its escape. And you observe they are casting on the pyre all his worldly goods, and many of their own most precious ornaments, as tributes of affection to their departed friend or relative; on the same principle as we, more civilized people, put fine clothes and jewels upon our dead," continued Kenmuir with a slight sneer. "When the body is entirely consumed they will gather the ashes, and, mixing them with pine pitch, daub them over their faces and bodies as mourning, and wear them until they gradually drop off in the course of weeks or months."

"How very dirty!" I exclaimed, involuntarily. "Do they never wash during that time?"

"Did the Jewish people not mourn in sackcloth and ashes?" asked Kenmuir, "and do you not cherish a lock of hair in your bosom, cut from a head that lies mouldering in some damp, beautiful nook, and helps to manure the flowers you plant upon it?"

"O, Kenmuir! how very matter of fact you are; in some things of earth earthy, whilst in others you are exalted to the seventh heaven."

Feeling my nerves quite thrilled by the painful minor tones of the death-dirge which, savage or civilized, breaks from the over-charged human heart, I begged Kenmuir to proceed or we should be belated reaching Galen's Rancho.

The rencontre with the burial of the poor Indian struck us both as ominous of the future we were about to meet.

Our thoughts brooded sadly over the gentle spirit fluttering on the verge of her funeral pyre in the once happy cottage of the Valley.

"You do not anticipate any immediate danger for Placida?" I asked fearfully.

"No, not within a few weeks, I hope; but hers is the only death I cannot bring myself to look upon with philosophy. Her life has been such a beautiful calm picture, like her name, without turbulence or disorder. She is the only person I ever knew who seemed to be ever with God and to lean upon Him. She reflected the purity and simplicity of celestial things, and truth and beauty are mirrored in her heart. She is the living soul of Naunton, and the spiritual life of his children."

"What a blank, what a dearth she will leave behind her!"

"I should like to know why the Lord takes her," resumed Kenmuir reflectively, as a humid glistening came over his clear blue eyes.

"He hath need of that delicate flower elsewhere," I suggested.

"Yes," said Kenmuir, grasping eagerly at the congenial idea; "He wants to plant her in a brighter vineyard even than this. The Lord has gardens of light of which these are mere reflections. He will not sacrifice so pure a blossom for the benefit of any of us: we are not worth it. I can easily understand that."

"Poor little Cozy!" I said, "my compassion is most excited for her."

"And probably you will have to exercise it, as Placida will no doubt leave her to you as a legacy."

Here we overtook Galen on the road; he, too, had been enjoying the storm, he said. He was carrying home on his sturdy black mule a fine deer he had just shot.

CHAPTER X.

AH-WAH-NEE.

WE SET OUT NEXT morning from Galen's Rancho. Considerable snow had fallen during the night, but only sufficient to make the splendid scenery more lovely. Every branch and spray was laden with its modicum of snow; often the yellow autumnal edges of the leaves showed all round a little tuft like an opal set in a golden frame. The sun was shining brightly, and the air was not so chilly as it had been the day before. So that Kenmuir was very positive in his prophecy that the snow would soon disappear, and that we should have a glorious Indian summer.

The trail was smooth and firm underneath its white covering, and the marvels of the road were a continual surprise and delight. The snow seemed to embellish everything and the air was so exhilarating, that had it not been for the thought of the poor sufferer in the Valley, we must have enjoyed it with the lightest of spirits.

When we reached Inspiration Point the whole panorama was a scene of enchantment. The mist was floating upward, tinged with all the prismatic hues. The granite towers of the Valley seemed to pierce into the blue vault with their fretwork of pine-trees all powdered with snow. Every nook held its tuft of downy plumes, and every vine trailing over the rocky ledges was tricked out with fairy-like grace and clearness.

The vast Hum-moo was like a colossal Milan Cathedral, with its thousand and one minarets, and pinnacles, glistening in dazzling whiteness on a ground of translucent azure.

The North Dome was a smooth cone of softest white, save where the sun's rays had decorated it with a cap of bright *cerise*. Tis-sa-ack was crowned with a diadem of unspeakable glory, and shone resplendent above all.

In view of so much natural beauty it was difficult to urge Kenmuir forward; he had that peculiar habit of standing stock-still and dilating on the manifold beauties and pointing them out *seriatim*.

I was obliged to repeat,—"Yes, I see it all; but we must keep moving, for Placida will be expecting us."

Upon this hint he would make a fresh start, but the whole way down the mountain was a series of exclamations of delight.

We put our mustangs to the gallop when we reached the level ground of the Valley, and the crunch of their feet over the iced pools and the ring of their bridles sounded sweet in the frosty air.

As we neared the homestead we caught sight of Oswald Naunton in conversation with Mrs. Nell. Radd, followed by Rollo, was mooning about in the distance, evidently in some disgrace from the solicitude evinced by his canine friend.

We soon caught the drift of the conversation, for there is some acoustic property in the Valley that conveys sound far and clear as the famous Whispering Gallery of St. Paul's, London.

"Of course I paid him the money for the skins, Nell," said Mr. Naunton.

"Ah, a course you did!" responded Nell, sharply. "I'd like to see the man as wouldn't back another to go to the devil right on end, and leave his wife to live on huckleberries. I make no account on 'em no hows."

"He said he wanted to buy groceries," pleaded Mr. Naunton.

"Now, Mr. Naunton, don't you go to tell me as you don't know that he always takes his groceries in a likid form! If it's grain, why it's whiskey; if it's molasses, then it's rum; and if it's berries, he'll take them in gin. It makes no sort o' difference to him, so it's likid. It's fortunate the Almighty didn't think o' making the sea o' liquor instead o' salt water, for he'd had it drunk dry if there's many such swallows as Radd's."

"Well, well," said Naunton, in a compromising tone, "he does not often get it, you know; but how came he by that dreadful scratch on his face?"

"Wall, I don't mind owning up that I do give him a claw-down now and then," said Mrs. Radd, imitating the action with her long bony fingers, as though they took an individual delight in the performance, as a musician will sometimes drum unconsciously on a table.

"I'm not the woman to go back o' what I do. When he comes worrying around spouting pottery and smelling like a whiskey mill, I know straight away that he bought no more groceries nor he can hold in a *mug*, and I do give him a claw-down."

Here Mr. Naunton perceived us and hastened to greet us.

"You are welcome, indeed, my good friend," he exclaimed, heartily shaking me by the hand. "The sight of you will make our invalid a new woman!"

"I'm darned if this isn't the folk from the city," said Nell, under her breath. "Good-day ma'am," she continued, aloud, making a bob curtsey, "but you've fann'd out well to come in through the storm to see Mrs. Naunton—afore she dies," she added in a whisper; "not that it'll help her, for she is a gone coon!"

"Nell!" called Mr. Naunton, looking back to where she stood, her arms akimbo, the most ungainly figure,—"don't you want to stay and make some light biscuits for this lady? She has not forgotten how good they used to be in the upper Valley."

"You bet!" cried Nell. "She's 'good fat.'"

Radd has once been a type-setter, hence Nell's vernacular.

"Tell Radd to remain; your huckleberry supper will not get cold," laughed Mr. Naunton, anxious in his heart to keep the pair in order to give them a comfortable meal.

Here Zanita came bounding along looking like a big dragon-fly. Her long thin arms and legs extended in opposite directions.

"That's my colt you are riding! He isn't a colt now, but he was once. Do you know it?"

"O!" she ejaculated, eying me attentively, "you are the one that came before with the man in spectacles and a big nose; you were mighty fond of adian-drums, but you can't have any now, they are all froze up. Give me a ride, won't you? You used to do."

Here we reached the cottage, looking sad yet beautiful in its frost-nipped vines.

So soon as I was dismounted Zanita had scrambled into my saddle and was off careering about wildly.

Placida lay on a lounge that had been constructed for her in the sitting-room, which, with this exception, remained unchanged. She looked as many consumptives do,—very sweet and beautiful, without any of those painful disfigurements which precede dissolution in other diseases. Her eyes were soft and clear, and her color was, if anything, brighter; and had I not known to the contrary, should have pronounced her stronger than when I first saw her.

Little Rosalind nestled at her mother's side making up a bouquet of late autumn leaves and flowers for her.

Mrs. Naunton received me with a glow of grateful pleasure that words failed to interpret.

I took a seat beside her, clasping her white slender fingers in mine, and in those moments I realized all the compensation which awaits on charitable acts, and with which we ought to be satisfied.

Mr. Naunton stood by rubbing his hands gleefully.

"We shall do now, my darling! This is the medicine we have been wanting. This is the strength you needed. Why, you are already worth ten per cent more than you were an hour ago."

And he stooped, partly to conceal the glistening drops in his eyes, and partly to stroke tenderly his wife's soft brown hair, which Rosalind had combed out all over the pillow. In truth, the flush of pleasure seemed to give the invalid new strength and life. Propped up with pillows she conversed easily, no cough disturbing her.

Kenmuir and the "squirrel" came in after a while, the latter explaining her absence on the ground that she had to attend to the horses.

"Neo-wah, the Indian, is not to be trusted! I have to attend to my colt *Jeroboam* myself," she said.

We passed a pleasant, happy evening. Nell doing wonders in the matter of cookery, and Radd in the new *rôle* of waiter, into which his wife unceremoniously thrust him, keeping us in continual merriment by his ludicrous blunders. Rollo also considered himself bound to make himself useful, and carried in a basket of fruit, and any other article convenient to be laid hold of.

"Ho! Radd; hold hard with the coffee!" cried Mr. Naunton, as the former was proceeding to pour it over the pudding, in mistake for a dark compound Nell had instructed him was "sarce."

"I guess you had better look smart or he'll sweeten your tea with salt," cried Nell, grimly, popping in her head, instinctively alive to the short-comings of her spouse.

"If there's a wrong way and a right one, Radd alus pitches on the wrong. I make no doubt he'll try to walk on his hands some day, just 'cause the Almighty has given him feet. If ever he's drowned I should never look down stream, he's certain to float up he's so contrary."

But Radd was too keenly sympathetic with the genial glow of friendship around him to be troubled by his wife's objurgations, and directly she was out of hearing proposed a toast,—

"Our welcome guest!" And after dinner, seated round the great hearth-stone, the pine logs roaring and cracking, his courage rose so high that he volunteered to entertain us with a song. We all caught eagerly at the proposition, and after a timorous glance toward the kitchen, Radd burst forth in his rich baritone, "Oft in the stilly night." The simple pathos of his voice and manner were truly delightful, and at the termination, all begged for another song.

Rollo looked doubtful, went and sniffed about the kitchen, then returned wagging his tail as an assurance that the coast was clear. Radd went on and sang us song after song, making the rafters resound with melody.

"This evening seems like old times," said Mr. Naunton, "and I will venture to say that we shall have many of them. For the snow will set in finally in a week or two, and then the Professor may bid good-by to his wife for the winter, for he cannot get her out until the thaw comes in the spring."

"I'm glad of that," cried the sprite. "Serve him right for letting his nose grow so long. Why doesn't he cut a piece off like papa does his beard?"

"Zanita," said her mother, "what did you promise me?"

"Not to talk, mamma," and she relapsed into quiet.

"That would never do," I resumed, laughing. "I must get back some way, for if I should leave my husband for a month he would be mistaken for a *debonnaire* instead of a professor."

Here we heard Zanita in high altercation with Nell in the kitchen:

"O, you are a right smart un, you are, but you're not a-going to put that here flat-tail rat into th' stove and make believe as I been a cooking on it for a ground squirrel. No, no, I haven't been around these diggins for more nor fifteen year not to know a rat from a squirrel!"

"You could not if his tail was cut off," persisted Zanita.

"You git!" retorted Nell, "or I'll cut the tip of your nose off."

"They ought to have cut yours when you were a little girl, like papa cuts the puppies' ears, to make you smart!"

Having delivered this parting salute, Zanita was seen bounding over the sward in a race with Rollo.

"Young varmint!" we heard Nell muttering; "no need to cut *her* ears. She's too smart, by far, already!"

"Radd," said Mrs. Naunton, "I wish you would whistle in Rollo; that child will be roving the country all night. She has not a bit of fear."

When we broke up for the night, Placida whispered me that she wanted to speak to me privately.

"Had you not better defer it until to-morrow?" I said; "after all this talking, you must need sleep."

"No," she replied, "I never can sleep until morning, and if you will remain with me Oswald will be glad of a night's undisturbed rest,—it is so long since he had one: he is so afraid of my not waking him when I want anything, that he never goes soundly to sleep.

"Now Oswald," she said, gayly raising herself upon her arm, "give me a kiss and go to bed like a good boy, and don't get up until you are called to-morrow morning."

The "good boy" looked very happy, and did as he was bid.

I drew the manzanita easy-chair close to the bed.

"I will rest for a little while," she said, and closed her eyes.

For about half an hour we both remained silent. I could not help observing then how much she had changed; how thin and wan she looked; and how cadaverous was the whiteness of her brow.

We were both roused from our reflections by a piercing howl from Rollo, repeated at momentary intervals until he was quieted by Radd's voice.

"Is it moonlight?" said Placida, "that Rollo bays the moon?"

"I think not," I said, whilst a cold shudder crept over me. I did not like that evil omen.

Presently she took my hand and gazed upon me with those deep dreamy eyes in which the soul's unfathomable mystery seemed to dwell, and said, very calmly, "I want to talk to you about my children. I felt that I could not go until I had seen you and spoken of them; but now I have very little time left here,—very little. I feel anxious about Zanita. She is a child whom her father will never be able to manage, for the reason that she can manage him; and she would, therefore, grow up quite wild and undisciplined. You know her peculiar temperament requires peculiar treatment, and also careful study to develop her remarkable talents and powers. She requires to be guided with a firmness that her father will never exercise over her. I feel that we owe more responsibility to her than usual from the circumstances which preceded her birth.

"Oswald chanced to have visited the Valley in one of his sketching rambles and he came back so thoroughly imbued with the marvelous grandeur that I caught the infection and resolved to accompany him on his next tour; and, finally, filled with the romance and poetry of our honeymoon, we talked ourselves into settling here. The effect upon us was as though we had been semi-consciously transplanted to another world, so highly was our imagination wrought upon by the weird and supernatural atmosphere which surrounded us and in which we freely reveled. I am sure sometimes, if our conversations could have been overheard by sober-minded persons, we should have been regarded as laboring under aberration of mind.

"We built up a fantastic fairy tale of our own lives and dwelt in it, until it became part of ourselves and our real existence. The commonplace outer world, as you can understand, living here in the Valley, receded from our view, and we felt as though an eternal separation had taken place; and for me it had so, indeed, for I have never quitted it,— never been outside these granite walls for eight years,—and now my body will never leave the Valley.

"We often said that it seemed as if we had died without the consciousness of the transition, and arisen in the future life; had advanced one step into that heaven we are promised and which I hope soon to see. I account for much in Zanita's disposition by these pre-natal circumstances, which give her a stronger claim than ordinary on my watchfulness and care.

"I know, my dear friend, that you will not hesitate to undertake any charge or sacrifice to accomplish a good work; and that if I tell you that I wish to leave my child to your sole care, and ask you to fulfill the duty from which I am taken, I may then go in peace and fully trust that I have done the best I could."

I took the shadowy form in my arms and promised to be a mother to her child.

Here Rollo set up another fearful wail and woke up Rosie, who came running into the sitting-room in her little naked feet to look for her mother. She crept closely to the tender embrace of Placida.

"O, mamma!" she sobbed, nervously, "I thought some one called out that you were gone, and I came to see. Dear mamma, don't go! say you will never leave little Cozy! Zanita says you will go."

"Not until the Great Father sends for me; but not now, my darling. I will not leave you; so go to sleep again."

Stroking her mother's hair with her little dimpled hands, she was soon asleep, and I carried her to my bed, for I had my old chamber with the door opening on to the sitting-room.

"I have only a few words more to say, and then I shall send you to bed, too," said Mrs. Naunton.

"I should so much prefer sleeping in this dear old chair by your side," I answered.

"Yes, it is very comfortable; many an hour Oswald and myself have slept in it together,—even, sometimes, with a young lady between us. He used to call it our nest," said Placida, with a sigh.

"I have mentioned the subject we were speaking upon often to Oswald; but he cannot bring himself to believe I am really 'going,' and will not discuss it. Yet he may understand what a boon it is to him when I am no longer here, to be relieved from the care of that child, and will appreciate it then as deeply as I do. For my darling little Cozy he will be all sufficient, and she will soon become so to him. Now farewell, dear friend! I am quite happy," she whispered, and pressed my hand with both hers affectionately. "Be sure we shall meet again. Now I am going to sleep," "sleep"—I thought I heard her murmur—"in God."

I sat by her several hours, and her soft breathing told me that she was peacefully sleeping.

I looked upon the inscrutable mystery of the fading out of life, but my mind failed to understand or realize it.

Was it possible that she was stealing away like the tints of a rainbow? Vanishing from our sight with the beams of the sunset,—silently moving toward heaven as the moonlight creeps up the cloud-capped dome of Tis-sa-ack? So it was, and a vague, supernatural fear seemed to thrill my whole being.

At dawn I returned to my room, having first awakened Mr. Naunton, to take my watch.

I had slept some hours, when I was aroused by Rollo's awesome wail. I stole softly into the sitting-room.

"She is asleep," whispered Mr. Naunton. I looked at her closely; she had not moved or changed. A celestial sweetness radiated the whole face, shadowed only by the long dark lashes which drooped over the semi-closed eyes. Her rich brown hair circled the saint-like head as in a frame, and on the parted lips lingered the ripple of a passed smile,—

"As though last by angels kissed."

But no breath came from them or stirred the delicate pink nostrils.

She was gone unknown to us all, we knew not why or whither. She had left us the semblance of a saint to look upon as an assurance that we had once possessed her; but the beloved Placida had flown, as she had said, with the "snow-flakes," and, with all things fair, and pure, and true, had returned to the hands of the Creator.

Oswald Naunton's grief was of the most frantic kind.

He refused absolutely to believe the fact, and wished to employ all sorts of remedies to resuscitate her, as from a swoon or syncope. Not until I took him forcibly by the hand, and made him approach and look at her, could he realize the calamity.

"Look at her, speak to her yourself; she will tell you how it is with her."

He gazed earnestly upon her.

"Placida, my mourning blossom," he gasped out.

"Death!" was the answer written visibly on every line of her face.

He beat his brow and tore his hair, and raved in a sort of frenzy, staggering about the house like one whose brain is surcharged with poisonous fumes. He was as madly drunk with grief as an opium-eater with his drug. He upbraided himself, the Almighty, and every one around in the most furious invectives; his judgment had no more control than that of a raving maniac. I was obliged to entreat Radd to carry the two children out into the forest, and keep them there for the day.

Poor Rosie had sobbed herself into a state of exhaustion; whilst Zanita, somewhat bewildered, was yet half enjoying the state of excitement.

She followed her father with a curious watchfulness that insured her mimicking the scene at some future time.

"Father's right mad because mamma is gone, isn't he? But she said she should go; she is gone to the Spirit Land, she told me so; and I'm to be good, and not tease Cozy. The rocks are higher there, and there are plenty of big waterfalls, and no bucking mules. I wish mamma had taken me. Mu-wah says they are going to put mamma in the ground like the cow that died; but they sha'n't; I'll dig her up again. I'll work all right, and Rollo will help me with his paws. She must be burnt on a big fire,—that's the way to the Spirit Land, Mu-wah says,—and have her heart taken out."

She was full of the excitement of the moment, and kept on discussing it with every one.

"Isn't papa mad?" she exclaimed. "Will he go on breaking everything in the house? I wish he would throw that pitcher of molasses at Nell's head. She would fly round like a wild cat."

Kenmuir wept softly like a woman, every now and then approaching the lounge on tiptoe to look at the dead. I had no time to indulge in the deep sorrow I felt, but every once and awhile had so far to yield as to have a good cry, and then resume my occupation.

Nell kept us all more or less in our senses and the commonplace, by constant suggestions about "decent folk having decent funerals, and how it was unlucky that there were so few people and no minister in the Valley to come and visit the body; that it was a right sweet corpse as she had ever seen;" whereupon Mr. Naunton swore furiously that no one should approach his wife but me.

Nell protruded her tooth, and sidled off into the back premises. Just then old Methuselah wandered up, looked in upon us from the lintel of the door, but was driven remorselessly away by the wretched husband, who accused him of the murder of his wife in having advised him not to take her out of the Valley when she first became sick.

He turned away, shaking his old mop head dolefully. I followed him apace to tell him that Mr. Naunton was quite beside himself, and knew not what he was saying.

"No, no," said the old man; "but when such young things marry and become mothers there is little hope for their lives. I always said how it would be. I suppose I had better come to the funeral though?"

"O, certainly; we shall need you to make one of the four to bear the coffin."

"I could carry her on one arm myself, little sylph-like creature! Just like the Princess Charlotte, heir to the British throne, who died the other day in her accouchement. Such children ought to be kept in pinafores, and not allowed to marry."

"Mrs. Naunton had been married nine years, and the Princess Charlotte must have been dead forty," I replied.

"Well, well, time flies. It's time I was thinking about getting married myself; but she married too young, poor thing! poor young thing!" and he wished me good day.

Three terrible days we passed beside poor Placida, waiting until her husband's paroxysm of grief should abate, or nature become exhausted.

Finally, toward the close of the third day, I noticed that he had at last fallen asleep in his chair, and, taking advantage of this to go outside the door to breathe the freshness of the wintry air, my eyes were further gladdened by the sight of the Professor, accompanied by Mr. Galen, of Galen's Rancho.

Without my knowing, the thoughtful Radd had been to Sonora and telegraphed to my husband the sad news; and, by a fortunate occurrence, he was able to start at once, knowing how much I should need his help and comfort under the painful circumstances.

The funeral took place next day.

Poor Placida was laid under the shadow of the great tombstone shaped "sentinel," the only monument Naunton would hear of; and, indeed, it was a magnificent one. It rose like a single slab of white granite, detached from the rest two thousand feet high, and its oval form always gave it, to my fancy, the shape of a tombstone.

I took some of her best loved flowers and planted them around her. Zanita behaved shockingly at the grave, uttering wild Indian yells, and protesting that her mother should not be put in a hole like a cow, but burnt on a big fire of logs that Mu-wah could make.

The Professor had recommended that she should be taken to the funeral, thinking it would have a subduing and awe-inspiring effect upon her. But as yet we had little idea of the wild spirit we had to deal with. Little Rosie, who was left behind, had formed the idea that the procession was some sort of ceremony to restore her mother to her usual state, and wept bitterly when we all returned without the coffin.

"O, where have you taken my dear mamma? Where have you put her? I would rather have her that way, quiet, and not opening her eyes, than taken away altogether. O, let me go to her!"

"She is gone to the Spirit Land," said Zanita, sententiously; "but I don't think she has gone all right, on account of putting her in the ground. She ought to have been burnt."

Rosie's eyes dilated with horror.

"And if you want to go to her, Cozy, I'll put you on a big pile and burn you up, and you'll go quite straight. O, wouldn't you blaze!" she cried,—"you are so fat!"

Poor Cozy burst into a fit of despair.

"Zanita," I said, "cease teasing the child. How can you be so cruel?" I took Rosie to my heart and soothed her.

I persuaded my husband to remain in the Valley as long as possible, for Oswald Naunton's sake; for although he was now calm and subdued from the effect of reaction, yet he was evidently a broken-hearted man, and would never be himself again.

The light of life had left him, and only existence remained; and O, what a weary thing is mere existence! Living until it is time to die. Life a hopeless waiting, and dread speculation of what the next may be.

73

CHAPTER XI.

MORE THAN A
HANDFUL.

SO IT WAS AGREED THAT we should take Zanita and adopt her as our own, or rather, as my own, for the Professor declared that although he did not object in the least to my having the child, yet he declined sharing any of the responsibility. She was to be wholly under my supervision and control, and I was not to apply to him for any advice or aid, further than the funds necessary for her maintenance.

"If," said he, "you consider, my dear, that it is your duty to care for and educate Zanita, and direct her mental growth, then by all means act as your conscience directs; but I am not imbued with the same opinion, and I warn you not to allow your heart to mislead you in this respect, under the very natural and feminine idea that it would be pleasant to have a child in the house to love and protect. Zanita is not the one to increase any one's happiness. And, excuse me for doubting that, even under your judicious treatment, she will ever make such a woman as a right-minded man would esteem and love. But, as I said before, if you think that your sacrifice for her good will prove her salvation, then, under such circumstances, I say you are the good and true little woman I have known you to be for fifteen years, and you shall carry out your noble intentions."

Accordingly we started with Zanita for our home in Oakland. This journey out of the Valley was one of the saddest rides I ever made in my life. Everything wore an aspect of woe: the iron Tu-toch-a-nulah himself had a crushed and bowed appearance, as though he grieved for the absence of the beautiful spirit that had flown away even beyond his cloudy crest. The trees, and the few flowers left by the autumn, seemed to droop and pine as for a lost friend.

It was one of those dying days of the year when nature seems expiring with a solemn mournful sob; bright, beautiful, and glorious as she had been for months, she was now a thing of the past. Hers is a state of transition: the end of one life and the birth of another. Human nature, whose existence is still protracted, has an internal sympathy with her dissolution, and longs to lie down and expire with her. Thus had it been with that sweet spirit, so tender, so intimate, so loving had been her fellowship with the Great Mother. The air was heavy with clouds. A few drops of rain now and then fell like our painfully restrained tears. The piteous sobs of poor Rosalind, as she had clung to all in turn, imploring to be taken to her mamma, and believing steadfastly that we were going to join her as we had all gone to the funeral, still vibrated in my heart. Every moan through the pine boughs seemed to bring the agonized cry to my ears, until my heart was so full that it ran over. I felt then that I would give the world to turn back, and take the child upon the saddle before me.

The Professor, who generally followed the tenor of my thoughts pretty accurately, though unexpressed in words, here rode close along by my side, and placing his hand upon my shoulder,—

"Come," said he, "bear up; you have done for the best; the child will be a comfort to her father, and it is the only consolation left him. She will be much happier in her old home than in a new one, and you have relieved them of a great trial in bringing away this one, who is absolutely enjoying, in her peculiar way, the lashing-up of her horse. If she does not break her neck over these rocks and stones before we get out of the Valley, I shall regard it as a special Providence."

I looked ahead, and there was Zanita curveting and whipping and curbing her horse on a path, not much more than half a yard wide, overlooking a chaos of rocks and boulders sloping down for a thousand feet.

"Zanita! Zanita!" I exclaimed, "stop lashing your horse; he will lose his footing and go over the precipice."

"Aunty," she called back, "he wants to go over, and I am trying to prevent him."

And she continued her exercise; fortunately the horse knew both his path and his rider, and pertinaciously refused to budge an inch off the track.

"Do you go to her, and take away her whip," I said to the Professor, as we exchanged glances of meaning that my trials had already commenced. "For, although the child is a splendid horsewoman already, and could ride a steeple-chase, yet I would rather see her anywhere than mounted."

Indeed my husband congratulated me when we arrived safely at Mariposa, there to take the stage for Stockton.

But our anxieties were only exchanged, and not removed; for having allowed her, under strict promise to behave herself, to ride alongside the coachman, she easily, with that soft winning look she knew so well how to assume when she wished to beguile a stranger, succeeded in persuading him to let her handle the reins, which she did with such skill and adroitness that coachee was amazed and delighted.

Presently we heard the whip going, and felt ourselves dashing along at a tremendous pace down-hill and around corners, the coach swaying to and fro until some of the inside passengers began to get alarmed, especially as we heard peals of laughter from the box.

"The driver must be drunk," said my husband, "but he has his horses well in hand. Did you see how splendidly we came around that corner?"

Suddenly we pulled up with such a jerk, that the impetus caused all the *vis-a-vis* to embrace each other. The Professor, putting his head out of the window, beheld Miss Zanita struggling with the driver in her refusal to give up the reins.

"Zanita, you must come inside if you cannot behave properly."

"He let me take the reins, and I drove splendidly he said," so pleaded Zanita; "and if you will allow me to remain outside I will not do so again."

We had not traveled half an hour before the elf, as my husband called her, was flourishing about on the roof and dangling the whip, to which she had tied a bunch of dry sedges, in at the windows of the stage.

"That ar' gal of yourn seems an imp of mischief," said a portly old gentleman in the corner, whose nose had been titillated by the sedges.

We had now to stop the coach, and have the imp brought in *bon gré mal gré*. It was a peculiarity of this child that she never fretted over anything, and no disappointment, or crossing of her purpose, seemed to afflict her more than two minutes. Her mind never dwelt longer on anything. If she were not allowed to amuse herself one way, she was fertile in improvising another. She had clung to her dead mother before she was put into the coffin, and had uttered wild yells, screamed, and fought, and bit in a frenzy to prevent the coffin from being lowered into the grave.

But the following day she seemed to have little, if any, remembrance of the tragic scene, and it was doubtful if the solemnity of her mother's death or absence affected her in any way. She was self-reliant and self-sufficient; and it was often a matter of doubt to me whether the normal affections had not been curiously omitted in her nature. She never nursed a doll, or fondled an animal, or caressed her sister. She would make the latter take a part in her play, but always to oblige herself. Yet once, when Kenmuir had harshly ejected Rosalind from amongst his botanical specimens, Zanita seized a chisel, and screamed with frantic passion that she would scalp him.

Being so much older than Rosalind, she ruthlessly took possession of whatever plaything she wished, indifferent to the lamentations of the little one. Yet, as a rule, she was not unkind, though tyrannical.

It boots not to tell of the hot water she kept our erst quiet establishment afloat in; nor would these pages suffice to narrate the ninety-ninth part of her escapades: how she rode astride down the banister, instead of stepping down the stairs; how she connived with the cat to catch a mouse alive, and put it into the meal barrel; how she would turn the water tap, and flood the whole premises; how it was impossible to keep her respectably clothed from any milliners. She never could be induced to take care of her costume; and of vanity, as far as *fixings* went, she had none. Gathers or trimmings were impracticable, the latter were always *en queue*, and the former *en feston*.

I had to take her in hand, and make her dresses in one piece, with as few seams or adornments as might be; nothing but back-stitching had a chance. Only on Sunday could I venture to dress her as a young lady to go to church.

Even then the Professor always declared he was ashamed to go out with her, for her hat could never be kept straight on her head, and often, if lost sight of for a moment, she would have it tied around her body, either as a pack or a breastplate, or strung over her parasol or umbrella, as though she were off camping again. In church she would persistently sleep and yawn aloud, or chew up the leaves of her prayer-book as if they were tobacco, making a tremendous display of spitting, and, if I gave her a handkerchief, would cough and bark until she drew the attention of the whole congregation upon her, and then she would flash out that elfish glance which expressed her highest state of enjoyment.

She had not been long in our quiet home in Oakland before most of my friends had come to condole with me, and delicately hint that she should be sent back into the wilds from whence she came. But the more difficult she was to manage, the more I felt that her father was unequal to training her: with her headstrong will, and relentless, fierce passions, she might drift into some fearful catastrophe or crime; while a judicious influence and pressure might subdue and guide her to some bright career; for that she was a child of magnificent talents and capabilities was undoubted.

Neither was it possible to conceal her mischievous proclivities from our neighbors; for if once admitted within their homes, there was no further safety for them or their belongings. She had sheared the tail and mane of the minister's gray pony, which, as his wife said, made it look such an indelicate, nude object, that she could never ride behind it again.

Her reputation was thoroughly spread, when, one day, having locked myself in my room to write letters, which having accomplished, I sought in the parlor and kitchen, and was told by the servant that she had not seen her, but believed she was playing in the back garden, or in one of the trees, her usual resort. She answered not to my call, nor was she in the garden, or in the house; every room was looked into, every closet was opened; nothing was found. Her hat was gone, and she was gone, and we were all non-plused. I then waited for a time, thinking she had ran in, perhaps, to some of the neighbors. After the lapse of a couple of hours, the Professor came home; but no Zanita.

He expressed considerable alarm when told of the circumstance, and suggested that a search through Oakland be instituted without delay. He arranged a plan, and we all turned out to carry it into execution. We dreaded such a beautiful child being decoyed into San Francisco, and that she would fearlessly go with any one for a sufficient bribe I did not doubt.

My husband took one street, myself another, and the servant a third. We had a young darkey called Beppo, or for short "Bepp," about thirteen years old, who served our small establishment as errand-boy and general skirmisher. He had been questioned at first, and his great round eyes opened so wide at the tidings of the disappearance of "Missy Zanita," that I was fain to say, as I often did, "Do close your eyes, Bepp; they'll fall out some day if you stretch them so wide." I now gave him directions to run all about the neighborhood, a jaunt of which he was usually very fond, and try to find Miss Zanita.

He showed his white teeth, and doubtfully rolled his head, which always seemed loose.

"Missy am not been done gone far away."

"How do you know—have you seen her?"

"I b'leeve missy an't been done gone far away."

"Nonsense!" I said, "go directly and look everywhere until you find her."

"I'se been gone, missis."

Two hours of ineffectual search and we became convinced, to our horror, that the child was not in Oakland; especially as in my travels I had met a lady who said that, from the description given, she had seen such a child going on to the ferry-boat, as she came off that day. She had not noticed her dress, but had been struck with her remarkable beauty.

Everything having been done that could be done in Oakland, and the police put on the *qui vive*, as much as could be effected with that body, myself and the Professor resolved to go over to San Francisco to trace the child which had been seen on the steamer, and communicate with the police in that city, and, as we could not conveniently return that night, we decided to remain there unless in case of her being discovered, when a telegram was to be sent; then we could hire a boat to take us across.

My heart sunk as I thought of the child wandering in the purlieus of San Francisco, and of the perils to which she was exposed: that she would readily accompany any one or enter any place I was sure, for fear was a quality which seemed entirely absent from her character. Even worse was the reflection, that she might choose to remain in any den of iniquity where it might suit them to keep her, with all her acuteness for concealing herself. I felt that, young as she was, it would take more than one adult intellect to compete with her in cunning devices.

As all these thoughts crowded upon me, I was utterly hopeless, and began to blame myself for bringing such a child out of her native forest. Communicating these thoughts to my husband, who, in spite of all his repudiation of responsibility, still behaved admirably in this emergency, he replied to my fears,—

"I would not make myself unhappy by entertaining those thoughts, my dear, if I were you; for I think it is ten chances to one that the child has hidden herself for the purpose of causing all this confusion, and that she will turn up in the quarter we least expect. Nevertheless, we must follow up this trace of her."

On the ferry-boat, no one who knew her by sight had seen her, but a porter at the San Francisco depot remembered a little girl with very bright dark eyes. I could scarcely keep the tears out of mine, as I heard this news.

"You know, my dear," commented my husband, "there are a few hundred little girls with beautiful black eyes who might be coming backwards and forwards to Oakland."

We finally traced the black eyes to the street-cars; there the conductor said that such a little girl traveled by his car and had paid her fare with a dime, but did not recollect where she got out. As regarding her dress, he believed she had blue ribbons in her hat. "No red?" said I. "Well, maybe it might be red. I could not be clear about that."

"What! not know blue from red?" I exclaimed, impatiently.

"Well, madam, I guess I can manage to get through without knowing. I havn't got to garnish my hat with either, and if I want to make our glorious flag, I've only to put the two together."

"But," I continued, in my anxiety, "can't you possibly recollect which? If it was blue, as you first said, it was surely not my little girl, and the dread of her having come over to the city alone would be at an end, and we could renew our efforts in Oakland."

"Wall," said the man immediately, "I guess it was blue; now, I am about certain it was;" and as my face brightened with the hope, he added,—

"I'm right certain it was the color of your bonnet ribbon."

"Good gracious, man!" I exclaimed, in despair, "that is violet."

"Wall, it's that, anyhow!" he persisted; so we went as wise as we came.

The captain of the police then told us he had seen, or heard of, at least six lost little girls, all with black eyes, and had no doubt but that he could lay his finger upon the one we sought in the course of twenty-four hours. He took down from my lips a minute description of her appearance and dress.

"Yah!" he exclaimed, running his eye over the page, "I thought I had her right off if it hadn't a-been for them 'slender limbs': now the little gal I have in my eye has stout legs and arms, and is a right-fleshy child." I went on with my description.

"Yah! I have her," he interrupted; "speaks rapidly, does she? No mistake," and he turned over the leaves of his day-book and ran down the columns with his finger.

"There ye are, madam. Black eyes, brown nose,"—

"Hair," I suggested, looking over the page.

"Quite right, madam; it is hair I was agoin'—straight down ye see. A quill nose,"—

"Aquiline," I put in.

"Just so; slender figure, brown dress. There you are," called the captain, triumphantly.

"Have you got the child?" I burst out, overjoyed.

"I guess I have; I guess I got just such a one in my eye."

"O, take us to her at once!" I exclaimed. "If you knew the anxiety I have suffered"—

"Here you are, madam! We'll go at once. I knew that child belonged to decent folks, professors like yourselves; so I kept her in my eye, though those people swore she belonged to a dead sister-in-law's cousin. Yah! I knew I should pitch upon it at last. I've had that case in my eye for the last ten days, madam."

"O dear!" I cried, clinging to my husband's arm, "then it can't be Zanita; she was only lost this morning."

"Not her!" exclaimed the captain, incredulously; and he again ran his finger down the column of the day-book. "Black eyes, brown nose,—nose—how? I mean a quill nose."

"It is of no use," I repeated; "the child was safe this morning under my care."

"Well, then, it's a case of mistaken identity," said the captain, "and I'll keep that child in my eye till her rightful parents does turn up. Now, madam, I will just take down how you came to lose her and where you think she is gone, and that is all that I will trouble you with this evening."

Having given our address in the city and in Oakland, and promising to call early next morning, for which the captain said there was not the slightest necessity, that he could lay his finger on her in twenty-four hours if she was in the city of San Francisco, and "if she wasn't, as a matter of course, why, he couldn't, that was all."

We returned to our hotel anxious and disconsolate; at least I was, but the Professor declared that he felt hopeful, as he had come to the conclusion that Zanita had not been in the city at all, and was safely in hiding in Oakland, for there was no place we could think of where she could be drowned or have fallen over.

"That child is the incarnation of mischief, and you will have to get accustomed to her vagaries and not worry about her, whatever happens!"

"Her poor mother never did," I replied, "and it seems as though she was the only one who could control her."

"Well, my dear," said my husband, in his consolatory way, "I think you manage her very well whilst she is by you, but unless you could influence her magnetically, and exercise some superhuman sort of control, I do not see how these untoward proceedings can be foreseen or avoided."

I never passed a more uncomfortable and restless night than at the hotel. I found it impossible to keep my imagination in repose for a moment. I was in spirit prowling all over the country, rummaging into every possible and impossible place. She might have fallen down somebody's well; she never could keep her hand from interfering with anything she saw. Had she walked out into the country and taken refuge in some barn?

I resolved to have all the out-houses and wells searched next day. Could she have wandered down by the beach and been carried off by the tide? She could swim like a fish, and I had a feeling that she could not be drowned.

After settling all my plans for the coming day I got a few moments of rest.

Early the next morning the Professor went around to the office of the chief of police, and to all the different places where we had given information the evening before, but without gaining any satisfactory result. The captain admitted he had not got her rightly in his eye, but would no doubt lay his finger on her in twenty-four hours. We, consequently, returned home weary and heart-sick.

Our woolly-headed page met us at the cars: from the grin on his countenance visible far away in the distance, I rushed to the conclusion that there was good news, and communicated my hope to the Professor.

"See how delighted he looks; they must have found her!"

"Bepp has a capability of always being delighted, and I doubt very much whether the seriousness of the affair has as yet penetrated both the wool and the cranium. I suspect his pleasure arises from having caught a glimpse of you in the cars."

"Is Miss Zanita found?" I called from the car window as soon as we were within hail. Bepp grinned assent and rolled his head in negative.

"What a tantalizing boy that is! Is Miss Zanita found?" I cried, jumping off the car and seizing him by the shoulder.

"Missy Zanita no found; she am been gone in the night."

"How do you know? If she came in the night she must be at the house now. Is she?"

"B'leeve Missy Zanita gone been in the night."

We hastened home, Beppo following, looking very serious, but no more intelligible. Martha, our girl, was standing at the door.

"Not the slightest tidings of her," she said, answering my inquiry, before I could utter it.

"What does that goose, Bepp, mean about the night?"

"I don't know," said Martha, coloring. "He fancies he saw her, or dreamed he did."

After some further talk we again took up the search. Martha went off on one expedition, and I started to hire a horse and buggy to be driven around the suburbs. I had not gone more than a hundred yards from the house, when I recollected that I might require more money than I had in my purse. I at once retraced my steps, opened the door softly with the latch-key, and was half-way up-stairs toward my bedroom, when I was startled by a fearful crash in one of the rooms below, which sounded as though all the crockery in the house had been broken. I thought of a strange cat having got into my china and store closet, and rushed to the spot.

The door was partly open, and there, astride the *débris* of my best tea-set, jam-pots, apples, peaches, dry tea, and coffee-beans, stood the lost Zanita, with a gleam of half discomfited mischief in her roguish eyes.

"Why Zanita!" I exclaimed, "where have you been?"

"Nowhere," was the prompt reply. "Has aunty just come back from San Francisco?"

"Certainly I have, where I have been looking for you. You naughty child! Where have you been?" I repeated. "Tell me, instantly."

"Aunty, I have not been anywhere,—not even into the garden to play whilst you were absent," cried the little witch demurely, attempting to make believe she had been conducting herself most exemplarily during my short stay in San Francisco.

"Where were you yesterday, and last night?"

"Sometimes in one room, sometimes in another."

I now recollected that we had all been away during the greater portion of the time, and that she had the full roam of the rooms to herself.

"What part of the house were you in when I was calling you?"

"I did not hear you calling," she said, with the most innocent look.

"How came all this breakage?"

"I was trying to reach an apple."

"You could not have broken the shelf trying to reach an apple," I said: and now the whole mystery flashed upon my mind. She had mounted the shelf and hidden away in the dark corner, so that a person coming from the light and looking in would not observe her; and when she had found the house clear had roamed about at large, concealing herself when she heard any one approach. Thus, probably, Beppo had seen her; but there was some Masonic understanding between them.

"Now, Zanita, tell me, were you not upon that shelf?"

"I was just camping there," she pleaded, at last brought to bay, "and I'll mend all the cups and saucers with pine gum, and I'll put a stanchion under the shelf, so that it won't break again."

"No," I said, "it will never break again when it is mended; for, in punishment of the naughty trick you know that you have played, you shall not enter that closet again for six months."

This was a terrible infliction, for it was her special delight to bring me fruit and cake from the closet, to which, no doubt, she helped herself. She made no murmur or to do, but just turned round and began to fit the china together.

Most of our friends were of opinion that she ought to receive a sound whipping, and that it would cure her of such exploits, but, besides doubting the wisdom of Solomon in general as to the use of the rod, in this *special* case it would have been the climax of evil. Fear of anything would never deter her accomplishing whatever she had set her heart upon, but a constant privation was what she could less endure. She was passionately fond of good things to eat, and for this gratification she was likely to sacrifice the other propensity to mischief.

At this juncture of affairs the Professor came in, and I hastened to inform him of the manner of the discovery. He was not a man of many words and said nothing, except his expressive little "Humph, humph!"

Zanita pretended hard to appear as though unconcerned in the conversation, but under her long dark lashes she was keeping a keen watch upon the Professor, like a wary dog guarding an enemy that might turn out dangerous. But she avoided meeting his eye. There was a struggle for mastery silently going on between the child and the man, very curious to observe.

He was making her aware that no such pranks could be safely played with him or anything appertaining to him. Unconsciously, she was trying to repudiate this impression, and reviewing in her mind how she could create a disturbance in his geological and botanical specimens. That she would fall foul of his study some day had been my fear and dread since she had entered the house. But my comfiture and pickle closet had been the first victim.

Presently the eyes of the silent and fierce combatants met, and Zanita received a glance which made her dark orbs droop and quiver. She turned away with that peculiar laugh of hers, half glower and half leer, and the contortion which came over her delicate and already expressive little face said as plainly as if spoken in words,—

"I see I must not come in collision with you, but there is mischief enough to beat outside your study, and I'll circumvent you in many a way you don't think of."

My husband and I exchanged glances of intelligence.

"It is very hard for you, my dear," he said, laying his hand on my shoulder, "but courage! you have to meet the ordeal you have undertaken."

"It seems to me," he added, sitting down on the lounge beside me, as he always did for a cozy chat,—"it seems to me a problem which I cannot solve. To start with the beneficence of Providence, it is a mystery that He should burden a poor child with such a character from no fault of any one that we can see, unless one is lugged out from some of the remote relics of her dead ancestors and bequeathed to her as a legacy, for neither her father nor mother had any of these peculiar traits. It is the unnatural development of the organs of destructiveness, secretiveness, and ideality."

"Admitted; but her mother was not secretive, perhaps a little reticent from timidity, but simple and truthful as a May morning, and her ideality was of the most spiritual and angelic character; and her father is as honest and upright as day,—a man without guile."

"Where, then, does she get her inaptitude, or, I may say, her incapacity, for truth?"

"It is her want of conscientiousness," I replied.

"Allowed," returned my husband; "but how are you going to supply it? Don't you admit that it is a misfortune to be born without conscientiousness?"

"Certainly I do; but by cultivating that organ and repressing destructiveness, I hope, in a measure, to counteract the misfortune."

"Well," said the Professor, smiling, "we shall see who has the best success: I with my cabinet, or you with your china closet."

Here we were interrupted by Martha's voice, exclaiming,—

"My, my! if you ain't a little cuss! I never did! I wish you were my child; I'd spank you while I could stand over you—that I would!"

"No you wouldn't," retorted Zanita; "I'd just put matches and powder under your bed if you were my mother, and blow you up in blazes."

"I'll bet you would; there's nothing impish that'll beat you. Where have you been?"

"Nowhere," cried Zanita. "I've never been out of the house. But *you* have; you've been out all night, and I'll tell aunty of you if you don't leave me alone."

"Drat the child! she must be a witch: how do you know?"

Zanita let fly her elfin fire, but said nothing.

Here I called Martha and explained the situation.

"And were you out, Martha?" I inquired.

"True for you, ma'am, I was: I'm sorry I left the house when you and the Professor was out, but it happened just this how. I fell asleep in my chair right early, and was awoke by a queer-like noise that set all my hair up, and I come out in a reg'lar perspiration: it was the strangest kind of thing. First, as though something had tickled my face, like the cat's tail, ma'am, but when I got up there was no cat, and I heard the *strangest* noise—well, more like the spirits in Purgatory than anything I can think of."

Here Zanita, her face buried in the sofa cushions, was shaking with suppressed merriment.

"Zanita! what is the matter; do you know anything about it?"

"No, nothing, aunty," said the child, looking up as grave as a judge, her great dark eyes troubled as though mischief had never been reflected from the same orbs.

"Well, ma'am, as I was saying, I just made tracks out of the door to fetch up Bepp, and then I bethinks me that if it was any of the brood of Satan, why a nigger might be the best to help him, both being of the same color like. So I just stepped into Mrs. Waddy's, next door, and found Jane sitting up, ironing; and she said, said she, that even with a hot iron she'd not like to face such a dispensation of Providence as spirits in Purgatory appearing in acshul presence as they are allowed to do, you know ma'am, on All-Hallow's Eve. So the long and short of it is, I slept with Jane, and I've not seen the cat this morning, and I do confess and believe that the devil and all his works have taken it."

At this avowal of faith another convulsion from Zanita confirmed the idea I had formed of this tragic story.

"Now, Zanita," I said, "tell me where the cat is!"

"You bet she'll know if any one does. I'm blessed if she ain't in telegrammatical communication with the devil, as is a growling lion as she is, always a talking about in them forests where she comes from."

"Where is the cat, Zanita?" I repeated.

Zanita cast down her eyes and twined her slender fingers, as she was in the habit of doing when seeking for a plausible subterfuge.

To my reiterated question she answered, "Oh, it was probably a tiger-cat, a great frightful striped thing that came down to the cottage at home in heavy snowstorms. Ah! Martha, it's a wonder it didn't tear your eyes out and your hair off, specially your waterfall that's just like a bird's-nest, and the tiger-cat would think there were young ones in it, and would eat it all up, and you too," she concluded, her eyes gleaming with delight at the horror and disgust expressed by Martha as she re-fixed her waterfall.

I could scarcely keep from laughing, but I said, gravely,—

"Zanita, that will not do. You must tell me where the cat is!"

"Well, then," she said, throwing her arms about me with her sweetest manner, "may I go into the closet again if I tell?"

"No! certainly you cannot; but you must tell all the same."

Having retreated behind her last fastness and unable to make terms, she yielded at discretion and whispered,—

"In the wood-shed."

"Come, then," I said, taking her hand, "let us find her."

We all went into the wood-shed, and there, as pointed out by my *protégé*, in a barrel, the lid heavily weighted by a lump of coal, lay poor pussy, still and lifeless, with my gilt leather cincture, to which a buckle was attached, drawn tightly round her neck.

To our mutual exclamations of horror, Zanita replied,—

"I put a pretty collar on her, aunty; you said she should have a pretty collar."

"Don't say a word, you naughty child; how could you be so cruel as to kill poor Kitty?"

"I didn't kill her. I only pulled the strap to stop her making a noise and waking Martha."

"Yes, whilst you tickled her face with pussy's tail!"

I took the poor kitten on my lap and unfastened the strap, and made Zanita stand and look at her while I appealed to her higher and softer feelings. I represented the suffering of the kitten and how playful and cunning she had ever been.

"She scratched me, once!" said Zanita.

I used my utmost eloquence, and pictured the death of the kitten in the most pathetic strain. It was all in vain; not a tear could I win, not an expression of sorrow or remorse flickered for an instant over her statue-like face. She coolly turned to Martha and said,—

"Martha, won't you skin it, just like you do the rabbits, and let me have the skin to make cuffs like aunty's, to wear in snow time."

I gave up trying to excite any tenderness as quite hopeless, and carried the cat to the Professor, who had been in his study all the time. To my great relief he pronounced the animal not dead.

"It is a case of suspended animation, and possibly we may resuscitate her."

The Professor went to work, with a little science and more good-will, and poor pussy was soon crawling about,—very languidly at first, but rapidly gaining strength, and bearing no malice toward Miss Zanita.

Children who are already callous to the delicate emotions, without a clear sense of justice or right, do not recognize the punishment of the rod as retributive, but only as an exercise of power which they set themselves to defeat by every means within their grasp. They do not resolve never again to commit the act for which they have been punished, but they determine to so plan and plot, to so lie and deceive, that they shall never again be caught. Thus they are not improved, but rendered ten times more vicious than before. Boys, especially, are often fearless and take delight in daring a danger, which, if incurred, will assuredly bring them pain. They know when they climb trees they may fall and break their limbs, and suffer weeks of confinement and agony; but *no boy* was ever deterred from climbing by fear of consequences, or from stealing apples by fear of a whipping, even though he has suffered from either: he merely acts with more caution in placing his footing, or waits till it is darker, or the owner of the apples more distant.

If Zanita had been whipped she would have taken the first opportunity of practicing the same infliction on the cat, or dog, or child over whom she might have control. I should have been in terror lest somebody's baby would be found beaten to death with the stair rod or hand broom, so vindictive and hard was her nature. Pain and suffering in another seemed to afford her absolute pleasure,—like the Queen Joanna of Naples, who is said to have had her lover tortured to death before her eyes. I did not doubt that my *protégé* possessed much the same disposition, and would exercise it with the same gusto when she had the power.

To counteract this idiosyncrasy I endeavored to exclude her from the sight or knowledge of any act of cruelty, for even the killing of bears, snakes, and wild animals, in her forest life, had already had a most baneful effect on her character. Life of bird, beast, or man was alike indifferent to her. She was as callous about her mother's death as about that of her favorite calf or dog.

"How did she die?" she would ask me over and over again, when I mentioned the subject. If I could have told her she had been shot, or fallen off Tu-tock-a-nulah, or drowned in the Mercede, she would have taken great interest in the subject; but she lacked sympathy and even appreciation of her sweet, saint-like mother. She could perceive no beauty in earth, or sky, or rock, or river, nor yet in her own exquisite face.

"Aunty," she said one day, "that little girl at Waddy's says I'm not as pretty as she is, because she has got light hair like Cozy. Isn't that rubbish? Who cares about being pretty! I can jump three times as high as she can, and throw a stone and hit any one chicken you like to say."

"No, indeed, I do *not* like 'to say'; and you must not throw at the chickens."

In many ways she had the character of a boy. She was never known to cry, and I have seen her, as a little one, bruised all over, show up her wounds and scratches, and even glory in them.

"You never had such a deep cut as that!" she would cry, exultingly.

Some days she would limp and explain to every one that a large rock had rolled over and crushed her foot.

CHAPTER XII.

BREACHES OF DECORUM.

BUT MY CHIEF AND MOST formidable difficulties arose in respect of her religious training. She was lamentably deficient in the organ of veneration, and as she had never seen a church or perhaps never heard of one, until she came to Oakland, it was difficult to teach her any sort of reverence for the holy building.

"Why is it naughty to laugh in church, aunty?" she would say to my lecture on good behavior in the sacred edifice.

"Because it is the house of God, and you ought to behave respectfully in it."

"Is God there?"

"Yes, He dwells therein."

"Mamma told me no one had ever seen God. Why didn't He have a house in the Valley?"

"No, no one has ever seen Him, for He is a Spirit, and invisible to human eyes. But He has promised that when even two or three assemble together in His name He will be amongst them."

"O, then it's for the people," cried Zanita,—jumping at once at the Quaker principle of a meeting-house. "Why doesn't God come here then when you and I, and the Professor and Martha, say our prayers?"

"He does."

"Then I suppose," she remarked, with a merry twinkle of her elfin eyes, "He wouldn't like me to laugh here; but I must laugh somewhere; perhaps then in the stable would be best."

She suddenly assumed a grave, anxious expression, as though she were really earnestly wishful to accommodate the Almighty. I could not keep my countenance, and was obliged to change the subject.

Not having been brought up to go to church, she could never be made to understand its importance and the gravity of the matter; and her keen and pertinent observations made it exceedingly difficult to inculcate the formalities of religion.

But a climax of all arrived shortly, when the clergyman himself was obliged to take her in hand.

There was a little boy, a neighbor's child, with whom Zanita would take it into her head to play for a week together, and then drop him, and take up with a little girl on the other side of the street. He was a chubby, sturdy little fellow, with innocent blue eyes, that never knew a glint of mischief. Being two years younger than Zanita, she made a complete cats-paw of him, compelling him to become the *particeps criminis* in all her mischief, and then, as with Cozy, made him the scapegoat. "Tommy did it," was always her defense for every misdemeanor.

One Sunday morning—I shall never forget it, as it witnessed one of the most absurd mortifications of my life—I had made her quite neat, and succeeded in keeping her clean until church-time.

"O, aunty, Tommy and I want to walk to church together, and his mother says we may."

"Very well," I said; "take him by the hand and walk straight, and don't touch anything by the way."

She started off. She wore a scarlet merino dress handsomely braided and trimmed, and a soft white velvet hat with white feathers—she looked dazzlingly beautiful; and people could not help regarding her admiringly when she went out in this costume.

The Professor and myself walked on to church, which was not two hundred yards distant. Zanita was not there when we arrived. Presently the Dicksons, Tommy's parents, came in. I had arranged the books, and found the Sunday of the month, when I became aware of a strange rustling, and something which sounded like a titter through the congregation. The minister had just entered, and fixed his large gray eyes on some object in questioning surprise. I hastily turned, and there were the children walking slowly down the aisle, hand in hand, as though duly impressed with the solemnity of the moment; but they had changed costumes. Tommy was arrayed in Zanita's scarlet dress; and she in Tommy's knickerbockers and jacket, covered with a formidable array of bright buttons; his little hat set jauntily on her hair, and the poor little fellow completely overpowered by the velvet and plumes.

Two such ridiculous little mummers never before tickled the fancy of a pious congregation. Tommy's dress was much too long for him, and Zanita's pants indecorously short. He walked on in good faith; but she was acting, splendidly, and no one could have told from her countenance that she was conscious of her grotesqueness.

The congregation had to bury their faces in their pews as at the first prayer. Mrs. Dickson and myself made a rush each to our metamorphosed brats, and bore them rapidly out of the church; Mrs. Dickson, who was a portly woman, becoming purple in the face with shame and horror, and the shaking of poor Tommy until he was the color of his dress. And both bid fair to have a stroke of apoplexy.

"Zanita!" I said severely, when we were outside the church, "I am ashamed of you."

"Tommy," she began, assuming a scandalized air,—"Tommy wanted"—

"No," I interrupted; "don't attempt to put the blame on Tommy; you know perfectly well you alone are responsible for the whole."

"Well, aunty," she cried remonstratingly, shifting her tactics, "you know you said yourself that Tommy should have been a girl, and that it was a mistake that I was not a boy. So I told Tommy what you said, and he said 'Yes,' and then of course I had to put his clothes on when he had mine."

"I'll give him a right good spanking," cried Mrs. Dickson.

Zanita laughed, and seemed in prospect to enjoy it. At Mr. Dickson's house, which was fortunately quite near at hand, we changed the respective garments again.

"Aunty," said Zanita, whose irrepressible temperament could never be subdued for a moment, "were not all the people naughty to-day in church?"

"Why?" I asked.

"O, they all laughed so much: wasn't it shocking!"

I explained that the shocking part was the one who had made them laugh.

The following day I intended calling upon our minister, and making what explanation and apology I could. But he anticipated me, and came in during the morning.

He said that the child had an extraordinary sense of humor; but that it ought to be repressed, and that he would like to speak to her. I sent for her. She came in biting the end of her apron, hanging her head, and affecting the greatest shyness.

The minister eyed her approvingly; he thought his imposing presence had subdued her; but I had no such hope. He was a large heavy man, with dark hair and bilious complexion: the most prominent feature of his face was a decided hook-nose; his eyes, of an exceedingly neutral gray, were set in a pair of tortoise-shell spectacles, which gave him the look of some wonderful and rare bird, such as one sees in museums. If Zanita did not perceive the comic side of this countenance it would be a wonder.

We had some trouble in getting her to approach him; she seemed so fearfully ashamed, and she did it so well, that the thought flew through my mind that she might possibly feel a little overawed.

"My dear little girl," said the minister, "I want to have a long talk with you. I want to show you what a wicked thing you did yesterday in church."

Zanita answered never a word. She stood on one leg, and examined the nails on the sole of her boot.

"Zanita, stand straight," I said.

She put down her foot and became rigid.

"Do you know, if you are naughty, where you will go when you die?" said the minister solemnly.

"When shall I die?" asked the child.

"I don't know; that is in the hands of the Almighty."

"Then I don't know where I shall go; that is in the hands of the Almighty also," returned Zanita. "Where will you go when you die?" she said, following up her advantage.

"To heaven, I hope," said the clergyman decisively.

"Then I guess we'll split tracks," and she laughed right in his face.

"Zanita," I interposed, "you must not laugh when you are speaking to the minister."

"Aunty, I can't help laughing; he is just like our jackdaw, and you always say you cannot help laughing at him, he looks so ridiculously wise."

I began to see the minister would make no way with her.

"My dear little girl," he resumed, "I came to talk entirely about your conduct yesterday. Do you know it is very wicked to assume male attire?"

"What's that?" said Zanita eagerly, pretending she felt anxious to be enlightened.

"Men's clothes, or boys'," he added, lest she might find a loop-hole by his want of explicitness.

"O," cried Zanita, "Nell Radd always wears her husband's pants when she travels over the mountains. I've seen her in them many a time, and I know they are Radd's."

"I am afraid she cannot be a very proper person," said the minister, evasively. The minister felt he could not pursue this question of "women wearing the breeks" much further, and being again out-flanked, said,—

"Well, I think the best thing you can do will be to learn your Cate-chism, and come to my Sunday class."

Zanita had been sucking her thumb, and now brought it out with a pop.

"That's drawing a cork," she said, "did you know it?"

"Say!" cried Zanita running to the door as I was politely bowing him out, "have you got any little girls?"

"Yes," he replied, "I have three."

"Have they got black rims around their eyes like you?" she asked with her elfish laugh.

I put my hand on her mouth, and pushed her behind me.

Our minister never wanted a second conversation with Zanita; but repeated, whenever we met,—

"Train up a child in the way he should go, and when he is old he will not depart from it."

CHAPTER XIII.

ZANITA'S SCHOOLING.

IT WOULD REQUIRE volumes to narrate the troubles, trials, mishaps, adventures, and vicissitudes I went through in my earnest endeavor to carry out the minister's precepts,—"to train up the child in the way she should go." This aphorism ignores entirely that the child had a way of her own, from which she was equally determined not to depart, and training in the ordinary sense was, therefore, quite out of the question. It was struggling, urging, persuading, forcing, coaxing, arguing; but as for all this putting her in the right way and fancying she would not depart from it, that was as effective as pouring water into a sieve and expecting it to remain.

I do not believe that the right way ever has an attraction for children; unless breaking the crockery-ware, scratching enameled surfaces, cutting triangular holes in a texture which the ingenious loom had contrived to make a compact drapery, be deemed right and proper. Some children have a propensity to stand on their heads, most of them for performing surgical operations on their own persons with purely mechanical instruments, such as cleavers, corkscrews, boot-hooks, etc.; few children who do not prefer wet shoes to dry ones if there is a puddle within their reach; few who do not try to possess exactly that object which they see cherished by their little neighbors,—stories of the man in the moon in no way abating their covetousness.

Thus training a child contrary to nature is very like training the spots on a leopard to grow in streaks, by constantly stroking them in the required direction. I do not know what effect the process might have if persistently followed; but it could not be much more hopeless than the training of Zanita in the way the minister said she ought to go; nor do I believe that Zanita, although a little peculiar, was altogether an exception. For most children are trained in the way they should go, yet it would be difficult to find the individual who has not departed from it directly he became his own master.

Most boys try smoking as soon as they leave school, and experiment in the use of spirits, simply because they have been forbidden. Their own sense, or sensation, may deter them from continuing the practice, but they do not abstain because they have been instructed in the right way and will not depart from it.

Habit is doubtless a wonderful director and guide; but some children, such as Zanita, are of such a volatile, erratic temperament, that habit seems impossible to them, unless under the form of regularity in irregularity.

With her instruction we had no difficulty; her perceptive faculties were so keen that she speedily mastered any task set before her. She had no taste for music, and, therefore, we did not urge her to learn; for to have made her practice so much per day would have been to attempt training her in one of those ways in which she would not go. It is certain that a man may lead the horse to the water, but he cannot make him drink.

With a view more to obtaining a little discipline than any amount of learning, of which she had already too much, I sent her to a day-school in Oakland; but soon discovered that instead of being trained herself, she was exercising dominion over all the other girls, little and big. She could tell a great deal they did not know of natural history, ornithology, and mechanics, and was quite beyond the control of mistress or tutors. She was soon expelled for determined insubordination.

She could not be made to understand this was a disgrace; but took it in her usual stoical way, and remarked,—

"Well, after all, aunty, I would rather you taught me; for you tell me about a great many more interesting things than they did at school."

For drawing she displayed no taste, if some little talent for her efforts consisted in strong caricatures. Her cattle would have lame legs, or broken horns, or too curly tails; and her faces usually squinted, or had teeth projecting like Nell's, or enormous beards flying, or mopheads like old Methley's, or any monstrosity she might chance to meet in the street. Not wishing to train this propensity I wasted no time upon her drawing, unless occasionally to get her a model, which she usually caricatured.

Another interval passed in which we kept her at home, and got on tolerably well upon ordinary occasions; for the child was never bad-tempered or fretful, never had recourse to weeping, or distressed herself about any reprimand or opposition. But upon any particularly important occasion, if we had friends visiting us, or if we went upon an excursion, Zanita was sure to come out in full force, and conduct herself shockingly, so that all my neighbors pitied me, and shook their heads, saying derisively,—

"Poor Mrs. Brown! she has a nice time of it with that child; and never corrects her either. It is strange how a sensible man like the Professor can allow his wife to carry out such vagaries, and the child no kith or kin to them. It's sheer romantic nonsense; just because her mother died up among those wild mountains, where it does not appear quite the thing for a respectable female to go, among bears and brambles of all kind; and makes the child that she has no more conscience than a squirrel. She jumped upon our hog and rode him round the lot, with her face to his tail; and our minister, who had just come from the East, took her for one of my children, and inquired if that was California sport. I never was so mortified in my life, and took the liberty of mentioning the circumstance to Mrs. Brown, who only remarked that Zanita was very primitive in her playfellows; never having had children she fraternized with animals."

One friend, however, took an interest in the wonderful precocity of the child; this was Mrs. Primer, who kept a very superior Young Ladies' Seminary at San Jose. She became charmed with Zanita's conversation about the habits of animals and plants,—information she had gleaned from Kenmuir,—and her shrewd remarks upon everything she saw. She regarded her escapades as mere *espieglerie* and evidence of genius. She was, like myself, fascinated with her brilliant imagination, and no doubt thought she would make her quite a show pupil if properly managed. But in that "if " lay the whole conclusion.

Willing to give her every chance, it was arranged that Zanita should go on trial for three months to Mrs. Primer's establishment.

Zanita in no way objected. She was ever ready for any change that promised her adventure; and she was no more troubled at leaving her home in Oakland than she had been at quitting her father and the Valley. Her self-reliance made her quite adequate to going among strangers, for she usually had the best of any encounter, and was perfectly fearless.

For the first three weeks, Zanita must have been on her best behavior, and displayed such talent that Mrs. Primer wrote me that she was perfectly enraptured with the girl, and was not surprised that I had adopted such a prodigy.

The letters that followed were not as enthusiastic; for although she could not cease from admiring Zanita's talents, yet she had certain powers that indeed might bring about a brilliant career, which were nevertheless dangerous in school.

Her power of mimicry, that might make her a great actress, thoroughly demoralized and disorganized the school; for girls when once set giggling are hopelessly beyond control.

Unfortunately one of the teachers, a person of great merit and erudition, was subject to a nervous affection of the face, causing a spasmodic twitching, which Miss Zanita had succeeded in imitating so amusingly, that whenever she practiced it the whole class were inevitably convulsed with laughter. To attempt to disgrace her by sending her out of the room was no avail, for, upon the first opportunity, when the class had become steady and penitent, she would boldly repeat her offense with equal success.

The following week I was informed that she had turned her attention to the Professor of French, an old gentleman of the *ancien régime* who was a snuff-taker, and usually drew out his tortoise-shell box, tapped and took a pinch of snuff before examining a pupil's *théme*. Zanita had procured a bit of oil-cloth about the same color, made a box, and audaciously imitated him in snuffing before his very eyes. The Professor felt very badly about it, and expressed his unwillingness to teach a young lady who could so ungratefully turn him into ridicule, the more especially as she had been his favorite pupil and best French scholar.

Moreover, Mrs. Primer informed me that Zanita's persistent insubordination was becoming detrimental to the discipline of the school; that she had acquired so much power over the risible faculties of the young ladies as to be able to throw them into a state of disorder any moment she pleased, and was fast making caricatures fashionable in the establishment.

It was useless to attempt to punish her, as she could not be made to feel that she was under any disgrace. If a task was imposed upon her she learned it with the utmost dispatch, and, as a matter of course, it cost her no trouble, and she never took it to heart as such. If she were confined in her own room, she seemed rather to enjoy it than otherwise; and being given dry bread she would eat it heartily, remarking that it was just like "camping out" when they never had butter, and Cozy used to cry for it. "I wish Cozy were here now; wouldn't she yell and make a bother."

Although Zanita was by no means indifferent to good things, yet upon occasion she could content herself with a dry crust and despise her little injuries.

Mrs. Primer concluded by saying that although still of the opinion that my *protégé* would make a most brilliant character, if properly trained, she could not believe that a school was the atmosphere that she needed; in fact she would contaminate half the class before her own reform could be accomplished. Under these circumstances she regretted that she must ask me to take my daughter away before the term specified had expired, and that she would prepare her to leave the following day but one, if I could kindly come for her, else she could be sent under care of some friend.

Thus Zanita returned, as blithe as ever; and was extremely diverting in her graphic descriptions of the boarding-school.

The Professor used to take infinite amusement from her eccentricities; there had from the first appeared to exist a kind of truce between them; she never played him any tricks, for she was too wily to make him her victim, and never evinced anything but stolid indifference to his teaching. But usually she was keenly alive even to the most abstruse of his conversations, and delighted him by her bright intelligence.

To my remonstrances my husband would reply,—

"My dear, she is a born actress and cannot help it. She must go on the stage, where she may play a part all her life long."

"She imitates even you, behind your back," I said, "and does it uncommonly well; with a book in hand, a pair of scissors for an eye-glass, her feet crossed upon another chair, and her mouth puckered up, just as you often hold yours when absorbed in reading."

The Professor laughed. "I would like to see her; I should then know how I look."

"The other day," I continued, "she had taken her *pose* after this fashion, but as *I* don't encourage her Professor, I therefore pretended not to observe the caricature, and said, 'Zanita! what are you doing with your feet upon that chair?' 'Surely, aunty, you can see,' she naively remarked. I had to ignore my question, and bid her put down her feet and the scissors."

The Professor chuckled at my dilemma.

"She is more than a match for you, my dear, I am afraid!"

I was anxious that she should still continue her French under the instruction of a native of the country, in order to preserve the good accent she had acquired; and hearing that there was a Parisian lady teaching in the best seminary in Oakland, I had no difficulty in having her join the class; and, as usual, her progress was highly satisfactory. With Martha to accompany her to and from this place, the arrangement seemed to answer for a time. She learned a good deal of science from the Professor, for my husband, although I say it, was a kind of encyclopedia which could not be approached without its imparting some valuable learning; and I attended to her general education.

Almost every year we were accustomed to make any excursion to the Mountains and Valley of Ah-wah-nee, and it was curious to note the progress of the two children. Zanita, though under the highest civilized training we could give her, remained as wild as the untamed deer of her native mountains; indeed, she would leap among the tall brackens with as much agility and zest as any young fawn; and I believe would have been as happy to winter in a cave as a cinnamon bear. Whilst Rosie grew in that exquisite feminine grace so attractive in adolescent womanhood.

During these periods I used to give as much attention as possible to Rosie's music and drawing, for which she had all the talent which her sister lacked; and, even as a child, her sketches from nature possessed that delicacy of touch and selection which reminded me of her poor mother.

I brought her all the books that Zanita had used, and her father, with this assistance, forwarded her instruction. So little Rosie progressed well, if not so brilliantly as Zanita; and was the happiest little fairy that ever dwelt in sylvan glades, and danced by moonlight round the mossy rings.

The great drawback to the new system of study was not long in developing itself, and grew out of Zanita's readiness to form acquaintances without any particular ceremony of introduction or choice of any special locality, or unusual circumstance or contingency. If she met a boy spinning a top, she would insist upon lending her assistance; or if she spied a peculiarly shaped box or bundle, she would promptly ask the possessor what it contained, and desire that it should be opened and let her examine. She once stopped a little girl carrying home a lady's bonnet, and instantly had it out of the box inspecting it, and declaring it was a "perfect fright"; she then put it on her head, to the amusement of passers-by and the dismay of Martha and the little messenger. Ere long she had introduced herself to half of Oakland and made herself very notorious.

CHAPTER XIV.

ZANITA AMONG THE NUNS.

"WHAT DO YOU THINK ABOUT nuns, John?" I said to my husband one day as I sat sewing in his study.

"I don't think about them at all, my dear; it would not be proper; you know they are vowed to celibacy," replied the imperturbable Professor.

"How tiresome you are! I mean, of course, as teachers. Some convents, I am told, give first-class education, and the moral training is quite unequaled."

"Indeed!" he said, dryly.

"Yes, Mrs. Dundas was educated in a convent, and you remember you said that she had more self-control than any woman you had ever known."

"I adhere to that opinion still, and I think you had better write to her and ascertain what she thinks of the suitability of such a school for Zanita, as I can easily see that her case suggested your inquiry. It is a subject on which I am not qualified to give you the smallest opinion. Conventual life is one which has never interested me."

In pursuance of this conversation I wrote to our friend, asking her opinion, and describing Zanita as closely as it was possible to define so singular a character.

In course of post the reply came, and was most satisfactory. She said that for such a disposition as I had delineated a convent would be most desirable; that she thought even Zanita would have some difficulty in withstanding the order and resisting the moral discipline in the atmosphere of high honor which pervaded these schools. The great secret, she went on to say, is the trouble the nuns give themselves for the benefit of their young pupils. They make a constant study of each character and disposition, never falling into the common error of believing that all children are alike and must be treated in the same way. A child's propensities are carefully observed, and every temptation spared her and avoided. The force of example is so strong, and the whole school in such perfect order, that a child must have an unwonted force of character to counterbalance it.

The control of a child is a perfect art, which the nuns of the Ursuline Order make a life-long study; and, like the Jesuits, their success in training the youth is quite marvelous. She ventured to predict that Zanita would not be expelled from the convent. She recommended a beautiful establishment near Santa Clara, and inclosed a letter to the mother superior of that nunnery in case I should wish to communicate with the establishment.

This I did, minutely detailing the points of Zanita's character, and the reasons for which she had been sent home from the various schools,—leaving entirely to their discretion whether they would undertake the education of my *protégé*.

I soon received an exquisitely written note, simple and yet elegant in diction, showing that letter-writing was certainly one of the accomplishments possessed by the Ursulines. It stated that they would be happy to receive the child on the usual terms—which, by the way, was little more than half of the terms of other seminaries; that the education and training of young girls to fill their different positions in life was the sole object of the Order of Ursulines; and that, in fulfillment of their vows, they had no choice but to receive all who applied, as far as the extent of their establishment would admit. They expressed a pleasant conviction that they should not have very much trouble, as I had anticipated; as from my statement she had never been subject to bad example, which they feared more than anything else in a child.

A few weeks after, therefore, saw us *en route* for Santa Clara, Zanita as usual full of wild anticipations and curious projects, especially as we understood there were some thousand acres of land attached to the convent, where there was not only a river but hills and trees. The nuns had a large farm, supplying almost all the wants of the establishment; so Zanita's prospects were exceedingly pleasing.

The Professor had also promised her that if she remained, and a fair account was rendered of her, he would send her a pony to ride provided the nuns had no objection.

As we drove up to the convent through handsome park-like grounds, my hopes revived; and when we entered the house,—so scrupulously clean, so airy and orderly,—I felt that I had entertained an unjust prejudice all my life against nuns; all my preconceived notions of monastic misery vanished at once before that cool quiet parlor into which we were ushered.

We had time to inspect the room whilst we waited for the lady abbess, or the mother superior, as she is called in this order. The walls of the apartment were tastefully decorated with specimens of penmanship, embroidered tableaux, sketches of the different points of view from their building, and crayon-heads,—performances, no doubt, of the pupils. There was a piano-forte and a harp, two or three magnificently embroidered *fauteuils* and footstools, the rest of the furniture being plain and neat.

Presently the door opened and the mother superior swept in with a graceful motion that took me by surprise, for I had never seen a nun like that before. She was a tall, distinguished looking woman, with long delicate features, and a soft womanly mouth, bespeaking great purity of character: her eyes were almond shaped and gray, with a steadfast, dignified expression almost overpowering. She wore a long black cloth robe which swept the ground; the sleeves of it, in which her hands were folded, hung long and deep from the shoulder half-way down the dress; a broad stiff collar encircled her throat, and descended low on the breast; a band of white was bound round her forehead, just above her straight penciled eyebrows; upon her head, coming to a sort of point in front, she wore a black opaque veil of some very fine texture; round her waist was fastened a small leathern strap as a waistband, from which was suspended a large rosary of olive stones brought from the sacred garden of the Mount of Olives, as I afterward understood, together with a large crucifix.

This imposing dress and dignified figure evidently produced some effect upon Zanita as well as myself. The superior received us gracefully, and with the polished manner of a woman of the world accustomed to receive guests. There was an impenetrability and a dearth of emotionality in her bearing which told of a latent power to rule and be obeyed. It was a face that seemed never to have heard of vacillation, though it was neither hard nor cold; a shadow of doubt never seemed to have crossed it. When she held out her hand to Zanita and drew her toward her, and imprinted a soft kiss on her forehead, I felt she had already decided the line of action to be pursued toward her pupil and, I believe, Zanita had some consciousness of this too, for there was an expression in her eyes as though a trifle overawed or puzzled.

She showed us over the house, and displayed Zanita's miniature bedroom, which was to be her own exclusively. "For," she explained, "we never allow two girls to room together."

She next took us into a pleasant little dining-room reserved for guests, and refreshment was served to us by one of the sisters. I was kindly invited to spend the night there if I wished; but I declined, not wishing in any way to influence the first impressions made upon Zanita, and preferring to resign her at once to their charge. I was eager also to tell the Professor all I had seen and the new experience I had passed through.

"I shall be very curious," said my husband, after we had talked over the day's event, "to know the result of this new experiment; it will be extremely interesting if those women, whom one is so ready to despise, actually control the child, if they cannot altogether change her. I would give a dollar to witness the first encounter between the superior and Zanita."

"It would be a study of human nature," I said. "For the former looks as though she had quite made up her mind about everything above and below the heavens. A woman who, if you told her that a new planet had been discovered, would remark, "I have counted them, and know their number, so you must be mistaken." She is satisfied that she was born to be superior of that convent, satisfied that it is the best destiny that could be provided for her, satisfied that she has the pleasantest convent in the world, that her community is exactly what it ought to be, and that the academy is the best school; she is not enthusiastic about it, but quietly settled in the belief without attempting to obtrude her views on anybody; a woman who would always do her duty, and even make great sacrifices without feeling them to be sacrifices; she would be kind to all but loving to none. She will never display any affection toward Zanita and never require any."

"And there will be one great source of power," remarked the Professor. "Zanita is not a child that requires any display of affection, and misuses it whenever she has the opportunity."

"And yet," I resumed, "the mother superior is a thoroughly womanly woman, without the slightest attempt at fostering the feeling of masculineness."

"That proves," said my husband, "that a woman may exercise unbounded sway if she have native power without assuming the character of the opposite sex. Your so-called strong-minded woman rarely becomes a ruler or exercises dominion over others; she is in a chronic state of antagonism without achieving any victories. It is the feminine woman who never allows her emotions to overcome her wisdom, and who holds to a purpose without vacillation,—whose power is, and ever will be, felt in the world."

"Yes," I replied, "I have no doubt that the mother superior reigns supreme in her little world, and her influence extends far beyond it. We never hear of a revolt in a convent, or under the monastic system; and this must arise from the marvelously sage ruling of the head of the establishment."

"If anything can upset them Zanita will," said my husband, laughingly, "for she has an absolute faculty for discovering a loop-hole through which she can create disorder. I do not know what phrenological organ you call it, my dear; I should name it the bump of revolt."

The mother superior had acceded with a smile to my urgent request that I might be informed weekly of Zanita's behavior; she thought there would be no necessity. One week was precisely like another in a convent, unless interrupted by some religious festival; but she assured me that everything was so carefully arranged that nothing like monotony was ever felt, either by nuns or pupils; and she doubted not that I should soon feel satisfied that my *protégé* was progressing well.

The bulletins of conduct came regularly every week for some three months. Zanita's short-comings and escapades were narrated with faithful accuracy; but no fatal results seemed to arise, or were prognosticated. I had, therefore, the pleasure of going to see her at the end of six months, and of coming away thoroughly delighted with the conventual experiment of training.

We left her there for twelve months without her returning home. She was fast growing into a beautiful girl, brilliant in every way. She had lost much of her ungainly and hoydenish manner, and acquired a graceful style wherever it was compatible with her erratic movements.

Now and then she would astonish her small world by some unimagined freak; but it was treated with impassive cold reprimand by the nuns, and the pupils soon came to regard *espiegleries* as a matter of course, and remark,—

"O, it is only Zanita at some new freak."

CHAPTER XV.

A NEW-COMER.

IT WAS ABOUT THIS TIME that a stranger made his appearance amongst us whose advent was to act upon our *ménage* and *entourage*, like acid poured into some alkaline liquid, setting us all into a ferment, fuss, and fume, and keeping our little community in this frothy excitement until each had accomplished his separate destiny in the drama,—until the curtain had fallen over the last act, and all was mute and still.

Yet this individual was in person the reverse of one adapted to fill such a *rôle*. He was no fire-eating, fiercely-bearded braggadocio, nor even the irrepressible man of wiry sinews, who never knows lassitude or reaction himself, and never permits any one near him to indulge in them. On the contrary, he was a quiet, elegant, undemonstrative young Englishman, whose femininely beautiful face took me captive from the first moment I beheld him; for in spite of my study of phrenology, physiognomy, and psychology, I am ashamed to say that I am frequently carried away by the more attractive claims of art, and my intense love of the beautiful.

The young stranger gratified these tastes to the full. His figure had reached that perfection of height—five feet ten—leaning more towards the Apollo than the Hercules; yet having withal a strength of grace and movement which was a constant and ever renewed pleasure to me to trace. His face was as fair as a woman's, with rich clear tints of red and white, which the moist climate of Great Britain alone produces in perfection. His almond-shaped hazel eyes were mellowed by long dark lashes. The contour of the face was a perfect oval, and the mouth and chin rivaled the Autinous. There was just that shade of haughty sweetness that bespoke the English aristocrat,—an unconscious expression of power, with a benign simplicity and gentleness.

"I think he is the most beautiful, but not the handsomest, young man I have ever seen," I imparted to the Professor, after narrating all these various points.

"Well, what of his phrenological aspect? You have only given me a highly colored picture *à la* Carlo Dolci."

I plead guilty at once to having been carried away by his beauty rather than by a study of his mental types. "But I am sure he is amiable and good, he has such a sweet and dignified expression; such a face as makes one think of his mother, and imagine her the perfection of beauty and nobility. I am sure he had a splendid mother,—one of those glorious English gems set in a court frame, such as we saw at the Queen's Drawing Room. Do you not remember the Duchess of Sutherland and the Hon. Mrs. Norton? Now I am quite certain he has had such a mother as that."

"And there is no line or curve about him by which you could decipher the character of his grandmother?" said my husband, quizzing me as usual. "Whether, for instance, she was fond of pickles, or took snuff?"

I ought to tell, according to the strict laws of narration, where the individual in question, whom we knew by the name of Egremont, was born, where he came from last, what he came for, and every detail and particular concerning his business and motives. But the reader must remember that we lived in California, where strangers started up like mushrooms in the night, and were recognized next morning as belonging to the state of things: no questions asked, no curiosity excited.

A man might be a dethroned prince, or defaulting clerk,—an East India merchant, or a peddler; no one took the least bit more interest in him whether he was a Professor from Oxford, or a policeman from Ireland. It mattered not; we asked no questions, and wanted no lies.

If the stranger chanced to be too great a villain, and the *too* could be stretched a long way, Judge Lynch and the Vigilance Committee attended to him; and the same result was arrived at, whether he was born in a palace or a pot-house: too much villainy came to the same end in California.

So beyond hearing that our friend's name was Egremont, guessing he was English by his complexion, that he was a gentleman by the polished case of his manner, that he had received a classical education from occasional sentences let fall, rather than paraded, in his conversation, we knew absolutely nothing of him: where he had sprung from, where going, or what doing.

But the latter was not very long enveloped in mystery, for it chanced that at this time I was working hard upon a manuscript of my husband's, recopying it for the press, and for this purpose generally shut myself up in his study, where, one morning, Mr. Egremont, expecting to find the Professor, came suddenly upon me.

Glad of the interruption by so pleasant a visitor, I asked him to remain. In the course of conversation I spoke of the tediousness of copying.

"I quite enjoy it," he said, "and if you would permit me to assist you it would be conferring a favor upon me, for I have ample leisure."

He looked so bright and earnest, I could not doubt that his wish was sincere.

"I cannot understand your taste," I said, "but I can appreciate the effects of it mightily, and shall take you at your word."

Thus, from thenceforth he became our constant visitor, and worked with an assiduity very surprising. More and more the fascination of his high breeding, and richly stored mind, grew upon me; and if, as the poet says,—

"A thing of beauty is a joy forever,"

I may here confess that his beautiful shadowless face was a constantly renewed enjoyment to me. Yet it set my science at naught. I learned nothing from it; it was like guessing at a picture; and no amount of study or scrutiny brought me to a decisive theory.

Then, as usual, I had recourse to my husband, for this is just a case where a husband comes in so useful; he is like a revised and corrected edition of one's self, to which one can appeal with moderate safety.

"I wonder who he is, and where he comes from, and how he got here?" I said, stopping my husband between two strata of feldspar and granite, which he was marking out on a map.

"Who, where, my dear—the feldspar? I'll tell you." And he was going to commence three millions of years before the Biblical date of the Deluge; when I cut him short with a shake; for I knew if I allowed him to start on that explanation, the history would last on and off for three weeks.

"No, no," I said, "I mean Mr. Egremont."

"I really do not know, my dear, who he is, or where he comes from. Why do you ask especially? Do you know where any of your California friends come from, or who they are at home?"

"No," I replied, "I should not trouble myself to inquire, but this young man seems very different."

"I find them all different. There is scarcely a place in the world where you meet more unique specialties of humanity than in California. Every man has his own individuality, his own history, his own experience, more distinctly than in older countries, where men have been bred and born more in classes, and have lived under the same influences. Here, also, we have draughted to us the more peculiar characters, for it is not the commonplace, jog-trot people of any community who launch themselves into the *terra incognita* of California: it is the adventurous spirit, the energetic enterprising man, who believes in putting things through,—himself included; the robust, healthy individual of thews and sinews, who feels he has strength to move mountains, or groove under them; the reckless class that make a dash at anything; the exploring mind, ever seeking for new wonders in nature;"—

"That's you," I interrupted.

"The desperado to whom any new country is a neutral ground, for a time at least, where he cannot mar if he cannot make a fortune; the unfortunate, who have tried everything and succeeded in nothing, who have a positive faculty for failing in whatever they touch. Then there are the wretched, who fly

'Anywhere, anywhere, out of the world!'

To them it is a *refugium afflictorum*, or they fancy so, which amounts to the same thing. Now when we have all these specialties forming an aggregate called society, I am surprised, my dear, that you should evince curiosity about any individual in particular."

"O yes; but he does not belong to any class you have mentioned, and his character is no less a puzzle to me than his face."

"Very well; then you find yourself right at home in your own sciences; you will have to make an analytical study of him."

I have often wished that phrenology could be reduced to a positive test, like astronomy or geometry; that we could put the human brain into a crucible, as we would a metal, and weigh the residuum of pure gold from the dross; a cow has a large brain, but it is not fine working matter; or that we could determine the workings of the brain as we do the movements of the comets and heavenly bodies in time and space; or, as in chemistry, analyze the component parts of the vegetable kingdom, and determine how much poison lies hidden in the sweetest scents and most delicate colors of flowers. In mechanics we are still further advanced. We can make a piston work in a cylinder, and a crank to turn a wheel, with the greatest precision. We know what work it will produce, what pressure it will bear, and how long it will carry out its function. But of ourselves or neighbors, of psychology, phrenology, ethics, or metaphysics we know comparatively little. If we put a new screw to a bolt, we know it will work until it becomes worn and old. But we know nothing of whether the machinery of an infant will work until it is a grown man. We speculate and ponder over ourselves, and grope about in semi-twilight. We feel sick or what is called out of sorts,—a vague, indefinite, wretched suffering, we know not where it begins or ends. We attribute it, or some sapient friend does, to iced lemonade, or clam chowder. But how often have we experienced this miserable *malaise* when nothing of the sort has passed our lips.

Thus a man becomes depressed and melancholy, and is said to be in love,—how, or why, or wherefore, he knows not, nor does any one else. He swears truthfully, no doubt, that he must inevitably worship Lavinia to the last moment of his life, and feels sure he shall meet her in a blessed land after death. He does, or does not, marry Lavinia; it is not material, for in three months he is entirely cured,—Heaven knows how, for no one else knows; he does not himself, the psychologist does not, the moral philosopher can give no better reason than the veriest old granny.

If we know little about our interior selves, we know scarcely more about our exterior developments. Phrenology and physiognomy divide the head, leaving us floundering vaguely. Lines and rules, and excellent theories have been laid down and duly studied; but yet we have not reached the first practical principle of singling out a murderer from a martyr, a sinner from a saint. True, when a great criminal is arraigned at the bar of justice, we all go to look at him, and express our conviction that we should have easily divined what he was—that he bears it upon his countenance. Yet every day we trust our goods with those who rob us, and our affections with those who trample them under foot, and toss them adrift in scorn.

"Why did not Providence," I said to my husband, "shape a man's nose so that a woman could tell if he were true or false, as we can tell the breed of cattle by the shape of their horns, or the quality of a puppy-dog by the strength of his tail?"

"Obviously an oversight in the design of Providence, my dear," said the Professor, gravely going on with his stratums.

From my babyhood my organ of causalty had been keenly engaged upon the human front divine. I used to take my little stool, and deliberately plant myself before every new visitor, and examine him with the widest eyes I could open. I noted with great exactitude the soft summer eyes, the cold wintry ones, and neutral eyes that said nothing at all; that one man had pink transparent nostrils, and another coarse hairy ditto. But my chances of kisses or *bonbons* rarely turned out according to my small theories.

Beautiful faces are the least to be relied on in man or woman. Whether the blaze of beauty acts like the sun, and dazzles the beholder, or that we naturally associate truth and beauty together, it is certain that this problem leads the physiognomist astray as well as the rest of the world.

The most tender and beautiful eyes that ever looked on this earth were those of Beatrice Cenci, the parricide. Eugene Aram had an exquisitely refined and gentle countenance. Auburn hair is thought to denote jealousy, yet Queen Elizabeth and Mary Queen of Scots were both sandy complexioned. The former was historically jealous, whilst the other displayed no such passion. Nero had a well-shaped face until he became too obese.

The beautiful face is therefore the most contradictory and bewitching to the student; like a "will-o'-the-wisp," it lures but to betray. The lines falling into the perfection of beauty, what should they represent but the perfection of worth? And we most of us plunge headlong into this supposition, and scramble out at our leisure, with most of our theories fractured.

The rose-bud mouth, the "wee bit mou," may close over a shameless frailty, as well as in the Fornarina. Is not that Adonis' moulded chin the symmetrical exponent of a noble, delicate, susceptible character, the exterior model of a youthful chivalric soul? Look at those bluish-gray eyes, the perfection of color and shape, with their long silken lashes veiling their fire and sweetness: a seraph could not look more tender, and on his coral lip hangs the divine afflatus of a higher sphere; dignity is enthroned on his marble brow. The phrenologist and physiognomist mark him down as little inferior to the Angel Gabriel. "Possibly," says the non-believer in science; "but I know that he is in the 10th Royal Lancers, and I'll back him for consummate deviltry against any number of 'ologies.' " And nine times out of ten the man of the world is right, and science is wrong.

Thus, in spite of my *savoir*, I was as much at sea as regarded my new amanuensis as I always declared my husband to be about his antediluvian oceans which rolled over the tops of the highest sierras, and from whence the present volcanic cones poured forth their fiery breath like Vesuvius and Etna from the blue bosom of the Mediterranean.

I am rather fond of a standing mystery upon which I can turn the sluices of imagination when I am at leisure. It is pleasant to have some inscrutable thing to ponder over; but of leisure I did not long have the enjoyment, for Zanita was to return from the convent for the holidays, and, if we found her sufficiently tamed, she was then to remain at home and study for the stage, should the early promise she had given of marked dramatic talent still evince itself.

Thus it fell out that one morning, while engaged with Mr. Egremont in my husband's study, the door was flung open with a bang, and Zanita presented herself backward, leading by the hook of her parasol two of my prime Muscovy ducks yoked together by her rosary twisted around their handsome green throats. Leda and her swans might have been sublime, but Zanita with her qua'-qua'-ing ducks was essentially ridiculous.

"Zanita!" I exclaimed, "you will strangle my pets; how can you be so mischievous?"

She turned and beheld a stranger, and for once I think regretted her freak. She would rather have appeared well to the handsome visitor; for a look flashed between them, as I introduced them, of undisguised, startled admiration.

Their eyes met with that glorious inter-commingling of soul which makes or mars in the hereafter either or both. I trembled as I witnessed this unexpected result, and my mouth became dry, as if preceding some imminent peril. The laugh caused by the ducks, which, poor things, still went waddling about the study, held together by the rosary, vanished; speech died away on my lips; a sensation of terrible anguish heightened the pulsation of my heart, and I was glad to send Zanita to take off her things, and Mr. Egremont to carry away the ducks to the yard whence Zanita had purloined them.

She had grown more beautiful than ever; her features had retained all their delicate symmetry, and her eyes were almost of unearthly splendor under the emotion; besides she had the *beauté du diable*, with all its indescribable loveliness, and I felt that unless I could turn her ambition and her beauty into some channel where it might have legitimate exercise, there was no calculating the calamities it might bring upon her.

Here was a commencement before she had been five minutes in the house. Those two, if thrown together, would inevitably make love to each other, and although he was charming, yet he might be a murderer for all we knew.

I concluded to drop my copying for the present; I was the more satisfied of the wisdom of this decision when I regarded how much I would be engaged with Zanita.

When I explained this intention to Egremont, thanking him warmly for the great assistance he had rendered me, the hot color mounted to his face in wave after wave, as though he had clearly divined every thought of my mind for the last half hour, and was ineffably pained by it.

A sad, pitiful look of reproach came into his eyes as of a child that had been wrongfully blamed. I felt my heart relenting, and a strong desire to trust him arising. Could I have spoken openly to him, and told him exactly my fears, I felt that I might have relied upon his honor, not to make or take any advance to or from Zanita. But what had I to rest my observations upon,—a single glance,—for not a word had passed between them.

I begged him to stay and dine with us as usual, and added that he must not believe that because I did not accept his further services that I should not be happy to see him at any moment of leisure.

I took him somewhat into my confidence, however, as regarded Zanita, her singular character, and my anxiety that she would turn out a genius for tragedy.

"Would you not fear the exposure of so much beauty to the temptations of a stage life?" he asked, keeping his eyes fixed upon the manuscript.

"No," I replied, "not if the love of her art became the ruling passion, as I think it would if she adopted it at all. I think she would glory in taking a leading position, and swaying a mimic world. I do not think that Zanita would be tempted out of her own course, whatever that might be. She is possessed of a super-abundance of power and talent, which I am anxious to throw into some safe channel; or she will assuredly fritter it away in an unworthy one. I would rather have her a Lady Macbeth on the boards than play the character in actual life. Her vivid imagination and vehement will must have a vent and course to deploy themselves, or they will revert upon herself and prove her destruction. Had she been brought up like her sister in the Valley, I am convinced that ere this she would have broken her own neck, or some one's else, for she was no respecter or life in man or beast, and least of all her own. I believe the good nuns have done all that is possible to do for her in guiding and training her wild and brilliant nature. But no education can fully subdue a spirit as recklessly daring, as wily and defiant as hers. Force of example, and propitious circumstances have done more than any amount of argument, reasoning, threatening, or coaxing could do; and yet you see her first impulse is not of affection to run to me, her only mother, and caress me, but to capture my pet poultry and torment them."

I noticed the color mounting in Mr. Egremont's clear complexion, as though the recurrence to the opening scene affected him unpleasantly, and the impression dawned upon him that she was not the most amiable character in the world. A mental resolve seemed to register itself, that he would not yield to the fierce fascination which had just beset him, as he intuitively perceived that it would be a *laiser magesté* toward me.

I felt inclined to stroke the beautiful soft face, and say, "Pray keep that resolution for my sake, for your own, for hers." But the words remained on my lips unspoken. Alas, why we do not follow our impulses! Half of them, at least, if attended to would save us many an hour's sorrow, and often avert fearful catastrophes. Children listen to their instinctive feelings, and rarely break their little necks, though a thousand dangers beset them. Animals follow their natural impulses and rarely go astray. What is that second self in us, which is swifter than our reason, and wiser than our educated faculties,—that sees without knowledge, and hears without a sound?

But the time went by, and the lost opportunity never returns. Resuming the conversation, I said,—

"The danger for a woman on the stage, I apprehend, arises from three causes: her poverty and isolation from her family and natural protectors; her heart sensibilities more exposed to be excited; and the temptation to her vanity,—the latter being the most perilous perhaps of any. Most actresses succumb from their inability to sustain the ordeal of hard work, poverty, and disappointment, which usually attends their early career on the stage. These Zanita would not have to submit to, as I should never leave her, and she would only appear as a *prima donna débutante*. As to her affections, I do not think she possesses enough of them to be under their control. Love, I do not believe will ever be her passion; nor vanity, the great yawning gulf which swallows up the fairest and brightest of womankind. She cares neither for dress nor gew-gaws, nor parade nor display. She would as soon go to a *fête* in her old garden hat as in the finest feathers of San Francisco. Frequently I have to leave her at home at the last minute, when she appears with her ink-soiled dress all in tatters as usual, thinking to accompany me down Montgomery Street, where she would hold up her head among all the overdressed belles, without an idea that she was not as comely as they."

"And perhaps she is right," said Egremont; " 'beauty unadorned,' you know."

"There is some truth in that, but I do not think beauty disheveled in dirt, quite applies. And yet I have seen 'Mad Tom' played when the actor looked much handsomer in his rags than in his velvet and satin robes."

But few women believe that, and however prepossessing one is, she will endeavor to improve herself by certain *fixings*; and falls into the error that the more expensive those "fixings" are the more they improve her appearance. She cannot understand that rubies are not more becoming than roses, or pearls than lilies; and thus to gratify her vanity she will sacrifice the real gems of her nature. But such a girl is not Zanita. If she were given a diamond necklace as a temptation, the donor would probably have the mortification of seeing her wear it wrong side out by mistake.

CHAPTER XVI.

A SHADOW
FALLING BEFORE.

OFTEN AND OFTEN I had had long and intimate conversations with Mr. Egremont, for I ever found him intelligent and conversable; but he never let fall a syllable that could enlighten me as to himself, his past career, experience of life, or future projects. He was a moving mystery in every-day life. I once asked him if his mother was still alive. He answered, "No." But the tone of his voice, the painful rush of color to his face, and the look of concentrated sorrow, made me eschew the subject for the future. Yet now that Zanita was come back to us it was the more dangerous that he should remain an *habitué* in our house.

The evening passed off pleasantly enough, considering the circumstances, for only myself had conceived alarm in the position. The Professor never could resist enjoying Zanita's brilliant sallies upon the poor nuns whom she quizzed, and had evidently, according to her own showing, tormented most unmercifully. Egremont strove ill to conceal his admiration; but Zanita made no effort to hide how much he pleased her. I expected her to declare openly every minute in her old backwoods' fashion, "I like you; I like you better than anybody!" But she said it with her eyes fifty times, and did so much mischief that I felt already in despair of fulfilling my position as guardian of her life's drama.

"Well, Zanita," said the Professor, "what was your last piece of mischief?"

And forthwith Zanita, thus encouraged, commenced,—"O, Professor! only fancy, I made all the nuns believe I was the devil got into the chapel right amongst them."

"I suppose she was the nearest approach to it those good folk have ever had to do with," said my husband, *sotto voce*, to me.

"How did you persuade them of that?" he continued, aloud. "I thought you had two vases of holy water at the door of your chapel for the express purpose of keeping him out?"

"So we have," she laughed, "and I got it thrown all over me for my pains. I first contrived to steal one of the nun's dresses and veil, leather girdle, and rosary, the whole paraphernalia, and dressed myself up in it. Then we have an old French sister named Xavier; she is terribly afraid of the *diable*, and is always making the sign of the cross to keep him off. In fact, I think she has a monomania on the point; for when she is sewing she lays her spools in the form of a cross, and when she peels potatoes she puts them cross-shape, all as preservatives against the evil one. She has a limp in her walk, is nearly hump-backed, and always wears a green shade, for she has weak eyes. I used to go behind her and imitate her walk. She has also a curious cracked voice, and speaks broken English. I could imitate her so well as to startle all the girls by crying out in her voice, *Voici le diable*! So I thought it would be capital fun to frighten all the nuns in chapel, when they got up in the middle of the night to go to matins. O, aunty! if you had seen me dressed you would never have known me, green shade and all; and I colored my face with coffee, and painted it in great wrinkles. The chapel is only lit by one dreary oil-lamp that time in the morning, and when the matin-bell rang I hobbled in the procession with the rest.

"Xavier is just my size, Mr. Egremont!" she said, casting upon him a brilliant glance which instantly produced a richer tint over his handsome face.

"When all was so still you could have heard a pin drop, and the lamp, swung by four long chains from the arched and groined ceiling, cast flickering, uncertain shadows over the nuns all kneeling and bowed in meditation in their carved oaken stalls, with the caryatides and separations, which, I always fancied, look like spirits in purgatory doomed to bear that weight on their heads, but, by this dim light, seemed like so many demons trying to carry off the stalls, nuns and all. The subject of the meditation, I must tell you, was 'Death, and the tortures of the damned.' "

"Surely," cried Egremont, "they do not require you to meditate upon such an awful subject?"

"O no! the girls never attend this service—only nuns; we are all supposed to be asleep in our beds. Just when I thought all their imaginations had become thoroughly inflamed with the horrors of the infernal regions, I gave an awful shriek in the cracked voice of Soeur Xavier, sprang to my feet, and hobbled a pace or two to show off my limp, and threw myself on my face in the most violent contortions. O, you should have heard how they all screamed 'Mon Dieu! Jesu Mariè! Joseph! Priez pour nous;' and called on all the patron saints in the calendar before they could stop themselves. How the reverend mother, in that awful sepulchral voice of hers, commanded silence. But I yelled harder than ever, '*Le diable! le diable*! he come *emporter* me! *enlever* me! yah-hi, yah-hi, I make one big sin; I no confess it, yah-hi! I put too much salt in the butter, the devil he take me. Him there! him here! *Cheres sœurs*, him blaze you all up on account of my sin!'

"The sisters had all rushed round me terrified, believing *Sœur* Xavier was at least possessed by the devil; some begging me to make an act of contrition; some saying the litany for the requiscent for me, and the few with presence of mind trying to quiet me and hold me still. One, thoroughly convinced of the satanic presence, rushed to the holy water and deluged me all over with it. I was terribly afraid my wrinkles would be washed off."

"I wonder the devil didn't really carry you off!" burst in Martha, who was coming to and fro in the room with the tea during the narration. "Sure, to be playing such a trick on them pious nuns as gets out of their warm beds to say prayers for such sinful minx as you, Miss Zanita! Why that's worse nor choking the kitten and tickling my nose with its tail."

Here Zanita gave one of her old sidelong glances of elfish delight. I verily believe the accomplishment of some torture to others was the only enjoyment she knew.

"Well, how did it end?" said the Professor, delighted with the vim of the story and the artistic talent with which it was narrated.

"Well," continued Zanita, "in spite of all the writhing and floundering I could do, they carried me to Soeur Xavier's cell."

"Should a' carried you to the pump," ejaculated Martha, who was a devout Catholic.

"And," continued Zanita, "they were putting me to bed when poor Xavier meekly put in, 'O, pray you please not put him in my bed; O, take him out pray, please!' All turned to look at the real Xavier, who now made herself heard in her own meek person, when they had thought she was kicking in fits before them. I do not know what would have happened next; perhaps, taking me for the imp of darkness assuming poor Xavier's form, they might have taken me to the pump or thrown me out of window."

"Sarve you right," said Martha.

"But the string gave way with which I had fastened on veil, *bandeau*, and green shade; and there I was, face and head exposed, with nothing but my coffee wrinkles left. I suppose I looked so odd that all the novices burst out laughing. Even Notre Mère, the lady superioress, you know, Mr. Egremont, who had been to the pharmacy for sal volatile, could scarcely keep a solemn face, and said, as she took me by the shoulder and marched me off to my own room, 'Mademoiselle, vous repondrez au moi.' "

"Did you not get fearfully punished?" asked Mr. Egremont, whilst the Professor indulged in a loud laugh.

"O no," replied Zanita, "they never punish there; that is the best of the dear old nuns. But I tell you, aunty, Soeur Dulcima talked to me about one thing, not scolding exactly or lecturing, until I felt as near like wishing I had not done it as I ever did in my life."

"That must have been a feat of Sœur Dulcima," I responded, dryly. "But if you can only personate Lady Macbeth, Ophelia, and Juliet as well as you did Sister Xavier, I shall forgive you as they did."

"I would rather play Romeo a great deal. I never could be so mawkish as Juliet and Ophelia."

"Do you think loving Romeo or Hamlet so absurd then?" said Egremont, making a desperate effort to look indifferent.

"No," replied the girl with perfect *sang-froid*,—considering that this was her *début* conversation on love with any young man,—"but the manner of it is ridiculous."

"Romeo, why art thou Romeo!" she mimicked to Egremont, whilst we none of us could restrain our laughter. I hastened to change the subject, not wishing her to enlighten him as to how she could make love after her own fashion.

After that evening Mr. Egremont rarely called; and my fears had partly given place to a pensive regret that I had been obliged to banish him from our society, and wishing on the whole that Zanita had not displayed such a decided fancy for him, or that she could be induced to restrain it within maidenly bounds, which I knew she would not. But, one day driving in Oakland, turning over these thoughts, the subject of them passed on the road before me. He did not perceive me, for there was a gloomy, wearied look on his face which never changed. There was something so graceful yet haughty about his carriage, that if I had seen him for the first time I must inevitably have fallen into speculation about him,—as I then did. The old conundrum proposed itself for solution. What could he be doing here? What brought him here? Did he really care about Zanita, and was he trying to live down the feeling without making any attempt to win her? I concluded that the latter was the case, for unless he had been self-conscious I had not said enough to drive him away in that sudden manner. Even the novelty of so beautiful and brilliant a girl as Zanita would naturally have been attractive to him. I was on my road to the ferry-boat to attend one of the Professor's lectures in San Francisco. I had vainly urged Zanita to accompany me. She did not like lectures on scientific subjects,—the geology of the cañons least of all.

"I know it off by heart, aunty," she pleaded. "Didn't we go with the Professor when he found it all out?"

I therefore left her at home reading the life of Rachel, whom I always fancied she resembled.

There was to be a late boat that evening, and the Professor and myself were to return by it after the lecture, which went off pleasantly,— as my husband's lectures always did. Afterwards we went to the hotel with some friends, took some refreshments—as I had told Martha not to wait up,—and then returned all together by the ferry.

The moon shone brightly on the bay, drawing its wavelets in rippled silver, and performing marvels of masonry on Yerba Buena Island, in shadowy towers, and castles, and cathedrals, which seemed traceable like embers in a fire.

"I feel strangely nervous and almost superstitious tonight," I said, passing my arm through my husband's. "I fancy I can see the figure of Zanita clearly defined in the moonlight standing on that pinnacle of rock, just as I have seen her stand at the very brink of Eagle's Nest or Pom-pom-passa."

"I see it too, and it is something like her," said the Professor.

"And there is Egremont rising up behind her," I said, tracing out the figure, "and about to push her over."

"I guess she'll be first with him, there!" laughed the Professor. "But there, they have both disappeared," as the boat veered round.

We parted with our friends at our own door. The Professor turned the key in the latch and pushed it open, and the whole passage was instantly flooded with moonlight. I lit the lamp, which had been left for us. I noticed the parlor door was partly open and the moonbeams slanting in. I went to close it, intending to go straight up-stairs to our room. I never can recall what impulse tempted me to look in, but my eyes rested upon a sight which instantly paralyzed my lips beyond the power to utter an exclamation. There, on the sofa, sat Zanita and Mr. Egremont encircled in each other's arms, like two statues carved in stone. The moon's rays, lying still over their placid faces, tinged them with the unearthly hue of two corpses, and showed their eyes, slightly open staring glassily. At this moment my husband appeared with the light: the vision changed at once and made them appear very much as though they had fallen comfortably asleep.

"Good heavens!" I exclaimed, recovering my breath. "What is the meaning of this, Mr. Egremont? Zanita, I am ashamed of you!"

But neither moved, though in my excitement I had spoken loud enough to rouse the "Seven Sleepers." I was about to rush upon Zanita and remove her forcibly from her position when the Professor laid his hand on my shoulder.

"Stop! my dear. Be careful; there is something very curious about this. It is not ordinary sleep." And he advanced and passed the light before their eyes. The lids never quivered, neither did the pupils move.

"My God!" I cried, with an awful dread stealing over me, "are they dead? My darling Zanita, speak one word!"

"They are not dead," said my husband, "nor is it even a case of suspended animation," feeling each pulse in turn. "Not sick," he muttered, "either, for their color is quite fresh and natural."

"Nor asleep," I said, "unless they are both somnambulists!"

"They must be under the effect of some strong narcotic," said my husband, "opium or hasheesh. Perhaps Martha can throw some light upon the matter. Where is she?" I ran up-stairs and awakened Martha.

"Do you know anything of Miss Zanita?"

"No, ma'am, unless she is asleep in bed. Why, is she lost again! Up in some other china closet, you bet!" suggested Martha, rubbing her eyes.

"Did you know Mr. Egremont was here?"

"No, I guess he's not, leastwise not of my letting in; for he called soon after you was gone, and said as he would not come in, which he needn't have troubled to, for I held the door in my hand and never budged an inch to let him pass; for I guess if I had Miss Zanita and he would soon have been up at some marlicks or other."

"Martha, dress quickly and come down-stairs! Something very strange has happened to Miss Zanita."

"I'd be more puzzled if it hadn't," responded Martha, hurrying on her things.

We found the Professor still experimenting upon the two statues, who sat rigid as though they had been frozen.

"Had we not better send for a doctor?" I suggested.

"I do not think it is a case for medical skill," replied my husband; and he added, "it might cause a great deal of scandal."

Martha declared she knew nothing of the event whatever. Until she had gone to bed at ten o'clock, Miss Zanita had not been moving about. No glass, cup, or spoon had been asked for, nor could we discover any pill-box, powder-paper, or glass, from which any mixture or drug had been taken. Mr. Egremont had his walking-cane in one hand, and Zanita had a lovely camelia in her right hand, their right and left arms lay loosely round each other.

"I am sure they were not speaking or moving around before I went to bed," persisted Martha, "and when I went to see the front door was all right on the latch, I noticed the parlor door ajar, and concluded Miss Zanita was abed."

"My lamb, my pet!" moaned Martha, terrified by the strange sight, throwing her arms round the still form of Zanita and stroking the pale Grecian brow, which, with its slight frown, seemed sculptured in white marble. "You shall tickle me with the cat's tail, or anything else you like, if you will only speak one word to your own Martha!" But poor Martha uttered a shriek of dismay, as this appeal was suddenly answered by Zanita, and Mr. Egremont simultaneously rising from their seat and looking upon us with a bewildered gaze.

Instantly the feeling of the impropriety of the situation flashed upon us all, and my indignation began to boil over and first found vent.

"Mr. Egremont!" I said, severely, "can you give any explanation of this?"

"None, madam," he replied, the words oozing from his blue lips as though they were thrust forth in agony. He had turned perfectly white in fact, almost a livid green, since he had awoke, and the miserable expression in his eyes seemed to appeal to the ceiling to fall and crush him. Shame, remorse, despair, complete self-abasement, were depicted upon every line of his person.

Not so Zanita; after the first stare of astonishment, she had fallen into that peculiar furtive look of hers when caught or arrested in any piece of mischief. The defiant, elfish smile was on her face, and, I must say, provoked me more than anything.

"Zanita!" I exclaimed, "how could you think of going to sleep on the sofa with Mr. Egremont?"

"Aunty," replied the invincible child, no more moved than if I had asked her where she had put a spool of thread, "I don't think I did go to sleep on the sofa with Mr. Egremont; at least I don't recollect it, if I did."

"My dear!" said my husband, coming to the rescue, "don't you think we had better postpone this investigation until to-morrow? Mr. Egremont"—he said, indicating that individual, who stood like a criminal listening to his death-warrant—"will no doubt be anxious to answer any and every question, and to-night will be glad of rest."

"Whatever you wish," responded the latter, "but I should feel grateful to have my explanations, few as they are, postponed until to-morrow." He advanced toward me and half held out his hand, but I was too angry to give any sign of being propitiated. "Be pitiful," he murmured; "do not judge me too harshly,"—and he walked out of the room bowing to us all, like the ghost in a magic lantern.

Zanita took up a candle. "Good-night, aunty!" she said, with a mischievous smirk; "good-night, Professor,—Martha!" and she skipped up-stairs with a bound.

"Wall!" exclaimed Martha, "if she ain't the little imperintest, audacious minx. I never did! she ain't afraid of man or devil!"

"No," commented my husband, "she has not a particle of fear in her composition!"—and we all retired to our chambers.

When the door was shut and the lamp set down, I put my two hands on my husband's shoulders. I needed his quiet strength very much that night.

"John!" I said, "tell me what is it? Tell me what you think?" He clasped his strong arms round my waist.

"My dear," he said, "I am not thoroughly satisfied myself what it is. I thought it might be some soporific, such as chloroform, which Zanita had chanced upon, and experimented with. But she, at least, has none of the symptoms of having taken such a poison, and I am inclined to think that it may be some singular effect of animal magnetism called mesmerism. The greater part of the phenomena exhibited, I am inclined to regard as a gross humbug. But there is no doubt that muscular insensibility can be produced by one person over another, the same as

ZANITA

by inhaling ether; and that such coma may last for a certain length of time."

"But how could they have both fallen into this condition?" I exclaimed. "How could they both have been mesmerized? Who could have operated upon them?"

"There is the mystery," said my husband. "I do not believe any one has been in the house; and yet I never heard of a case of mutual magnetic influence. I earnestly wish those two had never met, my dear."

"That thought has tormented me from the first moment they saw each other," I replied. "But what is to be done now that the evil has occurred?"

"As to that you must be guided by circumstances. That they met this evening by any appointment or evil intention, I cannot be induced to believe. And perhaps the best thing would be to give our sanction to their intimacy and thus denude it of that dangerous charm of secrecy."

"You had better question them separately, and I think, you will elicit more from either of them than I could. Egremont will speak more frankly to you, for a woman has a knack of arriving at the truth quicker than all the cross-questioning a man can put."

CHAPTER XVII.

AN APOLOGY
FOR LOVE.

THE NEXT MORNING I felt restless and anxious, expecting Mr. Egremont every moment. Zanita had resumed her perusal of the life of Rachel in undisturbed equanimity.

"Aunty," she said, presently, "won't you let me have a horse to ride? I feel so caged up in this small house and garden, I am sure it is that which gives me the headache!"

There was something so reasonable and yet so audacious in this request, at the moment when she ought to have considered herself in deep disgrace, that I paused before making her any reply. In that moment I perceived Mr. Egremont coming up the front garden. "Zanita, go to your room!" I said, peremptorily. She quickly descended from the back of the chair, where she had been perched like a squirrel, and left the room before Martha had attended the door. He came in looking haggard and worn as though he had not slept all night. After a cold salutation had passed we sat for some time in silence. I was trying to frame a speech sufficiently decisive yet without any acrimony, and nervously rejecting each sentence as it presented itself; but no sooner had I opened my lips to speak than he interrupted me with, "Pray, Mrs. Brown, do not upbraid me until you know all. I will tell you exactly as far as I remember, all that occurred, and then submit to whatever comments you may think fit to make."

"Proceed!" I said.

"I called here last evening to see you, and was told by Martha that you were out, and as she did not seem inclined to let me in, I did not ask for Miss Zanita but went away. As I passed the window Zanita threw it up and said she wanted to speak to me, and I must get in at the window, which invitation I gladly obeyed. We talked a few minutes before she asked me to take a seat on the sofa by her side. She asked me for the flower I had in my buttonhole. I gave it to her with a compliment. She looked so beautiful I put my arm round her waist and kissed her," said Egremont, wringing out the words as though he was at confession, and coloring like a girl.

"I am surprised, Mr. Egremont, that knowing the peculiar character of my ward, the anxiety I experience on her account, and the intimate footing upon which you have been received in this family, that you should wantonly enter upon a clandestine flirtation with Zanita!"

His handsome lips trembled and curved at this rebuke, and the hot color went and came painfully. He was silent for a few moments, and then said in a choked voice,—

"The *wanton* and *clandestine* both do me injustice. I was absolutely fascinated and bewitched by her beauty, as I was the first time I saw her. The interview was entirely unpremeditated. But I will resume.

"The idea occurred to me that I should like to exert control over her. I hoped I might gain her devotion, and I thought I would like to try to mesmerize her. I had no thought but a mere experiment. I said something of the kind to her; she replied, 'Take care, I may magnetize you, as the snakes do the rabbits.' I believe that is substantially all that passed; I have no recollection whatever of any symptoms of sleep coming over me, or of any premonitory consciousness that I was falling asleep, such as we usually experience; and I swear to you on my honor and conscience this is the truth. My feelings toward Zanita are honorable, and I will be to her whatever she may desire,—friend, lover, or husband."

"I am glad to hear you speak so frankly, and must accept your explanation, however strange and inexplicable it appears. May I ask, did you ever mesmerize any one before last night?"

"I have done so occasionally," he replied, the warm wave again mantling his brow. "But that was in the regular way of making passes," he added.

Unwilling to probe his suffering any further, I closed the interview, by saying, that the matter must rest upon Zanita's feelings; that, for my own part, I did not wish her to engage herself as yet, still less to rush into such extraordinary proceedings as that of the previous evening; that I did not think her at all calculated to perform the duties of a wife; "nor should I wish," I said, "to see you her husband, unless I knew more of you."

He winced at this last remark, and said,—

"Has there been anything in my conduct that you have disapproved of before last night?"

"No," I said; "but you must remember how little I know of your previous life, and the alarm I should feel at trusting such a wild unmanageable character as Zanita's with an entire stranger."

"Entire stranger!" he muttered bitterly, and wished me goodmorning, with the understanding that he was to return on the morrow to receive Zanita's answer to his proposition.

When I made what I considered a necessary explanation to Martha of the affair, desiring her not to mention it in the neighborhood, she exclaimed,—

"O, my eyes and Betty Martin! Ma'am, don't you go for to believe him. They were just a keepin' company a sitting up with one another, as is reg'lar among young folks. Why, when I was cook aright away down East, there was a young man as used to come along reg'lar at dusk a sitting up with our young lady, an' the parlor was always dusted a-purpose for them. An' Mrs. Fishgill she used to make us creep about as quiet as mice, fear o' disturbing on 'em. Why ma'am, it's quite natural like, only I don't see why they should a set so stiff at it. I thought they were dead. I'll be blessed if I did not!"

I gave up the argument again, recommending discretion.

"All right, ma'am; I'm not the one to be blabbing, about 'sitting up.'"

My interview with Zanita was not more satisfactory.

"Why, aunty, you know what passed last night very well; you have been questioning Mr. Egremont."

"Yes, my dear, and I want to see if he has told me the truth."

"O yes," she cried, "you want the equipoise of evidence. Well, aunty, he has told you the truth, for although he is an enormous falsehood on the whole, he never tells a direct lie. Now the difference between us is, that though I tell a thousand fibs I never practice deception, as he does."

"Zanita!" I said, "do not talk nonsense; come to the point."

"Well then, aunty, I called Mr. Egremont in and made him come through the window, as Martha had shut him out of the door. I asked him to sit on the sofa." She went on talking rapidly as though it were all a matter of course. "He had a flower in his coat, and I asked him to give it to me. He said he should have offered it to me before, as it perfectly resembled me,—'it was a scarlet camellia,'—but thought I did not care for flowers. I said I liked it, because it was *his* flower, and then he put his arm round me and kissed me, and I liked that too."

"Zanita!" I said severely.

"O yes, I like him better than any one except you, aunty."

I felt wretched, I had dreaded to hear this avowal, and had been hoping against hope.

"And would you like to marry him and become his wife?" I asked despairingly.

"O no, aunty! I could not be bothered!"

I laughed right out at this characteristic reply. Zanita never cared for any one more than would gratify her immediate purpose.

Of love, which in a woman consists of tenderness and devotion, her character was singularly devoid; they were emotions quite foreign and incomprehensible to her. Compassion for man or beast she knew not, and would as soon have strangled her lover as her pet kitten, and experienced no more remorse. When I laughed out at her queer reply, which, nevertheless, came so gratefully to me, she joined in with a terrible reckless glee, that looked almost fiendish upon that young beautiful face.

"O, Zanita!" I said, taking her delicate hand with its long taper fingers in mine. "My dear child, will you never learn to feel for any one but yourself, or reflect how much torture you inflict upon others in order that you may enjoy a small evanescent gratification?"

"What have I done to Mr. Egremont?"

"Zanita, you have done a very wicked thing. You have encouraged him to place his affections upon you, under the impression that they were reciprocated. You have schemed for and obtained from him the choicest and holiest gift a man can offer to a woman,—his heart and hand. And when you have succeeded in winning this, beyond his power to recall, then you reject scornfully the whole wealth of his soul which he has laid at your feet! My opinion is that a woman cannot be guilty of a more heinous and unpardonable sin. Heartlessness ought to be visited with equal reprobation as the weakness of over heartfullness. There is less real evil in the latter than the former."

"As regards Mr. Egremont," said Zanita, indifferently, "I don't think he has either heart or hand to give, so you need not lament the gift thrown away. He admires me because I admire him, and no more; he will not break his heart any more than I shall; and as to his hand it is no doubt given away long ago."

"What do you mean, Zanita?" for I fancied that with her usual trickiness she had slid into the latter suggestion the better to make out her case. She gave me one of her oblique furtive glances.

"You don't know that he has not a wife and children in England, or wherever he comes from?" she said.

"Nonsense!" I replied, reprovingly. "Of course he has not. But it is not of consequence, any way, since you do not intend to accept him. I shall inform him of your decision."

"Whatever you like, aunty," she said, carelessly, taking up the part of Lady Teazle she was studying.

"Aunty!" she called in her most coaxing voice as I was leaving the room, "can't I have a horse to ride?"

"I will see about it,"—and I left her.

When I rejoined the Professor in his study and recounted the various items of the *inquirendo*, he expressed himself highly satisfied with the result.

"I am heartily glad she has rejected him. She would have been the death of him," laughed my husband. "She would ruin a whole county of men if she were allowed to marry them; and I am very certain,—as I told you when she was a mere infant,—that she is not qualified to form the happiness of any one. She ought to content herself with being wedded to her profession, and I suppose that unless some prince or premier makes her an offer, she will not think it worth while to be bothered, as she calls it."

"She will never marry except from ambition or love of power," I said; "yet it is one of the strangest cases of attraction—I will not call it love—I have ever witnessed. It commenced from the very first moment their eyes met, and thus might be classified as 'Love at first sight.' But Zanita does not love him, and asserts that he does not care for her, and of course she ought to know best."

"And yet," mused the Professor, "you tell me he made a formal offer to marry."

"Yes, certainly; but I think he might be actuated by other motives than love. He possesses a great deal of that quality the French call *respect humain*, and would be very sorry to forfeit our good opinion; and the matter having been brought to a climax by the discovery last evening, he has seen no way out of the dilemma but honorable proposal."

"Very probable," said the Professor. "But admitting that to be the case, what is the attraction? How was the climax, as you term it, brought about?"

"That is a myth," I said, "which none of my *ologies* have yet elucidated. What is love? What, especially at first sight? A man sees a young woman bearing a noble part in her family, enduring patiently a great burden of misery, or struggling heroically with the rough current of the world. He admires, and pities, and reasons logically that such noble qualities if transferred to a more genial soil and planted round his hearth would make his home an Eden. The interest deepens into affection, the pity into tenderness, which is all natural, reasonable, and comprehensible. But that is the passion of love, only in certain minds: love is usually erratic, unreasonable, unruly, and unconquerable. It rushes down like an avalanche, we know not from whence, we guess not whither. It changes all things, transforms the whole face of nature, beautifying, glorifying, and gilding all it approaches. It makes the stars to shine out, and the moon to be intensely bright. What lover does not see the moon bigger than erst was her wont to be? The veriest clown picks gently the flower he has trodden under his hob-nailed shoes all his life, and carries it to his Molly. Nature seems in sympathy with this master-passion of love, which, at the same time, is metamorphosing and making as wild work in our interior and exterior world. The same vivid delusions prevail, as concerning the size of the moon, the brilliancy of the stars, and the beauty of the flowers. This may be called the poetic phase, where love idealizes and makes life a romance. Poets sing it, and artists depict it. Along with it troop a noble band of devotion, worship, self-sacrifice, admiration. We drink it in as an elixir, sometimes accidentally, but often consciously; and like revelers in champagne we know that intoxication is to ensue; we know that the whole world is to be turned like a kaleidoscope, from dull, prosaic gray to rainbow tints of gorgeous hue; we know it is the same old dull piece of glass, but yet it is mingled with such ecstatic moments of faith in the blissful *ideal*, and disgust of the dronish real, that we clutch the flowing goblet and sip and sip till our souls are wrapt in an elysium of bliss. This is all-absorbing love."

"Or harmless insanity," put in the Professor.

"Let us imagine it"—I went on, not heeding the sarcasm—"an essence something between spirit and matter floating in ambient air, neither all godlike nor fully human. We imbibe it with our eyes, and ears, and nostrils, and lips, and touch, and every trembling fibre of our whole frame."

"A sort of epidemic," suggested my husband, "infectious, like cholera or small-pox."

"You ought to be the best judge of that," I retorted, "for you have experienced the three maladies."

"Well," he said, "I hope the former has left more trace than the three little marks of the latter,"—placing his finger over three indented white spots on his forehead.

"But, John, I have not come to Zanita's case yet, and that kind of fascination is the most mysterious to me. She has no love for him of the description we have been speaking of, but still is irresistibly attracted toward Egremont and he to her. Do you not think, Professor, that the condition we found them in was a physical result of negative and positive magnetism operating as imperatively upon these two coming together as the detonation from an electric cloud?"

"That seems a plausible but very dangerous theory, especially if you think they might explode of spontaneous combustion," replied the Professor, who always worked out my nebulous theory by a little satire.

"They are thrown together by much the same magnetic attraction that draws the lamb to its own mother out of a flock of hundreds of sheep, though it has no mark by which to distinguish her from the rest. And I believe, that thousands of matches are made, and lives marred by mistaking that phenomena for love; for if we call it love among the animals, it ought not to be dignified with that name in human beings, because the soul has really no part in it, and I believe that either Zanita or Egremont, in spite of this attraction, would be capable of forming a real attachment to-morrow."

"I should be sorry for the object of such an affection," said the Professor; "but don't you think, my dear, that it would be an improvement if these negative and positive affinities could also entertain a little devotion and tenderness for each other? If the moon could grow a little larger for them as well as the ploughman, or the streamlets ripple out soft sayings to their longing ears, *par example?*"

"O, certainly! I should know the touch of your hand in a crowd, though I did not know that you were within miles of me."

For reply, my husband kissed me, and asked if I should know that, for a sapient little woman as I was. He said, he thought "even an unpoetical Professor of Geology might swear to that in the dark."

"Yes," I continued, "you must have noticed that some hands have the power to soothe in sickness whilst certain invalids are irritated by the touch of a nurse. You know what an objection your sister has to shake hands with strangers, because, she says, in touching some people she experiences the most uncomfortable sensation, amounting sometimes to a galvanic shock; and don't you think that sometimes, when my hair is emitting electric sparks, that if I laid it upon some persons they would feel some magnetic influence?"

"Without a shadow of doubt, my dear," said my husband, roguishly. "You used to wear a long curl before we were married, and one day the wind blew it round me, and after that I remember it was all over with me. Since Samson's time, long hair has been a mighty perilous weapon."

"Particularly," I said, "attached to a javelin, like the Spartan women."

The next day I felt uncomfortably nervous at having to break to Mr. Egremont the unpropitious news of his rejection by Zanita. I tormented myself to find the mildest form in which I could convey it and least wound his sensitive temperament. I rehearsed in imagination phrase after phrase, and sentence after sentence, with a view to making bad look better; for that Zanita had behaved badly I felt bitterly conscious, and how deeply he might take it to heart I could not decide. Sometimes I concluded that I would regard it lightly as a mere childish freak; at others, that I would treat it virtuously and indignantly, and condemn Zanita as a heartless coquette who was not worth grieving about. I even went so far as to think of offering my sympathy and influence to coax Zanita into a more amiable frame of mind. That was the most chimerical idea of all. The whole was cut short by the announcement by Martha of Mr. Egremont.

"He'll be come to fix up about Miss Zanita," suggested Martha, confidentially, "and no doubt keeping company reg'lar with him an' subdue her like. I know when I kep' company with Abimelech Jiggers I felt right badly all the time,—a low sinking like; and when he went away West to fix about some lot of land and wrote me to come on, I didn't feel like it, so I just put the letters in the fire that he might think I never got them,—post-offices is such uncertin things."

Still laughing at Martha's Irish solution of her anti-matrimonial difficulty, I descended to the parlor and made a thorough bungle of all I intended to say, becoming very hot and red in the process.

"I was quite prepared," answered Mr. Egremont, very coolly, "for your communication;" and a haughty sneer settled on his face, which both irritated and perplexed me. "Zanita having got into somewhat of a scrape with me I thought it best, out of respect for yourself and the

Professor, to make the offer I did, without the slightest idea that it would be accepted, and, indeed," he continued, tapping his boot with his cane, "with the slight knowledge she had of my position, I felt sure she would *not*."

"Then," said I, angrily, "it would appear that I am the only person in earnest in the whole affair?"

He smiled a faint sarcastic smile, which rapidly transfigured him to a totally different person. The gentle, sweet-faced Adonis suddenly appeared like some *blasé* guardsman, some callous *roué* seen lounging about most great cities. My eyes flamed up with vexation and surprise. "Under those circumstances, Mr. Egremont," I said, "I must beg you to avoid such *contretemps*, as you call scrapes, for the future. I had been considering how I could best spare your feelings in the matter; but now I perceive that you have none."

"I trust you will not judge me too harshly, Mrs. Brown," he said, resuming his soft captivating way, "and that in time you will think that this is really the best termination to the affair." He bowed gracefully with the old sweet smile, and left me.

"Well," I soliloquized,—for the Professor was out,—"he is gone, and the mystery with him; and I never knew anything more provoking and unsatisfactory in my life. If I only knew what he was or who he was. If I could decide to think well or ill of him, or come to any definite conclusion about him. The vague perplexity is tantalizing in the extreme. Why should Zanita hint at his being married? Why should he assume that if she knew his position she might act differently? How extraordinary that we had been upon such intimate terms, and discussing the nearest relations he could enter into with us, and we know absolutely nothing of him, and he had never let fall one syllable from which we could draw any conclusion."

The Professor laughed right out when I recounted to him the result of the interview. "He is quite right, my dear; this is the very best ending possible. If you can only write *finis* now, you have done well, and I congratulate you upon a very narrow escape from trouble."

CHAPTER XVIII.

NEW SYMPTOMS AND A RECOURSE TO NATURE.

FOR SOME WEEKS AFTER THIS all went on quietly at our home. We neither saw nor heard anything of Mr. Egremont. We decided that as the nuns had done all they could for Zanita she was to remain at home and study for the stage: first by reading with me, and afterwards with some tragedian.

She commenced the study well, and soon delighted me with the vivid conception she took of each character, old or young,—from Polonius, Ophelia's father, to Emilia, Iago's wife. She was skillful in seizing the identity, and where she could not personify she could mimic to perfection.

The saddle-horse she so much coveted had been procured, and she was such a fearless and skilled horsewoman that I permitted her to ride out alone, accompanied only by Beppo as groom, in the secluded park-like roads of Oakland. Sometimes she would visit her old school-mistress,—the matter of the expelling having been quite forgotten,—and would enchant that highly cultivated lady with her recitations from the poets. Mrs. Martinette made a point of calling upon me to express her strong conviction that Zanita was destined to become one of our greatest actresses; and that whenever I felt disposed to let her essay in a private rehearsal, her magnificent class-room would be placed at my disposal.

I was beginning to breathe afresh and see my future course clearly, when one morning Martha opened the parlor door with unusual precaution, and peering round stealthily closed it behind her standing with her back against it.

"Are you alone, ma'am?" she said in a sepulchral whisper.

"Why of course I am, Martha; what on earth is the matter with you?"

"Well, then, ma'am, I thought Miss Zanita might be around, for she is such a flipperty thing you never know rightly where she is; and I wanted just to say, ma'am, as Mr. Egremont's not visiting the house lately—is he?"

"Why no, Martha! How can you ask such foolish questions? I told you that as the young people did not care for each other the matter was at an end."

"Yes, ma'am," said Martha, wiping down her two red bare arms with her apron as though she had just come out of the wash-tub,—"yes, ma'am, you told me so; but it beats me if them two ain't a keepin' company right straight on."

"O, nonsense! Martha. What reason have you for supposing such a thing?"

"Where does Miss Zanita ride to?" she asked, briskly setting her arms akimbo.

"She rides about the roads and sometimes to the Academy."

"Pish!" ejaculated Martha, disdainfully; "no sir'ee, she do not!" she cried, forgetful of my sex in her vehemence. "She rides somewheres direct, and back same way, and brings that mare home in a sweat. 'Where's this you've been?' sez I to Beppo, 'to bring them horses all home in a sweat, sez I.' 'Them's not in a sweat, sez he.' 'Them is in a sweat, sez I,'—and I just wiped it off with my hand and threw it in his face to teach him to lie to me. And moresomever, ma'am, just you ask Beppo where they've went just after they've been, and you'll see the roundabout rigmarole he'll be telling you of nowheres at all."

"The next time they go out I will ask Miss Zanita," I said, "for I think you must be wrong in your suspicions. She had only to express the wish and Mr. Egremont could visit her as much as she desires."

"Bless you, ma'am! that's just her *contraryness*. She won't take what she can have, and will have what she can't get."

Having delivered herself of this lucid explanation, Martha wiped her arms again and returned to her kitchen, leaving me full of uneasiness; for although I could scarcely believe that Zanita had any rendezvous with Mr. Egremont, there was the danger that she had formed some other acquaintance; for discretion formed no part of her character, and to carry on anything on the sly was so much the negro propensity that Beppo would make only too ready an ally.

Satisfied that if there was any foundation for Martha's fear I should not elicit anything from Zanita, I resolved upon a strategem.

The following day, when the two horses were standing ready at the door and Zanita just preparing to mount, I suddenly notified my intention of riding with her instead of Beppo, and bade him change the saddle. Beppo was no master of the art of dissimulation, though an apt scholar; and his great wide open eyes, protruding to their utmost, showed how terribly he was disconcerted by this change of the programme. He cast an appealing look toward his young mistress, who stood carelessly switching her habit with her riding whip.

"Why, aunty! will you not be very tired? And you have company coming this evening."

"True, I had forgotten that; but I will go all the same."

Directly we turned into the main road both horses tried to break into a canter. Zanita checked her's, but I gave mine the rein and let him go. The animal shook his mane and went off as though intent upon doing his duty.

"O, aunty!" cried Zanita, "how fast you are riding; you will be quite tired."

But I never touched my rein determined to let my horse have his head and see where he would take me to.

After riding in this way for some time Zanita suddenly shot past me, for her mare was much fleeter than mine, which we used as a buggy horse, and presently I saw she was urging her mare to full gallop.

I screamed to her not to gallop, but keep with me; but she heeded me not, and was soon racing with the wind. The road was almost straight to the beach. She was a fearless rider and sat her horse so well that I felt no alarm. She looked so bright and beautiful as she flew on, that every passenger turned to look at her, and must have thought her the personification of a Die Vernon. Unwilling to lose sight of her I had now to urge my buggy charger, and he, nothing loth, did his best. But we had lost time, and just before we came in sight of the beach a curve in the road hid the runaway from my sight.

I rounded the point in time to see Zanita raised in her stirrup and waving her handkerchief, fastened to the end of her whip, like a flag of truce. She then turned her horse's head and was back at my side immediately.

"I wanted to get a glimpse of the beach," she said, "and you do not want to ride so far, I know."

"I am going on," I replied, without drawing my rein.

When we neared the beach a little skiff was putting off manned by a single sailor.

Could I be mistaken in that lithe, graceful figure! It was too far off to be very certain, but my emotions told me it was Egremont.

"Who is that in yonder boat?" I asked, turning to Zanita.

She shaded her eyes with her hand as if to take a better view.

"Which boat, aunty? You call all manner of craft boats. Is it the schooner, the cutter, the row-boat, or the man-of-war's boat with the captain in it? Sure enough!" cried Zanita, as if overjoyed with the discovery.

But the solitary boatman was now hidden by the sail, and the little skiff was bounding with joyous springs over the blue bay toward San Francisco. Zanita kept on chatting about the visit we had been asked to pay on board the English man-of-war lying off Buena Yerba. I made no reply, but turned homewards with a heavier heart than I had come. Both horses stretched out to take the same pace back. They had done their work, and evidently knew what was expected of them. If they could have spoken they could have told me how often Zanita had sped along that road at lightning pace. How often their spurning hoofs had struck the light from the flints as they tore up the stony road; how they had been running this race, poor beasts! for days and weeks, and were ever ready to do it again and again. No wonder they came home covered with foam. How often had that tiny white sail glided into the little cove or bay; and Zanita's genet could have told too, how often the handsome sailor had sprang ashore to lift the lady from its back, and afterwards stood stroking its soft nose and call it brave little mare. For he was always kind and affable and gentle to animals. But the dumb brutes are man's servants and his slaves; they do his work and keep his secret.

I needed no further enlightenment. I had seen enough. Zanita was keeping up her flirtation with Egremont, and the secrecy she was practicing could arise from no other cause than her *contraryness*, as Martha called it.

When I informed the Professor of my discovery he was more disturbed than was his wont.

"If she commences a practice of deceiving you, my dear, there is no knowing where it will end; and suspicion and distrust will keep you in continual anxiety."

"I should have expected more honorable conduct from Egremont. He must see what a wild thoughtless child she is, and he is taking advantage of it to amuse himself, not at hers, but our expense, for he knows that we should be the greatest sufferers from any *esclandre*."

Thus the amount of pain endured should be measured by the substance upon which it falls, not by the weight of the blow given. The organization, and the nervous system, regulate the proportion of suffering. A person of delicate sensitive temperament endures an excess of pain, both mental and physical, over the phlegmatic, obtuse person. Hence a public disgrace has killed many a man; whilst others seek only how they can best turn it to account. One man endures an agony from the amputation of a limb, whilst another could almost dictate a letter whilst the operation was going on.

"I fear we should never induce any dread in Zanita of what evil tongues might say of her proceedings. Whereas you, my dear, will never be free from pain for a single instant, until such contingency is put beyond all risk. Is it not so?"

"Indeed it is. To have my adopted child the talk of the place would utterly destroy my peace of mind; and to avoid this I must never lose sight of her; for her propensity to be in mischief is just as prominent as when she was a child."

"I think," said my husband, "you had better put an end to this affair by taking her home to the Valley for a time. It would change the current of her ideas, and probably turn them in the channel you wish."

"That would be the very best thing," I exclaimed. "But what will become of you left here by yourself?"

"O, I shall get on splendidly; hang the broom out, and have a good time generally with my bachelor friends."

I shook my head dolefully. I knew he was the last man in the world to be merry when left alone; that he would mope and grow sick; wear two odd stockings,—even if he were fortunate enough to find two; never have a handkerchief, and appear in a disreputable neck-tie; that all his linen would take the opportunity of my absence to go astray at the laundry. But he insisted upon sacrificing himself and his socks for the general good, —*c'est a dire* for Zanita's and mine. So it was decided we should start for the Valley immediately.

Zanita heard the news joyfully, and I was happy to think that no regrets for the handsome gondolier lingered in her mind. Our preparations were soon completed, and the Professor accompanied us to Stockton, partly to see a friend, and partly for the pleasure of a sail over the Bay of San Francisco, than which there is scarcely another to exceed it in beauty.

The city on its seven hills, like Rome, is more picturesque to look at from the water than pleasant to traverse: the beautiful coast-range of mountains, forming a wall to the golden gate, where alone the glorious sunlight seemed to be admitted; the soft green hills sloping like velvet to the very verge of the blue bay, and rising majestically to the two thousand feet of Tamel Pais and Mount Diablo; the pretty little towns and villages nestled in the cañons of the mountains, overshadowed by luxuriant mandrona and *quercus-virens*; the deep intense blue of the water, with the pink and gold glow of sunset; the sweet west breeze so fresh and pure,—

> "For of all the ways the wind may blow,
> I dearly love the West,"

all these combined make a sail on the Bay of San Francisco at sunset a dream of glorious beauty and delight.

"I never can decide," I communicated to my husband, "whether I like this or the Bay of Naples the best. To be sure the latter has Vesuvius, Capri, and Sorrento, which might be likened to Saneileto,—"

"Without the oranges," said my husband; "and I think there is a magical shade of light over Naples, which creates such enthusiasm, and which we lack here, though the sunsets are very fine."

"Yes, I remember what you mean: the after-glow,—the very poetry of nature. Do look at Zanita; she is nearly asleep, she cares no more for scenery than science."

"She has no poetry in her soul, obviously," said the Professor.

"I think it is very sad. I should pity a person more in being bereft of the faculty of drawing pleasure from the glory of God's works, than for being either deaf or blind. For nature to the appreciative is like sleep to the wakeful: it steals over us in our moments of bitter trial and harassing care, and wraps us in downy oblivion, and with imperceptible tonic opens the deadened senses to new delight and exhilaration. But this poor child would never know this balm in her *extremis*."

"Poor little child," mused the Professor.

"John," I whispered, moving near to him, as I always did when I wanted to gain my point,—"John, I wish you would try and exercise some of your kindly wisdom upon the child; for I feel she is beyond my control."

The Professor pressed my hand softly under my shawl, and replied,—

"My dear, I will do whatever you suggest to help you with your *protégé*; but I think in her management she more needs tact than wisdom; and of the former you have more than I; and in interfering I might only make mischief. Try the Valley first, and then when she returns we shall see if anything further is necessary."

"I have a sad presentiment or foreboding about her. I feel as regards her morally now, as I used to do physically, when she was a little girl in the Valley. She was always verging on some danger; always hazarding the brink of some precipice. If she was out of sight for a minute she was generally discovered hanging by her frock in some tree, or being carried down some gulch by the surging torrent. And now, if it is not the peril of Mr. Egremont, it will be something else. It seems a strange dispensation of Providence, that she cannot lead a smooth and natural life like other people!"

"Well, my dear, let us at least anticipate that once in the Valley of Ah-wah-nee, your lives will flow on as peacefully as the Mercede, when rippling between the banks of azaleas and lilies."

We remained in Stockton two days, and then having parted with the Professor, with much misgiving as to the state of his personal appearance when I should next see him, we resumed our journey, *via* Hornitas,—the Little Oven, so called in Spanish, from its intense heat, lying in the mountains very much like one. Or as Zanita called it, "*via* purgatory to Paradise, the Valley."

To ride behind four well-conditioned horses would seem, in the abstract, the most pleasurable way of travelling through a beautiful country. But practically this ride is one of the worst tortures that can be inflicted upon persons guilty of no crime recognizable by law as punishable. This coach is so constructed, that at every pebble as large as a nut, or hole to accommodate a taw, it rolls and pitches worse than a narrow screw-steamer in a chopping sea. You are jigged, and tossed, and bounced up to the ceiling, tumbled on the floor, wedged against the window, and scattered generally in all directions; churned up in the corner, or sent sprawling into your neighbors on the middle seat, and scratch your nose against a watch-chain, or lady's shawl pin. As this alternate beating and banging continues from twelve to sixteen hours, according to the road, you have very little definite idea of yourself whether you are a living, bruised, and crushed human being, or a palpitating mass of hogshead cheese. The only remedy for this is the alternative of having the stage crammed with nine stout inside passengers, a few children, and a baby or two to stop up the crevices; then you travel in the same style as poultry going to market promiscuously in a bag. You must either sit upon your neighbor, or he will make a cushion of you. You find some one's head pillowed on your shoulder, and a stray arm round your waist. Feet in general are in inextricable pell-mell, and woe to the wearer of thin boots troubled with corns. It is no use frowning at your *vis-à-vis* for making you a footstool, for it may be the individual in the farthest corner of the coach who has succeeded in intersecting his long limbs over the way. What canned lobsters must feel is easy to be realized by mortals travelling per stage on a hot dusty day in California.

CHAPTER XIX.

AU REVOIR.

NEVER WERE TWO ESCAPED negroes more joyous than we, when we were mounted on our horses to ride to Galen's Rancho. Fortunately, its most estimable owner was upon his way home, and accompanied us.

He was an old man who had lived the greater part of his life with Nature for his companion; he had lived so true and close to her that her beauty and purity seemed to permeate his entire character. Next to Kenmuir, we could not have found a more interesting companion for such a ride; and as we ascended higher and higher, four thousand feet, until we reached the Rancho, we appeared to be hourly invigorated by the pure mountain air.

The cares, vexations, and anxieties I had experienced in the city seemed to be fading away under the powerful stimulus of horse exercise and the refreshing beauty of Nature. I know of no better antidote for a weary and jaded spirit than a brisk gallop among the hills and byways of Nature's peaceful retreats.

Zanita was in high spirit, and looked radiant in beauty and power, as she always did on horseback. The old mountaineer could not help admiring her and remarking to me,—

"She does credit to you, Mrs. Brown, for although these mountains gave her talent and power, the refined bearing and culture come from you; we could not have given her these graces."

"You are very good to say so, but I think the nuns deserve the credit of the refinement you notice."

"It has always been interesting to me to trace," he said, "how much her birth amidst the stupendous grandeur of this scenery, and her life with it alone for so many years, have had to do with the formation of her character. Those children of Naunton's have always been a theme for curious speculation, and I am pleased to see such a pleasant result evolved."

"Yes," I said, "Zanita has turned out a very brilliant and attractive girl, and sets her own *cachet* upon whatever she does, but her nature still bears the impress of the wild, untrammeled character of the scenery;

142

she remains the uncurbed child of nature in spite of all we could do to make her conventional."

We passed the night at Galen's Hospice, and when about to start the next morning, on our twenty-five miles' ride into the Valley, Galen himself appeared leading up his own black mule.

"I am going to guide you myself," he said, "for I find that Bill is off with a stranger, an artist, who has come up to make sketches of the various points of scenery."

"I am very glad to hear that," I exclaimed, "because it gives us your company; also because we shall now probably have some fine pictures of this *luxe de beauté*. Who is he?"

"I don't recall his name, but he is a very pleasant gentleman."

"I wonder if we could have him give Rosalind some lessons? She inherits all her mother's talent for painting and music, and has accomplished some very creditable pieces with such little instruction as her father and myself could give her."

"So I understand," he replied. "She is growing up a very sweet and lovable little creature."

We were once more winding through the grand mountains, gorgeous in their wonderful atmospheric tints, and through mighty forests of centurian trees, many whose hoary locks denoted thousands of years rather than hundreds. To think of these giant patriarchs dwelling here for centuries, long before this Western Continent was dreamed of by Nor'lander or Spaniard,—when the limits of the toiling, bubbling, surging world of Europe comprised the *terra cognita*.

"Think of these majestic hosts that have encamped far and wide over this great land welcoming Columbus and Balboa to their mossy corridors and wide-spread leafy chambers, regaling them with their sweet gums and pine nuts, singing them to sleep by the rustling of their great feathery arms. They must have seemed to them like puling infants in contrast to their aged generation. They must have been as much astonished as these voyagers were."

"Yes," said Galen, "for I presume they had never seen a white man before."

"And do you think that the Indians are coeval with the *Sequoia* and the *Pinus ponderosa*?" I asked.

"I do. The Red man is a type of race which is gradually fading out from old age and decay in the same manner as the individual dies from the same cause. The Indians have ceased to multiply, yet there is little doubt that they once populated this vast Continent."

"Do not ride so far ahead!" I called to Zanita. But she was off and soon out of sight.

"I would ride after her," remarked Galen, "but I do not apprehend the slightest danger for her; still, if you feel alarmed, Mrs. Brown"—

"O no!" I returned, "she will be all right now, but we might as well all have kept together."

In about a quarter of an hour she came riding back to meet us, looking well pleased and as gay as she ever was. As we turned a point Galen exclaimed, "Ah! there they are!"

I looked in the direction he indicated and had no difficulty in recognizing the brawny shoulders of Horseshoe-Bill planted against a tree, his two hands thrust into the waist of his trousers, with a short pipe in his mouth, in the blissful enjoyment of life; near him was the figure of the artist partly concealed by a large white umbrella used to regulate the shade on his sketch. As my eyes rested on him he arose from his sitting posture and gave me a full view of him; my eyes surely had deceived me.

"Good heavens! Zanita," I ejaculated. "Zanita, is not that Mr. Egremont?"

"Yes, aunty. I saw him half an hour ago, and rode on to speak to him. He is making a splendid sketch," she replied, with the utmost nonchalance.

"Nonsense!" I said, angrily, "why has he come to the Valley?"

"To make sketches, I suppose, like any other artist."

"I don't believe he is an artist; if he is why has he concealed it from us?"

"You are a good judge, you can see for yourself, aunty," resumed Zanita, curtly.

As we approached Mr. Egremont, he advanced with that easy grace which was peculiar to him, and looked up at me with that unconscious sweetness that was always irresistible.

"Is not this glorious?" he said, surveying nature around us, and cleverly ignoring the awkwardness of our *rencontre*.

"Very," I replied, saying within myself, "What a consummate hypocrite you are;" for in the presence of Horseshoe-Bill and Mr. Galen I could not express myself aloud.

"You are right-smart at finding the trail now, Mrs. Brown, I guess," said Bill. "You remember how you were down on your luck first time as I brought you along; and how you wanted to put Kenmuir in Stockton mad-house." Here he laughed heartily, hitching up his waistband and enjoying the joke.

"That was your doing, Bill. Did you not tell me that he was an idiot?"

"Ha, ha!" laughed Bill, with an unction; "didn't he look like one, a moping and a mowing about the rocks? I didn't suspect as your husband belonged to the same profession."

"Moping and mowing idiots!" exclaimed Zanita, catching briskly at the blunder with her keen mischievous glance. "It's well the Professor does not hear you, and that aunty is so good tempered."

"I'm darned if I am up in the professions," said Bill, apologetically.

"Never mind; Bill, I understand what you mean."

We all rode on, Egremont mounting his horse and acting as my cavalier. He was ready with all those delicate attentions, those little easy flowing conventional speeches which entirely exclude any real and earnest conversation however important. Thus, partly owing to the interruptions of Zanita or Bill—Galen having taken his leave and returned when we were in charge of the guide,—and partly owing to Egremont's adroitness in warding off any special inquiries, I found no opportunity to ask the question which was natural and pertinent.

Long before we reached our destination he had so far insinuated himself into my good graces that I found myself talking to him in the old familiar way, and tacitly admitting his presence amongst us as a matter of course. Strange as it may appear, either by his influence, or the mysteriously soothing effect of the physical nature around me, my anger and annoyance at meeting him subsided. I enjoyed his presence as much as ever without any of the nervousness which had so depressed me when leaving San Francisco.

What would the Professor think, could he see me now, absolutely enjoying the very situation I had gone to so much trouble and inconvenience to avoid. My husband, I knew, would call it caprice; but I called it circumstances over which I had no control. What could I do? If I took Zanita back to Oakland they would again carry on their clandestine proceedings; here in the Valley, at least, I could exercise some supervision, and beside, as there was no other society but our own there was no fear of shocking proprieties. I had just to allow affairs to take their course, to permit the stream to flow on, since I was powerless to stem it. Yet how little I dreamed that my last move had opened a fresh dam which would ere long overflow and carry forcibly all along with its flood.

At first I imagined that Egremont could not stay long in the Valley, as there was only Mr. Naunton's house for accommodation; and unless he approved of his postulate son-in-law, Egremont would be forced to retire. But in the course of conversation it came out that Horseshoe-Bill had seen Kenmuir, who had agreed to receive the young artist into his tiny abode. So here again I was foiled, whilst Zanita had mastered the situation. "So be it," I said again to myself, for I saw no way out of the dilemma.

But time soon interfered with my philosophy. Rosie had grown quite tall, and looked quite a woman, and a very charming one. She had not lost her childlike, trustful expression, but it was mellowed by the dreamlike dawn of womanhood. Sweetness, resignation, and tenderness were all adolescent on her white brow, over which her little golden curls clustered coquettishly as if well knowing how pretty and privileged they were.

Her father had attended seriously to her education, and I was gratified to find her very little behind her sister in general information and cultivation. She quite excelled her in music and painting, and showed marked ability. She took a heartfelt interest in Mr. Egremont from the first; partly because he was really the first handsome stranger she had ever seen,—poor little bird!—in this secluded Valley; and eventually because he was an artist; her admiration was excited by his fine pictures.

"Ah, aunty!" she exclaimed, a few days after our arrival, her bright young face all aglow, "how nice it would be if I could go with Mr. Egremont and copy the same scene. I should observe how he composed his subject, and have all the benefit of his good taste."

My original idea of her taking lessons from the artist returned to me.

"If Mr. Egremont is agreeable," I replied, "I can see no objection; perhaps Zanita would like to amuse herself that way, and I feel inclined myself to do a little sketching; we could all go out in a party, each of us drawing our own conception, you only being under the tutelage of Mr. Egremont."

On being consulted the artist expressed himself quite charmed with the idea of helping Rosalind, always provided it was not to be considered professionally.

A fair day saw us all busy with frames and canvas,—Horseshoe-Bill displaying a talent for carpentering we had not expected.

"Wall! I guess I could make a right-smart pile of money if stuck at the trade; but I feel somehow like enjoying life backward and forward around these here diggins; it's mighty salubresome, I tell you."

"Why, Bill, I should not have supposed that you had to study your health," said I, laughing, as I surveyed his herculean limbs.

"I guess I am not to call sickly-like," grunted Bill, as he heaved a blow in chopping up a log that would have felled an ox, " 'but there's nothin' like preserving the Lord's blessings,'—as Kenmuir says. Bein' tied to one mill, ain't exactly to my fancy. I like to go where the Lord sends me," winking at Kenmuir.

"It's a long day since the Lord sent you on a message," quoth Kenmuir; "but if you'll come and help me to heave in a log at the saw-mill, I believe He will lead you to do that."

"All right! I'm your man," said Bill.

The sketching party came off quite a success. We turned out in full force, and selected "El Capitan" as a subject, viewed from a pile of *débris* on the opposite side under the Cathedral Rocks, as we called them.

Egremont sketched with the bold dash of an experienced artist, and the few first outlines gave promise of a powerful picture. Rosalind closely imitated, insensibly throwing in a sweet pathos of her own, for pictures, like music, imbibe the nature of the composer. I selected my own position, and drew as I had been taught at school. Zanita's foreground was filled in with a very ferocious grizzly bear, and the height of Tu-tock-a-nu-lah decorated with an eagle, which, according to the perspective, vied with "El Capitan" himself in dimensions. The face of the "Wandering Jew," which stands out upon that mighty rock, she was very particular to make distinct.

But soon finding herself eclipsed by the superior skill of the whole party, she threw down her impromptu easel and commenced painting a little smooth-haired white terrier, the property of Horseshoe-Bill, with bright patches of cobalt blue, the tip of his tail scarlet, which caused its master to exclaim when he saw the performance,—

"Wall! you're a rum 'un, I tell you!"

Kenmuir belonged to the pre-Raphaelite school, and drew and painted every flower and blade of grass and every feathery sedge just as it was in nature.

"A fig for your foreground!" he cried to Egremont and Rosie. "Those beautiful decayed silvery logs you have there, are a mile and a half away, and you can't seem them from your stand-point."

"But we have made a composition of them," said Egremont.

"Then do you think you can compose nature better than the Almighty? Man is the most arrogant biped that ever walked the earth."

"Why, Kenmuir!" exclaimed Rosie, "how bare your foreground looks."

"Bare!" echoed Kenmuir. "Bare with all those flowers in it?"

"They look like ten cents' worth of mixed glass beads, such as I used to buy in Oakland," cried Zanita, mischievously. "Look at my hog," she said, as she resumed her sketch. "There is only one pig in the Valley, and he ought to have his portrait taken just as he is engaged in grunting his opinion of the geological structure of El Capitan. Aunty, can you confer upon him the honorary degree of Valley worshipper? I'm sure he fully appreciates the beauties of nature from the expression of his sapient countenance."

But Zanita soon renounced the sketching expeditions; they were not sufficiently exciting for her busy brain, or her muscular activity. She renewed her horseback exercise, and easily induced Mr. Egremont to join her. Sometimes Rosie and myself or her father accompanied them; but Rosie was not fond of the actual exercise of horsemanship; but rather for the opportunity it afforded of compassing easily different *coup d'œils* of the landscape—this to me, also, was one of the greatest charms of riding in the Valley.

Every four yards on horseback brought new varieties of light and shade, and novelties of form, which we had not anticipated; hundreds of new sites for sketching subjects were ever presenting themselves: there was a *luxe de choix* perfectly bewildering.

"It is difficult to know where to begin," said Egremont, "and quite impossible to know where to leave off."

Every rock had a score of splendid forms, as seen from as many points of view; every mountain had fifty different shades and colors, as seen at different times of the day, or in peculiar phases of atmosphere,—all beautiful, all alike enchanting.

But this was not Zanita's pleasure. If there was a swampy piece to be found in the river, into that swamp she was sure to flounder, up to her horse's girth; and then she would whip and spur to get him out.

"O," she would exclaim, as she rode up to us bespattered with mud, "I had a terrible time to get Jeroboam out of that mud-hole."

"But Zani," replied Rosie, laughing, "why did you put him in? You know that is swampy land."

"O, I thought I could have got through on the edge," persisted Zanita.

She would ride full gallop under the low outspreading boughs of the oak-trees, her long silky hair flying loose, and catching round the leaves; Zanita with a jerk of her head carrying away the spray, or leaving a lock of hair suspended on the branch.

"You will share the fate of Absalom, some day, Zanita," I remonstrated. "Why must you needs ride through a place when there is not actually space, when you have the whole Valley to choose from?"

At other times she would throw me into a cold perspiration, by forcing Jeroboam over some brink of rock where there seemed not footing for a chipmunk—the sage beast carefully selecting his footing, while she would be shaking the reins, and calling,—

"Ho! Jerry, look lively; what are you stopping for?"

It came to be a jest before we started, to select a ride where Zanita could not get into mischief. To which she would retort,—

"Do let us find a place so secure that aunty can't get into a fright. Papa, let me have Mu-wah to lead my horse."

This was sure to provoke a laugh from Oswald Naunton.

Gradually the excursions became divided. I found more and more occupations in the house which required a woman's handiwork,—chairs wanting new chintz, windows needing new hangings, new sheets wanting hemming, and carpets renovating, table-cloths darning, and a thousand and one trifles which denoted a too young housewife.

In all these labors Rosie was only too anxious to assist me; patiently waiting to go sketching as the treat for her leisure. In the mean time Zanita, who could never be induced to sew ten minutes at a time, was away among the mountains, shooting with Mu-wah, or her father,— more frequently riding with Mr. Egremont.

Thus our family circle seemed to be flowing on as smoothly as the soft-flowing Mercede, meandering through the Valley,—so resembled it, alas! in other respects, when it dashes its foamy billows over the defiant rocks, hurling every weaker thing in its course to destruction and ruin. But now all was peace and summer sunshine; and, like the humming-bird trumpet flowers hanging over the cascade, we were all happy on the verge of a precipice.

True it was that I pondered inwardly upon the actual state of affairs between Zanita and Egremont. Whether they had come to any definite understanding as to their future, or whether they had agreed to sip the rosy minutes as they flew, and to let the future tell its own tale, I could not decide. To surprise a secret from either of them was hopeless, and their conduct offered no elucidation. Mr. Egremont acted with impartial gallantry to both the girls; he sketched with one and rode with the other, and was in every circumstance the pink of gentlemanly good-breeding.

Whatever tenderness he might feel toward Zanita, he was the last one to display it for the criticism and amusement of others. She alone would know the depth of his love, while outsiders, however observant, could only guess at it. Yet I had noticed that his gaze lingered over the peach-like face of Rosie—as she would lift her great blue eyes to his with an expression of baby-wonder,—with something more than artistic admiration of her beauty.

"But a man can't love two women at the same time," I said to myself, "and Cozy is but a baby, after all." I had faithfully narrated every circumstance relating to Mr. Egremont to Mr. Naunton, upon our arrival; but he had in his usual philosophic way laughed me to scorn, as I may say,—regarding it all a very good joke on the part of his favorite Zanita, unable to realize the smallest anxiety concerning her, and expressing absolute indifference toward Egremont.

"My good madam, you are too philanthropic by half. Zanita is all right; surely you cannot suppose her to be an object of compassion. She is as brilliant as a bluebird, and as frisky as a young kid. As to the artist, you acknowledge that you know so little about him, and are not even certain that he has a heart to lose; and if he has, he's big enough to look after himself. Don't trouble about them, Mrs. Brown; you are too good."

And Oswald Naunton went off, singing,—

> "Weep when you must, but now be gay;
> Life is too short to be sighing on."

Kenmuir took a different view of the case; but persisted in treating it as a good joke.

"He's in for it, as sure as death," he said, using his Scotch asseveration, as he usually did when excited. "I would not stand in his shoes for a hundred thousand dollars. Not I!" he continued; "for if he marries her, and you say he has offered himself, he will assuredly wish he had not before twenty-four hours are over; and the first journey he'll wish to take will be to Chicago. If he refuses to marry her, and thinks he'd like some one else,—my certis! but I wouldn't be in his shoes, that's all!" cried Kenmuir, enjoying the dilemma.

"I am not so sure about that," I retorted, a little piqued; "she is really not a disagreeable girl to live with. The Professor and myself never have any annoyance with her socially, and we are deeply attached to her."

"That may be; but you are not her husband. Why!" exclaimed Kenmuir, throwing himself back with his two hands grasping his waist-band,—"why I'd as 'lief be exposed to a female Puck, a Medusa, a banshee, an Ariel, a witch of Endor, all tied up in a bundle, as to be wedded to Zanita."

I laughed outright, as Kenmuir shook himself like Rollo, as if to get rid from any particle of chance of such an event happening to him.

"Very well, Kenmuir," I said; "nobody asks you to take up this bothersome bundle of confused natures. I am sure Mr. Egremont does not care to have you for a rival."

"I hope not," answered Kenmuir, suddenly becoming serious, and looking me in the face with an expression that made my color rise with an undefined consciousness of coming evil.

"Mrs. Brown," he said, earnestly, "I would move earth and heaven, and the powers of evil, if such there be, to secure the woman I loved from that beautiful specimen of humanity you have brought down here."

"I never brought him; but now that he is here, living with you, try to find out the good in him."

"The pure blossom opens to the sun," he replied, "and reveals its beauties to the day; it is only the bud that has a canker at its core that remains closed and secretes its imperfection."

These conversations had occurred the first few days after our arrival at the Valley; and weeks passed on over our lives, floating on as tranquilly, as peacefully as the web of yarn from cotton-wood trees, lying placidly on the breezeless air.

Sometimes, Sundays especially, Kenmuir would go botanizing, and occasionally Rosie would accompany him, returning laden with choice specimens and ferns culled from the high peaks around. These she

ZANITA

would tastefully arrange into bouquets with her mother's skill, though not as yet with her mother's science.

Returning from one of these excursions we all met together in the meadows at sunset: Mr. Egremont with his paint-box on his shoulder, Kenmuir and Rosie laden with tall fern branches, and Zanita careering with Mu-wah, fetching the cattle home, for she still delighted in her childish freaks. She would spring on her horse, with a piece of scarlet braid for a bridle, without hat or habit, and fly around with the Indian to drive the cattle to the milking corral.

"What a subject for an artist!" I exclaimed, as she approached us, her hair streaming on the wind, and her rich vermilion color dazzling over the white of her transparent skin, her dark eyes shooting back the golden rays of the sun. "She is magnificent!"

"As an Amazon, if she were large enough," replied Egremont with a slight sneer. "As a woman, or lady, she does not convey the type. But I know where I could find the model for a Ceres, or a Hebe, or a pure woman, if I wanted one," he continued, his almond eyes melting with a glance toward Rosie.

Kenmuir spun round on one heel, and whistled a stave of "Captain Jinks," commencing in the middle. Zanita rode up, jumped off, and threw the bridle to Egremont, whilst she walked on with Rosie, admiring the gigantic size of the ferns, making inquiries as to the exact spot where they grew.

Why should a thunderbolt have fallen amidst that pleasant group—why should each and all have been stricken down! I have seen a group of luxuriant oaks and pines embedded in sylvan grottoes of moss, and perfumed with violets, shriveled by a streak of lightning, and turned to ashes.

Why, why? But the answer cometh not.

CHAPTER XX.

A NEW BUD.

THE AUTUMN WAS CREEPING fast upon us in all its regal splendor: the oak-trees had here and there a bough of cream-tinted leaves, the maples were already every shade of yellow, and the wild cherry was gorgeous in crimson. The flowers had nearly all disappeared, excepting that an occasional patch of white violets enameled the mossy soil; but, *en revanche*, the ferns which had grown two or three yards high, were waving in a complete sea of burnished gold, flooding the whole Valley on every side. Whether it was mere force of contrast or actual reality, the rocks seemed to have become more dazzlingly white, and glittered in the sun, while the "Sentinel" shone like a white marble tombstone. The sky was of the deepest blue, and the hushed surging of the wind gave a solemn tone to the whole landscape. I was sitting beneath the great oak that overshadowed the cottage, trying to whittle out the sides of a pincushion from the yellow pine bark,—the cushion itself to be formed of *Sequoia*, which rivals emery for that purpose,—when my attention was attracted by the crunching of dried ferns. I looked up and saw Egremont approaching. He raised his hat as he caught my eye, but his face was grave and settled.

"I hope you are well this morning, and feel compassionate," he said, leaning his graceful person against the trunk of a tree adjacent to my seat.

"Quite well; but why compassionate?" I asked.

"Because I want you to be pitiful to me this morning. I have come to throw myself upon your mercy, and to ask your help to do what is right. I know I deserve all sorts of censure, but let me implore you not to be too angry with me. I am as much a victim to myself as to circumstances."

He pulled a handful of the gilded ferns and threw them at my feet; then sliding softly down and leaning upon his arm looked into my face with one of those sweet, imploring smiles which I believe no woman in the world could resist, unless it might be Nell.

"I want you to talk to me," he said, "as though I were your only son, and that I had no other friend in the world but my mother."

"What is it, Egremont?" I said, entirely mollified, as I placed my hand on his fair forehead.

"I have made a great mistake," he said, "one that may appear wicked, but yet a mistake. I never loved your adopted daughter, Zanita, never can love her, and if I had to force myself to make the attempt, should hate her with all the vehemence of my nature."

While he spoke his color came and went so rapidly that I dreaded he might take a fit. He clutched at the ferns and tore them in morsels; a fierce glare shot from under his long dark lashes which gave him the look of a maniac.

"There is really no occasion for this excitement, Egremont," I said. "Neither Zanita or any of us wish for any further intimacy between you."

"She does!" he said bitterly. "She cares no more for me than I do for her; and yet"—he cried, springing suddenly to his feet and poising himself in a defiant attitude—"her ambition would induce her to marry me for whom I am!" A light of scornful grandeur seemed to illumine his whole person, and I thought I had never seen so haughty and noble looking a man.

This speech naturally roused all my latent curiosity, and the mystery of Zanita's adherence to him.

"Have you then favored Zanita with more information than myself, in whom you profess to place confidence?" I asked, coldly.

"Shootee one big bird!" said a voice close to us. We both started. Fortunately it was only Mu-wah, the Indian, with an immense grouse as large as a hen, which he had just shot. I had necessarily to admire it, and then sent him off with it to the kitchen.

"But I have something more to tell you," continued Egremont, when we were alone.

"If I was so carried away by anger about Zanita, it is because I love Cozy. I worship her, and cannot live without her. In soul and person she is divine. The light of her blue eyes' radiance is all I need now and evermore. Do," he said, seizing both my hands and upsetting my pincushions, bag, and joinering tools,—"do give me one other chance in life! Do let me have her! for it all depends on you, and your whole life and her's shall bless this one moment of trusting. Tell me that you will regard me as you did before that fiend-like beauty crossed my path; let me start afresh with Cozy, as though all this delusion had never begun, and I will prove to you, in five minutes, that you have no reason, in a practical, worldly point of view, to refuse me; and you will not refuse to make us all happy, and everything shall be made clear, and all your speculations as regards me," he said, with a half smile, "set at rest forever."

He held my hand nervously with one of his, while he thrust the other into his breast, where he grasped something which he seemed only waiting to produce.

"I am not surprised," I said, "for I have noticed your feelings toward Cozy, but she is far too young; and it fills me with dismay to observe this passion you have conceived for these two poor children. Do you not think you are more their evil genius than they yours?"

"Not Cozy's," he said quickly. "It would be a delight to be torn by wild animals for Cozy's sake. She is the perfection of all that is lovely and exquisite, and I would rather be thrown from the top of Tu-tock-a-nu-lah than live without her. Tell me I may woo and win her; the rest of her life she shall tread on rose-leaves."

"I fear you have done that without leave," I said, gravely.

"Have I? Is she mine in heart?" he exclaimed, as his face glowed with fervent passion. "Great God be thanked!"

Ere I could open my lips to reply, a slight movement in the deep ferns arrested my attention. It was not Mu-wah this time, for the sun shone on the dark gleaming tresses of Zanita as she moved softly away on her hands and knees, very much with the motion of a bear. I caught Egremont by the arm and pointed to where the sun's rays fell on the shiny hair. He looked, reeled back against the trunk of the tree, and became as pale as death.

"She has heard every word," I said.

"She must have been there the whole time, and will be revenged on one of us," said Egremont, gloomily.

"You wrong her," I interposed. "She has never shown malice toward Rosie, and you can take care of yourself. But Zanita is not vindictive; she forgets too soon."

"Yes," he replied, "but her vengeance may be as rapid as her feelings."

I rose to leave him, feeling thoroughly discomfited by the morning's revelations.

"Tell me," he said, eagerly,—"tell me, may I hope? and, as regards myself, I will make everything satisfactory to you and Mr. Naunton."

"I cannot reply at once. I must have time for reflection. I will speak with you again in two or three days, provided you promise me you will make no positive advance to our dear little Rosie."

"It shall be exactly as you wish," he said, and bowed with that indescribable grace that was native to him.

I went to my room thoroughly bewildered and perplexed with contending emotions. Was it possible that after all he should turn out a fine character,—a man of position and fortune, perhaps a nobleman,—marry Cozy, make her happy, and a duchess? No man but an English nobleman had I ever seen wear such a look as he put on when he said,—"She would marry me for whom I am." Was it possible that Zanita, with her keen perceptions and vigorous intellect, had really fathomed the mystery and made up her mind to be a duchess? This seemed all absurd, yet the fact remained that here was a young man who had proposed to me for each of my adopted daughters, who pertinaciously persisted in concealing his position, family, and occupation; even now he asked my permission to woo my darling Rosie on the simple intimation that I shall be satisfied with all concerning him when he deigns to elucidate the question. Then arose the difficulty about the feelings of the two girls. Rosie was clearly in love with him in her gentle, delicate, caressing way. No man with a particle of tenderness and manhood could fail to appreciate the sweet, soft, affectionate, womanly nature of Rosie, let alone her dazzling beauty, which almost threw the brilliancy of Zanita into the shade. The effulgence of her blue eyes was truly, as he had said, irresistible, and the damask of her peach-like cheeks alluring to the touch; her full, rosy, laughing mouth would be sure to give her a dozen desperate lovers in any city to which she might be taken, who would only serve to tease and torment the child, for she had no ingredient of coquetry in her composition.

With Zanita, on the contrary, it was impossible to tell whether she was flirting or in earnest. So much was she a born actress that even I could not discover which was the play and which was the reality, and thus it defied my utmost skill to say if she did or did not like Egremont. Even in her escapade of the morning I vainly tried to determine whether she had been treating her imagination to the performance of a grizzly bear, or whether she had been maliciously and wickedly eavesdropping. I felt great reluctance to charge her wrongfully. If I mentioned the circumstance to her father he would be sure to adopt the hypothesis which favored Zanita, for he never could see a fault in her, and owing to his own frank and guileless nature could not be brought to realize the cunning of hers. "Her mother was as pure and open as day," he would argue, "and I am sure deceit is not one of my faults. Where can she have got it from? It cannot be a part of her nature."

This he repeated for the hundredth time, when, later on in the day I sought a private talk with him upon the welfare of the children and the present crisis of affairs.

"That is a psychological and ethnological question upon which I cannot precisely enlighten you, but there exists no doubt in my mind that Zanita is the child of some very remote ancestor, we will hope," I said, laughing, "and that her peculiar qualities are innate and not circumstantial. Everything that affection, example, practical or scientific training can do has been done, but all in vain; no effect has been produced upon her. She has no more conception of the beauty or righteousness of truth than she had when I first saw her as a baby. I never could make her love it, never teach her to admire it. She always liked fiction better than fact."

"That is so," replied Mr. Naunton. "She was always fond of the semblance of anything, and more delighted with the peeling of a fruit, put adroitly together, than with its unsullied bloom; and yet she is a great lover of nature, for see how she revels in the midst of it."

"I do not think it is love that stimulates her in anything," I replied. "The awe-inspiring, terrific grandeur of these mysterious rocks are congenial with her wild, daring imagination. She does not love their beauty, but glories in contending with their power. But to come to the practical question, What do you think ought to be done in the present emergency?"

"Well," said Mr. Naunton, stroking down his handsome beard thoughtfully, "I do not anticipate anything very serious will ensue. The cold weather will soon be upon us, and the first snow-storm will necessarily drive him out of the Valley. Zanita, I am sure, will not break her heart," said her father, smiling humorously—"that's one blessing! You see, madam, there is some consolation in that."

"Certainly," I replied, musingly; "but I never know what other worse thing she might not do, if seriously crossed in her plans or desires."

"O, she never has a plan, she is all impulse," said her father. "I wish to goodness she had!"

"Yes, her master of elocution tells me that if she would only carry her conception throughout the play, or even the character, she would make one of the finest actresses the world has ever seen. He says she has all the voluptuous grace of a 'Siddons,' with the weird power of 'Rachel.' But only fancy what she did at the private rehearsal we had among our friends. She had literally enraptured us all as *Lady Macbeth*, with her magnificent rating of her Lord, and when she came to the sentence, 'But screw your courage to the sticking point and we'll not fail,' she threw out a magnetic power enough to have swayed a kingdom, at which there was a unanimous burst of applause. She twisted her face to that elfish grimace she has, and stooped to tie bootlace, or garter, I really do not know which. The audience looked aghast for a moment, and then roared with laughter. The Professor of Elocution was furious, and declared that he would never give her another lesson, and my husband fears it would be quite unsafe to produce her before a real audience, as no reliance could be placed upon her not doing anything grotesque if the occasion offered."

Mr. Naunton cried out mirthfully,—"That is just like my Zanny. I fancy I see her do it. She never had the smallest sense of propriety, or of the fitness of things."

"We have digressed again," I said. "What do you think we are to do about Egremont and his offer to Rosie?"

"I would not do anything. I would just adopt Talleyrand's advice when consulted on a great crisis. He said, '*Ne faites rien.*' I don't want Egremont to marry either of my daughters. I don't quite fancy him for a son-in-law; he is not one of us; he is to me something 'uncanny.' He may be an artist, but I don't think it; he is on a different plane from anything we know in this country, and there is something about him as though he expected you to doff your hat and say 'Your highness' or 'Your grace.' "

"Just so," I remarked, "and however familiar you may become with him,—and you know I had him first as an amanuensis,—yet one never overcomes that sort of easy hauteur which surrounds him. He reminds me excessively of one of the royal dukes we chanced to meet travelling in Europe."

"No, no," resumed Mr. Naunton, after a pause, "we must just let him go about his business the end of this fall. My little Cozy does not want to leave her old father yet, and the child is too young to have formed any serious attachment."

Half a dozen yards from the window of the room where we sat, stood a gnarled and bowed tree, partially consumed by fire, which had left it jagged and picturesque, as only fire can chisel wood. It bore a fresco work of deep black charring, on the silver ground of the barkless trunk. One of its own mighty boughs, split from the junction, and fallen to the ground, had formed a perfect Gothic archway of some fifteen feet in height. A dead tree in most places is an unsightly object; but in the happy Valley even death is lovely. The oak leaves, in their sapless brown, are as beautiful as in their juicy green. The silver trunks of the denuded trees are as handsome as the golden bark of the yellow pine and unscathed *Sequoia*; and thus the archway, though in mouldering decay, was still rich in mellow coloring. Over it the trumpet honey-suckle hung a few bright flowers and variegated leaves,—for here nothing decays, it only assumes a new form. Just at this moment ap-peared under the archway, as if set in a frame, a picture of animate na-ture, that transfixed my gaze with admiration and anxiety. It was the figures of Cozy and Egremont standing together as only lovers stand. They were toying over a flower; and she was making some pretense at explaining its botanical properties; but it needed no diviner to find out that their thoughts were of each other, deeper and more intense than any subject of botany could inspire. Every now and then she would look right up into his face with those winning soft eyes, and the deli-cate blush which always hovered about her face when speaking emo-tionally. The sun's rays caught in the loose meshes of her hair and twined it into a halo of glory round her delicate head; her lips, like parted rose leaves, smiled ever as she spoke; the goddess of happiness sat enthroned upon her young face, which had never known a frown or a shadow since she had wept for her mother. How strangely has nature arranged these things. She seemed to possess, without an effort, all the lovable qualities her sister lacked; she had all the sweet reticence of modesty, combined with that gentle womanly yielding which makes a man believe such women angels. Egremont gazed upon her with ador-ing, reverential eyes; and the hot color came and went in alternate flashes beneath the transparent skin of his temples. But he would not have cast one shade of fear over that trusting face for the wealth of Golconda. He did not even attempt to touch the little dimpled fingers as they played about the petals of the flower; but he gazed on them longingly, and I half dreaded to see him snatch them, and press them to his lips. There was a subdued self-control about his whole demeanor, which contrasted forcibly with his abandon toward Zanita, and I could not help reflecting how much a man's disposition is formed by the woman he loves or who loves him.

"Look at that picture," I said, indicating them to Mr. Naunton. "Is it not exquisite? What a lovely couple they make."

"Very handsome," said he. "Only think of papa's 'chunck' having a lover to herself; for there is no mistaking that such he is."

"No, and I regret to see it. I very much fear they are both in earnest."

"Aye, they are young, they are young," he said, rising, and he left the room to look out some fishing tackle.

I hesitated whether or no to disturb them: I did not consider myself in duty bound to interfere with Rosie, as I should have done with Zanita, though I loved her fully as well; and her father seemed to think that matters ought to be allowed to take their course. Moreover, the picture possessed a charm for me that I hated to disturb. My eyes clung to it as though it were a last farewell look of some beloved object, and it was thus engraven indelibly on my mind, never to be effaced from that moment. It was not alone the exquisite grace and tenderness of the picture; but my heart seemed suddenly to yearn and weep over it. In that moment I felt I could forgive Egremont all his faults,—as one forgives the cold, mute face of the dead who have wrought us ill, although the stony lips ask it not, and were so defiant in life. As my eyes became humid with the big tears that filled them, the fair picture moved, and approached the little side window near which I was sitting. Egremont was speaking of his departure.

"When shall you have the first snow-storm?" he asked; "I shall have to leave you then or be a prisoner for the winter."

"O, that would be delightful," echoed Rosie in a joyous mellow tone. "The winter here is even more charming than the summer. You see all these rocks and mountains decked out with their choicest jewelry; every single ledge, crag, and projection has its share of gems, amethysts, pearls and rubies, and strings of opals suspended from cliff to cliff; then all the cedars and pines put on their furry white coats, and look so comfortable and happy, as though they dreaded no future storm thus clad; and all is so still and calm, that I have only to tread upon the crunching snow to make the most delicious harmonies. I often hear new tunes, that I can sing and play upon the guitar; and I will show you a thousand new pictures to paint."

Egremont beamed a glowing smile upon her.

"They would not let me stay all winter," he said sadly; "but you, Rosie, might come out with us. You have never left the Valley, never seen the great world and all the beautiful things which are in it. Would you not like to live in a splendid mansion, with frescoed walls, and marble pavements, and statues and vases all round, and glorious views from the windows of miles of green lawn, with the deer tamely grouping under the shadow of the wide-spread oaks; where the lakes are filled with gold and silver fish, so trusting that they will come and take the crumbs dropped from your hand; where there are gardens under glass, with every brightest plant, and flowers all through the winter; where a miniature world of brilliant-plumed birds will come at your call, and perch upon your finger; where the rich-toned voices of Italy come to warble to you, and the fine instrumentalists of Germany concert their grandest harmonies for your delight. Cozy, darling Cozy, will you not come to such a home and dwell there with me?" exclaimed he, with a gush of manly tenderness that made me tremble for our rose-bud.

A soft glow spread over her face for a moment, and then she looked up to him, her eyes like two blue violets melting in dew,—"Ah! do you live in such a lovely place? I should like to go, but," added she, "I should like to go anywhere with you, or stay here with you either."

"Always, Cozy?" he whispered, leaning over her with bated breath,—"forever, beauty?"

"Him catchee him horsee," cried Mu-wah, appearing on the scene.

"Well, put my saddle on," said Rosie, recovering herself, "and saddle the other for Mr. Egremont."

"Saddle him one other Miss Zany?" asked Mu-wah.

"No," said Egremont, decisively. "Excuse me," he said, turning to Rosie, "my interference; but I always feel so uncomfortable riding with Zanita. She is forever trying to break her own or some one's else neck. Tell me," he whispered, "what I asked you: will you go to the home I essayed to paint?"

"Should I have to leave father and aunty, and all of them?" sighed Rosie, a little dismayed.

"Dear child," he said, "do you remember your mother?"

"No, but I know all about her, and feel just as though I did."

"You know, then, that she left all behind to come into this wilderness with your father, when even her life was in danger from the Indians. Do you not believe that what your mother did was right?"

"O, indeed I do; papa always says that mamma was perfection."

"And you resemble her in every point," cried Egremont, tenderly; "so say you will come even before the first snow-storm."

"Is it very far?" asked Rosie, gradually yielding to her own heart and his importunity. "I am afraid papa would be so lonesome."

"He could rejoin us, and he would be so amused to see you in a long train-dress, and real jewels, instead of the frost ones you were describing; and we could give him plenty of fishing, and all the new books that are published."

I could not see Rosie's face; but I could imagine that some little glance of consent was given, for they moved away, and soon I heard their horses' feet.

CHAPTER XXI.

PEERING OVER THE EDGE.

HERE, THEN, WAS A DIRECT breach of his promise to me,—to allow affairs to remain *in statu quo*, until he heard from me. Yet he had acted with the same deliberate disregard of his word as in Oakland toward Zanita, and was urging Rosie to an immediate union, reckless of the effect upon her sister. To carry out the impulse of the moment seemed the sole aim and power of his character; there was no consistency in the basis. If he were sincere in the expression of his feelings when conversing with me, he showed himself the very opposite in his professions when he met with another.

I felt rather puzzled to guess the reason of their riding out together, for they had never done so before, Zanita having invariably been his riding companion,—Cozy going with him on the sketching expeditions, copying the same view, and, with his help, making almost as good a picture, for she had painted ever since she could hold a brush, and possessed admirable talent, inherited from her mother.

Nervous and excited with this momentous day, I betook myself to my good friend Kenmuir, at the saw-mill. "When your saw has cut through that log I want to have a chat with you," I said, and presently we were seated on the little platform, with the great amphitheatre of rocks around us in deep shade of cobalt blue. The nearer pine-trees were reflected with intense clearness of vivid green against the distant domes and pinnacles of the Valley. The air was fresh, though laden with odorous compound of bay and mint. There was always a solemn, sad sighing of the wind surging through the pines in this portion of the Valley, arising from the great current brought down through the trough of the Yo-semite Fall. To-day it seemed melancholy and almost wailing. "It sounds to me," I said, "like the wailing of Indian spirits over some funereal pyre."

"O, pshaw!" cried Kenmuir, "it is glorious! I love it! It fills me with rapture! It is the most perfect minor harmony that human ear ever heard! I fear you are not well if you feel so melancholy."

"I am mentally sick, that I admit, and so nervous I feel every moment as though some great calamity was about to befall us; as though the Sentinel might tumble over and crush us all."

"Let me see! Two thousand feet high, and calculating impetus of *débris*, would just reach us," laughed Kenmuir.

"Or a sudden waterspout," I continued, "burst over Yo-semite, as it did last year, when the water rose four feet in twenty minutes, and drown us!"

"Yes, but it did not drown *us*, for all that, last year, and might not this; and you would so enjoy it, for it was the most glorious thing I have ever witnessed. We heard a tremendous crash or explosion, as though a whole park of artillery had been fired, and the echo took it up, and repeated it from Tu-tock-a-nu-lah to Tis-sa-ack, for at least twenty seconds, and running out we saw the water leaping from rock to rock in a furious torrent, carrying down great pines (a hundred feet long) and boulders in its course, that were hurled over the top of the lower fall with such violence that they struck the giant trees growing at the foot and shivered them as if by a thunderbolt. The roar and booming was the grandest you ever heard, and the water rose in yon pool four feet in less than twenty minutes; but it did not destroy us, and your fears are quite imaginary. God has all these things in his fingers, and can take care of everything He has made."

I recapitulated to him the events of the day. He looked grave—a rare thing for him,—and seemed to come down to humanity with considerable pain.

"Man," he said, "is the only mistake, it seems to me, in the works of the Creator, and there does appear to be something radically wrong about him. It is strange to me if Zanita does not feel jealous and play them some trick. My poor Rosie! Rosie!" he said; "we shall have to be vigilant to shield her from any harm!"

"So she loves him," he said, with a sigh, after a long pause.

I could not help quickly regarding his face; there was a gentle regret upon it, as though some half-hope had faded out.

"At the risk of seeming inhospitable," he said, "the sooner you take Zanita out of the Valley the better. Perhaps Egremont will remain as long as the snow will permit him, or he may go out with you,—any way would answer,—but something must be done at once, or Zanita will torment them as sure as death. Their sketching excursions have not escaped her supervision, I know; she has often overhung a cliff where nothing but a squirrel would venture, to look at them under their umbrella; but, as you are aware, Egremont is not the man to take any freedom with a delicately refined girl like Rosie; he appreciates her too highly, and, I venture to say, her sister never saw a look or a movement to feed her jealousy; but she has watched them."

"How singular," I said, "for her to be jealous of a man she has refused and will not accept,—for I presume he was still following her when he came down here,—and if she had encouraged him, would never have thought of Rosie."

"It is not strange to me," he said. "Zanita never could love,—or even keep up the pretense of it, for long together; but she is gratified by attention, and strives to enthrall every one in her train. She chooses to rule and command. Don't you remember how proud and delighted she was, when a little girl, to lead that party of 'prospecting miners' up the Indian Cañon to Eagle's Point, and how angry she was with the one who stayed back to carry Cozy, and how she nearly killed him by rolling a piece of rock down upon him? I guess she feels much the same now, and, I rather think," he continued, "she has some high-fashioned notions about our friend being a great man in his own country, in which case she would make him marry her. She asked me the other day which was the greatest—an actress or a princess. I told her that, generally, the princesses were regarded as the highest, but that some actresses had been greater than any princess.

" 'How long would it take me to become such a one?'

" 'Eight or ten years.'

" 'O, bother!' she cried, and left me. I don't know what reason she has for not believing him to be an artist."

"He is very fond of it and very skillful, though it is strange that he did not mention his profession at first; but everything about him is strange, and everything about her goes by the rules of contrary," I said.

"The more reason," he answered, "that we should keep asunder these two remarkable freaks of human nature. Now you never see that amongst plants or trees; they grow in harmony together, and love each other's fellowship, and generally, if transplanted to a strange neighborhood, suffer long and bitterly, even if they do not pine and die. Moss is a most affectionate thing; it likes to cling and spread itself over the loved object. The giant, *Sequoia*, grow in family groups and frequent twins. Do you think if you cut one of those twins down the other would not pine and grieve? I know it would. But, here in human nature, two slim, beautiful young saplings, like Zanita and Egremont, fight and wrangle, and mar each other's symmetrical proportions, regardless of their mutual weal or woe. I can't understand it," said Kenmuir, "there's something radically wrong about human nature. I wish they were both safely out of this Valley."

"You are alarmed lest the Valley should be in any way injured by their contention," I observed, laughing.

"I should be sorry for them to injury the reputation of the Valley,— the noblest of the Lord's handiwork. For instance, I would not like any one to be killed here on these splendid rocks. I would not like them to spatter the blood, and dirt, and brains over this sublime coloring."

"O, do cease!" I exclaimed. "You have turned me so sick! How could you suggest such a horrid picture? My heart is quivering within me!"

"I am very sorry," he cried. "It was a mere fancy that rose before me as though I saw it. Pray forgive me! I ought to have remembered how nervous you are to-day."

"O, it's nothing!" I said, "mere weakness,—but I seemed to see the picture vividly, too."

"Let us talk of something more genial,—Rosie, for instance. Do you not think that her pictures are going to turn out real gems?"

"I do, indeed! I am going to take some of them to San Francisco, submit them to an artist, and dispose of them. It would be curious if the two sisters should distinguish themselves,—one as an artist, and the other as an actress."

At supper that evening Mr. Egremont did not join us, in fact he never did unless specially invited, for although Mr. Naunton in his hospitable way had asked him to make the cottage his home and the hut his lodging, he never paid a visit longer than a call unless so requested.

"Did you not ask Mr. Egremont to come to supper, Rosie?" I said, addressing her.

She blushed a sweet pink and answered, "I did not think of it, but I expected he would come."

After supper Zanita sat in the corner of the divan with her feet curled under her reading a book, the slight, habitual frown was rather more

marked than usual, and the lips were tightly compressed. It seemed
pitiful that a face so young and so beautiful should not enjoy more of
the sweet joyousness of youth; yet hers was a temperament constituted for suffering,—a disposition that was always chafed and restless;
her face in repose had ever a troublous expression, and all the enjoyment she knew was comprised in feverish excitement and in the accomplishment of some fierce design she had conceived, usually
bringing upon herself the antagonism of all around her. She naturally
made enemies instead of friends, and her own heart was inimical to her
surroundings, whether of man or beast. Poor, burning, sapless heart,
the milk of human kindness had never flowed through it to soften its
feverish intensity; it had never known the delights of affection or the
rapturous emotions of love, the tenderness of pity or the warmth of
sympathy. Ambition, strife, and dominion had possessed it from its
very cradle.

Zanita's pets had been her victims or slaves; her playmates, her tools
or servants; her relatives, the resources on whom she drew for her ne-
cessities, and when they ceased to fulfill that useful position they were
as nothing to her.

As these thoughts forced themselves upon me, my heart yearned
with compassion for the poor child, for it was not her fault, but her misfortune, that nature had dealt so hardly by her.

She was feeling more bitter and harassed to-night than usual; she
was aggravated by the loss of Egremont's attentions, even in the small
matter of taking a ride with Rosie; for the rides were part of her dominion, and although she had perversely chosen to make them distasteful
to him, she hated to have her rights abrogated,—she wished to command him with the power to pain unquestioned. She was now in the
throes of some new expedient to recapture his allegiance; and so self-
reliant and confident in her own power was she, and so unskilled in the
boundless tenacity of a real passion, that she had no other thought than
of reconquering the truant, rejected lover, and of bringing him again to
her feet.

It flashed across me also that memorable night, as I studied her
strange face, which had been a new volume for seven years to me, that
for one reason or other she would now marry him; perhaps he had daz-
zled her imagination with some ambitious picture of the future such as
he had drawn for Rosie, adapting the coloring to suit the taste of his

auditor, yet this hypothesis in no way sustained his indifference to the refusal of his offer and his present desertion.

Yet if she had resolved to marry him, as my convictions seemed to foreshadow, then would really come the tug of war. Would she control Egremont by her strong magnetic power, or would he, strengthened by a pure and holy love, adhere manfully and faithfully to the Rose-bud?

If he acted thus honorably, I thought I could respect him once more; but if, on the contrary, he should waver and yield to the fascination of Zanita and break our little angel's heart, I felt that I should lose all hope of the pair and renounce any further interest in the future Mrs. Egremont. But my present wish and hope was that he would take himself out of the "Life Drama;" altogether withdraw his thread from the woof of these two lives, and leave us to weave it out at our leisure for the greater good: "Mais l'homme propose, et Dieu dispose." All works together for a good end, our minister used to say when he found that any ends he had proposed for Zanita were utterly futile.

Rosie brought out her guitar, and throwing the blue ribbon over her graceful little shoulders, sang in her rich mellifluous soprano voice, "Ah scordali di me;" so clear and round was every note, so sweet and thrilling, that no doubt it would penetrate in delicious cadences to the little hut bathed in moonlight, where her lover watched and sighed for her; doubtless she thought so too, for a tender pathos was breathed in the refrain of "scordali di me," which came fresh from the young heart overbrimming with its first love.

Once she stepped quietly to the open door and peeped out wistfully. O, that yearning look for the beloved form for which we hunger! How many starve to death when the last look has been taken! Poor little Cozy, she looked into the moonlight in vain.

"Are you reading a tragedy, Zanita," asked her father, "that you look so stern?"

" 'Parisina,' father; but Cozy's banjo is spoiling the effect."

Zanita was no musician, and cared nothing for music.

"Cozy is more given to romance than tragedy," mused the father.

Kenmuir stepped in with the good news that he had seen an Indian who had met the Professor on his way into the Valley, and he might be expected in a day or two. Kenmuir made Rosie sing more love-songs, and at last the evening broke up, all feeling happy; the former whispered to me as he bade me good-night, " 'All's well that ends well,' you see."

CHAPTER XXII.

THE CREEPING SHADOW.

EVERYTHING WENT ON as usual next day until about noon, when I called to Zanita to come and read to me.

"Shall I do, aunty?" cried Rosie, starting up cheerfully.

"No, my dear; I want Zanita to rehearse with me. See if you can find her."

Cozy set off, but returned in ten minutes, saying she could not find her.

I went on with my work, thinking she would come in presently. At the end of two hours I again inquired,—"Where do you think Zanita can be gone, Cozy?"

"I don't know, I am sure, aunty. I have searched all her haunts, and she is not with papa, fishing. She may be gone for a ramble,—*camping*, perhaps,"—said Rosie, laughing, "as she always would do when we were children."

"She is the strangest girl for doing odd things that ever was," I exclaimed, going on with my work.

At our dinner hour I sent Rosie to look for Kenmuir. Probably Zanita had gone off on some expedition with him.

No, he had not seen her. "Stay!" he said: "did she wear a white dress?"

"No, a pink one. Perhaps you don't know the difference," said Rosie, laughing.

"Perhaps I do, Miss Pert! I thought I saw a piece of the same dress Zanita wore last night up among the ceanothus bushes, like a white fleecy cloud. I like that dress," said Kenmuir, "it is so much more graceful than these new-fangled fashions. I thought it was Zanita up there, though I did not see her face, and then I saw Egremont climbing up shortly after."

"Has he returned to dinner?" I asked.

"No," said Kenmuir. "Now Rosie, to satisfy yourself that I do know red from white, go and see if you can find the dress Zanita wore last night."

Rosie trotted off and returned laughing. "Her white dress is nowhere to be found, and her pink one lies on the floor just as though she had jumped out of it."

Kenmuir seized Rosie by the hand and imprinted a kiss upon the golden little curls on her forehead, saying,—"If you dare to question my knowledge of colors again I will cut off one of these."

"Then she has gone with Egremont," I resumed. "What on earth could possess her to put on a mull muslin dress to climb rocks and manzanita bushes? She will come home with it in ribbons, as of old." I spoke angrily, for I could not conceal my vexation that she had already commenced her strategic movement. I exchanged glances with Kenmuir, and we walked apart from Rosie.

"It is as I told you," he said; "she has made up her mind to have him or she would never discipline herself to sitting upon one rock all day watching him sketch."

"You are right," I replied, "and directly the Professor arrives we will leave, though we have to camp out at Mono again, and Mr. Naunton must do the best he can about Rosie and Mr. Egremont, for he is sure to remain behind if I carry Zanita off *nolens volens*."

Evening approached, and there was no appearance of the excursionists.

"I should not be a bit surprised," said Rosie, "if Zanita made Mr. Egremont camp out, just by way of mocking at his discomfort, whilst she will throw herself upon the bushes and sleep as though upon a bed of down."

"In a white mull muslin dress!" I exclaimed, irritably. "It will not look much like down to-morrow morning."

Rosie and Mr. Naunton laughed at this imaginative picture of Zanita next morning, but as daylight receded, and the moon rose, I became more nervous.

"I do not think you need be alarmed, aunty," said Rosie; "Zanita never had an accident, with all her hair-breadth escapes of flood and field, and if anything had happened to Mr. Egremont," she continued, her color rising at the mention of his name, "she would have been down ere this for help. I think there is no doubt now that she insistedupon camping out just to torment him, aunty, and show how brave she is."

"It is very wrong of her, and she shall never go out again with Mr. Egremont."

"It is too bad of her never to think how alarmed you would be, but I am rather glad she is not here to-night for I want to tell you a big secret, aunty," said Rosie, in a tremulous voice. She threw her arms around my waist, and laid her blushing cheeks upon my shoulder.

"What is it, darling?" I said, caressing her glossy hair.

"I want to tell you what Mr. Egremont said to me, I have been trying all day to do so but could not get courage."

She told me what I already knew, and then—how strangely events repeat themselves—I asked her the very same question I had put to her sister about the same man,—

"Do you love him, Rosie?" and the trembling answer came, "O, so much! aunty. I hope it does not seem ungrateful, but he is more than all the world to me—dearer than existence; and life without him would not be worth anything."

"And would you like to leave us all and become his wife?"

"Dear aunty! I should grieve to leave you and papa, and Zanita, and Kenmuir, and the Valley, but I would rather die than not be his wife when he wishes me."

I took the soft velvety cheeks between my hands and kissed them. I then said,—"Has Zanita ever spoken to you in confidence about Mr. Egremont?"

"No, aunty! you know she never gives me her confidence in anything. Why?"

"Because, my dear, perhaps she loves him too!"

"Zanita!" cried Rosie, with a start of surprise. "She never cares very much for any one, you know, aunty."

"No, dear, but she likes admiration, which to her is the same thing, and I think you ought to know that Mr. Egremont admired her once, when first he knew her."

"I am not surprised at that," she said; "Zanita is very handsome, and talented, and quite bewitching, when she likes,—but that would not trouble me. She intends marrying a prince,—she said so in her sleep one night,—and when I tease her about it she gets angry."

"I have reason to believe," I said, "that he came into the Valley on her account, and I feel, dear, that, for the sake of your happiness, it is somebody's duty to ascertain how he stands with Zanita. I cannot believe that a man can love two such opposite characters at the same time, and to be alternating from one to the other is simply disgraceful."

"O, aunty! you cannot surely look in his face and think him guilty of such conduct."

"My dear, that face is the greatest puzzle I ever met with in my life, and makes me inclined to throw physiognomy to the winds. If he should turn out dishonorable, and a hypocrite, I should never trust another beautiful face as long as I live. What does he mean by going out with Zanita and remaining out the whole day?"

"Aunty," laughed Rosie, "you seem to forget that Zanita may have insisted upon going with him, just for a freak, as she does everything else, without thinking or caring what the consequences may be."

"But he could return in proper time. It is incomprehensible, and, like everything else concerning him, bears the imprint of suspicion."

After a little more chat Rosie retired to her room, and seeing a light in Kenmuir's cabin, I walked over, for I was too uneasy and filled with vague conjectures, to sleep. The moon shone in mystic splendor, limning out distinctly the grandly fantastic rocks of Hum-moo, oxidizing its gigantic pilaster and minarets, like some wondrous temple erected for the worship of a fabulous humanity,—on the scale of the mastodon, still found in the iron grasp of the granite gorges. The opposite side of the Valley being in shade, was one solid mass of eberus, but from underneath the pines, obelisks sent long straight shadows across the meadows, raying them in alternate bars of light and dark.

As I crossed the Mercede, by the rustic bridge, the high ridges of To-coy-ee and Low-oo-too were clearly defined in the crystal waters,—the cedars on their summits transversed and standing on their topmost branches, pointed with feathery sprays to the lozenge-shaped moon, shining like a great Kohinoor diamond in the reflected cerulean vault. The owl's plaintive cry was reverberated from two antique cedars at either side of the bridge. They were pleading with each other over some momentous crisis in their lives.

"Doo-doo-doo!" sighed one.

"Doo-doo-doo!" echoed the other.

Birds and beasts, as well as men, have their troublous times, I ween, and their plans "oft gang aglee!" though Kenmuir seems to think it is only man who has got astray out of his orbit, or the ends for which he was created. My own idea, in which I agree with the Professor, for once, is, that nothing is lost or gone astray in the universe of creation,—that men and mountains, all fulfill their tasks as appropriately as mosquitoes and mastodons.

The Professor laughs at the idea of "mistakes," "blunders," and "miscalculations," and vexatious regret at having created this or that, and throwing it away in disgust. Whatever is, was intended to be, is our theory, and we have to make the best of it, unable at the moment to decide whether it will be good or bad in the long run.

I tapped at Kenmuir's window as I passed. He was sitting writing in company with two tree-frogs, who evidently took an interest in his literary labors. He opened the door for me.

"I half expected you," he said; "I know you are anxious. Come in and take a seat."

"No, thank you," I answered, as I noticed a third guest, in the shape of a pet rattlesnake, curled up in the corner over a watercourse which Kenmuir had encouraged to flow through his abode, in order to refresh some ferns which also had domiciled themselves under his roof,—"no, thank you, I would rather sit outside in the moonlight."

He pulled his old sheepskin chair to the step. Hung around the cabin were Egremont's small oil-paintings of the various points of the Valley. Somehow the sight of them brought a dimness to my eyes, the shadow of approaching wretchedness was so heavy upon me.

"I am sorry to see you so overcome," said Kenmuir, noticing my emotion; "you may need all your courage before long."

"And shall show more than I evince now!" I said. "What do you think of this state of affairs?"

Kenmuir settled his back against the door-sill, and looking steadily down into my face said,—"I fear they are off!"

"Eloped!" I exclaimed, springing to my feet.

"That's the proper expression, I suppose. I mean that."

"But they have no horses; they cannot have walked out of the Valley!"

"Not likely! but she would catch some stray horses, and they would ride bare-backed as far as Galen's Rancho, and then get saddles and go on to Mariposa, where they could be married."

"Good Heavens!" I exclaimed, stamping my foot. "How I shall hate him if he has done that! I would rather he had pitched from the top of Tis-sa-ack. What are your grounds for such a supposition?"

"Well," said Kenmuir, "they are these: if they had camped we should most likely see their fire, and I have been round looking. They are not out at Old Methley's, for I have been there; and then Zanita is far too good a mountaineer to camp out this weather without plenty of blankets and food. Now Egremont had nothing but his sketch-box when I saw him, and it is not likely he would allow her to carry a burden like an Indian squaw."

"She took nothing from the store closet," I put in, "because I had the keys all the morning."

"No," continued Kenmuir, "I will venture to say they are not camping out. If it were any one else but Zanita they might have lost their way; but she knows every foot of the ground, and would come back by this moonlight as easy as not. That they would remain out all night is too improbable, and I am quite certain they have not."

"No," I said, "that seems conclusive, and besides, Mr. Egremont would never dare appear before me again after such an outrageous proceeding; and I do not believe that Zanita, with all her influence, could make him do it. You do not suppose they have gone to Radd's," I suggested.

"No, there is nowhere to sleep there unless they turned Radd and his wife out; and Zanita would never put herself under the fire of Mrs. Radd's battery for a whole night: I am morally certain of that."

"Then what do you think ought to be done?"

"Do you want to stop the marriage?" he asked, hesitatingly.

"Why certainly I do; they are acting no better than two lunatics, and would tear each other to pieces before the honeymoon was over. Why, he expressed the utmost contempt and bitterness for her yesterday morning. I believe he must be subject to aberration of mind, and she is acting on some wild fancy; but she is under age, and we can surely prevent this marriage, and I shall have no hesitation in doing so: it is my duty."

"Well, then," cried Kenmuir, "I will saddle my Bucephalus, and meet them at Mariposa to-morrow morning, for they cannot have gone farther, and I know Judge Macmach well enough to get him to stay the proceedings."

"When will you start?" I asked. "It is no good consulting Mr. Naunton; he never has seemed to live clearly in this world since his wife's death."

"I am ready this moment, when I have taken the precaution to prevent the frogs continuing my manuscript with their legs dipped in the ink." He had been careful to tether a horse up, foreseeing that he might need one.

He was off in a few minutes. I listened to the horse's feet, as they resounded in the stillness for miles down the Valley.

When he was gone my heart sank lower and lower. I did not expect he would find them, although I coincided with him in his solution of their disappearance; yet I did not realize it in my heart. I am a woman of strong presentiments. I knew she could not have carried him off against his will, and yet they were gone together,—gone never to return it seemed to me; every hour appeared to make this more certain.

I put my ear to the ground. I could distinctly hear the scraping of the horse's hoofs over the rocky track round the Po-ho-no Fall. I almost wished I had started with him; it would have been less trying than this nervous waiting, this exhaustive suspense. In action, however terrible, I never feel that sickening dread which so overpowers me in moments of anxious anticipation. There is certainly no wisdom in meeting trouble half-way; but if I am sure that misfortune is approaching, I always feel inclined to rush *en avant* and contend for every inch of ground. To stand still, or even to fly, is equally impossible for me.

As sleep was quite out of the question, I resolved to make myself some coffee, write a little note to Rosie, telling her where I was gone to, rouse the Indian, Mu-wah, to accompany me, start for the Upper Valley, and put Radd on the search.

But the Indian was nowhere to be found, and I had to go in search of Rosie's pony and saddle him myself. I debated whether to rouse Mr. Naunton, and ask him to join me; but finally decided not to do so, as he would scarcely take my view of the importance of the case, and would probably retard me. Apathy and a good deal of indifference had grown upon him with years, and the death of his wife, who had seemed to be the better half of his soul; and, moreover, his faith in Zanita as a mountaineer was unbounded. That she could be lost, stolen, or strayed in the mountains, seemed to him an utter impossibility.

"You might search a week in these rocks in vain," he had said, when I had proposed seeking for her, "and she would walk in at the end of that time as cool as though she had only been out an hour. She is a real mountain child, the true daughter of Ah-wah-nee; she will never be otherwise, and it is useless to fret about her. She will be home probably by moonlight, and if not, by sunrise, and if not, to-morrow or the next day; but she must be let to come her own way."

175

I have often thought there was nothing so exhilarating as a ride in the early morning in the mountains alone. The freshness of Nature seems to descend over all, and fold us in her unsullied embrace; the nobility of the whole scene animates us, and dissipates those petty troubles which often pester us and destroy our happiness, as mosquitoes under a net defy the arts of the great god Somnus.

As I entered the sylvan tangle of the forest, the South Fork Cañon was dim in the matin twilight; but soon became roseate with incipient day, and ere I had ascended far up the rocky path which leads to the foot of the falls, bright flashes of slanting light shot through the trees, coruscating in golden beams, and when I emerged from the umbrose avenue of knotted cedars, the sun hung like a ball of resplendent fire between the rival domes of Tis-sa-ack and Tah-mah.

When I had reached the crest of the mountains, whence I could command a view of the two falls, and look down on the Py-wy-ack, whilst remaining on a level with the foot of the Yo-wi-ye, I drew my rein, and, as Kenmuir would say, "Let the grandeur and sublimity of God's untouched, unsullied creation permeate through every fibre of my existence." I had need of the sustaining power of the clear surging wind,—of the strength of the majestic cascade that rolls on from all time to eternity,—to crave the placitude of the mute moss that girdled with many rings the *pinus ponderoso* in sunshine and shower, and snow and heat, and cling to them in silent tenderness.

"Nature is a stern philosophic religionist.

'Thus it is. Thus it is best,' is her motto."

My soul took in this supremely divine message and felt composed.

Farther on a little bird caroling joyously, as though it would burst its little throat in its vigorous evolutions, gave me the idea to rouse the echoes. Possibly Zanita or Egremont might respond.

Upon the second trial I received an answer other than the echo. Alas! it was a male voice, and a baritone, whilst I knew Egremont's was a tenor, from his having joined with Rosie in duets.

I kept up the communication, in some vague hope that it might bring good news, and in the space of about ten minutes Rollo came bounding up to me; then I knew his master was not far distant, and shortly Radd appeared waving the hat with the torn brim, which, like the tower of Pisa, was always falling but never fell.

He welcomed me with a great display of gladness,—

" 'Hail Aurora, Goddess of the Morn,
    Whose rosy fingers ope the gates of day,'
"to thee I pay my *devoir.*"

"Mr. Radd," I replied, in plain prose, "I was on my way to see you, but I must rest here. I want you to make me a fire, and warm this coffee, and to have a very serious talk with you."

Radd looked into my face, read there my anxiety, and was silent. Gathering a few sticks, my coffee was soon warm, and sitting upon a mossy knoll at the foot of a wide-spreading evergreen oak, I made him my *confidante* as to the loss of Zanita and Egremont.

"We will hope it is not a tragedy, madam," he said softly,—and his face spoke that deeper sensitive sympathy which made me pity the husband of Nell,—"but unless it turns out as you fear, a wedding, I am almost afraid."

"O, a wedding," I interrupted him, "would be the greatest tragedy of all."

"Greater than death?" he hazarded, looking at me carefully.

I shrank a little from this fearful alternative. "Why," I asked, "do you put it so?"

"Because, madam, though I would not pain you by a heedless thought, yet you should not lose sight of the fact that the beautiful daughter of Ah-wah-nee has slept upon her mother's bosom too often, not to know that her mull muslin dress, as you term it, would be frozen about her at this season. Hence she has either got out of the mountains, as you say, for a purpose, or she is,—" and he stopped short and picked at the torn rim of his hat.

My eyes watched it, and thought it would come off; but my heart stood still, and I gasped out, "She is—what?"

"Returned to the bosom of her *mater naturæ,*" he said solemnly.

My breath came tightly for a moment. "Let us hope not," at length I said, pushing the horrid phantom from me.

"They have not been up here," he said,—"at least not through the Upper Valley; but they may have gone by Mono, and every inch of the road shall be searched this day; you shall not be kept in suspense any way. Have you anything about you that belonged to either of them? Rollo will find whatever he has once had a scent of, and if he gets on their trail will not leave it until he has run them down."

"There is a handkerchief I picked up a little way from Kenmuir's hut; it is marked 'Egremont:' " I handed it to him.

He looked at it carefully. "It is very fine," he remarked. "What is that square hole cut out over his name for? There has been something above: I can see the ink marks on the other side."

"Very curious," I said; "but I cannot divine why it was cut out."

"Well, madam, if you will return into the Valley, lest the family of our mountain sylph become alarmed, I will undertake to search all this portion of the rocks, and either find them or give you a positive assurance that they are not there."

Thus, without the trial of encountering Mrs. Nell, I wended my solitary way back again, Rosie's pony nothing loth to make such a short day of it.

CHAPTER XXIII.

OVER THE BRINK.

As I REACHED THE COTTAGE I heard Mr. Naunton's voice, exclaiming, "Where in the mischief are all the folks gone? Surely the fairies have been amongst us and spirited them away! There is Mu-wah off now, and Mrs. Brown, and Kenmuir, and only Cozy and myself left."

"Here I am!" I cried, riding up.

"Well, well," exclaimed Mr. Naunton, "wonders will never cease! So you have been for a matinal ride. Bravo!"

"Zanita returned?" I asked.

"Not yet. I am expecting her every moment."

"But where do you imagine she is?" I exclaimed, half provoked at his indifference.

"Well," he said, "it would take a great deal of imagination to say the identical spot where she may be, but if Mr. Egremont were not with her I should not take the trouble to think about it; but I do not exactly like her being away with him so long. I hope they have not found their way to any of the ranchos or settlements—it will cause such a talk. But I should think Mr. Egremont had more sense than that."

Here Rosie flew out and gave me a warm, rosy kiss. "I declare, aunty, I had become desperately alarmed about every one disappearing in such a mysterious way. I began to think there was some awful catastrophe about to peril the Valley, and that the Indians' evil spirit had come to assert his reign. But where is Kenmuir? I cannot find him anywhere."

"He has gone on the Mariposa trail, fearing they may have met with some accident," I answered, evasively,—for I could not wound Rosie by the dread suspicion.

"I don't see how they could manage an accident on that road, and without horses too," said Mr. Naunton, "unless they chose to jump over. There is no place where they could fall down that I know of."

"Do, aunty, come and take some breakfast, for you look as though you had not slept all night. Indeed, I do begin to feel very uneasy," she said, nestling close to me. "As papa says, if Zanita were alone I should not fear, for she knows exactly how to take care of herself; but Mr. Egremont would never remain out all night, I am sure, and must be withheld from returning by some unforeseen accident or misfortune."

Here old Methuselah came in to inquire if the young lady had returned.

"No," said Mr. Naunton, putting the best face upon the matter, "but we are expecting her in hourly."

"Because," continued the old man, "I think I can do a step or so of a score miles in the service of our Queen of the Valley, for never was a more daring, fearless mountaineer than that child, whose foster-mother was the great Yo-semite. Well," he said, diving inconsequently into his memory,— "there's the Duchess of Argyle,—called the 'Beautiful Duchess,'—who carried all the elections with her prowess, who won the wager with the Prince Regent, to raise a regiment in a shorter time than his Royal Highness, and won it, too, by giving every volunteer a kiss; then there is Mademoiselle Théroigne, who headed the populace of Paris, and rode on the cannon to Versailles. And to go back out of our own day: there was Joan of Arc; then, in semi-fact and fiction, there is the 'Daughter of the Regiment,' and 'Lord Ullin's Daughter.' But I'll back our 'Daughter of Ah-wah-nee, or the Great Yo-semite,' against them all. She can ride a wild horse, or shoot a grizzly, snare a skunk, catch a coyote, with any man in the Valley."

"Grizzly!" exclaimed Rosie, turning pale. "Ah, I never thought of that! Supposing grizzly has killed them! They had no arms."

"A grizzly!" echoed Mr. Naunton, contemptuously. "Why Zanty would be half-way up a tree before a grizzly could say Jack Robinson."

We all laughed; but mine was a mere catenation. I was thinking all the time of what other means could be devised to expedite the discovery for weal or woe. A silent inquisition of memory was rapidly going on through every circumstance and event, since the fatal meeting of these two exceptional persons in my husband's study; seeking vainly to detect a clew to the fearful climax which seemed impending, or to find some evidence which, followed, might lead up to the explanation of the mystery. More definitely asserting itself was an eager peering of the spirit into each ravine, and rocky defile or tangled glade. The impatient, palpitating soul could ill wait the tardy movements of the body, but was away over the distant mountains, scouring the Valley and austere heights, penetrating each umbrageous nook and dell, skimming down the rippling streams, where the cool waters might have tempted the fugitives to linger, glancing into every granite cave and under the tufts of plume-like ferns and drooping lichens.

It has always been to me a subject of speculation whether in this mysterious pilgrimage of the spirit out of the body it actually discerns tangible objects as revealed to the physical; whether in this intense mental search for Zanita it would recognize her presence, should she be on the spot it visited. We say, quite commonly, "O, I had lost an arti-cle, and could not find it for several days. I had an idea it was so and so, and sure enough! found it where I thought." Is it not possible the spirit messenger had searched it out?

Had Zanita been left behind, her prescient intuition would have discovered Egremont, and the latter appeared to have some kind of prevision by which he could sift out her hidden whereabouts. But my spirit wandered in vain, and saw them not. A dark cloud had fallen be-tween our worlds and parted us forever.

It must not be supposed that I trusted to this speculation alone. It was far too chimerical for the present absolute emergency.

So I quickly drew Methuselah on one side and expressed to him my fears that the young people had met with some serious accident; that they might be so injured as to be unable to move; and that I considered it necessary every exertion should be made to rescue them upon this supposition, for the thought of their lying wounded, without succor, was too horrible to dwell upon.

The old giant perfectly agreed with me, and arming himself with a stout hook and coil of rope, set out upon an exploration.

I began to calculate with Rosie what was the earliest time at which Kenmuir could return.

"If he went as far as Mariposa," she said, "besides scouring the country round, it would be a good hundred miles, there and back, to say nothing of the gyrations round to the different settlements, an-other thirty or forty. I fear we cannot look for him back to-night."

We went into Zanita's room to try to discern any indications of her having contemplated a longer absence, but all was as usual there. Her pink dress hurriedly thrown off, her book half open,—pencil and paper lying in it where she was making notes,—the last word half completed. That word was "Treachery!" The table stood underneath the window, and from it was visible Kenmuir's hut and the path leading to the great dome. She had doubtless seen the figure of Egremont depart, and had, in her impulsive way, resolved to go with him, and hastily changed her dress to the one she knew he admired, snatched her garden hat from the peg, where part of the lining still hung, and raced after him.

The appearance of her room was conclusive to my mind that there had been no premeditation. What she had succeeded in accomplishing afterward still remained wrapped in shadow. The marriage theory began to fade away, and my hopes from Kenmuir's journey to ebb low. The minutes passed like hours, and it seemed a whole week since I had given up expecting them the night before, and next to impossible that Kenmuir had been gone only twelve hours.

Weary and feverish I lay down and tried to sleep, but it was useless. My messenger was still out with the search-warrant,—now escalading cliffs impossible for humanity to have trodden, now sweeping under the falls where it would have been submerged and carried over the cataracts.

"Rosie!" I called,—unable to bear the supposition alone,—"do you think it possible they could have ventured too near to the fall?"

"I do not think it probable. I hope not!" said Rosie. "Mr. Egremont is never fool-hardy, and always tries to prevent Zanita from perpetrating these reckless exploits. No," continued poor Rosie, whose joyous face began to assume a pitiful look of a baby about to cry,—"I am afraid if they are injured it must be from the falling of a rock, either from under or upon them. I could not bear to entertain the thought at first, but it is gradually taking fast hold upon me." And she raised her violet eyes to the adamantine fortress in front of her with a sad, appealing look.

I had just closed my eyes again when she exclaimed,—

"Why here is Rollo coming up the path at full speed with something in his mouth. O, aunty dear, look! What is it?"

I sprang to my feet. Up came Rollo with the most bustling importance, wagging his tail, shaking his head, and wriggling his body as though he were conscious of being the most welcome guest and of rendering the greatest service. "If ever a dog rightly earned his dinner, that dog is myself," he appeared to say, as he delivered up to us the object he carried.

It was a piece of canvas, and although torn and scratched was evidently an oil-painting.

"It is Mr. Egremont's last sketch!" cried Rosie, turning white, "and O! is that blood upon it?" And ere I could catch her she had swooned away. I called loudly for help. Chang-Wo, the cook, appeared, fortunately carrying a pitcher of water. I took it from him and sprinkling it upon Rosie sent him for some brandy.

Rollo stooped over her and licked her face, much bewildered at the result of his achievement. She was soon conscious again, and the big tears rolling down her face.

"Courage, my darling! you must nerve yourself now, for there is much to be done. Thank God, we have a clew at last!"

"Where is Mr. Naunton, Chang-wo?"

"Him away, gone!" quoth Chang, in his monosyllabic style.

"Where?"

"Away! takee him long stick, takee him long rope, away!" and he pointed to the mountains.

"Poor papa!" cried Rosie, "he has really become alarmed; there must, then, be actual danger."

We examined the sketch together. It represented the half dome of Tis-sa-ack, and the point of the Clouds' Rest.

"Do you know it, Rosie?" I asked.

"O yes," she replied, "I was with him when he began it! I have the fellow copy on my easel."

"I am surprised he did not ask you to go with him to finish it. O, how I wish that your father or the Professor were here, for something must be done at once. Rosie, have you the courage to go with me?"

"Yes, aunty! I know the exact spot."

In another minute we had saddled the horses and were off at a brisk canter, Indian file, Rollo ahead, followed by Rosie and myself.

About three miles up the Valley Rollo diverged and made as for his own home.

"Rollo! Rollo! that is not the way," cried Rosie.

The dog hesitated, wagged his tail, and resumed his way.

"He wants us to go home with him. Never mind! push on, Rosie, for you know the spot."

Rollo stopped, looked wistfully after us, came slowly back a piece, stopped again, then took his own way, full gallop.

We were soon on the site whence the sketch had been taken. Rosie sprang from the pony.

"Here it is!" she said. "I remember it so well!"

"And there are evident marks of his having been here."

"I think these are our tracks," said Rosie, examining. "O yes!" she cried, and burst into an agonized sob.

ZANITA

I looked, and there in the disintegrated, fine granite was written the word "Cozy."

Poor child! I took her in my arms and kissed her softly.

"Do not grieve for this sign of his love. They have not been here or it would have been effaced. So let us go. I wish we had kept Rollo, for he would have guided us to where he found the sketch."

We mounted our horses and rode slowly home, silent and dispirited. A sudden flicker of soul's light had blazed up for a moment, and left us enveloped in deeper gloom.

"Ah!" exclaimed Rosie, suddenly jerking round in her saddle. "Here is old Mophead!" The name I had christened him years ago was familiarly used by the children; and moving at right angles toward our path, I saw something like a great bunch of tow.

"He has surely found something, or he would not have given up the search so soon."

He saw us and approached. His face had a grand old consequential expression, from which I rather argued favorably. He looked as though he would say, "I am the important personage in these matters; place yourself in my hands and you will not have long to wait for the solution of your difficulties." He flung his moppy head back in a stately way as he spoke,—

"I think, madam, that I have discovered a very important fact in this case. Do you not think this has something to do with the mystery?" And he produced from his bosom an ornament that glittered, and shot out rays of light back to the afternoon sun.

Rosie looked and turned away; she saw no connection between it and her beloved. But I took the bauble in my hand. It was a sort of star or cross, brilliantly set with diamonds in blue and white enamel, with a small piece of ribbon attached to fasten it to the garment.

"I have seen such ornaments in Europe," I said. "Where in the world did you find it?"

"No doubt, madam," he replied. "It is a foreign decoration. I remember quite well to have seen it pinned on the breast of high officers on board the *Bellerophon*, when the great Napoleon was laid low. It belongs somehow to courts and camps. Do you not think it formed a portion of the apparel of your distinguished guest? I found it tied round the neck of a Pinte Indian who was going up to the 'deer feast,' and I succeeded in getting it from him in exchange for a half-dollar. He told me he had just found it among the rocks, and I made him go back to

*184*

show me exactly the spot. I searched all about the vicinity, but could discover nothing more; but I had the Indian tied hand and limb in my castle in case he may have been murdered by the party."

"This," he whispered, approaching his great head which was nearly on a level with mine, though I was mounted on horseback,—"I brought this down to allay your uneasiness. Now I am about to start for the Upper Valley to get Randolph's dog. If you have anything which belonged to either of them I will carry it, to put the dog on the scent. He'll hunt out their traces if they are in the rock."

We told him how he had found the painting immediately after our vain search.

With great strides he was soon out of sight again.

I regarded the gemmed ornament attentively, and suddenly there flashed across me Mr. Egremont's movement when putting his hand into his breast and saying, "I can prove to you in two minutes." That it belonged to him there was not the shadow of a doubt in my mind.

We rode slowly home, thinking to be there when Mr. Naunton returned. He had not yet arrived, and again we were plunged into the horrors of suspense.

Rosie, after hearing my conviction that the gem was Mr. Egremont's, lay motionless with her face buried in the divan cushions.

"Do not despair, dear child! all is not lost yet. I feel as though they must find him very soon now. They must have had a fall, it would seem, from his things being so scattered about, but perhaps he is only disabled; and after an hour's rest, if your father is not returned, I will again start out for the Upper Valley with a few restoratives, and a good strong blanket to make a stretcher in case of need, for I feel, dear, that we must prepare for something of that nature. You must provide for our coming home. Have Mary keep the hot water ready. There is nothing like being prepared for the worst now."

I set forth again for the third time that day over the same path under the same feelings, only more intensified. They had risen slowly and gradually to the culminating fear that some more alarming, perhaps fatal catastrophe, had befallen the missing ones.

The little incidents above narrated had tended to dispel the lingering hope we all had cherished, that some unwonted freak of Zanita's might eventually unravel the mystery. We had dwelt upon the *espieglerie* of the china closet; and Mr. Naunton laid great stress upon the fact of her having once built herself into the potato-hole, where she made a fire, in performance of an Indian curative custom of the sweat-house. On that occasion fortunately Chang had gone to the hole for a supply of potatoes, and found her almost suffocated.

"Zanita is fertile in invention, and has struck a new lead of mischief we none of us can guess at."

But speculations of this nature were over. The picture had been torn from its case, and there were marks of blood upon it, and the ornament had been worn under the vest, if anywhere. I thought I would ride round by old Mophead's castle, in case he might have returned. I found only the Indian, bound hand and foot, who bellowed loudly when he saw me, "Wah-hi! wah-hi! go him away, go him away!"—meaning that I should unloose him and let him go.

He was an old man I had occasionally seen roaming about, whose soft handsome features we had often remarked. The very last time, I remembered Zanita had been with me, and had spoken a few words of Indian to him. I felt sure this man was no murderer, but possibly might know something concerning the missing ones.

I dismounted, gave him a drink of water, and asked him,—

"See young squaw?—talk Indian?"

He understood immediately, and answered, "Ugh! ugh! Mono," nodding with his head toward that direction. "Gone fetch him!" and he appealed to be immediately released.

This I dared not do, but it sent a thrill of pleasure through my heart I had not experienced for twenty-four hours.

"I go fetch big knife and cut your rope," I replied, smiling on him as I mounted my pony. He chuckled a response, and I rode off toward the foot of the mountain. I raised our mountain whoop several times, in order that the party might hear me and guide me to them. Soon I got a response from Radd,—for I knew his voice,—at the foot of the "Glacier Point." One side of this point, which projects into the Valley, is an almost vertical smooth surface for three thousand feet, which gives it the name of glacier. On the other side it presents a jagged, broken front formed of stern, bold rocks, clefts, and ravines,—a mass of broken stones, as though they had been prepared for building purposes. A few stunted shrubs of manzanita grow among them without an apparent soil for sustenance.

As I rode into this embattlement Radd approached me carrying in his hands some broken pieces of wood which I instantly recognized as the sketch-box.

"He has found these," said he, pointing to Rollo, "but there is more to come."

I left my horse and we mounted the *débris*. Rollo sprang from rock to rock with a plaintive yell that chilled my very soul.

I have heard the sharp excited cry of the fox-hounds on full scent in the English hunting field, and the still more bitter yelp of the bloodhounds chasing fugitive slaves in America, but the short gasping howl that burst from Rollo from time to time was the most distressful sound I have ever heard a dog utter.

Old Methley was eagerly following and urging him on with encouraging words. At last he bounded toward his master and delivered to him what turned out to be a bunch of paint brushes. Shortly afterward Mrs. Radd appeared on the shelving rock holding up a hat in her hand, which I immediately recognized. We climbed toward her. She said, as we all stood appalled at this evidence,—

"I know'd it was all up then—when I seen her ghost go a-gliding by last night."

"Woman, hold your peace!" cried Radd, with more severity than I supposed he was capable of assuming.

"Wall, it don't amount to much neither ways, if I says it or other folks says it; it's all up with them, and that's what's the matter; but I'll take my bible oath that I seen her ghost a-gliding through the moonlight in the Upper Valley last night."

"Is it not possible," I said, catching at this idea and comparing it with the Indian's assertion, —"that the form might have been Zanita's? She wore a white dress."

"And she all smashed up in the rocks," quoth Mrs. Radd, contemptuously. "Wall, them townsfolk have no manner of idee. Rollo never takes on like that but when he scents blood"—

"Peace! woman," vociferated Radd again.

Rollo was howling piteously over a deep cleft in the rock, and Methley's gaunt figure stood over him beckoning us like the genius of evil. We scrambled up the rugged steep at our utmost speed. The sun cast his last lurid beams over the peaks and jutting points, and tinged them with a deep blood-red, penetrating every niche and crevice.

We stood on the brink of the cliff looking into a fissure which was as if the rock had been split asunder. A slender streak of red, like blood, crept slowly down and down until it was lost in the abyss, and as we were kneeling breathless over it there was revealed to us a pallid face, still and mute, turned upward to the sky.

A great cry burst from every lip.

It was Egremont lying placid in the arms of death.

A heavy stillness came over me as I assisted to lower the ropes and hooks in order to grapple for him. Rollo paced about swaying his head, ever uttering his moans.

With much difficulty we raised the body from the depth of some twenty or thirty feet. Alas! we might as well have left it in its granite sepulchre. It was torn and mangled, and shattered almost piecemeal. His clothes were saturated with gore, to which fragments of granite had adhered. The skull was crushed, and only the beautiful face was left unexcoriated. The expression was calm and noble, and the beautiful arched lips and chin looked like chiseled alabaster. It was too sad for words and too solemn for grief.

We carefully laid him in the blanket and each holding a corner bore him down. Then Radd and Methley, cutting down two young saplings, bound the blanket firmly to them and lifted the sorrowful burden as the Chinese carry their loads.

"Do you not think we should continue the search?" I said, tremblingly, dreading to finish the terrible sentence.

"Rollo seems to have given it up," said Radd, "and I think he would not do that if there were any other scent to follow."

Radd, however, made the essay by once more ascending the rock, but Rollo looked after him wistfully, with an expression that said, "It is of no use." So we set out with our terrible burden.

Nell remained behind, saying she would take another look around, and I rode on in advance to prepare them at the cottage for the shocking catastrophe.

CHAPTER XXIV.

WAKING AND SLEEPING TERRORS.

IT WAS SOME RELIEF to my heart when, within half a mile of the house, I met my husband who had just arrived, and having been informed of the terrible crisis that we were in, he had come on to meet me.

"My poor Sylvia!" he exclaimed, as he lifted me from the saddle, the better to give me a fond caress.

I laid my head on the breast where I had found shelter from this world's sorrow for so many years, and burst into heavy sobs.

I could afford to weep now that he was present to act for me. This reliance, this help in need that makes a unity of love so precious, is the greatest boon granted us here below. For a few minutes I remained in his encircling arms, he stroking me gently and murmuring,—

"My poor child! you are overtried and overworked. Leave the rest to me."

But soon I was able to tell him of the dreadful discovery we had just made.

"Terrible!" he said—"very terrible! He must have fallen over the cliff and been dashed to pieces."

I calmed myself and we continued our march.

My husband speedily mastered all the facts in his clear way, and made a *resumé* which was some comfort to me:—

"No trace of Zanita having been found on the *débris*, the evidence that the woman saw her, combined with the Indian's Mono story, would go to show that she is safe and well somewhere, and will doubtless turn up in her wild way in process of time. But we must question the Indian with an interpreter."

Thus my good husband kept on talking all the way home; and so judicious was his treatment of my nervous excitement, that before we reached the cottage I was quite calmed and pacified, and able to undertake the painful task that lay before me of communicating the sad news to Rosie. She, poor child! rushed out to meet me and clung round my neck. She seemed to glean from my face that the mystery was solved. Her father had returned, and Kenmuir, looking jaded and worn, was just riding up.

"In vain," said he, shaking his head. "Unsuccessful."

On approaching me he too read in my face the preface to the awful disclosure, and was silent. I made him a sign that I must speak to Rosie alone, and motioned him to the Professor, whilst I went to my room followed by the poor child.

"Rosie, my darling!" I said, "a fearful accident has happened. He has fallen from the rocks and is very much shattered. They are bringing him home."

Rosie had uttered a little cry when I first spoke, now she interrupted quickly,—

"And Zanita?"

"We have not seen her. She was not there; but Mrs. Radd saw her alone last night, and she has probably gone off on the Mono trail."

Rosie's large blue eyes dilated with horror. "Gone off!" she cried, "and never sought help: left on the cruel rocks all torn and lacerated, to die! O, aunty!"—and her face flushed—"it is not possible!"

"We know nothing, dear, for certain. We have not seen her, but that is our conjecture. We shall learn more to-morrow."

"Can he not speak?" she said, after a pause.

"No, my darling, I fear we shall never hear his voice again."

Rosie was trembling all over, but rising with an effort, as though she dreaded to pursue the conversation, she said,—

"Aunty, let me get you some tea; you look as though you were going to faint."

"No dear, I shall not faint, but you may give me a cup of tea; and there's poor Kenmuir who has ridden some hundred and fifty miles, no doubt, without ever being out of saddle."

I went into the sitting-room. Kenmuir was standing with his arms folded and head dropped down. There was a dark shade of sorrow on his usually bright face.

"O, Mrs. Brown!" he said, "how grieved I am for that young man. There was something noble in him that I could not but like,"—and then he added, in a whisper, "my soul shrinks back affrighted from the solution that my judgment gives of the event."

"Good God! What?" I said.

"No, no," he murmured, clasping his hands, while the big drops of sweat oozed out from his forehead,—"I cannot tell you my suspicion. We will wait."

"Be ready to prevent Rosie from seeing the corpse," I said. "They are to take him to your hut, and you must sleep here."

"O, that makes no difference," he said; "I would as soon remain near the poor boy dead as alive, but I think we ought to try the Mono trail at once, and when I have taken a cup of tea and an hour's rest I will start again."

"O, impossible!" I exclaimed. "You must have already ridden one hundred and fifty miles."

"Nearly that, for I diverged to the Mariposa Grove and Big Trees, and several sheep ranchos, and three horses broke down under me. The first thing is to examine the Indian, and learn where he last saw her. I dread being too late again. If I had gone off on that track last night I might have saved him. Poor lad! his handsome young face will haunt me many a day."

Here Rosie appeared with the tea. She pressed Kenmuir's hand affectionately. There was still a rigidity about her face that was more alarming than the most violent burst of grief,—a wild, horrified look, which made her blue eyes assume a shade of black.

I looked out, fearing she had seen the arrival of the party, but they were not in sight.

"What has she seen? What does she suspect?" I said to Kenmuir, as she turned to seek her father.

"My God! not what I do, or she will go mad," he said, passing his hand over his brow.

What did he suspect? I had not the courage to press the inquiry. I felt that I had borne as much as I could, for that day, of horrible excitement. My head was beginning to feel as in a dream of hideous phantasmagoria.

Mr. Naunton was much shocked, but on the whole somewhat relieved when he found that it was not his own child, and felt quite sure that now Zanita was safe somewhere.

Presently Kenmuir intimated that the party was coming. I beguiled Rosie into my room at the other side of the house; for there is something about the appearance of a corpse, however enveloped, which at once tells the sad fact that life is no more. Some shrinking consciousness we have that there has taken place some supernatural change, which has a sort of repulsion and terror for us; and I wished to spare my darling this shock if possible.

It was only a few moments before Kenmuir rapped at my door, saying,—

"Mrs. Brown, you are wanted."

Then turning to Rosie, I said, "They have brought him home, dear child, and I am going to him; remain here unless I send for you; try to prepare yourself for the worst. I can give you no hope."

The same look of horror passed over her face, which she strove to hide in the pillow as I left her to attend the corpse of her lover.

It was found impossible to remove any of the clothes; so mutilated was the once graceful form, that it seemed held together only by the garments. We wrapt him in a sheet and tied a linen cloth about the head, leaving the fair white forehead uncovered.

Ah! how beautiful he looked in death. I stooped and kissed his closed eyes, with their deep long lashes resting on the rounded cheeks where the remains of his brilliant color yet lingered, and my tears dropped softly on those curved and haughty lips which had appealed so piteously to me but the day before.

> "O life, so few the days we live!
> Would that the boon which thou dost give
> Were life indeed."

But here was the end of the sad life drama, in which we had all played our parts; and there lay the hero, with his secret forever locked within his marble lips. O, that they had told it yesterday, he had now been alive and happy, with our Rose-bud in his bosom; for then he would never have gone with Zanita, who, no doubt, allured him into that mad danger. It was the opinion of all that he had fallen backwards from the projecting pinnacle of rock, which shelved out over the Valley from Glacier Point. No doubt he had turned giddy and lost his balance.

"I think we ought to make a strong oak coffin, lined with cedar, and send him to his friends," said Kenmuir.

"There is the difficulty," I said; "we know absolutely nothing of his antecedents."

"Under the circumstances, I think we ought to look in his desk."

We had taken from his pockets a few keys and trifling articles, and with one of them we opened the desk. There was a great deal of poetry, which seemed original, in his handwriting, and some letters, of no importance, addressed to Mr. Egremont. Only one contained a striking and mysterious inclosure. It consisted of a second envelope addressed to "His Highness the Prince Augustus of Cumberland;" the letter was written in a delicate female hand, and commenced, "My dear husband." The whole letter was a strong pathetic appeal to be taken back in the name of their former love, and of their child; but the tenor of the communication left the impression that it had not been written by a wife or a lady. It concluded with a curious demand for a larger allowance. There was no date or address to this document; it was signed by the pet name "Maggy."

Was it really addressed to our poor friend; was that his true name, and did he preserve his incognito from some circumstantial necessity? All was a deep and terrible mystery; but many expressions of Zanita's now recurred to my mind, which led to the belief that she, at least, had fathomed its depths. When she reappeared, no doubt much would be explained.

In the mean time old Mophead had gone to bring up the Indian, in order to have massed together all the knowledge of the language which the three possessed,—Naunton, Kenmuir, and himself.

Bill, who had come in with my husband, was a carpenter as well as a guide, and he set about the melancholy task of making a coffin. Poor Mr. Naunton walked away, saying, in response to some suggestion from Bill, "I cannot give any directions about that work; it takes me right back to that day when my sweet saint went to her home in heaven, and left the Valley but a gloomy wilderness to me. If she had taken the two little ones with her, I should have been thankful; then we might all have gone together."

Methley here came in with the Indian, now untied. The former was shaking his old mophead dolefully.

"I make no account of him," he said. "Where is Mu-wah? He says that Mu-wah knows all about it; but he has certainly seen our little lady on the Mono trail, unless the scamp is making up the story; and I can't, for my life, see why he should."

Mu-wah was not visible—had not been seen by any of us. Ah Chow said he had never returned from the deer feast; but this the Indian denied, and said that he had. It was nearly certain that the Indian knew whatever Mu-wah knew; but was possessed with the notion that Mu-wah should reveal it himself, and again volunteered,—"Him fetch him."

He was promised a dollar if he brought Mu-wah back before morning, for we all conceived the impression that Mu-wah was some way in league with Zanita in assisting her hiding.

We all went to take an hour's rest. I looked in upon Rosie; she was lying quite still, with her face in the pillow, but she looked up as I approached; there was no sign of weeping, but her eyes wore the same awe-stricken expression.

"Aunty," she said gently, "may I see him before—before"—and her soft lips quivered so that she could not finish the sentence. She made another effort and said, "I know what that hammering is; they are putting the nails in my heart!"

That loving little heart had divined all. I pressed her in my arms, hoping that she might be moved to tears.

"Rest to-night, darling, and to-morrow you shall see him; his face is still beautiful."

"Is it?" she answered, and the lips again quivered and prevented farther utterance.

I lay down, but sleep, in the soothing oblivion which brings repose, visited me not. My soul seemed to go into a semi-trance: that mystic land of shadows, where our bitterest sufferings in actual life are intensified by a vague helplessness which seems to surround us. The mountains of granite which we have to traverse are endless, and boundless as the despair with which we continue to struggle to ascend them; the sky pours down a flood of hot lava, or freezing snow, which annihilates us, and yet we seem to be surviving in death. We have no power, we give up and succumb under our misery; we cannot lie down and die—this luxury of despair is denied us.

I have often thought that if man is doomed to eternal torment for his crimes, this vividly conscious dream of agony must be the realization of it; for bitter as was the misery of our actual life at this moment, my dream was wrought up to be fifty times more wretched. Every spot I had visited on the previous day I was again toiling over, with feet more heavily weary and a heart bursting to overflowing.

Poor Egremont's condition was more mangled, and the wretched portions of his limbs were constantly falling away; his face was distorted, and excruciatingly painful. Yet I had to look at it, and I had no power to seek relief by turning away. The Indians were jabbering, like the blue jay, an unintelligible tongue, yet we were compelled to find out what they said.

At last my soul, having traversed the dark paths of yesterday, continued the journey onward in search of Zanita: over the rocks and through the Upper Valley, where I seemed to see her in company with Mrs.

Radd,—gliding like a ghostly phantom, whom we cried to in vain, and could not reach or touch, though we strained every nerve and sinew. She yet floated away, and still we had to follow, and follow in an agony of dread and anguish. Hither, thither, over rugged boulders, over great barriers of fallen trees, whose ragged arms pointing upward made a *chevaux-de-frise* over the boiling rapids of rushing torrents; under the cascades of the Upper Valley, flowing from the endless melting snow of the huge sierras; through the green rippling river, which, when we entered with our naked feet, seemed no longer water but coiling green and purple snakes, that hissed and sputtered as we passed.

Still the soft white semblance swept on; the folds of her muslin drapery, like the gauzy mist of the falls, left nothing in the eager grasp but moisture. Now we thought she was taking the Mono trail, anon that she would sweep up the inaccessible cañon of the outlet of the Valley. Yet as she is wafted toward the bare frowning side of Tis-sa-ack, there comes an indefinable superstition over us,—that we are chasing the goddess herself, and no longer Zanita. Up the side of that bold and austere height she rolls like a fleecy cloud of morning mist: what mortal steps can follow! yet stop we cannot. Will Death enfold us in his cold embrace at last? No, we must go on, on.

Our drooping forms are hurried on toward the fearful edge where six thousand feet overhang the Mirror Lake.

If she is mortal she must be dashed to pieces there, and we must share her fate; for we seem to have gained on her, and nearly touch her. On, onward she flies, and we pursue; nearer, and nearer to the edge,— and now she is on the brink. We can see the surging world below more dizzily before us, and the lake shimmering in the moonlight.

One plunge, and she is over! But I have caught the white dress, and hold it firmly in my grasp,—the piece is left in my hand!

I awakened with a stifled cry.

"O, husband! she is in the lake."

"Who, dear?" he answered. "You have had a nightmare, and woke me with your cry."

"Zanita!" I gasped, wiping the perspiration from my brow. "I am persuaded that she is in the lake."

I had grasped the sheet so convulsively that the marks were still fresh. The Professor endeavored to persuade me to sleep again.

"O no!" I exclaimed, "not for the world; such agony I never experienced in my waking moments—a perfect hell of torments. Besides, they will all be ready to go out on the search again, and I am determined to go to the Mirror Lake."

I related my dream excitedly to Kenmuir, though not to Mr. Naunton.

"Do not let this idea distress you," said Kenmuir, who nevertheless spoke as though he believed it every word,—"it is only a dream, and I had an idea myself of going there."

I noticed the same dark look in his eyes, of which he seemed conscious, for he looked away as he continued: "I will follow the trail you have dreamed of, and will come out on the shoulder of Tis-sa-ack, which walls in the lake; you and the Professor can go there by the Valley route, and then, if we can find nothing, we can all go up to the cañon together toward Lake Tomaya, and on to the Mono trail to meet Muwah; and then I think we shall have encompassed her round."

Thinking I would not awaken Rosie if she was asleep, we stole off quietly: Naunton and Kenmuir together on foot, and the Professor and myself on horseback. Ah Chow, who seemed aroused to the consciousness that the affairs transpiring were very important, and that he ought to be equal to them, had prepared a cold roast fowl, which he divided between the parties, and insisted with a kindly smile upon our taking, saying,—

"Him muchee care of Missy Rossy."

"Take care of her, good Ah Chow," I said. But I hoped we might return ere she was fairly awake.

CHAPTER XXV.

IN HER
MOTHER'S ARMS.

THE MOON WAS JUST AT her second rising above the Sentinel; it was a waning moon, which makes the commonest things of earth look unearthly. She cast a weird light over the north dome and royal arches; and the manzanita, which cluster upon it, looked like the cavernous entrance to some enchanted castle or hobgoblin's cave—every dark archway was deeper and more unfathomable; and the round white dome, shining distinct in the bright light, completed the hallucination that this rock was some vast fortress of midnight ghouls and uncanny spirits.

Now and again we heard the sharp yelp of a wandering coyote as he prowled in search of prey. When we entered on the wooded rocky path, unearthly figures seemed starting out of every projecting rock, or half concealing themselves behind the trunks of trees; so strong was the impression of my dream upon me, that I could not deter myself from riding around the strange objects to ascertain really what they might be. The charred trunks of trees presented the most hideous spectres to my distracted fancy; and when a deep guttural sound reached my ears, I grasped my husband's arm with fright.

"It is only a bear," he said; "he will not molest us: do not be alarmed. I have my revolver in case of need." It was a relief to know it was anything so near humanity as a bear, for they rarely take the offensive, and generally run away when attacked.

I was fast losing my self-control. As we trod the steep rocky trail leading to the miniature lake, it seemed peopled with strange fantastic figures, which the water in the early summer had hidden from view, or only partially revealed, but now were left bare in the dry season: they were grotesque limbs of trees and rocks, scored deeply by the water at its various heights. The horses' hoofs sounded hollow as though passing over some subterranean world, and sent a dismal reverberation to the vast tower of See-wahlum, which marks the entrance to the Mirror Lake.

As I knew the trail better than my husband, I had gone in advance, it not being wide enough to admit of two abreast. My attention was directed to the careful guiding of my horse down a difficult bit of road over a slope of flat rock, down which he had to slide. As we turned the corner of the great portal into the mighty coliseum of granite mountains, the arena of which is the brightest Mirror Lake, set in, as it were, to reflect the whole, I expected to see it as I had done so often, with the dome of Tis-sa-ack reflected, and the brother peaks of Tocoyæ, Hunto, and the smaller tower See-wahlum, communing together deep in the bowels of the earth, all nodding gravely with each ripple, like a state cabinet in solemn conclave on the affairs of the upper world.

As I turned the corner, I raised my eyes, and the whole view of the lake was before me. I uttered a piercing cry, which the five echoes took up, and heralded around; shrieking from cliff to cliff, from tower to dome.

> "As though the fiends from heaven that fell
> Had pealed their banner cry of hell."

For there was my dream revealed in stern reality before me; there was the shadow of the great mountains bending their giant heads together, and there lay Zanita stretched on the mirror, the centre figure.

There was scarce a ripple on the lake, the silver sheen of the waning moon played over its surface and mingled with the folds of the white robe which lay floating upon it. The face was like whitest chiseled marble, framed in the dark locks which waved loosely around, and fell in long silky meshes over her bosom. She looked like a lovely picture on a silver disk, set in the depths of some bottomless gulf. Her hands were by her side, and her delicate taper fingers interlaced with the water, as if she were playing with quicksilver. Her eyes were closed, and the penciled eyebrows made a stern line across her Olympian brow. There was an expression of firm endurance about the small mouth which had never deigned to complain.

Long ere my eye had taken in all this, my husband had thrown his strong arm round to support me on my saddle; and we sat together gazing down upon her mute and motionless. All hope and all action were at an end; Death had held her for hours in his icy clasp. Calm, placid, and beautiful, around her the mighty death watchers towered up solemn and mournful in the melancholy moonlight; underneath them, as she floated on the silver sheen, the stars shone out in the deepest blue, and her home seemed bright down there.

The water of the lake had fallen perceptibly, having a broad band of white sand, which gleamed in the pale light like polished ivory, making a framework for the green fringe of willows that bordered the lake.

I felt stupefied and palsied at the discovery, and as though all energy of motion had suddenly left me. I had no wish to touch or move the phantom-like scene. It seemed as though my life and the world were come to an end, and that all was consummated; my whole soul and faculties seemed entranced in my gaze. I felt no poignant grief or violent sorrow. I had no sudden burst of anguish, of dread, of regret, or of horror. It seemed as though I had become perfectly resigned to all that had transpired, and had no aspirations beyond. I was in close unison with the placid melancholy of the waning moon,—still, cold, and death-like.

How long we sat our horses in this way I know not, my husband holding me softly to his breast. He knew well the condition of my overwrought system and brain, and knew best what to do. Presently I was roused by his saying,—

"Isn't that Kenmuir and Naunton?"

I lifted my eyes for the first time from the scene; and followed where he pointed to the sloping shoulder of Tis-sa-ack. We could descry the figures. The Professor waved his handkerchief, and they returned the signal; but they could hardly have discovered what lay in the lake.

"He had better see her thus," I said; and my husband raised his voice, and shouted, "Come here!"

The echo answered in sepulchral tone, "Here!" and a second cried pitifully, "Here!" and a third more mournfully, "Here!" and a mocking sigh, as from distant regions, echoed, "Here!"

I shuddered, and looked again in the lake, where the tall bowing heads of the mountains pointed to the figure that floated on the centre. "Here!" they seemed to say,—"here is our child, the daughter of Ahwah-nee, returned to her native home." Again I shuddered, and looked up to Tis-sa-ack. They had seen it all. Naunton stood with his face buried in his hands; he was not fascinated as I was: the grandeur and immensity of death overcame him. Kenmuir was urging the descent; a few yards before him, my practiced woman's eye lit upon something that was not a shimmering moonbeam playing on pulverized granite; it was a strip of soft mull muslin; it hung and fluttered from a contorted bough of chaparral, and then I knew how it had happened: from thence she had fallen, and was dead before she reached the water. All this I knew, but said it not; we sat still again for another half hour, till the crackling of the branches announced the arrival of the two men, when I heard the convulsed sob of Mr. Naunton. It seemed to nerve me into life again, and an acute sympathetic pain grappled my heart. I jumped from my horse and approached him.

"Ah! don't leave her thus," he moaned.

"See," I said, "look how beautiful she is; this is not death as we regard it; it is only a change as the oak-leaves change, and the ferns are golden, and the water dried into silver sand. The child of the mountain! See how she sleeps in her cradle of glory."

But he could not raise his head then, and never more, for the mountain tops never again saw his brilliant eyes, or the heavens his upturned face.

"Come away, then, and they will bring her." I led him by the arm, and we mounted our horses and rode away.

Kenmuir had not spoken; but I noticed that the fixed dark expression was still on his face, which the dusky light made almost ghastly.

We paced home slowly and in silence; dumbness seemed to possess us all, and reign over every other emotion. It might have been the shock, or the peculiarity of the circumstances, or that the tenderest passion of love was not awakened by the elf-like child. It was more a mystic entrancement than tender affection. No heart-wrung cry of sorrow was heard from any one, and I felt that the scene was too appalling and grand to weep over. I thought Rosie would be the one to cry aloud.

As we passed Kenmuir's cabin I noticed Ah Chow sitting on the step almost smothered in a whole bolt of white calico which I had brought from San Francisco for sheeting. I gazed with stolid wonderment upon him. Surely, I was getting light headed! What could the man mean by unfolding my bolt of calico? Uncertain if I saw aright, I jumped off my horse and approached him. He pointed mysteriously toward the door with his thumb.

"Missy Rossy muchee sorry!"

By degrees I comprehended that it required "muchee" calico to make mourning according to Chinese fashion. Somewhat relieved as to my own state of mind I stepped into the hut, and there lay our Rosie half seated, half extended on the bier, her long fair curls bestrewing the cold immovable face of the dead. I put my arms around her.

"Come, dear little one, come home with me!"

She arose mechanically without uttering a sound, and passed out with me. Ah Chow stood aside hesitating with the funeral calico. I shook my head to forbid any demonstration, and he submitted with that patience peculiar to Asiatics.

As Rosie did not make any inquiries as to our success in finding her sister, I resolved to withhold the terrible truth from her as long as possible. When she arrived at the house she threw herself upon the divan and buried her face as before.

I went in search of Horseshoe-Bill to send him to meet my husband and Kenmuir. I soon heard his voice in high confabulation with Mrs. Nell and Mophead, who were helping him with his joinering.

"I can't see no manner of use in putting of him in two coffins: he can't want a Sunday and a week-day suit. He has nothin' to do but lie there until the trumpet rouses him up at the last day, and I suppose the Almighty'll attend to finding his missing pieces, as He does for other folks. I don't see no difference with this."

"It is my opinion," said Methley, "that he ought to be buried with military honor; for the decoration I found is similar to those I saw worn by high officers on board the *Bellerophon*."

"O, you dry up with your millingtary blesserings. He's just one of your British adventurers as come over here a-swindling of honest folk with their titles and foldermirigs. I make no count on 'em, nohow! I'd jest bury him like other folks. Wall! I reckon he'll have to be sent home to his folks in England, and he'll need more nor one coffin to keep him all there. I reckon he's a right to that, for he forked me out ten dollars when I brought him in here," said Bill.

"Ah, I guess you know which side your bread is buttered; but I guess it's as likely he's not left directions for the superior 'commodation o' two coffins to be paid for."

"You bet your life he has!" responded Bill.

I notified my presence, and explained in a few brief words the misfortune which had befallen Zanita.

"Well, well!" cried Bill, passing his sleeve over his face ostensibly to dry the perspiration, but really to wipe the tears from his eyes,—"I'd a backed that young'un against a thousand dollars never to have missed her footing. What could have ailed her? She must have been off her feet."

"There!" broke in Nell, triumphantly projecting her front tooth,—"there! did I tell you or did I not? I guess I don't say much as isn't gospel! When I see her ghost come a-flyin' and a-callin' for help through the Upper Valley, I knew how as she was burglariously murdered, and I'd as lief bet a cinnamon bear-skin against a cent that this here Britisher, with his jewels and hifalutin airs and 'commodation of two coffins, is at the bottom of it."

We all stared at Nell in horrified silence. I felt the tight grip on my heart again and my breath coming heavily. More horrors! never to cease accumulating in this memorable twenty-four hours.

"I did hear 'em a pitchin' into each other right smart one day when I was fishin' down below the Po-ho-no Falls," said Bill. "Darn me! if he didn't jest rear and tear like a real lunatic; and she kept on a jeering and a spiting him. Then I thought I'd better be on hand to see fair play for Miss Zany, if he should think o' layin' hands on a woman. There's no tellin' what them furriners 'ill do. Now I wish I'd been on hand day 'fore yesterday. I don't believe in her falling down there."

I turned away faint with this new suspicion. Old Methley followed me sympathetically, and shaking his great mop like a good-natured lion tried to console me.

"We must not lightly cast suspicion upon a distinguished member of a friendly power like Great Britain. Of course if he had survived we should doubtless have been under the necessity of confining him in my castle, and I should have posted myself as honorary guard until everything had been cleared up—as it was thought fit to do with the Great Napoleon at St. Helena,—just to keep him out of mischief. But now that he is dead I would not dishonor his grave."

"But supposing he were alive," I said faintly, "would you think he had something to do with Zanita's death?"

"I should say that he pushed her over the shoulder of Tis-sa-ack in a fit of passion."

"Good God!" I ejaculated. "How, then, do you now account for his death?"

"Suicide," replied my companion, deliberately; "suicide, madam. You remember some little time ago," continued Methuselah, falling back on his memory some fifty years,—"the British Prime Minister, Lord Castlereagh, whom Byron satirized as 'Carotid Artery-cutting Castlereagh?' "—

My heart was too riven with anguish to enter into the discussion, and he continued,—

"But I would bury him with honors if he cannot be sent home to his friends."

"What!" I said, anxious to put to the test he suspicion he had expressed,—"would you confer honor upon one whom you believe to be a murderer and a suicide?"

"We do not know for certain that he is, madam; but the suppositions are strong, that having been seen last together alive and found dead apart, that they did not each fall from a separate rock by accident. And no mountaineer will believe that our young Vestal of Tis-sa-ack fell from her high altar, or that she flung up her young life willingly. Her father, for one, will never believe she fell by accident. On the other hand, this British stranger going alone to such a narrow slip of projecting rock as 'Glacier Point,' and falling therefrom, after parting with his sweetheart, indicates suicide. You know best, madam, if he had any motive for committing this damned deed?" cried the old man, excitedly.

I dared not answer the question. The uncontrollable vehemence Egremont had shown when last speaking of Zanita rose to my memory and kept me silent.

Methuselah, with delicate perception, changed the subject.

"How is poor Naunton?" he said. "How does he bear it?"

"I greatly fear it may be his death," I said. "He does not seem able to endure deep grief."

"Some of us are not," he replied. "It kills the soul if not the body. Seventy-five years ago I was a young man and wooed a young girl. We kept company in New England fashion,—became one life, one heart, and one soul. Well! she died. She went away, and took with her that part of my soul which she alone possessed; and here I stand alone, and have never been the same man since and never shall be again!" sighed old Mophead, "for I am getting old. I've never been the same man this seventy-five years."

Mr. Naunton was still in his room, and as I received no answer to my knock I judged it better to leave him to himself.

Fortunately when the sad *cortège* arrived we were able to bear the poor girl to her own little room without the knowledge of father or daughter.

"I guess I'll fix her up an elegant corpse!" cried Nell. "It would be real *mean* to bury her as you did her mother!"

"I don't think her father will allow her to be touched, but you can ask him."

"What! bury her in them sink-rags? Well, if he isn't a queer cuss, you bet your life! He's as *contrairy* as Dick's hatband, as went nine times round and wouldn't tie! I guess we'll have a right-smart time with him afore we get her buried, anyhow! As to t'other," she continued, wagging her head in the direction of the cabin,—"I make no account of fixin' a corpse that's mashed up like hog's head cheese. He'll be all right if he gets his two coffins. It's all them Britishers cares for!"

The "smart time" prophesied by Nell soon came about, for although Oswald Naunton was not violent as he had been at the death of his wife, yet grief had transformed him into a different man. He remained shut up in his own room, refusing sympathy, and food, and conversation on any point.

I was anxious to know where he would like his child buried, and if Egremont was to be laid alongside,—awaiting instructions from his friends. After many ineffectual efforts, I succeeded in procuring the laconic direction,—

"Bury her with her mother!"

"And Mr. Egremont—shall we lay him by her side?"

"No! Curse him!" thundered Naunton, rising and pacing the room with long strides. "Pitch him into the deepest pool in the river! Burn him on the top of the highest mountain, and cast his ashes to the winds! Fling him over the Po-ho-no Fall! Cast him into hellfire forever!" shrieked the wretched father. "My child! my beautiful child!"—and he covered his face with his hands and moaned aloud.

It was useless to offer words of consolation. The conclusion his mind had arrived at was evidently that of Nell and Methley,—the terrible one that his child had been murdered by the English stranger, and the anguish and horror of the thought was driving him mad. There was no comfort for him but time.

From the father I went to the daughter, and, to my surprise, found her in eager conversation with Kenmuir, the latter half supporting her with his arm. They were gazing into each other's eyes with the same appalled expression of dismay I had noticed from the first, as though they had seen some fearful spectre which froze up every other emotion. They became silent as I approached, as though they had resolved to spare me the *vision*, whatever it might be. It could not be the same idea as the father's, or Rosie would never have spent the night by her dead lover, had she believed him to be the murderer of her sister.

I next sought my husband, my refuge under every emergency; for I was fast losing my presence of mind in this rush of inscrutable events.

"Dear John," I said, "is not the mystery of this tragedy terribly crushing? I feel almost overpowered by it. What is the suspicion which is transfixing poor Rosie and Kenmuir with horror? Do you know?"

"Yes," he replied; "and if you feel that you can bear it, I will tell you all about it. But mind I do not agree with the hypothesis, nor still less with that of Mr. Naunton. I do not agree with any of them. I take a different view altogether." He always did take a different view of everything from every one.

"We met the two Indians," continued the Professor, "whom Radd was bringing in. Mu-wah is nearly out of his senses with some great fear which has seized upon him, and is altogether incoherent. His companion corroborates with a nod and a grunt every incongruity that Mu-wah asserts."

"What do they say?" I broke in impatiently.

"I am coming to that, my dear. In substance nothing more than that they saw Zanita and a white man out on Palel-lima, or Glacier Point. 'They muchee talkee,' which means they were disputing, I suppose."

"Good heavens," I exclaimed, "surely she never pushed him over?" And I seized my husband by both arms, in my eagerness to bring out the fatal secret.

"Be calm, my dear. I made that stipulation with you, you know. Rosie and Kenmuir suspect what you have just intimated. Of course without premeditation, but they think that she gave him a push in her impulsive, fierce, bitter way. A very slight push would send a man backwards from that point."

"Fearful, fearful!" and a rush of tears came to my relief.

"But," continued the Professor, "Radd says that there are man's foot-prints leaving the point; and the Indians are rather confused in a statement that they saw them upon the Mono trail. Now my impression is, that Zanita had been in one of her aggravating moods; that she had taken him to Glacier Point to show him the 'kingdom of the earth,' which he might possess if he wedded her, and subsequently carried him on to Tis-sa-ack; that there she ventured to the very brink for the sole purpose of tormenting him; that he, under terrible fear, had attempted to withhold her,—the most fatal thing he could do under the circumstances; that she, in defiance, and scorning his help, had missed her footing and pitched headlong over the brow of Tis-sa-ack. The piece of her dress hanging on the bushes denotes she has fallen, and I do not for one moment entertain the idea that Egremont has murdered her. If you will think of it, my dear, such a thing is not at all compatible with his character."

"Well, then, who has murdered him?" I said, repeating the word inadvertently.

"I do not see any grounds for the supposition that he was murdered," reasoned the Professor; "that is where all draw illogical deductions. It in no way follows as an inevitable sequence that because a man is found dead in the cleft of a rock a few thousand feet below a platform, upon which he was last seen alive, that he has been murdered."

"Then you think, like Methley, that he committed suicide?" I cried, becoming every moment more confused in my ideas.

"No! certainly not: why suicide? He had sought Rosie's affection, and obtained it. He did not care for Zanita, who was the obstacle, and she is suddenly removed from his path. Why should he destroy himself? The thing is preposterous. Why is it that human nature ever delights to duplicate horrors? Don't you see, my dear, that when the rash girl fell from his grasp he could not follow her; but had to retrace his steps at his greatest speed, under the utmost excitement and anguish, to seek for help in the Valley. Mechanically he would retrace the track she had brought him. He would come round that sharp curve on to that dizzy height unexpectedly, and at a random speed; would suddenly perceive the danger of his position, launched, as it were, between earth and heaven. His brain would reel, vertigo would ensue; he would overbalance, and have passed into eternity in less space of time than it has taken me to describe it. Few mountaineers would walk out upon that narrow projection of rock without nerving themselves for the feat; even Kenmuir would not *run* out upon it; and for a person unaccustomed to mountain heights to rush upon it without warning, and in a great state of mental excitement, every nerve and muscle strained to the highest tension of haste and suspense, would obviously result in certain destruction."

"Then you believe it to be a series of accidents happening in a sort of sequence?"

"Unquestionably, to my mind accident is the solution of the whole terrible affair," replied the Professor.

I cannot say that this view of the matter thoroughly convinced me; or that I quite coincided with Kenmuir or Methley; my mind remained in an undecided neutral condition, more painful to the nerves than any positive conviction. For the mind accustoms itself to the most painful catastrophes; but uncertainty goads like an open sore that heals not.

My poor Zanita, without being "*fixed up*," was laid, embalmed only in our pity, beside her mother,—her father, Rosie, and Kenmuir declining to attend the funeral, although, as I well knew, from different motives: the former, because he could not bear to look upon his grief; and the other two, because they did not dare that others should witness their want of it.

Poor Rosie shut up her gentle soul within herself, and seemed to have no confidence to impart the dreadful secret that had darkened her young life to any one but Kenmuir, who shared it with her. Mr. Naunton kept his room, and was unapproachable to my husband, myself, or any one, and after the funeral I felt that I had no longer any mission in the Valley. Old Methuselah had taken possession of the double coffin with the remains of the mysterious Egremont, and had hidden it away from the father's vengeance in one of the moss-clad grottoes in the rocks, a natural mausoleum, where it may remain to the present day, for we never were able to discover his relatives, or any one who knew him more than casually.

He had appeared as a mystery, and so remained to the end, and was one of a class of the extraordinary characters which may be met every day in California. He might have been a prince who had forfeited his principality, or the son of a princess who had made *disgrace* his portion, or a murderer, or an escaped felon: we never knew more than that. He had the manners, breeding, and education of a gentleman, if not the principles.

But now the end had come, the past was irrevocable, and my husband sought by every means to divert my thoughts from dwelling upon it. We soon, therefore, took our farewell of the Valley of Ah-wah-nee forever.

CHAPTER XXVI.

FINIS.

WE RETURNED HOME; but my health and nerves had received a shock which I could not overcome, and months of weary restless suffering passed on. My heart was too full of sorrow to enjoy anything, and thus the monotony of my life was fast eating into my natural vitality.

At length my husband proposed our going to Europe; not, as he said, entirely on my account, as he did not wish me to suppose myself so ill; but because there were several geologists for whom he had the highest respect, yet with whom he was most anxious to hold an argument.

Thus four months after the tragedy of the Valley saw us landing in Southampton. Change of scene and habit wrought that marvelous revolution in my feelings which no medicine, spiritual or material, could accomplish.

The Professor disputed to his heart's content; and then went on to Switzerland to make more explorations.

"My dear," said my husband one day, pulling out a pocketful of dirty stones, "I do not think this mountain air agrees with you. You are looking sick and weary again."

"It is not the air, " I said, "but the recollections which the scenery recalls. It makes me nervous; I cannot deny it."

"Let us go to Italy!" said the Professor. "We will see the Thorwaldsen Lion, and then we will depart."

We were gazing on that far-famed work of art in rapt admiration, when a firm hand was placed on my arm, and, turning, I beheld the glad honest face of Kenmuir. Only the face, for the rest was a travelling suit of Tweed, and leaning upon him was the graceful figure of Cozy.

Explanation was scarcely necessary. They were on their honeymoon trip, "Walking in fresh gardens of the Lord," as Kenmuir phrased it; for in nothing else save his Scotch suit was he changed from the moment I had first seen him upon that fatal point of Palel-lima.

The news from the Valley was the usual tidings of death and marriage,—the former, poor Mr. Naunton, and the latter, their own.

Nell and Radd went on as usual, Rollo assisting in the household, and pioneering Radd when he had sold too many skins to see his own way. Old Mophead would doubtless live as long as the famous Dr. Parr; and even the present generation of babies may hope to see him if they visit the Valley of Yo-semite some twenty years hence.

Horse-shoe Bill conveyed travellers into the Valley, never failing to relate, "That horrible mash as took place of two human beings in this here spot!" The traveller would examine the place where love and jealousy had wrought out their ends, gather a flower, and sigh, "Alas, poor Zanita! What a poetical name! Is there any more champagne? Do their ghosts haunt the place?" and so pass on.

And thus we all pass on through light and shade,—through life's joys and crimes,—till we come to the end, and the Angel of Death writes up

FINIS.